A MOTHER'S WAY

ROMANTIC TIMES REVIEWERS' CHOICE AWARD WINNER
LISA CACH

"[Lisa Cach's] ability to create toe-curling tension makes for a must-stay-up-and-read-till-dawn story."

—*Romantic Times*

"[Ms. Cach writes] beautifully crafted, erotically charged scenes and [has a] light, humorous touch."

—*Booklist*

THREE-TIME P.E.A.R.L. AWARD WINNER
SUSAN GRANT

"Sizzling . . . Susan Grant proves that hers is a potent and versatile new talent."

—*Romantic Times*

"Susan Grant's talent for fast-paced, intelligent, sensual stories is undeniable."

—*The Romance Reader*

USA TODAY BESTSELLER
JULIE KENNER

"A true original, filled with humor, adventure and fun!"

—*Romantic Times* on *Aphrodite's Kiss*

"*Aphrodite's Kiss* is . . . full of surprises and just plain good old-fashioned entertainment. . . . A delightful reading experience."

—*Romance Reviews Today*

ROMANTIC TIMES REVIEWERS' CHOICE AWARD NOMINEE
LYNSAY SANDS

Ms. Sands "is talented at creating endearing romps!"

—*All About Romance*

Lynsay Sands "will make you laugh and turn up the air-conditioning."

—*Romantic Times*

A Mother's Day

Romance Anthology

❤

Lisa Cach, Susan Grant,
Julie Kenner, Lynsay Sands

LOVE SPELL BOOKS ✦ NEW YORK CITY

A LOVE SPELL BOOK®

March 2002

Published by

Dorchester Publishing Co., Inc.
276 Fifth Avenue
New York, NY 10001

ISBN 0-505-52471-6

Visit us on the web at www.dorchesterpub.com.

THROUGHOUT THE AGES, MOTHERS HAVE ALWAYS HAD
THEIR WAY . . . .

A Mother's Day
Romance Anthology

♥

1353
Mother, May I?
by LYNSAY SANDS

For Mom. Miss you.

Chapter One

London, England
1358

"Mother!"

"Oh, dear." Lady Margaret of Fairley paused, then fixed an unconcerned smile on her face and continued brushing her hair as she listened to her son stomp his way through the small sitting room off her bedchamber. By an effort of will, she managed to keep from starting when the door crashed open behind her.

She studiously ignored him as he stormed across the room to where she sat by the fire, but grimaced as she felt him loom above her, breathing fury down the back of her neck. She waited for a count of ten as he glared and snorted at her much like an angry bull, then glanced over her shoulder and offered a bland smile. "Good morning, son. How are you this fine day?"

The question evidently agitated him. His face flushed an angry red and his expression grew even more furious. Yes, she thought, she could see why the French were terrified of this hulking man. "How am I? How *am* I? God's teeth, woman, how do you think I am?"

"Hmmm," she responded mildly, turning back to the fire. "*Some*one awoke on the wrong side of his bed this morn."

"Not *I!*" he snapped. "I was in a perfectly good mood . . . until my audience with Edward."

Lady Fairley opened her eyes wide, feigning surprise. "Did it not go well?"

"Did it—" He broke off to mutter a few choice words.

She gave him a look of mild reproof. "Please, Jonathan. 'Tis not very chivalrous to speak so around ladies. Are you not a knight of the Order of the Garter? Were you not taught better back when you were a squire? Perhaps instead of sending you to train at Westcott, your father should have taken you in hand—as I suggested. He never would listen to me, that stubborn—"

"Mother," Jonathan interrupted with an obvious attempt at restraint.

"Yes, dear?"

"What did you say to the king?"

"Me?" She stared at him in a show of innocence that merely made his eyes narrow.

"Aye. You. I know you had something to do with this."

Judging that it was time to show some irritation of her own, Lady Fairley set down her brush with a clatter. "Something to do with *what*, Jonathan? You have not yet said what has occurred. Why did the king call you here to court?"

2

Mother, May I?

She watched the struggle waged on her son's face with interest before he blurted, "He has ordered me to marry! *Me! The Scourge of Crécy!*"

"Oh." She turned back to the fire and resumed tending to her hair. "Is that all? For a moment you had me concerned." She sensed rather than saw the way her son slumped behind her, deflated by her unconcerned response.

"Is that *all?*" he echoed with dismay. "King Edward has given me two weeks to choose my own bride ... or he will. Two weeks! He wants me married by month's end, *and* to have begotten an heir by next summer." She turned and saw fury suffuse his face at the very thought.

"Oh, bother!" she remarked, drawing his attention back to her.

"Oh, bother?" he repeated.

"Well, really, Jonathan. Do you truly think *I* needed to do anything to bring this about? Ha!" She turned her nose up and sniffed delicately. "It hardly needed my attention, surely? Your father and brother have been gone for five years now, leaving you the lord of Fairley—an *heirless* earl. I am only surprised that King Edward has let the matter go so long. Fairley Castle is on the border of Scotland. Strategically, it is an important keep. Of course he wants you married and your bride bearing. And with all the fighting you do ... Should you die, the only person to take your place is your cousin Albert. You *know* what a fool he is. So does the king. He would hardly want Albert as lord of Fairley and its lands."

"Well, a babe is scarce likely to do a better job," Jonathan grumbled, shifting irritably.

"No, but if there is an heir and a widow, Edward may

Lynsay Sands

put whomever he wishes in your place, either as chatelain, or as a new husband for your bride. Without a widow and heir, Albert will inherit."

Jonathan looked pensive, obviously overcome by the truth of her words, but he scowled as she nonchalantly gave up her brushing in favor of donning jewels and a headpiece. It was her finest headpiece, and one she generally saved for special occasions. Eyes widening slightly, he took in the dress she wore, the way she had pulled up her hair, and . . . Yes, he'd just realized that it was not natural color on her cheeks, but a smuggled French rouge she'd put there. She knew she looked lovely, and younger than her fifty years.

"You are primping!" His words were a dismayed accusation.

Lady Fairley felt herself flush and thought it a rather nice touch as she tried for a slightly guilty expression. "I am not primping," she disagreed with great dignity.

"You are wearing your best jewels."

Beginning to feel her mouth twitch with self-satisfaction, Lady Fairley rose in a display of impatience. "They match my gown. One likes to look one's best at court." She ignored the way he squinted suspiciously at her, and instead of commenting she walked out into the sitting room. Her maid Leda burst in from the hall.

"Here you are, my lady."

"Ah, good," she murmured as the girl rushed forward with a small decanter. Her son watched her take the container, then sniffed suspiciously when she unstoppered it.

"Perfume!" The accusation was shot like an arrow from a bow.

"Aye," she answered, applying it liberally while Jona-

4

than watched in horror. She knew the source of his dismay: she had not bothered to apply perfume since his father had been stricken by the plague. Which was why she had been forced to send her maid out in search of some. She hadn't even brought any with her to court, because there wasn't any from Fairley to bring. All the scent she had once owned had dried up over time. Now it was part of her scheme.

"Thank you, Leda." She handed the perfume back to her maid and continued on to the door, not at all surprised when her son followed.

"Where are you going?" he asked.

"To visit with a friend," she responded gaily.

"What friend?"

"I believe I am past the age of needing to explain myself, Jonathan," she said with mock exasperation. She opened her chamber door, then stepped into the hall. "However, if you must know, I am going to visit with Lady Houghton and her daughter." Seeing the consternation on his face, she fought a smile. This was all going according to plan.

Jonathan had followed her into the hall before comprehension at last dawned on him. She'd convinced the king to order him to marry, and now she would thrust another friend's daughter under his nose! She'd been trying this for years, and he'd managed to sidestep every move to see him wed. In fact, if he never saw another—

"There is no need for you to accompany me," his mother spoke up, ruining his theory quite thoroughly. "In any case, is there not something of more importance that you should be doing? Two weeks is very little time to find a bride—and here at court, things must be doubly difficult. There are many other knights as handsome and accomplished as yourself, my son. If you want to make a good alliance, you really should not waste time following me."

Jonathan was so startled by his mother's pronouncement that he stopped walking and simply gaped at her back. She continued down the hall.

"But what of this friend's daughter?" he blurted at last, hurrying to catch up once he recovered from his shock.

"What of her?"

"Do you not wish me to consider *her* for my bride?"

"Oh, no. She would not do at all."

"What?" He gasped, scandalized. "You have shoved every eligible daughter of every friend under my nose for the last five years. Now here is one you—"

"I have introduced you to every eligible and *suitable* daughter of friends of mine," his mother corrected sharply. "And I have run through the entire list. Now you are on your own."

"You are giving up on me?" he cried, unsure whether to be relieved or injured by such a possibility. Not that he wanted his mother thrusting would-be brides under his nose, but he wasn't sure he wanted her indifference on the subject, either.

"Not at all, son. I shall support you in your choice; I simply can no longer aid you in your quest. Now"—she patted him affectionately on the arm—"go find yourself a bride to please the king, and leave me to my friends."

Jonathan stared at his mother in bewilderment, then he noted that the hand she had patted his arm with was now patting her hair. She was primping again! She hadn't primped since his father's death. Something odd was going on.

"I think I shall accompany you to meet your friend's

daughter," he announced as she started away again.

"No!" Lady Fairley shrieked, coming to an abrupt halt. He'd never seen her so agitated. She regained her composure quickly, though, replacing the alarm on her face with an irritated scowl. "I mean . . . I told you she is not suitable."

"Oh?" He eyed her curiously. It had been his experience that nothing short of a questionable virtue was enough to make a woman unsuitable in his mother's eyes. At least lately. To be fair, she had been much choosier at first, when producing possible brides for him to consider, but as the last few years had passed and he had shown a distinct lack of interest in the marital state—especially in comparison to his fighting on the Continent—his mother's desperation had begun to manifest itself. She had begun to parade any woman with all the necessary parts before him. And the "necessary parts" did not always include attractiveness, personality or even all the usual limbs. His mother had grown quite desperate. Virginity had never been a point she overlooked, though. Lady Fairley wanted grandchildren from her own son, not someone else's.

"Is this girl free with her affections?" he asked. His mother turned a horrified expression on him. "Of course she is not free with her affections. Elizabeth raised her properly! The girl is as pure as a babe."

"Hmmm." This was interesting. He found himself intrigued by his mother's vehemence. "Is she betrothed, then?"

Irritation flickered on her face, but she did admit with obvious reluctance, "Nay. Her betrothed was taken by the plague."

"Is she without title or dower?"

Much to his surprise, irritation flickered on Lady Fairley's face once more. "Nay. Her father was a wealthy baron. There is a sizable dower."

"Well, then, why is she unsuitable?"

"She is . . ." Her expression fluctuated briefly, torn between irritation and reluctance as she struggled for an explanation. Jonathan was shocked beyond belief when it finally popped out: "Puffy."

"Puffy?" he echoed with a laugh.

"Aye. She is large. Too voluptuous, if you must know. And she is far too intelligent and strong-minded. She would not do at all. She even reads," his mother added with distaste, giving a delicate shudder. "Nay. She is perfectly nice, but not for you. She—Oh, look! There is Lady Griselda of Epton. I understand that her parents have not yet secured her a betrothed. Little coin for a dower, I gather," she added in an aside. "But you hardly need concern yourself with that. Why do you not go see how she would suit?"

Jonathan's eyes nearly fell out of his head. He knew quite well that his mother positively loathed the young lady. For some reason, that had once added to the girl's attractions in Jonathan's eyes; he had courted her briefly. Very briefly. The girl had an amazingly high, screeching voice. Which was a shame, really. Otherwise she was quite lovely. Still, a man would have to be completely deaf to put up with her, and Jonathan was far from that.

Of course, Lady Griselda's voice was not the reason his mother did not like her. She claimed the girl was spiteful and sneaky, a heartless witch who wielded gossip as men wielded swords.

Realizing that while he stood there goggling, his mother was doing her best to escape, Jonathan rushed forward. She was moving at a fast clip as she turned the corner ahead. When he followed a moment later, it took him several seconds to spot her. This palace corridor was busier than the one leading to her rooms, and Jonathan suspected that she had put on a burst of speed the moment she was out of his sight. She was a good distance up the hall, half-hidden by a quartet of servants coming toward him.

Proceeding to hurry, himself, Jonathan ate up the distance between them with his longer stride, quickly reaching her side. The glance she threw him was not welcoming. She ignored him as they reached the stairs, then traversed another hall. Finally, at the door he knew led out into the royal gardens, she paused to give him a harassed stare. "Are you not going to go look for a bride? You could hardly wish Edward to choose one for you."

"I have plenty of time for that," he argued. "I want—"

"Oh, aye. Plenty of time," she interrupted scathingly. "A fortnight."

Ignoring her sarcasm, he moved forward and opened the door, gesturing for her to proceed. His mother glared at him in frustration for a moment; then, seeming to realize that he was unaffected by her mood, she let her breath out in a disgruntled whoosh and marched outside.

Alice was the first to spot the approach of Lady Fairley and her son. At least, Alice assumed it was the woman's son. Margaret of Fairley had spoken a great deal about the man, describing him as tall, dark, and handsome, very strong, solid like his father. She had also given various other flattering descriptions. Most of them appeared correct. He was tall and dark. He certainly looked solid and strong as he marched along beside his much smaller mother. Seeing him, Alice believed everything she'd heard about his campaigns against the French. As for him being handsome, it was hard to say. His face was scrunched up in a scowl as they neared, a scowl that seemed to deepen with every step as his mother verbally berated him.

Alice tilted her head and watched the pair curiously. The petite older woman appeared to be shooing her son away like some pesky fly, her hand waving vaguely in the air as she spoke in aggravated tones to him. The man that Alice assumed to be Lord Jonathan appeared unmoved by her gestures or her words; he followed Lady Fairley forward, pausing whenever she did stop to wave a finger at him, then following again. It was all rather curious, amusing even, and Alice's lips stretched into a smile as she watched the unlikely pair approach.

"What has you so amused?" her mother asked curiously, then followed Alice's gaze. She positively beamed as she espied her friend and the man approaching. "Oh! There is Margaret. And look, young Jonathan has accompanied her."

Alice caught the meaningful expression that her mother cast Uncle James, and had a moment to wonder at it, but then was urged off the bench she occupied.

"Let Lady Fairley have your seat, dear. Respect your elders."

Alice rose automatically and shifted away from the place where her mother and Uncle James were settled. The move made her the first to greet Lady Fairley and her son as they approached.

"Oh, good morning, my dear," the noble woman murmured, and Alice felt her expression reflect her confusion at the cool tone the woman used. Lady Margaret was usually as warm and pleasant as could be. Her coldness now was somewhat startling to Alice and took her aback.

The woman gave the man accompanying her an irritated glance, then introduced him. "This is my son, Jonathan." Her smile was decidedly forced and unenthusiastic. "Jonathan, this is Lady Alice of Houghton."

"Good morn, my lady," he said. The smile that accompanied his greeting was brilliant, making the man's hard face almost handsome as he took her hand and bowed over it.

"Good day, my lord," Alice murmured, smiling politely back even as Lady Fairley added, "He very kindly walked me here, but he cannot stay. He has a task to fulfill for the king."

"Oh, what a shame," Alice murmured politely, her gaze moving curiously from the woman's grim face to that of her again-scowling son. The two staged a silent war with their eyes.

"There is no need for me to rush off right this very minute," Lord Jonathan countered at last. "Certainly, I can afford to spare a few moments to get acquainted with my mother's dear friend and her lovely daughter."

Alice could not help but notice that his charming words merely seemed to agitate Lady Fairley even more. With an exasperated wave, the older woman turned away and almost flounced over to take the seat Alice had just vacated. Apparently the introductions were over. It was hard not to notice and wonder at the fact that Lady Fairley had very obviously neglected to introduce her son to Alice's own mother. Or to her uncle, whom Alice's mother had most mysteriously insisted accompany them on this morning constitutional. Usually her mother was embarrassed by the man, who was something of a court dandy. And more surprising than her uncle's presence, was the sudden warmth that Lady Fairley was showing him. Not that Alice would expect the noblewoman to be rude, but from where she stood, Lady Fairley appeared to be almost gushing over the man, which was entirely bewildering. Alice had not thought the usually dignified woman capable of such effusive feeling, especially over a man like Lord James of Houghton.

Putting this curious turn of events away for later consideration, Alice glanced at Lord Jonathan to find the man glowering at the others with obvious displeasure. Alice peered from son to mother just as Lady Fairley paused in her conversation to glare back at her son and—if she wasn't mistaken—at Alice as well.

"Come stand by me, son. Or better yet, tend to your quest."

Alice gasped at such bossiness, but Jonathan, rather than appearing upset or insulted, just smiled. The smile held a degree of affection, but there was also a median of contrariness. "Nonsense, Mother. I know you are concerned with the completion of my appointed task, but tomorrow is soon enough to start that endeavor. Besides, I can hardly leave Lady Houghton's daughter standing alone here. There is no room for her on that bench you are sharing, so I must stay to keep her company—'tis the chivalrous thing to do. Speaking of Lady Alice," he added slowly, a strange smile coming to his face, "you were hardly fair in your description of her. She is much lovelier than you claimed."

If Alice blushed at this unexpected compliment, Lady Fairley flushed an even redder shade, one that turned almost purple as her son went on: "How was it that you described her?"

Alice peered from son to mother again when Jonathan

paused; she was aware of undercurrents here, but didn't understand them.

"You never mentioned that her hair held all the colors of a sunset: mellow golds and fiery reds. Or that her eyes were the clear blue of a cloudless sky. What *was* it you said?" The knight tapped his chin thoughtfully, and all the while his mother grew more straight-backed and tense. Alice simply grew more and more flustered.

"Oh, aye, I remember now. You commented on her figure. What was it you said? She was . . . lush? Round and rich like a berry brought to full ripeness?" Alice wasn't sure how to take such a compliment, but before she could react, Lord Jonathan went on. "No, no. It was something else you said. What was it?"

Lady Fairley looked ready to burst out of her skin. Instead she blurted out, "Oh, go sit over there with her if you insist. Just do be quiet."

He smiled and bowed to his mother, then Lord Jonathan moved to take Alice's arm. He turned her solicitously toward the bench on the opposite side of the path. "Shall we sit over here, my lady? I promise not to embarrass you with any further compliments."

"Er . . . aye. Thank you," she murmured, as bewildered by the exchange that had just taken place as she was flustered by the words this handsome lord had used to describe her. No one had ever described her hair or eyes so prettily, and his description of her figure . . . well, gentlemen were not supposed to comment on a lady's figure. Alice now knew why. His words had sounded seductive and almost carnal. But surely that was due only to his reference to fruit and ripeness and such, she thought a little faintly. Glancing over her shoulder, she saw that her uncle now sat, seemingly forgotten as her mother and

Lady Fairley huddled together, some secret satisfaction on their faces. The two were holding a whispered conversation.

"Pray forgive my mother's moodiness," Lord Jonathan murmured, drawing her attention back to him. "We have had a disagreement."

"Oh." Alice seated herself on the bench and proceeded to direct her eyes everywhere but at the huge man settling beside her. It was funny, she hadn't found him particularly threatening upon first seeing him, but he suddenly seemed so . . . male. Embarrassed by her own silliness, she cleared her throat uncomfortably. "I had noticed that she seemed a tad out of sorts."

"Aye."

Alice forced herself to glance at him, only to see that his eyes had gone back to the trio on the opposite bench. Apparently he didn't like what he saw. A small scowl tugged at his features, making his rugged face seem harsher. Surprised, Alice followed his gaze. It seemed Lady Fairley's discussion with Alice's mother was finished, and she and Alice's uncle James were now in the midst of what appeared to be a rather intimate tête-a-tête. Lady Houghton appeared to be dozing in the sun beside them.

"Your uncle . . ." Jonathan asked. His voice was harsh, and Alice turned a questioning glance on him as he continued. "Is he married?"

"Nay. He is widowed. His wife died several years ago, shortly after supplying their only son. He never bothered to remarry."

"Why?"

Alice blinked at the question. The man sounded almost irritated that her uncle hadn't wed again. "Well," she answered slowly, "I suppose his affections were never engaged by any of the eligible widows. And then there was never any apparent need . . . until his son and my father died." She had his full attention at that announcement, and answered his silent question: "They were both taken when the plague struck."

"Ah."

"Aye." She let her breath out on an unhappy sigh, then went on: "Uncle James inherited Father's title and the responsibility for Mother and myself."

"The plague took many," Lord Jonathan said with quiet sympathy. The words made Alice's eyes fill with tears before she could stop them. She had lost a younger sister, her father, her cousin, and her betrothed all in one fell swoop to the plague. The extent of her loss had seemed unbearable at the time. It was still a terrible ache within her. Yet while it was still painful, her anguish had eased a bit with each of the last five years. At times like this, however, the old sorrow caught her by surprise and overwhelmed her. Perhaps that was why she now so loved to lose herself in books, poetry. . . .

Embarrassed by her own unexpected display of emotion, Alice glanced away and blinked her eyes rapidly to clear them, wiping surreptitiously at the few small drops that had overflowed to roll down her cheeks.

"What have you done now, Jonathan? You have the poor girl crying."

Alice straightened and shifted to the edge of the bench to make room as Lady Fairley suddenly plopped herself down between them.

"It was nothing he did," she defended quickly. "I was just explaining about my father, sister, cousin, and betrothed all being taken by the plague."

"Oh. Aye. Terrible, that. Jonathan's father, brother, and betrothed were stricken by it as well."

"Oh, dear. I am sorry," Alice murmured.

"Aye. So am I." Lady Fairley's eyes briefly misted over; then determination settled on her face. "In fact, that is the reason we are here at court."

"Is it?" Alice asked politely.

"Aye. Well, 'tis the reason Jonathan is here. I was already here enjoying a nice visit with you and your mother. 'Tis so nice to be able to get out and about after a long, dreary winter like the last."

"Aye," Alice agreed. " 'Twas a harsh winter. There was so much snow our men were castle-bound at one point. They had trouble even getting out through the snow to hunt. We were quite desperate for meat."

"We had the same difficulties," Lady Fairley acknowledged solemnly. "That is one of the problems of living in the north."

"Aye."

"I was most eager to get away from Fairley by the time the snow melted. Which is how I happened to be here when Edward sent for Jonathan."

"Oh? The king summoned him here?"

"Aye. I had no idea what it was about, but it turns out that His Highness has decided 'tis time Jonathan weds."

Alice's jaw began to drop; then she caught herself. She couldn't imagine the husky knight being ordered to do anything! "I . . . see," she said finally, at a loss as to what else to say.

"Aye." Lady Fairley heaved a sigh that ended with her glaring at her son. "Jonathan has dallied about the project and the king has run out of patience. He has two weeks to find a bride, else His Highness will find one for him."

"Oh . . . my," Alice said softly, her eyes shooting to Lord Jonathan's face. The man, who'd been silent since his mother's appearance, was looking quite irritated and miserable.

" 'Tis quite a fix," Lady Fairley confided unhappily. "Jonathan . . . well, he really is no good at this sort of thing. He prefers jousts and combat. And me, I am of little use. He has already refused to consider every single young woman of marriageable age I have brought before him. I suppose 'tis not surprising. After all, I am an old woman. I hardly know what young people are thinking nowadays, let alone what such young bucks as my son would find attractive."

Alice glanced over at the knight, wondering herself, but he hadn't been paying attention. Without answer, she began, "Oh, aye, well . . ." Lady Fairley suddenly brightened and grabbed Alice's hands. "I have a brilliant idea!"

"You do?" Alice asked warily, suspecting she would not like what was coming.

"You are young and would have a better idea of the kind of bride Jonathan would like. Perhaps you could help him, Alice."

"Me?" She peered at her mother's friend with surprise. This was not something she knew anything about at all!

"Mother," Lord Jonathan suddenly hissed in warning, but the woman ignored him.

"Oh, I do not think—" Alice began.

" 'Tis a *fine* idea."

Alice snapped her mouth closed and turned disbelieving eyes to her mother. Lady Houghton was suddenly standing before them, beaming. "Mother—"

" 'Twould not be any trouble at all, I am sure, Margaret. Alice would love to help you with your son. Why, she

Lynsay Sands

knows plenty of lovely young women for Jonathan to look over. She's been here at court for some time now."

"Look over?" Alice frowned, feeling herself react with indignation at her mother's phrasing. "Rather like looking over falcons, choosing one to hood and bind?" She wanted to be wed someday, but not chosen like property—and she imagined other girls felt the same.

"Aye, it is rather like that, is it not?" Lady Fairley agreed, to Alice's horror.

"Daughter, you can make a list and arrange for Jonathan to meet with those he finds to his taste," Alice's mother enthused.

" 'Tis perfect!" Lady Fairley cried, then turned to pat her son's arm soothingly. He looked wary as she said, "You see, dear? With Lady Alice's aid, you should have a bride in no time."

The knight's only answer was a long, drawn-out groan. Alice sympathized.

Chapter Two

"Mothers!" Wrinkling her nose in irritation, Alice waited impatiently for the list she had just finished writing to dry. Thanks to her mother's volunteering her for the task, she had spent the better part of yesterday and most of this morning seeking out the names of every available lady at court—a sorry task, to be sure. There were a dozen other things she would rather have been doing, most of them away from here.

Once, she had been perfectly happy back at Houghton Castle, reading, walking the fields, spending her time in solitary pursuits. Then her mother had begun to worry that she enjoyed her own company too much and insisted on her coming here to London. That had been bad enough in itself—Alice had little patience for the preening and backstabbing she'd discovered went on here at court—but now the dear woman had promised to help her find a bride for Lord Jonathan. Not that it should be so difficult

19

a task. The man was good-looking, strong, and was un-questionably a renowned warrior; the court's ladies would line up to be introduced. But what had possessed her mother to volunteer Alice for this endeavor? Good Lord, her preference for her own company and lack of friend-ships with other girls her own age had been part of her mother's excuse for bringing her here. How was she now expected to know everyone, and who would be suitable for a man such as Lord Jonathan?

Well, she supposed she had done well enough in mak-ing up a list of the available ladies. All it had taken was a little cleverness. Alice had sought out several of the loudest gossips at court and merely mentioned the task she'd been set. Now she had a lovely list. All she had to do was present it to Lord Jonathan and her chore was finished. Just thinking of the man conjured his face, and she found that disturbing. She paused in waving her list to dry it, and contemplated his features in her mind's eye. The man really was quite handsome. And he had been kindness itself yesterday . . . when he hadn't been scowl-ing or frowning at his mother.

She smiled slightly at the memory, then stood. Oddly enough, she had found the scowls endearing. At moments, they had transformed the ragged knight into nothing more than a sulky and suspicious child. And it was clear that the man adored his mother, despite his stormy expres-sions.

"All finished?"

She glanced up as her mother entered the room. Alice looked at her list. "Aye. You may take it to Lady Fairley now."

"Not I." Her mother smiled. "I have an audience with the queen. You shall have to deliver it. I believe my brother mentioned meeting Lady Fairley and her son in the stables. No doubt you shall find them there if you hurry."

"The stables?" Alice stared at her mother, aghast. "But Uncle has hated horses ever since—"

"Ever since his mount threw him into that tree, breaking his leg," Lady Houghton finished impatiently. "Yes, yes. I have heard that often enough from him. Yet it appears he is willing to visit and perhaps even ride the beasts to please Lady Fairley. Speaking of which, you had best be off before they are away and you miss them."

"Oh, but—" Alice cut off her own protest. Her mother was no longer there to hear it; she had rushed out of the room. Realizing that there was nothing for it but to see to the duty herself. Alice allowed herself a moment of distaste, then quickly rolled up the parchment she held and set off.

Neither Lady Fairley nor Alice's uncle were about, but she did find Lord Jonathan outside the stables. He stood, staring out into the distance, a frown once again clouding his handsome features. Alice paused for a moment to take in his youthful expression, amusement twisting her lips as she gazed upon him. Then, realizing that she was wasting prime reading time—her mother could hardly complain about her loafing around reading if she had an audience with the queen—she took a deep breath, straightened her shoulders, and started forward.

"My lord," she began. "My mother said I might find yourself and Lady Fairley here. Fortune has apparently smiled upon me, for here you are."

The knight glanced around at her words and gave a quick nod. "Aye. Here I am. Unfortunately, my mother is not. She is off on a picnic with your uncle."

"Ah, well . . ." Alice hesitated, as startled by his disgust at that idea as she was by the knowledge itself. Really, she found it difficult to wrap her comprehension around the idea of Lady Fairley being interested in James. The man was a twit. She could not imagine that a woman who had raised such a handsome and strong son as Lord Jonathan would be interested in such a fop.

Pushing the concern aside for later consideration, Alice offered Lord Jonathan a smile. "I suppose it matters little; I can place this in my lord's hands as easily as my lady's."

"What is it?" the big man asked, giving her his full attention as he took the scroll.

"A list of all the eligible ladies presently at court. There are quite a few as you can see."

"Quite a few?" The knight gaped at the list as he unrolled it. "There are at least forty names here." He gave her a pointed look.

"Closer to fifty, actually," Alice agreed, stepping back and preparing to make her escape. "Perhaps you could weed through the names and scratch off those who are obviously unsuitable. Then arrange meetings with the rest and—"

"Brilliant!" Lord Jonathan interrupted. He was looking at her in a way that made her heart flutter. "You and I shall go on a picnic . . . to weed through these names together."

"A picnic?" Alice stared at him blankly. "Oh, I—"

"Well, I hardly know these ladies," he reasoned. "I shall need your assistance in learning of them. And you have proven to be a rather quick girl. Come." Ignoring her weak protests, the big man grabbed Alice's arm and rushed her into the stables. "We must get mounts, but then I know just where we will go."

Mother, May I?

* * *

"Bloody-minded horse, bouncing me around like a sack of wheat! I swear, my arse is the color of—Oh, I suppose I should not be mentioning such things in your presence, my lady."

Margaret rolled her eyes. James had been complaining since they'd ridden away from the palace into the king's woods, and often with very little concern for the delicacy of his wording. Lady Houghton's brother was rather cruder than she'd expected for a reputed court dandy, and were it possible to use an alternate plan now, she might have considered it. But it was too late for that. Jonathan was already responding beautifully. As she'd expected, her son did not at all care for her recent attentions to James of Houghton. She knew that, as she did for him, her son had very high standards regarding the caliber of anyone she would consider marrying. As if she would ever replace Jonathan's father; what she wanted was grandbabies!

Lady Fairley paused. Looking about, she drew her horse to a halt in a small clearing and dismounted. Waiting until she had both feet planted firmly on the ground, she spoke patiently while removing the two bags she'd attached to her saddle. "I thought we would picnic here. It is as nice a spot as any."

The man stared at her, nonplused for a moment, then gasped. "Good Lord, you don't really intend to picnic, do you?"

"Well, aye, James. 'Twas the idea." Lady Fairley shook her head with amusement. Proceeding to dig out the woolen blanket she'd requested from the king's household for this endeavor, she asked, "Is that a problem?"

"A problem? Of course 'tis a problem!" the old dandy

23

sputtered. "Picnics invite all manner of pests and bug infestations. And there are wild animals out here, Margaret. They will be attracted by the smell, and we shall be forced to fend for our very lives over a scrap of cheese and mutton."

Margaret didn't even bother to roll her eyes at his exaggerated claims; she merely began to lay out the blanket. Calmly she said, "We shall survive, I am sure."

"But—"

"Do you wish to marry your niece off or not?" she interrupted impatiently.

Grimacing, the dandified lord of Houghton grudgingly dismounted.

Lady Fairley nodded with satisfaction as she settled on the blanket. "I thought so."

"Hmm." Lord Houghton's face twisted as he ambled over to where she was now pulling out several items from her bags. He eyed the food greedily, yet still managed to sound irritable as he added, "Aye, of course I want the lass married off. I love my sister and daughter, but Elizabeth has always had a sharp tongue, and Alice has recently shown a distressing tendency to follow in her mother's footsteps. The last thing I need is *two* harping women about!"

Lady Fairley smiled. Betty *had* always been rather sharp-tongued. The woman wasn't a shrew by any means, but she was honest. Especially around those she knew well, she did not curb that honesty with kindness. Her lazy, unambitious brother, who had stumbled into her husband's title, had been the recipient of such treatment on many occasions.

If Alice was showing signs of a similar personality to her mother, it was all as Lady Fairley wished. The last thing she wanted was a sneaky, conniving daughter-in-law. Or a pliant one. She liked to know how things truly lay, and she hoped never to have to wonder with Alice. True, the girl had so far been reserved and quiet, but Margaret believed that was just a show of good breeding. With the right encouragement, the lass would become the brave, thoughtful young woman that Margaret believed would be the only good match for her son. After all, didn't he need someone to challenge him every once in a while, as she herself had done all his life? And a wife needed to be honest, like Alice's mother. And she needed to be someone with enough of a sense of self to be naturally attractive to her son.

A rustling in the bushes caught Lady Fairley's attention, and she glanced into them suspiciously. Her gaze narrowed as she caught a brief glimpse of eyes peering through the branches; then they disappeared.

Aha! she thought with satisfaction. Jonathan had followed . . . as she'd hoped. Also, as she'd expected, he had appeared to be irritated with her choice of companions. *Perfect.* Of course, she'd hoped to have Alice along with her son as well—she'd figured that the best way to get the two together would be to have her son in as many situations with the girl as possible—but everything was a matter of timing, and she would be able to work with this.

Wait! Fate appeared to be smiling on her plans. Margaret was suddenly aware of a light pink cloth showing through the underbrush, and she was fairly certain it was not from anything her son would be wearing.

Turning back to the lunch she had just set out, Lady Fairley murmured under her breath so that only Lord Houghton could hear, "We have visitors."

Much to her amazement, rather than finish sinking

down onto the blanket—as he had been doing—the old nobleman straightened and pulled his sword inexpertly from its scabbard. He whirled in place, calling anxiously, "What is it? A wolf? A boar?"

Rolling her eyes at his panicked reaction, Lady Fairley tugged at his breeches. Impatiently she said in a hiss, "Sit down, you old fool. I meant my son and your niece."

Really, she must love her son to be putting up with this clod: Looking slightly embarrassed, Lord Houghton promptly resheathed his sword and settled on the blanket beside her. He grumbled, "Well, you could have just said so."

Her mouth tight with irritation, Margaret tried for a discreet glance toward the bushes, but she couldn't see anything. Hoping that the pair hidden there had missed Houghton's odd behavior, she sought out and found the strawberries. Now she would enact the second part of her plan.

"What are we doing?"

"Shh," Jonathan hissed at Alice, squinting at the pair in the clearing, trying to sort out what was happening. Lord Houghton had jumped up and done a brief spin on the blanket with his sword drawn—as if preparing to fend off a horde of bandits.

Was the old fool trying to impress his mother by acting out made-up tales of bravery? If so, all would be well. Lady Fairley was nothing if not a bright woman, hardly the sort to be impressed by such posturing—especially by such a jester as Lord Houghton. The man was no match for Jonathan's father—now, there had been a true knight and husband!

Reassured, he once more peered through the bushes.

Mother, May I?

His mother was leaning close to the silly Lord Houghton, offering him a strawberry. Oddly, she didn't just hold out the bowl for him to take; she was urging a fruit toward his lips as if he were a babe needing to be coddled.

"What is happening there?" Alice asked impatiently by his ear, making him grimace.

He felt confused himself. "That is what I am trying to figure out! Why is she feeding him like that? Is your uncle so decrepit he cannot feed himself? Must he be fed like a babe?"

Alice moved close enough to peer through the foliage at the couple on the other side. She shrugged impatiently, then said in peevish tones, "She is not feeding him like a babe; she is feeding him like a lover."

"A lover?" He stiffened. "That's impossible. My mother would never do something like that. Besides, I don't see what you mean, anyway."

Alice glanced through the brush again, then looked at him, wide-eyed. "You truly don't see what I mean?" Sighing, she gave an irritated expression he didn't understand, then struggled to her feet. "Wait here."

"What are you doing?"

Alice ignored him and pushed through the bushes out into the clearing. Deaf to his panicky hissed protests, she walked straight over to the couple on the blanket. Smiling at the startled glances her arrival caused, she greeted them cheerfully. "Good day, Uncle, Lady Fairley. I was wondering if I might beg a strawberry from you."

"A strawberry?" they both echoed in bewilderment.

Alice nodded solemnly. "Aye. I wish to show Lord Jonathan something, but I need a strawberry to do it."

"Oh." Lady Fairley and Lord Houghton exchanged a confused glance; then Jonathan's mother reached for the

27

bowl of berries and held them out. "Take as many as you like, dear. We have plenty."

"Thank you." Alice took three and then turned away.

"My dear?" Lady Fairley called.

"Aye?" she asked, turning back.

"Whatever are you *doing* here?" Jonathan thought his mother looked embarrassed.

"Oh, well," Alice explained. "Mother said I should find you by the stables, but instead I found your son. I gave him the list of prospective brides I made up at your request, and he insisted that we come out here for a picnic to look them over."

"A picnic?" Lady Fairley repeated in seeming bemusement. Jonathan felt his annoyance rise.

"Aye." Alice's expression turned confiding. "I fear he neglected to bother to bring the picnic, however."

"Ah." Lady Fairley smiled. "Well, the two of you are more than welcome to join us. We have plenty," she announced.

"I shall be sure to tell your son that," Alice promised. On that note, she whirled away and rushed back through the bushes. As she returned, Jonathan began softly banging his head against a nearby tree trunk. Alice merely arched her eyebrows in response. She shook her head and moved to again sit at his side.

He turned to her at once. "We were supposed to be spying on them—" He broke off abruptly, silenced by a strawberry she popped into his mouth.

"I am aware of that, my lord," she answered as he automatically chewed, then swallowed. "I am not a complete nodcock."

"Well, then why—"

Another berry quieted him.

Mother, May I?

"Aiding you in finding a bride is one thing," she snapped. "Aiding you to spy on your mother and my uncle in their private moments is quite another. Now . . ."

Alice held a third strawberry out, then smiled in a way Jonathan could only describe as seductive. It was startling enough to make his mouth snap closed. All thoughts of his mother and Lord Houghton disappeared as Alice leaned forward and rubbed the fruit lightly across his lips. "Another succulent, sweet, juicy strawberry, my lord?" she asked.

Jonathan felt his eyes widen incredulously at the girl's husky tone, but his jaws remained stiffly closed. Her perfume was drifting around him, soft and enticing, and he was hard-pressed not to notice the way she was leaning forward, affording him a lovely view down the neckline of her gown. His eyes were drawn devotedly to the soft, luscious mounds of her breasts, which were pressed affectionately together and upward as if ready to leap out of her clothes at him.

As he continued to simply stare at Alice rather dazedly, she drew the berry away from his mouth to her own, luring his gaze to her full, soft, and very kissable lips. He watched her lick very deliberately at the rounded red tip of the fruit and found himself swallowing. Hard. Then she closed her mouth slowly around it. As juice began to run down from one corner of her lips, Jonathan's body tightened in response. His eyes greedily followed the trail that slid down her chin, and he had the sudden insane urge to lean forward and lick it away. Before he could act, though, the girl's own tongue slid out to catch the dripping juice. Jonathan swallowed harshly, aware that his breathing had become fast and heavy; his body was reacting as if she had licked and nipped at him!

Her demonstration apparently over, Alice straightened, her expression promptly becoming businesslike again. She popped the rest of the berry into her mouth and chewed energetically. "You see?" she asked as she swallowed. Her whole demeanor had changed. "Hardly the way one would feed a baby."

Jonathan blinked. He was completely and thoroughly aroused, his body hard and full of desire from her little show. A feeling of frustration overcame him. Worse, he suddenly realized, his mother was feeding that oaf on the other side of the trees in the same way. If it was giving the old man the same ideas it was giving Jonathan—ideas like licking the sticky, sweet juice from Alice's soft lips, pressing her back into the grass and—

He rose to his feet with a roar, drew his sword, then charged through the bushes.

Alice stared after Lord Jonathan in amazement, then rushed to her feet and stumbled in pursuit. She reached his side as he paused at the edge of the blanket on which the older couple sat. His hand was clenching his sword, his chest heaving with every breath, and his eyes were darting furiously between his mother and her companion. Those two turned startled gazes up at him.

"Oh, lovely. You decided to join us."

Alice couldn't help but notice that despite the welcome of the words themselves, Lady Fairley sounded far from pleased by Alice and Jonathan's arrival. In fact, the woman was actually glaring at her son. Which was quite odd, Alice decided, since she was sure the invitation earlier had been sincere.

Before she could consider the matter further, Jonathan dropped abruptly onto the edge of the blanket and set his blade down, poking Alice's uncle with its tip in the process. Alice was trying to decide if it had been an accident or not, when the knight reached out to grab her hand and yanked her down, nearly into his lap.

"We are pleased to join you," he claimed, grasping Alice's shoulder to steady her and bestowing an enigmatic smile upon his mother. Then he reached forward, retrieved a strawberry from the small wooden bowl on the blanket, and turned to Alice. "A strawberry, my sweet?" he asked.

"What?" Alice's head shot around to face him, her eyes wide, her mouth gaping slightly. Jonathan popped the berry inside. He then pushed her jaw to chomp on it, before turning to smile at his mother.

"We thought 'twould be nice to enjoy a picnic while we consider my plight."

"Aye. So I heard." Lady Fairley's gaze seemed to narrow on her son with displeasure. "I also hear you forgot the food for this picnic."

"A slight oversight," Jonathan explained through clenched teeth. Then he gave a brilliant smile. "But how is a man expected to think of such petty things with a beauty such as Alice about?"

At that claim Alice's mouth dropped open. She found a second berry popped inside. Jonathan gave her a smile she didn't like and gently pushed her mouth closed. Alice couldn't help it; her eyes narrowed on the big knight suspiciously. Really, it was completely unkind of him to bandy about such compliments when he didn't mean them! Cruel, even. Obviously he had just brought her here as an excuse to spy on his mother!

Swallowing the fruit in her mouth, she turned to speak to Lady Fairley. "Aye, my lady, you understand. Unlike women, 'tis difficult for a man to think of more than one thing at a time. Why, I am constantly amazed that they can walk and converse at the same time. . . . Well, I am amazed by those who can," she added dryly. Turning, she found Jonathan glaring at her. He seemed surprised by her attack. Alice glared right back.

Their staring match was interrupted by what sounded very much like a laugh from Lady Fairley. Alice glanced at the woman, who suddenly burst into a fit of coughs and throat clearing. "Perhaps we should have a look at that list," she suggested after she was through.

Nodding, Alice glanced toward Jonathan expectantly. Scowling and muttering under his breath, the young knight pulled out the scroll he had been given and handed it to his mother. Lady Fairley unfurled the parchment and looked the names over consideringly. "My, 'tis quite a selection, is it not? You are quite fortunate, Jonathan!"

Alice's uncle grunted, leaning over to peer at the list. "Half of them are snaggletoothed hags or harridans. But that still leaves quite a selection."

"Aye." Lady Fairley nodded. "Perhaps we could remove some right now. Shall we go through them?" When no one dissented, she settled more comfortably on the blanket and started to read off names.

Alice sat quietly, listening to the roll of eligible women, but was a bit amazed when Lady Fairley followed each name with a favorable comment. Some of the girls were perfectly lovely, or acceptable in both personality and looks, but really, many of the women Lady Fairley was praising were . . . well . . . *not* praiseworthy. Either Lady Margaret had no clue of the women at court or she simply wanted her son to be married to anyone. While Alice found that a particularly awful concept, she forced herself to keep her thoughts to herself. This was none of her business, after all.

She could stand it no longer, however, when Heloise of Brock's name came up. When Lady Fairley commented that the woman was "such a friendly lass," Alice could not restrain herself. She muttered under her breath, "*Friendly* is right. The girl has been 'friendly' with almost every single one of the king's guards."

Much to Alice's chagrin, despite having simply breathed the comment, Jonathan overheard and gave a guffaw of laughter.

Lady Fairley looked sharply at them. Alice sat up straight, trying to adopt an innocent expression. She suspected she failed miserably. Much to her surprise, it was her uncle who saved her. He nudged Lady Fairley curiously and asked, "Who else is on the list, Margaret?"

Alice saw Jonathan stiffen at Lord Houghton's familiar use of his mother's first name. She sighed inwardly. This was all quite ridiculous.

"Lady Rowena," Lord Jonathan's mother read, then glanced up to smile at them all. "Oh, she is a delightful young girl—such a lovely personality. You really must consider her, Jonathan."

He waited until his mother turned back to the list, then raised an eyebrow in Alice's direction. She hesitated, not wishing to be rude or say anything to draw Lady Fairley's quiet ire again, but really, she decided, it would be too cruel not to give some warning regarding Lady Rowena of Wilcox. The woman was sweet as molasses, but her looks left much to be desired. Rowena weighed as much as Alice's uncle's prize cow, and unfortunately resembled it as well, with large, bovine eyes . . . which were crossed. Giving in to a devilish impulse, Alice nodded, then puffed out her cheeks and crossed her eyes in imitation.

A startled laugh burst from Jonathan's mouth, drawing another sharp glance from his mother. The older woman's eyebrows drew down in definite displeasure. Alice lowered her head repentantly, grateful when Lady Fairley continued.

She had gone through three more names, and was praising Lady Blanche for her gentle kindness, before Alice dared glance up. As she did, Jonathan raised his eyebrows questioningly.

Alice shrugged. She had yet to meet Lady Blanche. Jonathan's response to her signal was to waggle his eyebrows, then jerk his thumb toward himself and nod. Alice took that to mean he *did* know the woman, or at least knew of her. She presumed she was correct when he next sucked his bottom lip and the better part of his jaw back, leaving his top teeth naked and protruding outward, while squinting unattractively in an imitation of the lady in question.

Alice couldn't stop the laugh that spilled from her lips then. It was conjured mostly by how silly he looked. She tried to stop and covered her mouth, her gaze shooting guiltily to Lady Fairley, who'd glanced up again from the scroll.

"Well," the woman said irritably, rerolling the parchment from which she had been reading. " 'Tis obvious that we shall not get anything done here today. That being the case, we may as well pack up and head back to the castle. Perhaps you three would be good enough to make a start while I . . . er . . . go for a little walk and clear my head."

Eager to redeem herself, Alice nodded and began to make quick work of the task while Jonathan's mother disappeared. Alice's uncle sat back in a relaxed pose, making it clear he thought this a woman's work. Surprisingly,

Lord Jonathan assisted, rewrapping the untouched cheese in its cloth and tossing the unbroken bread in the sack. They were finished quickly and were left to sit and wait on Lady Fairley. She took an inordinate amount of time.

Alice was just thinking the woman might be in distress and need assistance when she suddenly reappeared. Lord Jonathan's mother stumbled out of the woods on the opposite side of the clearing from where she'd entered, looking slightly ruffled and a touch out of breath. Alice noted that with some confusion—she'd assumed the woman had gone on a call of nature—but had little opportunity to comment as the men, apparently more than ready to leave, were immediately up and preparing to do so.

"You know, I believe I have had a wonderful idea," Lady Fairley announced as Jonathan helped Alice refold the blanket upon which they'd sat. "Perhaps we could arrange a dance tonight. Invite all the eligible women. That way, you could make up your own mind as to who is fitting, Jonathan."

Alice glanced at the knight to see how he took the suggestion. She was less than surprised to see it wasn't well. His eyes were wide with what appeared to be horror.

"Mother, may I suggest you not" he began, but Lady Fairley didn't let him get any farther.

"Thank you, son," she said, taking the blanket he held. She slid it quickly back into the bag she had brought, then moved to reattach the bag to her saddle. "Now, you two had best go retrieve your mounts."

Jonathan frowned, then nodded as he watched his mother settle on her horse. "Aye. We shall return directly."

Alice remained silent as he took her arm and led her out of the clearing.

35

They had tied the steeds some distance from the spot where they had originally come to sit, and Alice realized now that Jonathan had not wanted the horses to alert the older couple to their presence. Of course, she hadn't known what he was up to at the time. He had ridden out hard from the palace, holding on to Alice's reins as if she might turn and ride back if he did not, then had suddenly stopped and cocked his head as if listening. After telling her to wait where she was, he had ridden off, leaving her alone for a few minutes. It was only after he'd reappeared, suggesting she dismount and proceeding to tie the horses to a tree branch, that he'd let her accompany him farther. He'd led her off through the bushes then to the spot he'd chosen from which to spy.

Alice's honest nature had balked at the infringement of their family members' privacy as soon as she'd realized Lord Jonathan's intent. In fact, she had been looking for an excuse to let the couple know of their presence when she rushed in to borrow the strawberries. Well, that, and she'd suddenly given in to a desire to see what Lord Jonathan would look like while she was feeding him.

At any rate, the upshot of their actions was that they had a bit of a walk before they reached the horses . . . or, to be more exact, *Jonathan's* horse. Her own appeared to be missing.

"What the devil?" Spotting the lone animal, Jonathan rushed forward through the trees. Alice was hard on his heels. Reaching his mount, the big man looked it over, then examined the branch where the stallion's reins were still tied. "Damn! Someone has stolen your horse."

"Do you really think so?" Alice glanced around nervously. "Perhaps he merely came untied and wandered off."

"Nay. I tied him well. I was sure to tie them both well." Jonathan freed his mount, scowling around the area. "Someone has to have taken yours."

"Oh, dear." She glanced around the woods to the tree where her horse had been tied. "Well . . ." She brightened. "I can ride back with my uncle. They are waiting in the clearing, after all."

"Aye." Giving a nod, Jonathan put a foot in the stirrups of his horse. Alice turned to start back through the woods, but then she heard him call.

"What are you doing?"

Glancing back over her shoulder, she answered, "Heading back to the clearing to—" Her words were cut off as her foot was caught on a branch that sent her tumbling. Embarrassed and muttering, she quickly started to push herself onto her knees, then froze at the sight of a bit of blue cloth snagged on a branch near her face. It was the same blue as Lady Fairley's gown. A moment later she was caught under the arms and lifted unceremoniously to her feet.

"Are you all right?"

Alice glanced up in surprise at the concern in Lord Jonathan's voice. He wasn't looking at her; his gaze was traveling down her body in the wake of his hands as he checked her over to be sure she wasn't injured. She flushed at the familiar way his fingers skimmed over her, and took a quick step back, nearly tumbling again.

"I am fi-fine," she got out a little breathlessly as he caught her arms to steady her. "Really," Alice added when he continued to look concerned. After a brief pause, he swallowed and nodded, then turned to grab at the reins of his mount.

Her gaze moved distractedly back to the small swatch

of blue cloth on the ground by her feet. She was about to draw Jonathan's attention to it, when she was suddenly caught by the waist and lifted onto his horse.

Alice promptly began to protest. "Oh, really, my lord. There is no need for us to ride. I can walk back to the clearing. I—"

At last she gave up her protests, mostly because he was ignoring her. He mounted in front of her and drew her hands around his waist.

"Hold on," he instructed.

Alice nodded against his back, breathing in deeply to try to steady her nerves. It was rather novel to be in such close proximity to a man. She had never done so before. Unmarried women were simply not allowed such familiarity. Of course, this was an unusual circumstance, and . . .

Her thoughts died as she breathed in the scent of him. He smelled of the woods and the river and . . . male. It was a surprisingly pleasant mix, she decided, breathing it in again as her fingers interlocked at his middle. Feeling the muscles of his stomach bunch and ripple, she flattened her fingers over them to get the full sensation, then, realizing what she was doing, stopped breathing in embarrassment. Her fingers stilled.

Of course, Alice couldn't go long holding her breath. She managed to do so for the short ride back to the clearing, but there the breath left her in a slow hiss. The place was empty. Lady Fairley and her uncle had not waited for them; they had apparently ridden on ahead. Alice recalled the small swatch of cloth she had spotted near the horses and pondered silently, wondering why Lady Fairley had been by the horses. Surely *she* hadn't untied Alice's mount and let it go? Had she really been so annoyed with Alice as to wish to have her walk back to the castle?

"Well, we shall have to ride quickly to catch up," Lord Jonathan said.

Alice glanced at the back of his head, then pressed close and held on tightly as he spurred his mount into a trot. She didn't hold her breath this time. Instead she sat, her breasts pressed against his back, her hands clutched at his front, breathing in deeply of his scent.

She was enjoying it so much, it took her most of the ride to realize that despite his words, Jonathan wasn't trying very hard to catch up to her uncle and his mother. He had the horse going at a trot, but a rather slow one, really. They had ridden here faster. She was so startled by the realization that she loosened her hold and started to pull away, but he stopped her by catching her hands with one of his own.

"You had best hold on," he said. "I would not wish to see you fall."

Alice wondered at the husky note to his voice, but decided to merely enjoy the ride. She relaxed against him.

Chapter Three

Jonathan managed to keep his smile in place as his toes were trampled by yet another dance partner, but only just. He could honestly say that even the siege of Calais, where he had suffered a wound to the stomach that had caused him immeasurable pain and nearly killed him, was preferable to this hell his mother had arranged.

His bridal feast. That was what she called it. She had arranged for the celebration with the king, and now Jonathan was suffering through it. His first complaint was with the name. Shouldn't it be called the groom's feast? It was *his* feast, and *he* was the proposed groom, after all. Yet nay; his mother claimed it was to find him a bride; therefore it was his bridal feast.

Jonathan's face twisted with disgust. As silly as the name was, the actual event itself was worse. His mother had managed to finagle the use of the great hall in the palace. The king and queen were in attendance.

Mother, May I?

Jonathan's eyes slid unhappily to the glowering monarch and his wife. Edward had been sternly glaring, mostly at Jonathan, since arriving. He supposed it was to show how seriously His Majesty meant his orders to be taken. Jonathan was getting the message.

Another stomp on his toe drew his attention back to his dance partner. He sighed inwardly. The woman was myopic and a venerable four-and-thirty. Jonathan was thirty, himself, and so he supposed she was not *that* old—but she was well past the age considered prime for childbearing. She should have been crossed off the list at the picnic, but, in the end, no one had been crossed off that list. His mother had left the whole thing intact. Every woman at court was in attendance here tonight.

Looking around, Jonathan found his thoughts wandering to Alice and their ride back to the castle two days earlier. He instinctively sought the Houghton girl out where she stood with her mother, her uncle, and his own mother near the king and queen.

Much to Jonathan's surprise, he had found himself preoccupied with thoughts of the lass ever since that day. And not just any thoughts. He kept recalling her husky voice as she'd pressed that cool, sweet strawberry to his lips, could still smell the scent that had drifted off of her, ensnaring him in its erotic spell. And the vision he'd glimpsed of her delectable breasts, too, they kept rising before his eyes, blinding him to all else around him. Then, there were his sensual memories from their return trip that haunted him. If he concentrated, Jonathan would swear he could still feel her arms around his body and her breasts pressed against his back.

Yes, he had found himself undoubtedly aroused by that ride. His body had reacted to this girl as it had to no other, and that very fact had left him somewhat embarrassed and discomfited once they reached the stables. Jonathan had found himself avoiding Alice's gaze, as if she might read the less-than-sterling thoughts that had been tumbling through his mind. So he had done a fine job of avoiding her ever since.

It hadn't been difficult, he thought with sudden annoyance. The girl had hardly sought him out.

Another crunch of his toes drew Jonathan's attention back to the reel. Fortunately, the musicians ended the song, saving his dance partner from his exasperation. Gritting his teeth, he walked the lady back to her mother, then glanced around the waiting horde with a sigh. There were countless women in this room, and three men. Two, he corrected himself as his gaze slid to where the king had been standing just moments before. Having done his duty by making an appearance, Edward and his wife had apparently taken themselves off to more amusing entertainments than watching the Scourge of Crécy dance with more willing damsels than there'd been French at that victory.

Scowling at the thought, Jonathan let his gaze roam to Lord Houghton. As the only other man present, the old bugger might have lent some assistance with this mob, he thought with resentment. Instead, the velvet-clad old fop appeared glued to his mother's side. Houghton had been hovering over Lady Fairley all night, leaving Jonathan to usher snaggletoothed female after nasty old crone onto the dance floor under the watchful gaze of some fifty want-to-be brides and their mamas, aunts, and other chaperones.

The two times he had dared beg for rest, returning to the trestle tables for his ale mug, he had found himself surrounded by that crowd of she-wolves. Subjected to their titterings and twitterings as they bombarded him with long, lavish dissertations on their skill at embroidery and such, despite his sore feet, Jonathan had quickly resorted each time to dancing again, simply to get away.

Becoming aware that his partnerless state was once again making him a target, and that the maternal swarm was closing in, Jonathan murmured his excuses to the nearest she-wolves and swiftly made his way to where his own mother, Alice, her uncle, and Lady Houghton stood. "Mother, may I—"

"Ah, Jonathan!" his mother interrupted gaily. "This.is a wonderful success, do you not think?"

"Nay, I *do not* think," he snapped, which, wiped the self-satisfied expression off her face.

"What?" she asked in injured tones. "But it is working beautifully."

"Nay. It is working horribly," he corrected.

"But—"

"Mother, there are at least one hundred and fifty women here."

"Well, aye," she agreed soothingly. "But only fifty of them are really of any concern; the rest are merely here to chaperon the girls."

"Still, fifty women and one man are not exactly even odds, are they?"

"Oh, Jonathan," she pshawed. "You are a warrior. Surely you can handle this gaggle of females. Besides, you are not the only man here; Lord Houghton is in attendance." She pointed that out and moved closer to the man, running her hand down his arm in a possessive manner that made Jonathan's skin crawl.

Jonathan snapped, "Well, he may as well not be for all the good he is doing."

"Jonathan!" Lady Fairley turned, obviously shocked by her son's bad manners.

He was beyond tact. "Do not 'Jonathan' me. Lord Houghton has been standing here slobbering over you all evening while I have had my feet danced off, my toes crushed, my ears talked away, my best tunic stained by several clumsy wenches too busy blabbing to watch where they were going, and . . ." He paused to sniff experimentally in Alice's direction, then said in a snarl, "And damned if my sense of smell has not been ruined by the rank bodies or overindulgence in perfume by half of the noblewomen of London!"

Alice bit her lip at Lord Jonathan's outburst, her urge to laugh nearly overwhelming her. She peered curiously at Lady Fairley to see what the woman's reaction to this would be. Margaret of Fairley stood for a moment, mouth agape; then, much to Alice's amazement, her face crumpled like a child's.

"You never appreciate *anything* I do for you, Jonathan. Here I worked so hard at getting permission to hold a feast for you—you know the king feels indebted to you if he'll arrange for this—then attaining the room, arranging the food and drink and inviting everyone, and all you can do is—"

"Oh, I am sure your son appreciates your efforts, my lady," Alice found herself stepping in to say. Guilt had washed over the man's face. "I think he is merely stating that he is a bit overwhelmed. Perhaps 'tis expecting a lot from him to entertain so many women at once. Mayhap 'twould have been better had you invited some men to help with this endeavor."

"Exactly," Lord Jonathan said. "Finally, a woman with some sense."

"Are you suggesting that I have no sense?" Lady Fairley asked with icy politeness. Alice nearly laughed aloud at the poleaxed look on the knight's face.

"Nay, nay," he began quickly. "Of course not, Mother. I never meant to suggest—"

When Lady Fairley opened her mouth in what Alice suspected would be a furious blasting, she couldn't stop herself from intervening again. "I am sure he meant no insult, my lady. It is obvious he is quite worn out from doing his duty this evening and is not thinking straight. Perhaps it would be best if he were to take a stroll in the night air and let his thoughts clear."

"Aye." Jonathan leaped at the proffered escape. Yet, rather than simply slipping away, as she expected, he latched on to her hand and drew her with him. "A little walk through the gardens will be of great assistance in reviving me."

"Oh, but I do not—" Alice protested as he drew her away from the great hall.

"Come. Your presence will keep those other women from following to harass me," he insisted.

As he pulled her along behind him, Alice made a face at his back, but there seemed little use in arguing. Besides, she too was quite ready to get out of the feast. This had been a terribly boring evening for her; standing on the sidelines, watching Jonathan dance with a multitude of ladies. The entire time she was recalling how it had felt to be pressed close to his body, and the scent of him as they had ridden back to court after the picnic.

Alice sighed as those memories enveloped her again. They had a nasty tendency of doing so these last two days, and she didn't at all understand why. She had never before had such problems, never before been plagued by the memory of any single event, but it seemed these days her mind was constantly full of Jonathan and their time together.

"Thank the Lord."

Alice was drawn from her thoughts to find that they had finally made their way outside. Falling into step beside him, she breathed in deeply of the night air and felt herself relax. It was only then that she realized she had been rather stiff and tense all evening. She'd found it irritating to watch Jonathan trip about with all his whirling maidens. Some part of her had even thought it terribly unfair that he hadn't asked her to dance, at least *once*. . . .

Just so she could compare it to how it felt to hold him on horseback, she assured herself quickly. But Alice knew that wasn't true. A part of her was quite unhappy that she wasn't under consideration to be Lord Jonathan's bride, and she couldn't help but wonder why. Not to mention that she couldn't understand why his mother seemed to like her fine when Jonathan wasn't around but showed definite signs of annoyance whenever he was in her company.

"Watch your step."

Alice jerked her attention back to where she was walking, just barely managing to avoid stepping in a dark mass of something unpleasant.

"Where are we going?" She glanced around a bit anxiously. Normally she would not be alone like this with a man. Even the son of a family friend. Actually, now that she thought of it, she was flummoxed that her mother wasn't trailing behind, acting as chaperon. Glancing over her shoulder she saw that no, there was no one following, and yes, they were definitely alone. Most unusual, she decided with confusion.

"The stables."

Alice turned her attention forward again at that answer. "Why?"

"I thought we might go for a ride."

Alice brightened at the thought—sitting behind him again, her arms around him, their bodies pressed close together—then caught back her enthusiasm. Firstly, he likely intended her to be on her own mount. Second, it was not very safe to ride at night. A horse could easily make a misstep and be injured. Also, this simply was not a good idea. What if someone caught them out here? What would people think of her virtue?

Sensing her resistance, and that this time it was a true resistance, Lord Jonathan paused to glance back at her. Her solemn expression seemed to jog his memory about propriety, and he sighed unhappily. "I suppose a ride is out of the question."

"Aye," Alice quietly agreed.

He nodded in resignation. "I just thought it would be nice to ride with you again. I enjoyed it the other day."

Alice blinked at that awkward admission. He wasn't looking at her when he said it; his gaze actually danced everywhere but on her, still, it took her a moment to recognize his sudden shyness, and to realize that he was sincere in his claim. He had enjoyed their ride as much as she had!

"Perhaps . . ." she began, then paused. He was finally looking at her, and his gaze was trained on her mouth. It caused an odd tingling to start in her lips, and breathlessness overcame her. She could not have spoken had she wished. When he started to sway nearer, Alice felt her ability to breathe evaporate altogether. She was absolutely, positively certain he was about to kiss her. She allowed herself to sway toward him in response.

"Jonathan! Oh, there you are! I told James I thought you had gone this way."

Alice and Jonathan leaped guiltily apart and swung around. Lady Fairley and Alice's uncle were approaching through the darkness.

"Mother." The word was almost a groan on Jonathan's lips. Alice could sympathize completely. She felt rather like making a similar noise herself at the moment. His mouth had been so close to hers that she had felt his breath on her tender, tingling lips. But that promise was apparently not to be fulfilled tonight.

"I have decided to forgive you," Lady Fairley announced. She reached them and slid her arm through her son's. "In fact, I have decided you may even be somewhat . . . well, not *completely* wrong about tonight's endeavor."

"Oh?" The knight definitely sounded wary, Alice thought distractedly. Her uncle silently drew her hand onto his arm and they followed Lady Fairley and her son back from the stables.

"Aye," Alice heard Margaret say. "In fact, I have decided to have another feast."

"Another one?" Lord Jonathan came to an abrupt halt.

"Aye. Another one." His mother laughed at his obvious horror and drew his arm back under hers to drag him along. She added gaily, "Two, in fact. Now I just have to speak to the king."

While Jonathan had spent the two days between the picnic and yestereve's feast avoiding Alice and the confusing feelings she stirred in him, the first thing he did upon awakening this morning was to go in search of her. He found the girl breaking her fast in the great hall, where it appeared almost every other guest at court was also eating. The room was overflowing with people, and the benches groaned under the weight of their numbers.

Alice sat at one of the upper tables, her mother on one side, a leering ogre Jonathan didn't know on her other. Striding forward, he managed, with a scowl and an elbow, to make the fellow, one who sat entirely too close to Alice, shift over enough to allow him to squeeze between them.

Alice twisted on the bench in surprise as he unintentionally jostled and nudged her, trying to claim the small space available. Much to his pleasure, the action left her chest smashed against his. Jonathan found himself quite enjoying the situation for the few seconds it lasted, then the girl blushed bright pink and turned to face forward again.

"Good morn, my lord," she said.

Jonathan smiled at the strangled sound of her voice, knowing she was embarrassed. He also knew that his own voice would come out similarly at the moment if he used it—but not from embarrassment. The brief and intimate contact of their bodies had left him almost instantly aroused. Clearing his throat, he grunted in greeting and concentrated on the food and drink set before him. He allowed his body to recover before turning his attention again to her.

Those few moments allowed her to recover her composure, he saw. The red had receded from her face, and a slightly dreamy expression had replaced the embarrassed look of only moments before. "Do you have any plans for the day, my lady?" he asked.

49

"Nay. Why do you ask, my lord?" She glanced at him curiously, then, as he shuffled through his mind for an answer that eluded him, understanding came to her face. A crooked smiled claimed her lips. "Oh, of course. The list."

"The list?" Jonathan repeated blankly.

"Aye. No doubt you wish to go over the list again . . . now that you have interacted with some of those on it. So that you may cross off those you found unacceptable," she added when he continued to stare blankly at her.

"Ah, yes," he murmured. His eyes fell back to his trencher as he contemplated that. It hadn't really been why he'd sought her out this morning. He couldn't say why he had; he'd simply wanted to see her. He had been pondering kissing her since his mother had interrupted what he was pretty sure would have been a hell of a kiss. Of course, he couldn't be positive he would have kissed her. He hadn't really been thinking at that point. At least, he hadn't been thinking, *I am going to kiss her*. Mostly he had been thinking that her lips looked full and soft and tempting, and that they probably tasted as good as they looked, and—

Well, this is neither here nor there, Jonathan told himself. The point was, he had spent a good half of last night imagining a kiss he hadn't given her. The other half *had been spent* dreaming that he *had* kissed her . . . and more. He'd had terribly lascivious dreams, full of Alice's naked, creamy flesh in his hands and mouth, enclosing his hard—

"I had no plans for the day and would be pleased to assist you in this matter."

For a moment, Jonathan thought she meant in the matter he had dreamed of. His heart nearly leaped through his chest with gratitude at the thought, and his body instantly became hard again. He gave his head a shake, peered at her innocent, smiling face, then realized she must mean she would be happy to go over her list with him.

It hadn't at all been the reason he'd sought her out, but he supposed it was the reason he *should* have sought her out.

"Wonderful," he said, frowning at the huskiness of his voice. Clearing his throat, he tried again. "That would be very helpful, thank you."

"If you are through breaking your fast, we may even do so now." Much to Jonathan's horror, she actually started to rise. Grabbing her arm, he stopped her when she would have moved away from the table.

"I, er . . ." He peered down at his lap briefly, then realized that the action was likely to draw her attention to the unfortunate state of his manhood. He raised his gaze abruptly. Clearing his throat, he murmured, "I am not through eating."

When her gaze moved with confusion to his trencher, Jonathan noticed that he had absently consumed every last bite of food that had been set before him.

"I am oddly ravenous this morn," he explained lamely, but she nodded and relaxed back into her seat. Breathing a sigh of relief, Jonathan gestured a servant over and requested more food and another drink. He then glanced at Alice with a smile. Noting the sidelong looks being shot at the two of them by Alice's mother, Jonathan leaned forward and said, "I trust you are feeling well this morn, my lady?"

"Oh." Lady Elizabeth of Houghton flushed. "Aye. Thank you, my lord. And you? Are you prepared for the day's endeavors?"

Lynsay Sands

"Endeavors?" he asked cautiously.

"Aye. Preparations for your next feast."

"What?" Jonathan had no qualms about letting his horror show. Another feast? Over his dead body! He would never again willingly suffer the tortures he had experienced the evening before. He had only refrained from arguing last night because he'd assumed the king would never agree to such activities in his palace. It seemed his mother had more persuasive power with Edward than he'd imagined.

"Oh, dear." Alice's murmur drew his questioning gaze, and she explained, "I had quite forgotten about the feasts. I promised this morning to assist your mother with the preparations."

"That is unnecessary," he said. "I really do not think that another event will be necessary. The last, while not completely unhelpful, was something of an ordeal I would rather not see repeated."

"Oh, but that is why I agreed to assist. I wanted to be sure that it would not be another like last night's debacle," she explained earnestly. "This time, only appropriate women shall be invited. And half of the attendees shall be men, to help balance things out. This way, the other men may entertain the others while you concentrate on one lady at a time. You see?" She smiled at him brightly. "I am sure it will work out much better."

Jonathan grimaced. He was not reassured by the news, but it seemed he had little choice in the matter. Worse, it appeared that Alice was now throwing herself into helping his mother find him a bride.

Now, why did that idea annoy him so much?

Chapter Four

"Oh, I am so sorry, my lord. I am so clumsy."

"What? Oh." Jonathan tore his gaze away from Alice to force a smile for the young woman with whom he was dancing. The throbbing in his toes told him she was apologizing for stomping on his foot. It was the first time Jonathan had been so stomped all evening, but he had hardly noticed the action. His attention had been riveted on Lady Houghton's daughter—and the man presently leading her across the dance floor.

Damn his mother and her never-ending plans! he thought irritably. Muttering some polite comment about his dance partner's misstep, he turned his gaze back to Alice. This was the second bridal feast—the result of several days of work carried out by his mother, himself, Alice, and her mother. Lord Houghton had been present, as well, but that was all. The man was a layabout who apparently considered any manual labor to be beneath him.

Jonathan sighed inwardly. Normally there were a thousand and one other things he would rather have done with the last few days. Certainly bickering over what food and drink to serve at these bloody feasts his mother kept planning was ludicrous for a warrior such as himself. However, none of his alternate pastimes would have included Alice's presence. She had pledged to assist his mother, and that meant that, for him to spend time around her, he'd had to assist as well. And Jonathan had found himself hungering for Alice's presence.

Actually, the lass had managed to make the past two days fun. She and Jonathan had talked and laughed their way through his mother's orders, enjoying each other's company and working together. As he'd suspected, Alice was a clever woman, and her witty turn of phrase and irreverent sense of humor drew Jonathan like a moth to a flame. He only hoped he did not get burned.

"Oops. I have done it again."

This time Jonathan did not need to be told, he'd definitely felt the crunching of his toes as the reel brought him and his partner together again. Had it been a deliberate stomp, with a twist at the end to inflict the most damage? It did not take a lot of thought to realize that the delicate little brat he was dancing with was annoyed with his lack of attention.

He would have been enraged once, but Jonathan was honest enough to admit that he *was* being rude in his lack of attention. He likely even deserved his dance partner's attacks, petty as they were. In truth, he had been rude to almost every single maid he had danced with, what with his gaze and attention being taken up as they were by Alice and her suitors. The wench had hardly sat a dance out. She was forever fluttering around the floor on the arm of one lordling or another. Why the hell had he allowed his mother to invite so many damned men? he wondered irritably. And did they all have to be so bloody attractive?

The third stomp was the final one Jonathan was willing to suffer. It was also the most painful of the three and left him limping as he escorted the little brat off the floor. Leaving her to complain of his distraction to her mama, Jonathan sought out his own mother, intending to do a little complaining of his own.

"Ah, there is my handsome son."

Jonathan grimaced inwardly at his mother's words as he paused at her side, but he gave a polite nod to the group of noblewomen gathered about Lady Fairley. He was beginning to feel like the pride of a stable, being presented for possible stud service.

"Here you are, my dear."

Jonathan did grimace openly as the ever-present Lord Houghton appeared with a drink for his mother, but in truth, it was more from habit than anything else. It was now clear the man was nothing more than a nuisance. Jonathan was positive his mother had more sense than to do aught but dally with the oaf's affections. Of course, if she suddenly decided to marry the bastard, Jonathan would have to kill him, but he would worry about that when and if the time came. At the moment, he was more concerned with Alice's antics.

"My, this was a brilliant idea, Jonathan, and a fine success. Do you not think?"

He nodded absently, hardly hearing his mother's question or the cooed agreement of the surrounding women. He irritably watched yet another man lead Alice through a reel. She was a graceful dancer, her body perfectly in tune to the music. She put all the others to shame.

"Do you not think so, Jonathan?" his mother asked again.

"Hmm?" He glanced around to find a dozen expectant faces turned toward him. He nodded distractedly, then commented, "Lady Alice appears to be quite popular, does she not? She has danced with nearly every man here."

His mother waved that away impatiently. "Really, Jonathan. Whatever does it matter whom Lady Houghton is dancing with? She is not the one who needs to marry. You are. Now, why do you not give Lady Jovell a turn on the floor? You have not danced with her yet."

Jonathan frowned at the suggestion, but he was too polite to give any insult by refusing. He took the arm of the spotty-faced girl who stepped out of the group and led her onto the floor. Fortunately, the chit was the quiet sort who did not seem to desire conversation while dancing. She also didn't seem to mind that his gaze was trained on Lady Alice and the bevy of beaux vying to dance with her. Of course, that may only have been because she spent the entire dance with her head bowed, watching her feet.

At least she did not treat him to a sound foot-stomping for his inattention, and that was something to recommend her, he decided as the music finally ceased.

Afraid that his mother might try to push another young maid on him, Jonathan made returning Lady Jovell a quick business. He merely escorted her back to the group around Lady Fairley, then hurried away, pretending he did not hear his mother when she called.

He moved off in such a rush that he nearly ran over Alice. Steadying her with a hand, he beamed brightly, his first real smile of the night, and promptly took her arm.

"Ah, there you are. Come. Dance with me."

"Come here, come there, come dance with me," Alice muttered, and Jonathan glanced down at her with concern. There was an opening on the dance floor, but he paused, facing her, to await the music.

"Do you not wish to dance with me?"

"Oh." She smiled wryly. "It is not that, my lord. Although I am a bit winded and was hoping for a chance to rest."

"Then what—"

"You have a tendency to order me about, my lord," she pointed out dryly. "Rather like a lackey. And while I realize that I agreed to assist you, I had not realized that it was to be in such a subservient position."

"Subservient?" The expression he gave her was aghast. "I hardly look upon you as a servant."

"Nay?" She raised an eyebrow, a wry smile tugging at her lips. " 'Tis my error, then."

The music began, and they both fell silent as the dance started. The steps first distracted, then separated them as they hopped and skipped through several partners.

The moment they were back together, Jonathan cleared his throat and said, "You said you were hoping to rest. Would you prefer—"

"Nay. I am fine, my lord. I may rest after this dance."

"Ah. I am not surprised that you are weary. I had noticed that you appear to be quite popular as a dance partner."

Jonathan wished he could retract the words the moment they left his mouth. The comment had definitely sounded rather peevish, and the curious look Alice sent him before the steps of the dance drew her away from him again made clear that she had taken notice of it. It seemed an eternity before the dance returned her to him.

"I was rather amazed myself at my popularity," was her mild comment as they moved together through a simple alman.

"Amazed?" He scowled at her. "There is nothing to be amazed about. You are a beautiful woman, intelligent and witty. Of course you are popular." He did not sound pleased by this admission, even to himself.

"Do you really think so?"

Jonathan glanced down sharply at her almost whispered query. The girl's eyes had gone all soft and dewy. For a moment he was positive that she might cry just from his giving her such a compliment; then he spared the time to toss another glare in her uncle's direction. Obviously the wretch did not waste time complimenting Alice as he should. As anyone who loved her—and in whose care she had been left—should do.

"Aye," he said quietly. "I think you are all those things and more, Alice."

"Do you think we might slip outside for another walk?" she asked.

Jonathan blinked in surprise, his mind suddenly awhirl with possibilities. A romantic walk under the stars? A chance to claim that kiss he had missed out on two nights before? Then he noted Alice's expression as she apparently realized just what she had suggested. Fearing she might retract the offer, he headed quickly for the door.

They were just about to slip out when his mother and Alice's suddenly stepped into their path.

"*There* you are!"

Jonathan closed his eyes. He was becoming heartily sick of that phrase.

"Alice, your mother is not feeling well, and she would

like you to accompany her back to your room."

Jonathan wasn't at all fooled by the claim. He could clearly see the determination in his mother's eyes. He had also taken notice of the startled expression on Lady Houghton's face before she managed to cover it with what he supposed she believed could pass for the pathetic expression of an ailing individual.

"Oh, Mother!" Alice was immediately at the older woman's side, offering her arm for support. "Is it something you ate, do you think?"

"I, er, I am not sure, dear." Lady Houghton's gaze jumped to Lady Fairley, then away. "It may be. I simply feel awful."

Lady Houghton was a lousy thespian, Jonathan decided. He sighed unhappily as his chance to get Alice outside, alone under the moon and stars, slipped away.

"Well, come, we shall get you above stairs and put you to bed." Casting a regretful glance in Jonathan's direction, Alice departed with her mother, leaving Jonathan to turn an irritated glance on his own. Before he could catapult the accusations swimming around in his head, however, she drew forward a young sticklike figure in a dress and smiled brilliantly. "This is Lady Estemia Kolpepper, my dear. You have not yet had the chance to dance with her."

Outmaneuvered again, Jonathan gave his mother a look that promised retribution and took the arm of his latest offering.

Jonathan was heartily sick of seeing Alice fly by on the arm of some man or other. It did not matter that he himself had danced with equally as many women. The fact was, she was far too popular with the men in attendance at this, his last day of bridal feasting, and he did not like it.

The dance finally ended and Jonathan escorted his latest partner off the floor. He left her in the general vicinity of where he had collected her, then strode purposely toward Alice. He'd had quite enough of dancing with clumsy oxen and spoiled mama's girls. Jonathan had also had quite enough of watching Alice dragged across the floor by every lecher at court. Had his mother deliberately invited every ne'er-do-well who gathered around the king?

"Oh, Jonathan." Alice beamed on him when he paused before her. "Have you met Lord Roderic of Somersby?"

"Nay, and I do not wish to," was his abrupt answer. He swept her out onto the dance floor as the musicians started again.

The first song had ended and a second begun before he noticed the way Alice was shaking silently at his side. For a moment, his black mood was displaced by concern that she might be crying or some such womanly thing, but then he glimpsed the expression on her face. It was mirth she was attempting to subdue that was making her shake so.

"What the devil do you find so amusing?" he asked.

"You," she answered promptly, a laugh slipping out before she could stop it. "You look like a sulky boy. What has gotten under your cap, my lord? Not enjoying this bridal feast?"

Jonathan growled at her gentle teasing, his gaze moving hungrily over her sparkling eyes and cheerful grin. "No, but I notice *you* have been enjoying it."

"If you think so, my lord, I fear you are sadly mistaken." She spoke so cheerfully, for a moment Jonathan wasn't sure he had heard right.

"Are you saying you are not enjoying the feast?"

Her smile slipped and she sighed. "My lord, my feet ache, it is positively stifling in here, and if I have to listen to one more grand tale of bravery in battle, I shall surely die of boredom."

For some reason, her litany of miseries cheered Jonathan somewhat. He found himself smiling at her in return.

"My lord, are you aware that the music has changed again?" When he stared at her blankly, she explained, "This is our third reel."

"I had not noticed," Jonathan admitted wryly. "After three days of feasting and dancing, all the songs are sounding the same." He leaned forward and confided, "I have been judging the length of a dance by how many times my feet were stepped on."

Alice was amused by Lord Jonathan's admission, but the man had obviously not taken her point. "Well, I fear your mother has noticed even if you have not, and she appears to be growing irritated."

Her dance partner glanced over toward his mother, but his only reaction was to tighten his hand on hers.

She decided to try again. "In fact, she is beginning to look quite vexed. Really, my lord, I take her point. Is this feast not about finding a bride for you? 'Twill be difficult for you to do so should you continue dancing with me, neglecting the women brought here for you to consider."

"I need consider the matter no further. Any one of them is interchangeable with the others. Besides, I like dancing with *you*. You do not step on my toes, you do not breathe garlic into my face, you do not spill food on me, and you can converse."

Alice blinked once, twice, then ventured, "Converse? I take it you have found some of the women—"

"Unable to string two words together that have more than four letters in them. And many of them are deceitful. You should hear what they say about each other!"

"Oh, dear." Alice bit her tongue to keep from laughing. Then she became worried. "Oh, my. Your mother is headed in our direction. I suspect she is about to tell you that you should be dancing with the others."

Lord Jonathan glanced over his shoulder, his expression becoming irritated. He promptly began to walk Alice in the opposite direction.

"What are you doing?" she asked in surprise.

"I am getting us out of here."

"Oh, but—" Alice began. She got no farther as Lord Jonathan picked up the pace. He hustled her out of the great hall, and a glance over Alice's shoulder just before they slipped through the door showed Lady Fairley pausing, hands on hips, eyes narrowed, as she watched them flee. She did not look at all pleased. Once again, Alice was reminded that the woman positively did not see her as bridal material for her son. She found herself inexplicably saddened.

Lord Jonathan slowed to a walk once they were outside, and Alice glanced at him curiously, peering at his face in the moonlight. His distraction was obvious, so she left him to his thoughts and they walked in companionable silence for several moments; then she recognized the path he had taken. She smiled slightly.

"The stables again, my lord?" she asked with quiet humor.

"What?" He sounded bewildered, then glanced around and seemed to realize she meant their destination. He shook his head. "Nay."

Despite his negation, they continued silently in that general direction, but Alice didn't question him further. She noted, however, that he was rubbing his stomach absently, his gaze and face working as if he were resolving some problem. Quite suddenly he asked, "Are you hungry, Alice?"

Startled by his use of her given name, it took Alice a moment to digest his question. She considered it seriously and nodded with some surprise. "Aye. Actually, I am."

"As am I. Come." Taking her hand again, he tugged her off the path they had been on and along another, this one leading around the back of the keep. He urged her silently through a door there, pressed a finger to his lips, then led her along a dim hallway that grew warmer as they went.

"Wait here," he instructed, bringing her to a halt outside a set of double doors. He slid through.

Alice obeyed for all of a minute; then curiosity got the better of her. She cautiously eased open the door, and wasn't at all surprised to see that the doors led into the kitchens. And what a huge kitchen it was, she thought with awe. Houghton Castle had a rather large scullery of its own, but this had to be at least ten times bigger. Alice supposed that it was necessary here at the palace. Certainly Houghton Castle, even with all its servants and men-at-arms, still had nowhere near the number of people to feed as did the palace.

Her gaze skimmed the small army of servants cleaning up the kitchens, until it came to rest on Jonathan. The big knight stood talking to a man she could only guess was the head cook, who was eyeing him with a jaundiced eye and shaking his head firmly.

Jonathan, Lord Fairley, was not the sort to take no for an answer, though. As Alice watched, he talked and talked and smiled and charmed, then finally resorted to bribery. He pulled out a small sack of what Alice guessed were coins and pressed them on the man—whose attitude abruptly changed. The chef transformed from a narrow-eyed, grim-faced man to a jolly little cherub who pressed a basket on Jonathan and led him around stuffing food into it. Alice eased the door closed again.

When Lord Jonathan stumbled back out to rejoin her some moments later, he was bearing an overflowing basket and had a skin of wine tucked under his chin. Alice chuckled at the slightly stunned expression on his face, then relieved him of the wine.

"Accommodating fellow, was he not?" she asked with amusement. They moved up the hall.

"Aye, once I showed him some coin." He shook his head. "I think I may have been overgenerous."

Alice laughed softly. "Well, it did appear a hefty sack you offered him."

"I was so hungry, I would have given him half of Fairley Castle . . . and had begun to fear I might have to. He was not eager to indulge us." He chuckled.

Alice grinned at his tired jollity, then leaned toward him, poking at the contents of the basket as they walked. "What did he give you?"

"Everything." Lord Jonathan slowed a bit to adjust for her slightly staggered gait; she was trying to continue forward while twisting about to investigate the booty. "It would be easier to say what he did not give us."

Us. Alice left off poking through the basket, her gaze shooting quickly to the knight's face, then away as the word played in her mind. *Us. As if we were a couple*, she thought slowly as they exited the keep the same way they had entered. The idea pleased her immensely. In fact, the amount of pleasure it stirred in her was somewhat shocking. *Us.* She found herself smiling for no reason at all as she followed Jonathan through the darkness.

"Here. The perfect spot."

Pausing as he did, Alice glanced around the location he had chosen: a small clearing deep in the royal gardens. Two benches stood on either side of the path, one not far from a statue that seemed to gleam silver in the moonlight. It was that piece that finally told her where they were: this was the same clearing where she had first met Lord Jonathan, where he and his mother had joined her, her mother, and her uncle that first morning.

Her eyes slid slowly over the statue now. During daylight it appeared sweet, the woman bearing a sad, loving expression. Now, with moonlight casting shadows over it, it looked different. Rather than poignant, the statue's expression seemed seductive, that of a woman calling to a lover. The gown, which had seemed perfectly respectful and demure in daylight, seemed to cling and emphasize a lush shape.

"Ah."

Alice turned her attention from the statue to Jonathan. He had settled on the bench they had occupied that first day, and he was withdrawing items from the basket and setting them in the center of the bench. Giving up her position before the statue, Alice moved closer, smiling as he oohed and ahhed over their treasure. It appeared he hadn't paid much attention to whatever the chef had pressed into the basket, for he was obviously pleasantly surprised by many of the items he set out.

"Ahhhh, a feast worthy of a king." He sighed as he placed the last foodstuff on the bench and set the container aside.

"My, yes." Alice gazed over the fare with wide eyes.

"Just how heavy was that purse you gave the chef?"

"Too heavy, apparently." The big knight chuckled. "Come sit."

He patted the empty portion of the bench, on the other side of the food from himself, then lifted a chicken leg and offered it to her as she sat. Alice accepted the offering, surprised to find she truly was quite hungry. They ate in companionable silence for several moments; then, as their hunger eased, they began to talk.

Alice was eating a fruit tart when it happened. The pastry crumbled slightly as she bit into it, smearing some of the berry filling on her cheek by the corner of her mouth. Chuckling, Jonathan leaned forward to catch up the sticky goo with a finger, then unthinkingly stuck that finger into his mouth. Apparently affected by the action, Alice stared at him, wide-eyed. Her expression made Jonathan aware of what he had just done, and their gazes met in one meaningful moment of silent communication.

"It is a pleasant night," Alice blurted then, setting the rest of her tart down on the bench.

"Aye." Jonathan gazed around, then up at the sky. "A clear, starry night, though there is a cool breeze. Are you chilled?"

Alice started to shake her head no, then realized that she was absently rubbing her upper arms. She shrugged. "A little. But not enough to wish to give up this lovely evening."

Jonathan frowned, not wishing her to suffer discomfort, but not wishing to bring an end to this interlude, either. He took a moment to marvel over the fact that she had admitted as much, herself. But then, he had noted that natural honesty in her quite early. Alice had a strong sense

of truth and honor. She had staunchly refused to participate in spying on his mother and her uncle, Lord Houghton. After a hesitation, he removed his cape and settled it
around her shoulders.

"Oh, but then you will be cold," she protested, trying
to remove the gift.

"Nay, your very presence warms me," he said quietly.
Replacing the garment around her shoulders and smiling
at the softening of her expression, Jonathan hesitated, then
used the cape to draw her closer.

This time there was no sudden arrival of his mother or
hers, no interruption to stop him at all, and he let a small
sigh slip from his lips as his mouth settled over hers. Her
mouth was as soft and pliant as he expected, and he spent
a moment just enjoying the warm feel of her before sliding
his tongue out, questing for hers. Much to his pleasure,
her lips opened at once. He suspected it was more from
surprise than an understanding of what he was request-
ing, for while she allowed her mouth to slide open, she
started to retreat at once in surprise.

Smiling against her mouth, Jonathan lifted his hand to
the back of her neck, ending her retreat, then kissed her
as he had imagined doing since the picnic. After one startled moment, Alice joined in. Her response was definitely
lacking in skill, but was enthusiastic nonetheless. Jonathan
spent several moments teaching her. By the time the les-
son was over and he broke the kiss, they were both breathless and panting.

"Oh, my." Alice gasped shakily as they stared at each
other in the moonlight.

"Aye," Jonathan murmured. He brushed a thumb gently over the side of her face; then, because he simply
couldn't resist her passion-swollen lips, he bent to kiss her

again. She was a quick learner; this time there was no need for tutelage, and she opened her mouth without his bidding, inviting him to deepen the kiss. Her boldness made the blood surge in Jonathan, but when she shifted instinctively closer, pressing her upper body into his, he gave up what little restraint he had and let his hands begin to explore. The hand at the back of her head slid down over the curve of her shoulder, sliding partway across her arm before drifting around to cross their bodies and cover one breast.

Alice promptly stiffened, her breath catching on a small gasp that briefly sucked the air out of his mouth; then her kisses became more frantic. Her arms wrapped around his neck and clutched almost desperately there as he squeezed and fondled until he could feel her nipple grow hard through her gown.

"Oh, please," she said softly against his cheek as he let his lips break away from hers. He slid them along the curve of her jaw. "Oh, ahhhh."

Jonathan smiled against her throat as her head dropped back, her breath coming in violent little pants as he sucked and nibbled at her tender flesh. Then she raised her head abruptly, desperately seeking his questing mouth for another kiss. Jonathan gave her what she wanted, his kisses less gentle and more devouring. His other hand slid down her waist and across her hip over the material of her gown then slowly shifted around to the inside of her leg. She didn't seem to notice what he was doing at first, her senses preoccupied with his other caresses, but when he reached the apex of her thighs and touched her there, she jumped, breaking the kiss with a start. Her eyes went round and uncertain.

Jonathan kept his hand still, allowing her to get used to

its presence, and managed what he hoped was a gentle smile before he again brushed his lips lightly over hers. When she remained passive under that caress, neither protesting nor participating in his kiss, he brushed her lips again. He let his mouth drift over to her ear and set to work, nipping and tugging at the soft, plump lobe, then at the sensitive spot behind.

"Ohhhh." The word came out on a quavering sigh as Alice melted beneath his caresses. Jonathan felt relief rush through him. He was hard with desire from just their kisses, and he felt sure he would die if he had to stop now. She was an innocent, of course, and he knew he could not take this too far, but he felt sure that he could control himself. He would just go a little further, enjoy this beauty's awakening passion a little more. Touch her, and taste her, and . . . Dear God, he wanted her as he had wanted no other woman before. But Jonathan knew he couldn't take her innocence. He renewed his assault on her throat and ear, then began to apply pressure between her legs, pressing the material of her gown against her. Rubbing slightly, he slid his tongue into her mouth once more.

Alice was dying of pleasure. Her eyes were open, staring blindly up at the stars above as Lord Jonathan did delicious things to her. She knew he should not do these things, but her body was clamoring under his gentle assault, and she seemed helpless to stop him. In fact, when the hand between her legs slid away, she nearly sobbed in protest. She caught her lower lip between her teeth to prevent such wanton behavior.

Her teeth bit down in surprise when Alice felt his hand actually touch the naked flesh of her calf. He had not stopped, but had dragged her skirt up and slid his hand under to glide gently over her knee to the sensitive skin of her thigh. A nervous giggle slid from her mouth into his, and she squirmed slightly from the tingles radiating out from his caress. His hand returned to its former position—between her legs. And this time, there was nothing to shield her from his touch.

Alice moaned long and low into his mouth, bucking slightly beneath this new caress as his fingers dipped into the slick core of her.

The sensations racing through her then were overwhelming. Alice was hardly aware when he used his other hand to drag her lower body across the remnants of their picnic. She was soon thigh-to-thigh with him. His mouth covered hers again, and he pressed her back as his touch became more aggressive.

They hardly noticed their tumble from the bench. Lord Jonathan took just enough notice to twist them so that he landed on the bottom with her splayed atop him; then he rolled her onto her back, his mouth dropping to cover her breast through her gown.

Alice felt the moist heat through the cloth, then heard Jonathan curse before he removed the hand between her legs to use both hands to tug at the top of her clothing. Missing that touch, Alice promptly began to help him, tugging and shimmying until her breasts were bared to his attentions. She groaned and arched when his mouth latched onto one swollen nipple, then twisted and arched again as his hand found its way back under her skirt and moved directly back to where she wanted it. The combination left her completely mindless, a twisting, trembling mass beneath him.

"Please," she said in a gasp, reduced to begging. "Please, oh, Jonathan, please."

She thrust into his caress instinctively, her hands moving over what she could reach of him; his head, his hair, his shoulders and upper arms. She thrashed her legs restlessly until he cast one of his own over hers, nudging them apart and holding them still at the same time. Then she felt something begin to press deep into her, and she bucked in shock. Alice glanced down, thoroughly confused when she saw that Lord Jonathan still lay half on her and half off, fully clothed, only his hand between her legs. It took a moment for her to deduce that it was his finger inside her, and it was such an odd sensation that she went still, unsure whether she liked it or not. She did know that she missed his caress of a moment before, but then the caress started up again, similar but different, and she cried out in gratitude. Some part of her mind was guessing that he was using his thumb, but for the most part, her brain was beyond caring or thinking what he was doing so long as he didn't stop. She began to shift and thrust into his touch, clenching her hands into his hair to draw his mouth up for a kiss she desperately needed.

He accommodated her, and the kiss was as fiery and passionate as she'd yearned for. The next moment, Alice tore her mouth away to cry out as pleasure ripped through her. Her inner muscles contracted and vibrated, her thighs clenching around Lord Jonathan's hand, her arms and fingers tightening, her heart seeming to stop. When she regained herself enough to become aware of what was going on around her, it was to find Jonathan gently holding her, murmuring calming words as he pressed gentle kisses on her face.

"I—" Alice began, feeling shame and embarrassment

71

slowly make their inevitable appearance, but her lover shushed her at once. He pressed a soothing kiss to her lips.

"Jonathan!"

Their kiss ended abruptly at that scandalized cry. A scramble ensued as Lord Jonathan quickly tugged her skirt down and sat up, shifting to block Alice from view. She tried desperately to straighten her gown.

"Mother!" There was no mistaking Lord Jonathan's outrage at this interruption, Alice decided as she struggled to right her clothing with hands that shook with humiliation.

"Do not 'Mother' *me* as though I am the one in the wrong, son. How *could* you?"

"I think you had best come with me, Alice."

Finished with her gown, Alice stiffened at those words. She sat up to peer reluctantly over Lord Jonathan's shoulder. A little sigh escaped her at the sight of her mother with Lady Fairley. It just figured the woman would be here to witness her daughter's shame, Alice thought unhappily. The only positive point at that moment, it seemed to Alice, was that Uncle James was not also in attendance.

"Alice."

Grimacing at her mother's tone of voice, Alice got reluctantly to her feet and moved around Lord Jonathan to follow Lady Houghton as she turned abruptly and started back up the path.

"Wait! Alice."

A glance over her shoulder showed Jonathan struggling to his feet to pursue her. Eager to be away from the scene of her humiliation, Alice did not stop, but she did slow down enough for him to catch up. Much to her relief, her mother continued on, unaware that her daughter was no longer on her heels. Alice had one brief moment in which she thought she might get a word alone with Jonathan to reassure herself that he did not think as poorly of her as everyone else apparently did, but it was only one moment; she glanced back to see Lady Fairley step into her son's path.

"Let her go!" the woman said, in a hiss. "I have told you all along that girl is not good enough for you, and now here I find her tossing about on the ground with you like some tavern wench out for a quick roll in the hay."

That was all Alice needed to hear. She had found Lady Fairley's treatment of her to be strange all along. The woman was pleasant enough when her son was not around, but cold when he was. Alice had wondered at that behavior, but now she understood. Lady Fairley disliked her. That dislike was obvious in the woman's tone just now. And her words had left little confusion over why.

Turning away, her eyes burning with tears, Alice ran through the darkness to catch up to her mother. The sweet interlude she had just experienced with Jonathan was suddenly a dirty, shameful thing, and the brief hopes for the future it had engendered in her died an abrupt death.

"Do not say another word or I swear, Mother, I shall—" Jonathan paused and swallowed the bile in his throat, trying to swallow his rage along with it. He had never felt anything close to the fury that had swamped him as his mother had insulted Alice. He had even actually started to raise his hand, preparing to slap her for saying what she had, but then had caught it back. Clenching it at his side, he told himself that Alice had left; the words could not hurt her so long as she had not heard them—and she would never hear them. Ever. Now he took a deep breath and glared at his mother coldly. "I am aware of your feelings regarding Alice. You have made them clear many times. However, I suggest you attempt to get over them, because first thing on the morrow, I intend to ask her to marry me."

On that note, he turned and strode briskly from the clearing.

Chapter Five

"Alice!"

"Oh, damn," Alice muttered under her breath, recognizing that voice. She didn't need to look over her shoulder to know that Lord Jonathan was riding up behind her; she could hear the thunder of his horse's hooves. To be honest, she had rather hoped that taking herself away from the palace for the day would help her avoid him. One day: that was all she had hoped for, one day to compose herself and prepare to have to face him after last night's shameful conclusion.

It appeared it was too much to ask for.

He drew up alongside her and reached over to catch at the reins of her mount. "I have been looking for you all morning," he said accusingly as he drew her horse and his own to a halt. "*Everyone* has been looking for you. Even your mother had no idea where you had gone."

"I thought a ride would be nice. I . . ." Her words died

abruptly when he suddenly leaned across the distance separating them and pressed his lips to hers. For a moment Alice went stiff, but then she softened with a moan and kissed him back.

"Good morn, my lady," he murmured huskily a moment later.

Alice opened her eyes. "Good morn," she answered solemnly.

"I would like to thank you."

His words made her blink. "For what, my lord?"

"For last night."

She immediately flushed with a combination of embarrassment and shame. He then urged his mount closer, attempting to hug her and pull her off of her mount onto his own at the same time, but she evaded him by urging her mare sideways. "Please, my lord. I—"

"Surely you can call me Jonathan," he chided gently, allowing her to escape him for the moment.

"I think it would be better if I did not."

"As you wish," he said mildly. "Howbeit, once the wedding is over, I will insist on your calling me Jonathan—at least in private."

Alice stilled, her uncertain gaze finding and locking on his. "The wedding? You have chosen a bride?"

"I have chosen you. If you will have me."

For one sweet moment, Alice's heart seemed to dance out of her chest with joy. Then, as thoughts of Lady Fairley intruded, it landed back in place with a bump that caused her actual pain.

"Alice?" Jonathan asked worriedly when she remained silent. "You *will* marry me, will you not?"

"Nay."

"Nay?" He stared at her blankly. "But . . . I realize we

have not known each other long, but I thought that we got along rather well, and—"

" 'Tis not you, Jonathan," she said gently. "I would marry you in a heartbeat, were it not for—"

"What?" he asked, catching her arms as if expecting her to flee.

"Your mother," she said quietly.

Lord Jonathan's hands dropped away weakly, his expression becoming one of defeat. "My mother."

"I am afraid so. She dislikes me greatly. I know that."

"Nay, she—"

"I heard what she said last night," Alice interrupted, bringing his protest to a halt. She watched rage flood over his features; then he paled and glanced away. A helpless look overcame his face. She guessed it meant that he realized he could not argue; she had already overheard the truth.

" 'Tis not my mother you would be marrying," he said finally, an almost pleading look on his face as he turned back.

"Nay. I know. But did I marry you, I would have to live with her and her dislike of me forever." Pained by the look in his eyes, she reached out to caress his cheek gently as she tried to make him understand. "I love you, Jonathan, but I could not bear a life with a mother-in-law who hates me. My mother had that. My father's mother made her miserable. She made us all miserable with her constant and open hatred of my mother when I was young. It was like living on a battlefield where words were used in place of swords. I could not bear that. I am sorry.

"And I know you love your mother. I saw it in the way you were so protective of her when she was with Uncle James. I would do nothing to see that relationship destroyed." Retrieving her reins from his slack hands, she turned her mare and started back toward court at a canter. She didn't look back at the possible future she was leaving behind, and Jonathan let her go.

"Mother!"

"Oh, dear." Lady Fairley rushed across the room, plopped onto the stool by the fire, and snatched up her hairbrush just as Jonathan crashed into the chamber.

"Good morn, son," she said waspishly, pulling the brush through her hair with studied indifference. "I suppose you have proposed to that girl?"

"Aye."

Margaret barely restrained herself from leaping from her seat with a victorious shout, and had to take a moment to calm herself before she could speak. "And when is the wedding to be?" She asked at last, affecting a sneer. Five years of planning, and at last her scheme had met with success!

"Never. She refused me."

Lady Fairley leaped to her feet after all, but her roar was far from victorious. *"What?"*

"I said, she refused me," he repeated.

"Well, why?" Lady Fairley gasped. "Surely she does not think herself too good for you, does she?"

"Nay. She thinks she is too good for you," he snapped.

That took her aback, and Margaret sank onto her stool in dismay. "What?"

"Alice knows you do not like her. She overheard your slurs and insults about her last night."

"Oh . . . I see." Lady Fairley bit her lip under her son's accusatory glare, then rallied. "Well, that hardly matters. 'Tis not me she will be marrying."

"Which is exactly what I argued. However, it seems that Lady Houghton, her mother, apparently suffered under a hateful mother-in-law who did not like her. Alice's grandmother made Alice, her mother, and father miserable with her hatred of Lady Houghton. Alice has no wish to repeat history . . . so refuses to marry me. Because of you."

"Oh, dear. I had forgotten about that," Margaret muttered under her breath. She frowned.

"What?" Jonathan glanced at her sharply, and Margaret turned her glower on him.

"Never mind. I shall take care of this," she announced, setting down her brush.

"What? How?" he asked sharply, following her to the door.

"I shall have James find her and send her here to talk to me."

Her big knight of a son threw his hands up helplessly. "Oh, *that* will be of great assistance. I may as well go tell the king to pick me a bride. You shall scare her off completely if you interfere."

"Nonsense." Margaret smiled, sure she could help. "Have a little faith in your mother."

Alice lectured herself grimly all the way to Lady Fairley's chamber. She really had no desire to see the woman who had ruined her happiness, let alone speak to her. However, her uncle had found her in the small alcove where she'd been indulging in self-pity and tears, alternately berating herself for giving up the happiness she might have enjoyed with Jonathan, and assuring herself that she had made the right choice. A mother-in-law who hated her would have made both their lives miserable.

Always having been uncomfortable with tears, her uncle had shifted anxiously about, his gaze landing everywhere but on her as he had announced that she was to go directly to Lady Fairley's chamber. He had made it clear that this was an order from her mother that was not to be brooked and that dallying was out of the question.

For one moment, Alice had considered rebelling against her uncle's command to visit Lady Margaret, but then had decided she did not have the energy. Now she found herself pausing outside the door of the nasty witch who had ruined her life. She had no idea why she had been summoned here, but had no doubt it had something to do with Jonathan. Alice supposed it was possible that he had informed his mother of his intention to propose, and that this was some attempt by Lady Fairley to be sure Alice said no when he did. Of course, there was no need for such a request now, but perhaps Jonathan had not yet informed his mother of Alice's refusal. Which left it up to her to do. *Great*.

Taking a deep breath, she pasted a nonchalant smile on her face and tapped on the door.

"Enter."

Alice grimaced at the command, but quickly replaced her anger with a more pleasant, though less honest, smile. She opened the door.

"Ah, Alice." Lady Fairley stood up from her seat by the fire and started across the room. Oddly enough, she wore a welcoming smile on her face. Which served only to make Alice warier. "Thank you for coming, I—"

"You need not fear, my lady. I am not going to marry Jonathan," Alice blurted. The older woman's smile faded and she halted as if struck by a lance.

Quite sure the woman would be grateful to hear the

news, Alice was wholly unprepared when Lady Fairley roared, "Oh, yes, you are!"

Alice blinked in surprise, sure she had misunderstood. "I beg your pardon?"

"My dear girl, I have worked too long and too hard to get the two of you together to have you refuse Jonathan now."

Alice gaped. "Excuse me?"

"You heard me. Sit down."

Confusion reining in her poor, woolly mind, Alice sat on the nearest item of furniture, the end of Lady Fairley's bed. She watched in bewilderment as Lady Fairley began to pace.

"First off," Jonathan's mother said abruptly, "I wish to know if you love my son. Or think you can grow to love him."

"I . . . yes," she stammered, too bewildered to lie. "I do."

"Good." But the satisfied smile that came to Lady Fairley's face did not reassure Alice. "I can explain. Jonathan is a wonderful boy: intelligent, charming, handsome, loving . . . every mother's delight. But he does have one flaw. He is as stubborn and contrary as his father ever was."

"That would be two flaws, my lady. And I have already noticed them," Alice agreed. Lady Fairley knelt down by her side at once.

"Of course you did, you brilliant girl!" She took Alice's hands in her own as she rose and settled on the edge of the bed next to her. "And even with these flaws you will love him."

"No one is perfect, my lady. And as flaws go, stubbornness and a contrary nature are rather typical of men."

"Aye." Lady Fairley sighed. "However, I doubt you have quite grasped the depth of his stubborn and contrary

81

nature, especially when it comes to myself. I fear Jonathan is . . . constantly suspecting me of some scheme or another. And . . . well, were I to point out that the sky was blue, he would swear it was orange simply to avoid agreeing with me. Especially if he thought he might find himself ensnared in some imaginary plot."

"Oh, dear." Alice patted Lady Fairley's hand sympathetically. "That must be trying."

"Oh, my dear, you have no idea." Lady Fairley shook her head tragically, then heaved a sigh and went on. "So, seeing as how he was dallying about finding a bride, I—Oh!" She interrupted herself, giving a nervous laugh. "I mean, when the king gave the order for Jonathan to choose a bride within two weeks, well, I decided it was time I took a hand in his future. Two weeks is a very short time to find a bride. I knew he would take no advice from me, so . . ." She shrugged helplessly.

"So you schemed and plotted to aid him in the endeavor," Alice suggested.

"Aye." Lady Fairley beamed at her, apparently missing the irony in Alice's voice. "Your cleverness is one of the reasons I felt sure you would be perfect for him. And I did know you would be perfect, my dear. Oh, I introduced him to the daughters of various other friends, but I knew they would not catch his interest. I was simply giving him something to measure you by, knowing you would come out shining above the rest. Of course, I could not introduce you the same way. He would have rejected you whether he was interested or not, simply to confound me. I had to find a way to make him wish to be around you . . . So, your mother, and I—"

"Uncle James," Alice said softly as the realization struck.

Jonathan's mother nodded. "I fear I was not much taken with your uncle; however, he really did come through for us. And, to be honest, he was really only necessary the first day or two. After that, I do not think Jonathan cared so much what I did. My plan was working beautifully; his attention was wholly taken up with you."

Alice digested that slowly. "Am I to understand that the courtship that you and my uncle were indulging in was all a sham meant somehow to convince Jonathan to ask me to marry him?"

"Aye."

Alice briefly chewed that claim over, then asked bluntly, "Why? You detest me."

"Detest you? Nay, child! I adore you. You will be a wonderful daughter-in-law. Why, you are clever and sweet and honest to the bone, and . . ." Pausing, Lady Fairley framed Alice's face with her hands and allowed a true affection to show through. "Alice, had I had a daughter of my own, instead of a son, I would have liked her to be you."

Alice felt tears well up inside her at that kind claim, but shook her head with confusion. "But I heard you telling Jonathan—"

"I am sorry, my dear." Lady Fairley interrupted with sincere regret. "Jonathan told me that you overheard me last night, but I never intended for you to be privy to that nonsense. What I said then was not at all true; I was simply misleading Jonathan. I was hoping to raise his interest by making him think I did not care for you."

"I see," Alice murmured, gazing down at her hands.

A moment of silence passed as Alice considered all she had learned; then Lady Fairley could stand it no longer. "So? You will marry my son?"

Alice lifted her head slowly and peered at Margaret for a long time; then she nodded. "Aye."

"Oh, lovely!" Jonathan's mother exclaimed, hugging her happily. "You are perfect for each other. I know you will be happy together. I—"

"On one condition."

Lady Fairley stiffened. "Condition?"

"Aye. As much as I appreciate that you love Jonathan, and that you want only the best for him . . . And as much as I appreciate how you got us together, I really must insist that the interference stop here, this very moment. I will not marry Jonathan if it means spending the rest of my life worrying about what you are up to."

"Oh, my dear." Smiling, Lady Margaret patted the girl's hands affectionately. "I will be more than happy to stop my interfering. All I wanted in the world was to see my boy happy, and I knew he could be very, very happy with you. Now that the two of you are together, there is no longer any necessity for me to interfere. I can happily retire and enjoy my golden years."

Alice relaxed and smiled. Her eyes growing misty, she squeezed the older woman's hands. "Thank you, then. For everything you have done."

"You are more than welcome, my dear." Lady Margaret hugged Alice briefly, then sat back and smiled. "Now, Jonathan is waiting in the garden where we found you last night. Go drag my son out of the misery your refusal has sunk him in. I promise, this time I shall not interrupt."

Beaming, Alice rose quickly and rushed from the room.

Lady Fairley watched the girl go, then opened the chest beside her with a pleased sigh.

"What are you doing now, Margaret?" Elizabeth of Houghton slid out from behind the curtains that had been hiding her for the past several minutes. Her best friend since childhood was drawing a piece of parchment and a quill and ink out of the chest.

"Setting to work on a plan to get Alice with child. All we need are grandbabies to make things perfect."

"From what I saw when we *finally* interrupted those two last night, babies will not be a problem," Elizabeth said dryly. She moved forward to look over her friend's shoulder at the list being written.

"I told you, it would not have done to stop them too early. Had Jonathan not already intended to wed Alice at that point, we would have been able to use what we saw to force them to marry. Which would not have been possible had we interrupted earlier," Lady Fairley said, sounding a touch irritated. "Besides, while they may be enthusiastic about the endeavor, one can never tell how the matter of fertility rests with the two of them. A little help in that area will not hurt." Then she glanced up with a twinkle in her eye. "I spent the better part of the winter investigating which herbs increase a woman's fertility, and which a man's ardor. . . . Just in case."

"When you were not plotting how to get the two together, and corresponding with me on the details of that plan?" Elizabeth asked dryly.

" 'Twas a long winter, was it not?" came Lady Fairley's response. "And 'tis always nice to have a project to occupy the mind during such long, bitter winters."

"Hmm." Lady Houghton shook her head at her friend's antics, watching her draw up a list of ways to encourage grandchildren. "Did I not hear you vow mere moments ago never again to interfere in the lives of our children?"

"Oh, well. And I shan't . . . except for ensuring that I get grandbabies."

"But you swore on your honor." Lady Houghton taunted.

Margaret gave her a dry look. "Elizabeth, darling, you know that a mother lets nothing, not even her own needs, not even her honor, stand in the way of her child's happiness . . . and getting her grandbabies."

"Alice!" Jonathan leaped to his feet the moment he saw her approaching and silently blessed his mother for whatever it was she had said. Things must be fixed, for that was the only reason he could see that Alice would be there. He knew he was right when, as soon as she spied him, a smile bloomed on her face. She picked up her pace to run into his open arms.

"Oh, thank God," he said softly, holding Alice close and swinging her around in a half circle before setting her down. Peering down into her face in question, he asked, "Mother straightened everything out? You will marry me?"

"Aye." Alice laughed happily. "She explained everything, and really, she is a dear, Jonathan. You are very fortunate."

He goggled at the claim. "A dear? Fortunate? She nearly lost you for me."

"Nay. She loves you very much, Jonathan. And were it not for her help, we would not be together."

"Her help? Ha!" He scoffed at the very idea. "She did everything in her power to turn my attentions away from you. Had I listened to her, we never would have even met. Why, that first morning, she did everything in her power to dissuade me from accompanying her to the gardens where she was to meet you, your mother, and uncle."

"Which only made you more determined to accompany her," Alice pointed out gently.

Jonathan stopped his pacing to turn slowly toward Alice. The truth dawned on him. "She manipulated me."

Alice nodded apologetically. "She knew that if she asked you to accompany her to meet the daughter of a friend, you would balk. And that if she acted at all as if she thought I was suitable, you would find some excuse not to be interested in me. So she—"

"Played me false. She acted as though you were thoroughly unsuitable in her opinion and . . ." He narrowed his eyes. "Your uncle?"

"A trick, I fear," she admitted with more apology. "His attentions were false, something they stirred up between the three of them. It was intended to keep you around us long enough for you to get to know me."

"Your mother was in on this, too?" he asked in horror.

"Well . . ." Alice grimaced. "Your mother said that she was not, but I suspect she was: Mama is the only one who could have convinced Uncle James to participate."

"Damn." Jonathan sank slowly to sit on the bench. Alice peered at him, obviously worried.

"Jonathan? Are you all right? Has this changed things? Do you not wish to marry me after all?"

"What?" He glanced at her distractedly; then what she had said sank in. He leaped to his feet again. "Nay! I mean, aye! Aye, of course I still want to marry you. I just . . . well, I—" He made a face. "It is discomfiting to know I am so easily played by the woman."

Alice seemed amused by that comment when he suddenly whirled on her. "Did she admit to involvement in getting the king to order me to marry?"

"Er . . . well, no. That did not come up." She frowned

87

briefly, then moved to stand in front of him. "But does it really matter, my lord? I mean, you do really want to marry me, do you not? 'Tis not simply a case of having to marry, and I am the most likely candidate . . . is it?"

Recognizing her fear, Jonathan took her hand. The last thing he wanted was for her to believe such nonsense. "Nay, Alice. You are not simply the most likely candidate. Even were there not a pressing need to marry, I would surely want to wed you. And most likely just as swiftly. In case you had not noticed, my passions become carried away whenever you are about."

She ducked her head and rubbed her fingers over the knuckles of his hand. "Actually, I had not noticed, my lord. It appeared to me last night that you were the one in control, and that I was the one carried away."

"That is only because my mother interrupted us," he assured her. "I kept telling myself that I could not take your innocence, that your satisfaction must be enough until I could get you properly wed to me. . . ." He grimaced. " 'Struth, I was a heartbeat away from ravishing you there on the ground like some lowborn wench."

Alice blushed, but smiled. "And are you sure you will not mind being married to such a wanton as myself?" At his uncertain look, she quietly admitted, "I fear I do not think I would have minded being ravished there on the ground. In fact, I would not protest should you wish to do so now."

Jonathan felt his body harden and tighten at the very suggestion. He swallowed thickly. Damn, just the thought of it had him ready for action. Hesitating briefly, he glanced around, gauging the odds of getting caught. They might be getting married, but they weren't yet. He wouldn't see her shamed before he—His thoughts died abruptly as he became aware of Alice's hand drifting down toward the more than obvious bulge between his legs.

"Perhaps," she murmured, meeting his startled gaze boldly, "you might even teach me to please you as you pleasured me, my lord. Your mother promised not to interrupt us this time."

"Oh, Alice, my sweet." Jonathan laughed. "Whether my mother was involved or not, you are definitely the right bride for me."

She smiled widely at those words and took his hand to lead him around the bench and toward the bushes behind it. "I am glad you think so, my lord. I, too, think we shall be terribly happy together."

"Until my mother next interferes," he added dryly.

"Oh, nay." Alice paused and leaned into his chest, her expression serious as she slid her hands up around his neck. She drew his head down for a kiss.

Jonathan's legs nearly gave out at the shock of her aggression. His lovely lady was a very quick learner! He let his arms slide around her and pressed his hands against her bottom, urging her up against his hardness. Her tongue delved into his mouth and explored with an abandon that left him trembling. He actually moaned aloud when she broke the kiss and leaned back to murmur, "She has vowed never to interfere again."

"Oh, that is all right then," he whispered huskily, then claimed her lips once more.

Jonathan had little real hope that his mother could fulfill that vow. The woman simply did not know how *not* to interfere. Still, he would keep that little tidbit to himself. He had no intention of scaring off the woman he loved. He was rather hoping that by the time Alice realized his mother simply did not have the nature to keep that promise, Alice would love her enough to overlook it. Lady Margaret of Fairley was a woman who grew on a person, and her intentions were always the best. She loved her son and wanted what was best for him. And this was one of the few times Jonathan agreed with his mother. As his new bride-to-be led him farther into the surrounding trees and bushes, he conceded Alice *was* definitely the best. And despite her interference, or perhaps because of it, so was his mother.

1750
The Breeding Season
by LISA CACH

To Sheri

Chapter One

Bath, England
1750

"It's not that Evelina is a *bad* girl. She has no wickedness in her," Mrs. Johnson said, and worked her lips over her false teeth, testing the firmness of their seating before taking a sip of her chocolate.

"No, of course not," her good friend Mrs. Highcroft replied, trying to disguise a delicate scratch at her scalp as an adjustment of her pristine lace cap. Mrs. Johnson was not fooled. "She has high spiwits and no discipline, is all."

Mrs. Johnson frowned at the implied criticism, and sat straighter in her stays. She could never decide if her friend's speech impediment was real or affected, and at the moment the sound of it annoyed her greatly. "I was as strict as a general. I sent her to that boarding school that promised the severity of a convent. I kept my eye on

93

her every waking hour. I lectured her on morals and propriety. I did everything a mother could! It is not my fault that she behaves with all the breeding of a common country wench."

"I was not faulting *you*. Never you, my dear! You know I would not, not when I have such a failure of my own, in Chawles."

"And he such a handsome boy," Mrs. Johnson said, and shook her head over the tragedy. She still held her cup of chocolate, and the movement sent a wave of it sloshing onto the skirts of her gown. "I would never have thought he would grow to be so awkward and retiring."

Mrs. Highcroft narrowed her eyes. "He is not awkward when in his element."

"My dear, I meant no offense. . . ."

A tight smile twitched Mrs. Highcroft's lips. "Although even I admit that his element is most often the barnyard."

"Oh, dear." Mrs. Johnson smothered a smile that would have shown her teeth. She shifted, trying to rearrange herself within her dress. A bit of boning was poking her most cruelly under her arm. "Tell me again that this will be the solution to both our problems."

"It will be. It *has* to be. Our childwen are misfits of society, and it would be too cruel a God who would not let them balance and improve each other, and give us surcease from our worries." Mrs. Highcroft half turned in her seat, her perfectly pressed silk gown rustling, and searched the parlor as if truly expecting to see her son standing like a side chair in the corner. "Now where *has* my Chawles gone to? He's likely wandered off to your back garden to converse with the chickens."

"And I fear it may be another two hours before Evelina considers herself garbed for visitors." Mrs. Johnson gave up on finding comfort within her stays, and sagged against them. She noticed a fresh spot of chocolate on her skirts, and dabbed at it with a handkerchief. "Neither Evelina nor Charles is going to come easily to this."

Mrs. Highcroft turned back to her and lifted her chin, her tone imperious. "They are our childwen. They will do as we diwect."

Mrs. Johnson murmured a noncommittal sound. She wished she could be so sure.

"A pox on it! Sally, come help me. I can't get the cursed thing off my fingers," Evelina said, her fingertips sticking and coming undone, then sticking again as she transferred a paste-covered scrap of black taffeta from one digit to the next.

"Miss, you've been summoned three times now. Your mother will be cross if you do not descend at once."

"I cannot go down with this great red spot upon my forehead—Mrs. Highcroft has brought her son. He will stare at it." She tried to press the moon-shaped black patch over the blemish, but it wouldn't stick. "It is not fair, I tell you! By the time I grow out of blemishes, I will have wrinkles and gray teeth."

Sally came and peeled the patch off Evelina's paste-smeared fingertip, and with an extra dab of fixative settled the patch into place over the blemish. "There, now. All hidden."

Evelina frowned into the mirror. The center of the forehead was not the most seductive of locations for a crescent moon, but what else was to be done? Mama had taken away all of her ceruse, that mixture of white lead and vinegar that gave a porcelain complexion to those who used it. Mama had said it would destroy her skin.

95

Pah! Destroy her skin? How could one destroy that which was already riddled with blotches?

But there was no more time to fuss about it. The Highcrofts might leave before she managed to get herself arranged to her satisfaction, and that simply would not do. She wanted to see Charles.

She had met him twice or thrice before, when they were children, but had not seen him for many years. He had been lately at Oxford, and she, of course, had been locked up in that horrid boarding school with teachers who would have been better employed as Newgate prison guards.

She didn't remember much about Charles: he was four years older than she, and it was enough of an age difference that as children they had paid no attention to one another. She doubted she would recognize him.

Old memories were not the reason she was eager to see him, though. He must be twenty-two now. Full-grown. A man. That was reason enough.

Heart thumping in anticipation, she stood and gave one last check of her flowered, cherry red gown. Doubtless Charles would appreciate her French tastes, unlike Mama. He had been out in the world, not mired in the country, and would recognize sophistication when he saw it.

She descended the white stone staircase to the first floor, imagining how he would be dressed. He probably wore only the most expensive imported powders on his wig, and a waistcoat stiff with silver lace. His jacket and breeches would be a peacock blue velvet, he'd carry a cocked beaver hat under one arm, and his stockings would be a spotless, blinding white with a trace of embroidery up the sides. He would smell of the finest perfume, and be wearing shoes with red heels and silver buckles.

Not that any of that really mattered. He was a *man*—and it had been at least a week since she'd been allowed near a young one. It really was *trop mal* that Mama had caught her kissing that Kingston boy, and thrown such a fit. And even worse was that the kiss had hardly been worth it—Kingston's lips had been as wet and soft as a raw oyster, and just as cold. She would have to rank that kiss well near the bottom of her list.

If Mama knew just how much she loved men—their smell, their height, their strength, the deepness of their voices, and the hunger in their eyes—Evelina would be shipped back to that dungeon of a boarding school, *immédiatement*. Girls were not supposed to sow their wild oats and follow where their lusting bodies led them; only boys were allowed such fun.

A pox on that! When the time came, she had every intention of being an honorable, faithful wife, but that meant her only freedom was *now*. Her only chance to steal kisses was *now*. Her only opportunity to flirt and cast glances, to allure and seduce, to know men in all their glorious variety, was *now*—before the chains of matrimony forever locked her away from such entertainments.

And now here was a man in Evelina's own home. *Manna from heaven!*

"Mama! Mrs. Highcroft. Please forgive my tardiness," Evelina said, prancing with what she hoped was an elegant step into the parlor. "And Mr. Highcroft, what a . . . pleasure to see you again . . ." She trailed off, her voice dying and her steps slowing as she took in the sort of man that Charles Highcroft had grown to be.

Oh, dear. Perhaps someone had let a field laborer into the parlor by mistake?

He wore no wig. His dark brown hair was pulled back by a ratty old ribbon and left to hang like a horse's bobbed tail, and there was not so much as a speck of powder upon it. Locks of his heavy hair had come loose around his face, and with his head bent shyly forward they half-concealed his features.

His lashes were dark and lush beneath arched brows, his nose straight, his jaw strong and with a clean, lean line. He might almost be a handsome man, if he had a bit of grace or self-assurance. Her assessing eyes roamed over his body, taking in the broad shoulders and trim waist. His figure was not bad, for all that it was languishing under drab brown garments that were two decades out of date and looked twice as old. The man wore his stockings *over* the knees of his breeches, for heaven's sake! That mode had gone out during her father's time.

And he wore boots. *Boots!* She was better off not looking at those, or at the bits of dried muck that clung to them.

She continued to stare at him, and without so much as a bow in her direction or a word of greeting, he turned away, going to stand at the window that overlooked Queen Square. Her lips parted in astonishment at the blatant rudeness.

"Evelina, dearest, we'd about given up hope of you," her mother said, and patted the space beside her. She obeyed the summons and sat, happy to ignore the country clod at the window, and the faint odor of farm that lingered after him. Perhaps she would have to rethink adding Charles to her list of conquests. She had standards, after all.

"What a curiously vibrant color you are weawing," Mrs.

Highcroft said in her thin, nasal voice. "I don't know that I've ever seen the like."

She sensed that the comment was not entirely complimentary. *The purse-mouthed old hen!* But Evelina smiled sweetly when she replied. "Thank you. I have always admired your own sense of style, and like to think that I model my choices after yours."

"Ahh . . . thank you, my dear."

Ha! There was nothing like a compliment to confuse an enemy. Although Mrs. Highcroft had always been friends with Mama, Evelina had more than once thought that Mrs. Highcroft considered herself superior to the Johnsons, and in a position to cast judgments. Never mind that Mr. Highcroft had made his fortune as a merchant—a peddler of pots and candles, no less—whereas Papa was a gentleman, with lands that had been in the family for five centuries!

A look passed between Mama and Mrs. Highcroft, and Evelina narrowed her eyes, sensing that mischief was afoot. No doubt Mama had been speaking about her in her absence, asking her old friend for advice on how to handle her wayward daughter. She had long suspected that the boarding school had been Mrs. Highcroft's idea. Mama was too softhearted to have come up with such a draconian notion on her own.

Mrs. Highcroft raised her pointy nose and called her son: "Charles, come here. Don't hide behind the curtains like a sulky child."

Evelina peered over her shoulder at him, feeling a twinge of sympathetic embarrassment for the fellow at being ordered about like a five-year-old. With Mrs. Highcroft as his mother, he was probably under tighter rein than even Evelina was, as a female.

99

With his gaze on the floor he slowly walked back to their little group—he might as well have been approaching his executioner, Evelina thought—and sat next to his mother, perching on the edge of the settee as if afraid of breaking or soiling it. He rested his hands on his knees, one of which began to bounce up and down with nervous agitation.

What a backward sort of creature this was! If a girl ever kissed him, he'd likely fall to the ground dead of the fright. It was cosmic justice that immaculate, socially ambitious Mrs. Highcroft should have a son such as this.

Evelina smiled to herself, and touched her mother's arm in a gesture of solidarity. She and Mama were more than a match for Mrs. Highcroft *et fils.*

Mama patted her hand and smiled at her. "Dearest, we have a wonderful surprise for you. For both you and Charles."

"Oh?" She was wary of surprises. The boarding school had been a surprise. From the corner of her eye she saw Charles's knee go still. Maybe he had learned to be wary of them, himself.

"Charles is going to be your escort."

"He is? To where?" What manner of evil was this? God in heaven, let it not be to someplace her friends might see her.

"Not to one place, dear. Everywhere, for as long as we are in Bath. Balls, musical evenings, house parties, shopping, rides into the countryside, visits to the baths. Anytime you leave this house, Charles will be at your side."

"I do not think so," the young man suddenly said, his deep voice rumbling into the daintiness of the parlor, startling them all. A pocket of silence formed where his words ended, as they gaped at him. It was as if a horse had spoken, so unexpected were words from that quarter.

"Neither do I," Evelina said into the silence. "What a ridiculous idea. I shouldn't think that either one of us would like such an arrangement."

She briefly met Charles's eyes, seeking confirmation, then blinked. She'd thought his eyes would be brown, but they were blue-green, set off by his thick lashes. Boys should not be allowed to have eyes like that; they were much too pretty. She herself should have eyes like that.

He looked away, his cheeks coloring with what was either embarrassment or anger. She wondered if he often defied his mother, and guessed that he was more the type to avoid confrontations by staying out of her sight.

"What either you or Chawles want is not our concern," Mrs. Highcroft said. "This is what you both need. Chawles, you have spent entirely too long in fields and stables. It is time you pwacticed those social skills I have tried so hard to teach to you. You need to be looking for a wife, and you will never find one if you don't learn how to speak to young ladies."

"And you, Evelina," Mama said. "I'm afraid that you need an escort to keep you out of trouble. After that last incident, I simply cannot trust you out of my sight, not even if you have Sally with you."

"Mama! It was only a kiss!"

Her mother's hands fluttered. "Only! Only, you say! It was far too much, and well you know it. Well-bred young ladies do *not* exchange kisses with men to whom they are not married."

"Then how am I to know which one is worth wedding? I shouldn't like to go through life enduring clammy, sloppy kisses each morn and night."

"Evelina! You will not speak of such things!"

But the devil was in her, and she would not stop. "Charles would not be scolded so if he did the same. He would be praised, I think."

"Licentiousness is never to be praised!"

She cocked her head and smiled at Charles. "Perhaps I should turn my attentions to him," she threatened. He met her gaze with widened, horrified, beautiful blue-green eyes. His lips looked as though they might be rather fine to kiss.

"You will do no such thing!" Mrs. Highcroft said, puffing up like an angry bird. Then she looked at her son and settled her feathers. "But if you did, I doubt you would have any success. Chawles has yet to show the weactions of a normal man."

Charles abruptly stood, hands clenched at his side, the muscles of his jaw flexing. Evelina's heart skipped a beat at the size of him, towering over them all. He looked so gloriously angry, so poised for action, she forgot for a moment the disgraceful state of his yellowed stockings. He should get angry more often, if this was the transformation it wrought.

"Enough, Mother. I am no longer a child, and will not stay here to be treated with such disrespect in front of your friends." He turned and stalked toward the door.

"Yes, you will!" Mrs. Highcroft shrieked, panicked by the unexpected rebellion. "Or you can bid farewell to your mares and foals!"

Charles stopped and turned back to stare at her, in his eyes a hardness that had not been there before. "They are mine," he said, his voice a cold threat.

Evelina shivered, enjoying the spectacle. What would it be like to have a man be as possessive of her as Charles was of his horses? It really was a pity that his attachments apparently ran more to animals than to women. There appeared to be a certain attractive potential to the man, under the shyness.

Mrs. Highcroft continued screeching. "The line was not started with your money, nor are they fed with it. Your father will give way to me in this. We'll auction evewy one of them, and he'll invest the money wherever he wishes. You know how much he adores any chance to invest money."

Charles's stance was rigid, and he took no further steps toward the door. Evelina guessed he was assessing the truth of his mother's words, and not liking the answer he reached. She waited to see what he would do and, as the moments stretched out, the tension grew. It got to be too much for her, and she had to break it.

"You may be able to force Charles to your bidding, but there is no such hold on me."

"Isn't there?" Mrs. Highcroft asked. Evelina heard her mother sigh beside her. The sound sent a rush of cold anxiety through her.

"If you do not leave the house with Charles," Mama said, "then you do not leave the house. You do not leave your room. You do not receive letters or visits from friends."

Evelina gaped at her mother, who gave her an apologetic smile before continuing. "And there will be no new clothes."

She gasped. "Mama!"

"I am sorry, but you leave me no choice. And truly, dear, would it be so terrible to do as we ask? Left on your own, you would shortly earn yourself a reputation. You will be the better for a bit of restraint, and will thank Mrs.

Highcroft and myself for this, in time. It is for your own good."

"Like the boarding school was?"

Mama squirmed at that, but her lips held the stubborn line that indicated she would not budge. Evelina had learned long ago how to read the nuances of her mother's expression, and this was going to be one of the rare times she could not be persuaded out of her decision.

Evelina sank, her shoulders slumping, and looked again at Charles. His eyes met hers, and they exchanged a silent cry of helplessness. Their mamas had won.

Chapter Two

Charles marched down the pavement, barely conscious of the scene around him, having no destination but that he get himself far from the house on Queen Square, where his mother still sat with her coconspirator, Mrs. Johnson.

Damn her! Damn her for knowing how to manipulate him, and damn her for treating him as if he were yet a child, unable to decide what was best for himself.

And damn his own self, for having assumed that what was his, was truly his. A gentleman was not supposed to work—that had been drilled into him by Mother his entire life—and yet that very circumstance left him at the financial mercy of his parents. The fact that Papa had earned most of his fortune through trade was Mother's deepest shame, although she obviously was not above using the fruits of his labor to get what she wished.

Damn, damn, damn. It was the realization of his own

powerlessness that made him furious, far more than what was being demanded of him.

Although that alone was bad enough: parties and dances, and the constant company of a gaudy butterfly of a girl. A Spanish inquisitor could have devised nothing worse.

"Charles! God's bodkin, will you slow down?"

The voice startled him out of his self-absorption, and he stopped. Evelina Johnson trotted up beside him, the wide hoops of her skirt bouncing, the ridiculous moon in the middle of her forehead peeling up. Her maid remained several respectful steps behind.

He had forgotten they were with him, and he realized Evelina must have been nearly running to keep up with him. His error came as no surprise; he knew he was hopeless when it came to polite behavior, and especially to behaving with ease among women. He had an innate talent for saying exactly the wrong thing, and over the years his embarrassment over his ineptitude had caused him to avoid more and more the situations where he was likely to humiliate himself.

"My apologies," he said, and then resumed walking at a slower pace.

She made a noise in her throat, and when he looked at her she was bobbing her head around as if trying to convey some sort of message.

He stopped again. "What?"

She sighed and stepped around him so that she was on the side of the pavement nearest the buildings, while he was by the road. A dim memory stirred in his mind that this was how a gentleman and a lady were supposed to walk together.

"My apologies again," he said. He glanced at her, checking to see if there were any other basic rules he was forgetting, and when she gave him a little smile he flushed and resumed walking.

"Where are we going?"

"I don't know." The sound of hammers and shouting workmen seemed to follow him wherever he went, pounding at his head; on almost every street there were new houses going up, and walking toward the edge of the city meant walking through a morass of construction, as Bath spread into the surrounding fields.

"If you have no destination, then would you mind if in our wanderings we passed by the Blue Ball, in Stall Street?"

"What is the Blue Ball?"

"A marvelous shop. They have all manner of ointments and perfumes, and excellent hair powders from France. Maybe you would like to buy some?"

He snorted. "Maybe not. I have no wish to turn my head into a powder puff, trailing dust wherever I go."

"It would be better than looking like a medieval serf, Charles."

She used his first name the same way his mother did, as if he were a small boy in need of correction. He should have been Mr. Highcroft to her, and no matter the dullness of his social skills, he recognized her use of his name as an insult rather than a sign of cozy familiarity. "Is that why you bury your own head in talc, *Evelina*, to avoid being mistaken for a peasant?"

"What a rude boy you are! I knew you would not recognize fine taste when you saw it; I knew it even before I met you!"

"I do not see what is such fine taste about turning your hair the color of my grandmother's."

"I wear my hair as the French do, and you would do well to follow my example. At least I do not look like a common country bumpkin."

"The country girls I've seen look far fresher for wearing their own hair, clean and shining in the sun."

"So you *do* notice the fairer sex, then? Your mama would be happy to hear it."

He felt his face go hot. "My mother knows little about me."

"She knew well enough how to manipulate you. What are these horses for which you are willing to endure my company?"

"You would not understand." He was in no mood to explain anything to this twittering little hummingbird.

"Dear me, no, I probably wouldn't. I haven't a brain in my head, you know. I have to have dear Sally tell me if it is morning or night when I wake, I am so easily confused."

Despite his bad temper, he felt his lips curl in the hint of a smile. He'd managed to rile her. He glanced at her and suppressed a laugh. She could have no notion of how silly she looked, being cross while that cresent moon fluttered in the breeze, attached now to her forehead by only a single point. He noticed the red blemish she had been trying to conceal, and felt a bit of his usual bashfulness with women fade away. She had her vulnerabilities, just as he did.

"I had the good fortune to gain possession of a granddaughter of the Godolphin Arabian. You've heard of him?" he asked, feeling the familiar stir of excitement that came whenever he thought about the line he was trying to create.

"No. I do not know much about horses."

108

"Ah, well. Never mind."

She laid her hand on his arm, and her dark eyes looked up at him with amusement. "Sometimes the point of conversation is to impart new information. Some even find the unfamiliar to be interesting. Tell me, what is the Godolphin Arabian?"

He hesitated. She did not look like someone who would care a halfpenny about his breeding ambitions. "I do not wish to bore you."

"That's very gallant of you! Most young men are content to blither on whether their companion shows true interest or not. If you decide to listen to my advice about the hair powder and allow me to do something about those dreadful clothes you're wearing, we'll have you charming the garters off any number of young ladies."

He didn't know if she was joking or serious. And what was wrong with his clothes? Whatever momentary comfort in her company he had gained was gone, replaced by the familiar queasy anxiety.

She was still talking. "But to return to the topic: what is the Godolphin Arabian?"

This, at least, was one subject on which he could converse. If she became bored, he decided, she would have no one but herself to blame. "He is one of the three pure Arabians to appear in England over a quarter century ago. The Earl of Godolphin purchased him from a Quaker who had found the stallion in Paris, pulling a water cart. The horse had originally been a gift to Louis the Fourteenth by the sultan of Morocco."

"How did the Quaker know the stallion was special?"

"The Arabian is a distinctive horse, and the Barb is an extraordinary example of his breed. The story goes that it was the abuse the animal was suffering at the hands of its owner that prompted the Quaker to buy him, and that it was the former slave who had come with the stallion from Morocco who told the Quaker of the horse's history."

"Where was the slave while the horse was pulling the water cart?"

"Lurking nearby, I take it. He had been doing his best to watch over his beloved stallion, and after hearing the slave's tale the Quaker brought him to England along with the horse."

"What a dramatic story! Who would have thought a horse could have led such an interesting life? It's worthy of a romantic novel."

He felt a bit of confidence return. She'd liked the story— she was smiling!

"And your mare? How did you obtain her?"

"She belonged to an acquaintance at Oxford, who got into debt. He was afraid to ask his father for money—it had gone badly for him the last time he had done so— and he knew I was enamored of the horse. He sold her to me for a painfully large sum."

"Why are you smiling like that?"

"I was just remembering. His father was more furious that the mare, Desert Rose, had been sold than he likely would have been about the debts. My Oxford friend tried to buy her back, but I will never let her go. Never! She's mine now."

Evelina sighed and gave him a look he did not understand. "I think your mother may be correct, and you are in need of a wife."

He didn't know what had prompted her to change the topic. "There is plenty of time for that. I do not see why I need one now."

Which was, to some degree, a lie. He did not know what

he would do with a wife during the day, but he had more than enough thoughts on how they would spend their nights. His friends had often paid for the favors of women, but he had been too embarrassed to do the same. And then, just as frustrated desires had finally been enough to win over native shyness, one of his friends had become infected with syphilis. The thought not only of carrying such a burden, but of possibly passing it on to a future wife was too horrific for him to accept, and he had made the difficult choice of chastity over pleasure, promising himself that once married he would make up for missed opportunities.

Perhaps he *did* know what he would do with a wife during the days. Why limit himself to nights?

"Of course you need a wife. Every man does," Evelina said with certainty.

He didn't know what to say to that—how could he engage in any argument without treading upon topics unfit for discussion with a young lady?—so he turned the conversation back to her. "I should think that you need a husband more than I need a wife. I don't know why your parents do not marry you off rather than take the trouble to set me as a watchdog upon you."

"I am certain they plan to, once they find a suitable fellow. Since I am their only child, they are cautious in their selection. Papa wants to know that his family's lands will be cared for after he is gone."

"You must be giving them nightmares, worrying you'll end up carrying a fortune hunter's child." The comment slipped out before he had time to think better of it. Charles Highcroft, master of the ill-considered word! He would do better to keep his mouth shut and never speak.

"I have my virtue, sir! I may dance and flirt and steal

111

kisses, but I know my value and do not give myself freely, not to anyone!"

"Why steal the kisses? Why let others think you a strumpet? You make it more difficult for your parents to find a match for you. Or is that your intention?"

"Of course not! I am the one who will have to live with my husband; I should hope he is the best they can find."

"Then you are doing nothing to help. I should not want a wife with such a reputation as your mother claims you are building for yourself."

"And I would not want a husband who wears his stockings over his breeches and gets along better with horses than with people!"

An angry silence descended between them, and though they still walked side by side he felt as if there were a stone wall between them. He had no notion of how to bridge it, or even if he wished to. Got along better with horses than with people, did he?

Well, perhaps so, but she needn't throw it in his face like that. And what was so terrible about how he wore his stockings?

Did he do nothing right?

Their route had taken them to the bridge over the river Avon, where they stopped to take in the prospect, and where he briefly considered the joy that might be had from tossing Evelina over the rail. Likely he would lose his horses for certain, if he did.

From the bridge's span he could see a stoneyard and wharf across the water, and the horse-drawn railcarts that went up the hill to Prior Park, and the quarries. His father was growing even wealthier by investing in the buildings those stones would construct, but all Charles saw when he looked at the stoneyard was noise and disruption.

"The wharf spoils the view," Evelina said. She had her arms crossed and a petulant look on her face. The maid stood silent and watchful, a few feet away.

He knew that he was likely more the target of her mood than the wharf, but he felt an unexpected relief that she had broken the silence. He would try to be agreeable, to make up for his own comment on her apparent strumpethood. "You enjoy the countryside?"

"It has its beauties."

"I always wished I had grown up in the country rather than in London."

"And I wished the opposite. Although I do admit, when I was away at school, I missed our fields and woods terribly."

"Did you?" He leaned one elbow upon the wall of the bridge, regarding her with interest. He had not thought that one so obviously concerned with dress and makeup would be of a temperament to appreciate natural beauty.

"Of course." She gave him a look he could only interpret as wicked. "I was better able to slip away on my own in the woods, and to meet whom I pleased."

He stared at her, aghast, and she started to giggle, her hand coming up to cover her ruby-painted lips.

"Charles, there's no need to look at me so!" she said when she caught her breath, and lowering her hand she pushed him lightly on the arm, as if he were a dull-witted brother. "I was teasing. I was far more likely to meet a crofter's daughter and play house in an old tree trunk than I was to be making mischief with boys. Although there *was* that one young fellow who was willing to drop his breeches and let us look, if my friend and I would lift our skirts in exchange."

"D-did you?"

"We made him go first, and then ran when it was our turn. We laughed whenever we saw him after that; he was always trailing after us, complaining that we had to pay our debt."

"Poor sod."

"You'd rather I had lifted my skirts?" The smile was still playing around her lips.

"No, I—" He fumbled, flustered. "I imagine the fellow was probably half in love with you, and received poor treatment for it."

"If he was half in love with me, he should have tried picking flowers instead of dropping his breeches. No, I doubt it was love that he had on his mind."

She was altogether too wise for a girl of eighteen. He felt the less worldly of the pair, and realized she probably had more experience of the tender interplay between man and woman than he. If ever she were to steal a kiss from him—not that he wished she would try!—she would likely laugh at his ineptitude, and then go searching for one better able to meet her hunger.

Although, given the chance, he was certain he would learn to please a woman as well as any other man, if not better. Only not with her! He could not even tell the color of her hair, so covered was it in powder, although the warm dark brown of her eyes she could not hide.

He thought she might be a pretty thing, if not buried under all that makeup. She was willful and improper, and far too ready to speak her mind, but she was also plainly not one to hold long to a grudge or a bad humor, and had a ready laugh. Perhaps spending a bit of time with her would not be entirely the tribulation he had assumed.

"Could we go to the Blue Ball now?" she asked. "I think I have had enough of the view of the wharf, and there is a new edition of the *Ladies' Guide* that I wish to purchase. And while we are in Stall Street we can find you a new black ribbon for your hair. That one you are wearing is a disgrace."

Then again, perhaps spending time with her would be a torment of unforeseen proportions.

Chapter Three

"You needn't gloat, Mama." Evelina was in her room, helping Sally to pack up a basket of entertainments she would be taking with her on her outing with Charles.

"Evelina, my darling, I wouldn't think of it. But I am glad to see that you will be out enjoying the fresh air. It must have been tiresome for you, being indoors all week."

"A drive into the country with Charles Highcroft will be nearly as great a bore, I expect." She had tested Mama's resolution this past week, making several attempts a day to leave the house and pestering her with complaints, in hopes of wearing her down. Mama had answered the assaults with the blank solidity of a castle's curtain wall, and eventually outlasted the siege.

"Mind that you don't alleviate your boredom by trying to kiss the man. I won't have you practicing your flirtations on him."

"I thought the very point of setting him as my watchdog

was his indifference to feminine wiles. Are you worried he might behave less than honorably?" Now, there was an interesting thought. It might be entertaining to see if, instead of fainting dead away at an advance, Charles responded with enthusiasm. And then what a state Mama would be in!

"No, of course not," her mama said, sounding very worried indeed. "All the same, you are to behave yourself." She paused, and then shook her head, as if laughing at herself. "But what was I thinking? No one, not even you, would wish to kiss such a loutish, homely sort as Charles."

"He is not loutish in the least. He is shy, and there is a certain backward charm to that." She was prompted to defend him by a perverse sense of loyalty to her fellow sufferer at the hands of manipulative mothers. "And I think he could be handsome, if he would take more care with his appearance."

"Nonsense. He is uncouth. But since you think that he is not devoid of appeal, I find I must absolutely forbid you to kiss him. And perhaps you should limit your outing today to no more than an hour."

"Mama! You must allow me more than that! Please!" She could not bear to stay inside for yet another day. Ten minutes ago she had been bemoaning her fate at being stuck with Charles, but now he was her deliverance from incarceration, and she wished she could be off with him at once.

"It would be safer to keep you at home."

"Please, Mama. I must go out; I simply must."

"Well . . . as long as you do not think of Charles as anything more than a chaperon. I know that Mrs. Highcroft would be as upset as myself—perhaps more so—to hear of a dalliance between the two of you."

"Would she! The arrogant old cow, she probably thinks I am not a good enough match for her precious son. Well, if he doesn't start to listen to my advice on dress and behavior, you can be sure that all she'll find for him will be the worst sort of fortune-hunting harlot."

"Evelina! You are too frank in your speech."

"But it is true, Mama. The Highcrofts are merchants at heart, and they will buy their son a wife, likely one with a pretension of rank and a money-hungry family. Poor Charles, he has no happiness awaiting him in marriage; that is for certain."

"You should not be calling him by his Christian name."

She was saved from a reply by a footman announcing Charles's arrival. *Thank God!* She had best make her escape before Mama changed her mind yet again. "I must go."

"You will behave yourself—"

"He is waiting; I must go! Sally, my hat!"

Sally came and tied on the straw, flat-crowned bonnet, covering her tiny lace cap and her close-dressed, powdered curls.

She hurried down the stairs, Sally following behind with her wrap and basket. Charles was waiting in the foyer, playing with his hat and sneaking uneasy glances at the impeccably dressed footmen to either side of the front door. He looked up at the sound of her heels on the marble stairs, a nervous smile pulling at his mouth.

"Good day, Mr. Highcroft! What a pleasure to see you again!" she said, with an exaggerated politeness completely at odds with their last meeting. She winked at him.

He blushed. "Miss Johnson." He fidgeted, apparently at a loss for further words, and then suddenly put his hat on, the left side of the brim wavy from the mangling of his hands and drooping down over his eyebrow. And just

118

as suddenly he took it off again, and bowed to her in belated greeting.

There was something adorable about his shyness. It made her want to wrap her arms around him and nuzzle his neck. It also brought out the imp in her, that liked to startle and surprise, and to see his cheeks change color.

She reached the bottom of the stairs and curtsied in return, and then held out her hand, waiting until he lifted his forearm for her to lay her palm lightly upon. A footman opened the door and Charles led her outside, to the carriage that awaited, with the coachman perched high on his seat and a Highcroft footman in blue livery standing by the lowered step.

She smiled at the footman, who grinned back, then went stone-faced when Charles glared at him. Once they were all installed inside, and the carriage had begun to move, Evelina leaned toward Sally. "He was a handsome fellow, don't you think? Such lovely dark eyes."

"I can do better than a footman." Sally sniffed. "I wouldn't settle for less than a head gardener, with his own cottage—or better yet a butler."

"But he *was* handsome."

"He was that," Sally admitted.

"But not as handsome as you," Evelina said, turning her attention to Charles. "You are by far the finer figure. And you are wearing the ribbon we bought!"

"We had a bargain, after all," he muttered.

"Indeed we did." She had finally persuaded him to buy a new ribbon after promising that, in exchange, their next outing could be to wherever he wished. "And look at your stockings, properly tucked away. Next we will have to go to work upon your hat and waistcoat."

"I like my hat the way it is. It keeps the sun from my eyes."

"As if that were the purpose of a hat! No, we must have your outward appearance match the dashing fellow I know to be hiding inside, and that means a cocked hat and embroidered waistcoat. Come, what would you like in exchange this time? Shall I agree to go riding? Fishing? Or would you perhaps like . . . a kiss?" The offer was out before she could think better of it, and her heart tripped in a mixture of embarrassment and the hope that he might say yes.

What nonsense! She did not wish to kiss him. It was Mama who had put the idea into her head, with her forbidding it.

"No, certainly not!" he said.

She made a face. "You needn't be so very adamant about it. A young lady might feel insulted."

"I doubt other young *ladies* trade away their favors."

"God's bodkin, Charles, you are a prudish sort. A simple peck upon the cheek, as a sister would give her brother, that was all I offered." Although he did have lips with the perfect amount of fullness, shaded with just a hint of color. It might be very nice indeed to kiss those lips, and to lay her hand upon the broad chest beneath his drab waistcoat. His legs looked long and strong, making her palms itch to run along the muscled thighs . . . or even to sit upon them, and wrap her arms around that stiff neck, her hands playing in his dark hair. Her breath grew short with excitement.

"In trade you could promise instead to stop leering at servants," he said.

"You would take away all my fun. What harm is there in a little leering?"

"Or better yet . . ." He smiled at her, and it was a wicked smile of a sort she had not seen before on his face. She felt a thrill run through her.

"What? What would you have me do?"

"Stop wearing your powders and paints."

She gasped, her excitement turning to horror. "I could not!"

He shrugged. "And I like my clothing as it is."

"That is not the same at all. I am à la mode. You are not. I am trying to help you."

"And I, you. I should think you would find many more men willing to be kissed if you did not have purple cheeks or the dead skin of a corpse. And what *are* those things above your eyes?"

"Mouse-skin eyebrows," she said softly. His comments went straight to her heart, wounding her. "I look pretty with my powders and paints," she said in a weak show of defiance, but her voice betrayed her with its quaver.

"Pretty as a painted pagoda, perhaps, but not as a lady."

"That's not nice, Charles," she said, and tried not to cry. Hearing the words from him hurt far more than if they had come from Mama, who was constantly on her about her cosmetics. "I don't know that you should be any judge of what is attractive."

"I don't know why I should not be. For all that you and my mother seem to enjoy treating me as a boy, I am a man."

"And I had thought a kind one." A tear slipped down her cheek, her throat tightening.

"Are you crying?" He peered at her across the shaded carriage.

"No!" she said on a hiccough, and searched for a handkerchief. Sally handed her one, and she dabbed at her face, trying not to smear the black that was dripping from her eyelashes.

"You *are* crying." He sounded appalled. "Ah, damn. I'm sorry, Evelina. I didn't mean to make you cry."

"You've a cruel heart, to tell a girl she is ugly," she said amid her tears.

"Evelina, I'm sorry! That is not what I meant! I'm a lout, with no command of his own tongue. I did not mean to hurt you." He reached across and took the hand without the handkerchief, patting it awkwardly between both of his. "I think you're quite beautiful, under all that paint. I wish I could see you better, is all. You have pretty eyes, and a lovely smile, and your figure is excellent. I'm sure you don't need powders or false colors to be the fairest lady in all of Bath."

She sniffed back her tears, holding the wet kerchief to the end of her nose. "Truly?"

"I may be a clumsy lout, but I am not a liar."

He had stopped his hand-patting, and hers now rested motionless between his warm palms. She gave one of them a gentle squeeze. "You have a smoother tongue than you give yourself credit for." She withdrew her hand and mopped the last of the moisture from her face. The kerchief was covered in black and pink. She almost laughed at the sorry spectacle she was sure she now made.

"Am I forgiven?"

She nodded. She didn't know when she'd gotten as sweet an apology from anyone.

He sat back, still wearing a frown of concern. She slid her foot beside his and nudged him, and when his brows went up in surprise she smiled slightly, to show she was not going to hold it against him.

He nudged her back.

She grinned.

With Sally's help she repaired the worst of the damage to her face, wiping away the black from under her eyes and down her cheeks, and evening out her skin tone with a fresh application of powder. She had no other makeup with her, and felt half-naked with her pale cheeks and lips, and lashes that held only the faintest trace of black. At least her mouse-skin false eyebrows were still in place.

"Where is it, exactly, that we are going?" she asked. She was glad now that they were heading into the countryside, where no one would see her.

"To our country house, Highcastle." He said the name with a grimace, as if the very sound of it was distasteful. "I thought you might like to see Desert Rose."

They were driving all this way to look at his mare? It was a good thing she'd brought her own basket of entertainments. What did she care about a horse? But Charles looked both uncertain and hopeful as he waited for her response, so she smiled. "That will be delightful. I should like to understand what about her has inspired such devotion in you."

"And I thought we might walk in the park afterward. There are several ponds and temples and whatnot. It's supposed to be diverting."

She laughed softly. " 'Supposed to be'? You do not find it so?"

He shrugged. "I like the fishing pavilion well enough."

"A place with a purpose."

"Yes."

"I shall have to teach you the joys of idleness, I see. We ladies are fond of lounging, after we are exhausted by our shopping, and we like it even better when there are suitors gazing upon us with adoration, feeding us sweetmeats."

123

He looked at her with some alarm.

She nudged his foot again, and smiled. "I'm teasing. Still, there is some fun to be had wandering through an unfamiliar park. Were the temples your mother's idea?"

"My father bought the house just three years ago. The park was already in place."

"Ah."

They lapsed into silence, and before long arrived at the estate. There was an overstated grandness to Highcastle, but knowing there was no family history attached left Evelina immune to its intentional impressiveness. Charles seemed embarrassed when they drove by, keeping his face turned half-away from the newly rebuilt facade.

"You don't like the house?"

"It has fine stables," he hedged. "I told the coachman to bring us straight there."

It was on the tip of her tongue to ask if the house had been his mother's choice, but she decided it would be done with petty motivations. There was no need to embarrass Charles more than he already was about Mrs. Highcroft's snobbish, socially ambitious ways.

A thought fluttered at the back of her mind: it was strange that Mrs. Highcroft should have chosen her as the companion to polish off Charles's rough edges. She showed such superiority toward Mama. . . . Were her true feelings, then, those of inferiority? And did she have ulterior motives to this pairing?

The thought dissipated before it had fully formed, as the carriage pulled to a halt. She told Sally she could wait where she wished, and let Charles lead her into the stables.

And what stables they were!

The ceilings were vaulted, and would not have been out

of place in a church. The stalls were of a rich, dark wood; each horse had its own wrought-iron manger; bronze plates mounted above each stall gave their names; high windows were open to let in the spring air; and everywhere was the clean, fresh scent of hay and horse, and enough stable boys to be sure that no horse would have to stand more than a moment near its own manure. "You did not exaggerate. They are fine stables indeed!"

"What they shelter is finer still." He was standing taller, and yet seemed more relaxed than she'd ever seen him, a quiet pride in his eyes. His plain hair and simple clothing no longer looked dated and inappropriate in this setting, and his shy clumsiness had been replaced by a graceful ease.

The handsome man she had guessed lurked within was suddenly right before her, and she felt a warm rush through her loins. Good heavens, but he was beautiful. As she gazed upon him she felt tinglings begin in unmentionable places, and knew a nearly overwhelming urge to press herself against his body and nibble where his jaw met his neck. And to dig her hands into his hair. And to invite his tongue into her mouth, where she could suck on it and—

"This is Winter Wind, who you can see has traces of the Arabian in the slope of her shoulders and the shape of her head, although her ancestry is undocumented. . . ."

He had no idea how utterly delicious he was. She watched his hands as he stroked them down the back of another horse, strong and long-fingered. His mares knew him, whickering at the sight of him, nudging out with their soft noses. He was gentle with them, speaking softly, and yet showing a quiet confidence that made her body melt with desire.

125

"Am I boring you?" he asked, suddenly breaking off his narrative.

"No, not at all."

"Are you certain? You haven't said a word since we came in."

"Please, go on." She could watch him all day. "Where is Desert Rose?"

"Out in the paddock, with some of the other mares. Come, I'll show you."

He led her to the end of the stables, and as they were passing the doorway to the tack room she glanced inside, then stopped as her eye was caught by a drawing pinned to the wall. "Wait, Charles, if you please," she said, stepping into the room.

"What is it?"

There was not just one drawing, but several scattered around the walls of the room, above the mantel of the fireplace, between racks of dangling harnesses, even on the back of the door. They were done in both charcoal and in ink, and all were of horses: horses running, standing, jumping, tossing their manes, mares with foals, and foals on their own, struggling to rise. Each had the name of the horse written at the bottom, but there was no signature.

"These are wonderful. Did one of the grooms do them? You have an artist in your employ, if so! And one better suited to paintbrushes than horse brushes!"

"Er, no, they weren't done by a groom."

She turned wide eyes on him. "Then who?"

His face colored.

"You?"

"I wouldn't have put them up, but the men say they like them. They're nearly as attached to the horses as I am."

126

"I like them, too. Very much. Would you do one for me?"

His face, already pink, deepened to scarlet. "You would want one?"

"Oh, yes. There is such emotion in them, one would almost think they were human. Look at this mare with her foal. With a few lines you have managed to convey care and concern, and yet at the same time a sense of her curiosity at this young creature that is hers. I wish I had half your talent."

"Do you draw, then?"

"A little. Mostly I play with watercolors." She felt a bit of blood rise in her own cheeks. "I brought a set with me today, in case there should be an opportunity to use them. Being in the country, you know, with such pretty scenes . . ." She hoped he would not guess she had expected to be bored. One might as well bring a novel to the dinner table; it was as insulting!

"Then let us make an exchange. I will do a drawing for you, if you will do a watercolor for me."

"You would have the poor end of that bargain."

"Then you should be happy to agree, if you are to be so much the winner."

"I shall be an embarrassed winner."

Her shyness over her artistic abilities seemed to encourage him, and his smile was as bold as any a rake ever gave a naive virgin. His blue-green eyes met hers and held them, until she felt a warm wetness between her legs, and, embarrassed and flustered, had to look away.

Maybe it was for the best that Charles was backward in so many ways; the young ladies would stand no chance against him otherwise. *She* would stand no chance against him. He would be corrupted by the female riches on offer.

Lisa Cach

She had the sudden, possessive urge to keep him in his ratty old coat and uncocked hat, so that no other would see the treasure beneath the unassuming clothes and try to steal him from her.

Which was ridiculous. He was not hers, and this morning she would have sworn on her miraculously extant virginity that she would never *want* him to be hers.

To steal a kiss, though . . . that might not go too strongly against her former opinion of him. And she couldn't imagine that he would mind. He might not think much of her face paints, but he was still a man, and what man ever minded a kiss?

"Let's go look at Desert Rose," he said, and led her from the tack room, and from the privacy it offered. Her kiss stealing would have to wait.

A half dozen mares were prancing around the paddock, in the center of which was a free-standing stall, almost like a cage with solid wooden walls four feet high. Over the top of the walls could be seen the back and head of a roan horse.

They leaned on the rail of the paddock fence and Charles pointed out Desert Rose. He started describing her attributes, but it was the horse in a box at which Evelina could not stop staring.

"Why," she finally interrupted, "is that horse in a box?"

"That's, ah . . . the teasing stallion."

"I beg your pardon?"

"He's there to tease the mares."

She laughed. "Well, yes, if I were a mare I might find it amusing to see a stallion in a box, but I assume that there is some aspect to the situation that I fail to grasp."

"I don't know that an explanation would be in the best of taste."

She raised her brows. "Now who is teasing? You do nothing but whet my curiosity with such a statement."

He fidgeted and made an embarrassed noise in the back of his throat. "If you are offended by what I am about to explain, you will have no one to blame but yourself."

"I promise to stop you if I feel in danger of fainting at whatever scandalous information you are about to impart. Come now, no more hesitation. Tell me."

He sighed and then straightened, and his voice when he spoke was as emotionless as that of a schoolteacher, as if he could somehow make the words less shocking that way. "We are trying to determine when the mares are in heat. That is, when they are ready to breed. There are certain signs they display at that time, but only if there is a male, a stallion, nearby."

She burst out laughing. "It is exactly the same with females of the human sort! A group alone will gossip and eat and loll about, but put a male amongst them, and suddenly they are fluttering their fans and casting glances, and taking only the daintiest of bites from their cakes."

"The signs a mare shows are a little different," he said, his lips twitching with suppressed humor. "Although I admit that there is winking involved."

"Mares wink?"

"Not with their eyes, and that is all I will say about *that*."

She frowned as she tried to puzzle it out, then watched the mares as one by one they approached the box and either pranced away again, or stood and let the stallion touch his nose to her. One mare raised her tail, and even from twenty feet away Evelina could see the flashing of pink as the mare moved an unknown muscle within her exposed sex.

Lisa Cach

Evelina turned wide eyes to Charles. "Winking?"

"I refuse to answer."

She laughed. "I shouldn't like to imagine the young ladies of Bath winking so. What a frightful sight that would be!"

He mumbled something.

"What was that?"

"I said, 'That opinion depends upon who is watching.' "

"Charles! I am appalled!" And then she dissolved into laughter again. "Tell me what they do if they are not ready to breed."

"At worst the mares will kick or bite, but otherwise they will simply ignore him."

"I think it might be the stallion's fault on occasion, if all does not go as he wishes," she said, looking up at her host.

"It is the mare's cycle that determines the mood of the encounter. The stallion has no control over it."

"That is what he tells himself. Perhaps he should try harder," she suggested. "He might find her more receptive than expected."

Their gazes met. "Are we still talking about mares and stallions?" he asked hoarsely.

She winked.

His eyes widened. "Yes! Right, then! Let's walk, shall we?" he said, stumbling away from the rail. "Where has your maid gone? Shall she come with us?"

Evelina laughed and followed him back through the stables.

Chapter Four

Evelina sighed, and he watched the movement of her chest beneath her fichu as the breath left her. "I don't know when I've ever seen such a lovely place, Charles."

Her pleasure was his own. "I was hoping you would like it."

They were walking down a shaded path beside a brook, one with moss-covered stones on its banks and lacy ferns dipping their deep green fronds down toward the clear, cold water. Sally, of course, followed a few steps behind, and if it were not for her presence, he was not sure what he might have tried with Evelina.

Since the day at Highcastle they had seen each other twice: they had spent a day in Bath, going to a public breakfast, to the Pump Room for the atrocious, supposedly healthful mineral water, and to the Abbey to read the inscriptions on the tombs; and he had taken her to the theater one night, and surprised himself by enjoying the performance.

Most surprising of all, he had begun secretly lusting after Evelina with a force that was frightening—and which he constantly feared she would detect.

It had been that conversation about horse breeding that had undone him, and the wink that could have had only one meaning. Since then every moment, both waking and dreaming, was consumed with thoughts of taking her to his bed. He felt like that pathetic stallion trapped in a box, unable to satiate his desires.

When she'd looked up at him with such hunger, and then winked—winked! With the mares in the paddock doing their own winking right behind her!—he had been so startled he had reacted in exactly the opposite way he wished. He had run from her, instead of dragging her back into the stables and tossing up her skirts, having at her like a sex-starved stallion. That was what he would have *liked* to have done.

Not that he would have, given the chance to do it over again. He hoped he was enough of a gentleman not to despoil a virgin, however willing.

The rest of the day, though, had done nothing to help his state of arousal. They had walked the circuit of the park, taken a picnic in one of the mock temples, and then frittered away the rest of the day with conversation and reading aloud from one of the novels Evelina had brought with her.

He had been like one drugged, listening with half-closed eyes to her soft voice and watching each movement of her hands and face, the rise and fall of her chest as she breathed. He had let his eyes dwell upon the bit of white-clad ankle that showed beneath her hem, and considered what it would be like to let his hand follow that stocking up beneath her skirts to the dark, warm moistness above.

He had looked for an opportunity to steal the kiss she had offered, but Sally was with them then. He could do nothing under her watchful eyes, and Evelina had made no move to dismiss the girl. He had wondered if Evelina might be aware of his frustration, and amused by it, and kept the maid there on purpose.

They were in the country today because Evelina had insisted that it was again time to do something that *he* wished. What he wished had nothing to do with ambles beneath the trees and gentle conversation, but such would have to do.

A secret, cowardly part of him wondered if, were Sally to wander off for a while, he would have the nerve to take Evelina in his arms. Or was he using the maid's presence as an excuse not to risk being turned away?

They came out of the woods and followed the path up a flower-strewn hill to a lone oak at the top, under which awaited their art supplies and a picnic lunch.

"If I did not know better," Evelina said as she settled herself on the spread rug, "I would say that you are beginning to enjoy spending time with me."

"That is utterly ridiculous," he said, trying for a jocular tone. "I prefer horses to people, as you have said yourself."

"They are not much for conversation, horses."

"Neither am I." When he was with Evelina, though, that was a bit of a lie. She had a way of coaxing him to speak, drawing words from him when he would otherwise remain mute.

She passed his paper and charcoal to him, and set her own paints and brushes and water jar around her. "Do

133

you think you might stand humanity long enough to do a portrait of me? You still owe me a drawing, you know. And I shall do a painting of you."

"Wouldn't you rather paint the landscape?"

She held the end of a brush to her lip, as if considering. "No. You make a much more interesting subject."

"I shan't like being stared at."

"Nonsense. Men love to be the center of attention."

"Not all men."

"Yes, all men. But as you shall be staring at me in return, you will have nothing about which to complain."

An invitation to stare at her: that could not be considered bad. It was a pity he could not ask her to pose in the nude.

They did a number of drawings and paintings of each other and of the scenes around them, complimenting each other's work, and exchanging questions on technique. Evelina had a talent for the use of color that, in his perception, made up for any weaknesses in perspective.

The time passed in languorous pleasure, and he wondered what had filled his thoughts—and what he had done to fill the days—before he met her.

Chapter Five

"You are looking almost pwesentable, Chawles," his mother said. "I had my doubts that that Johnson girl could effect any changes, but I see that she has. Soon you'll be ready to spend time with weal young ladies."

He had stopped by the drawing room to wish her a good night before he left to join Evelina and her parents to attend an assembly. He regretted the courtesy, his mother's words pricking at him and stirring up a defensive anger. Malign Evelina, would she? "Are you implying that Miss Johnson is not a lady?"

"Heavens, no, I would not say such a thing, however warranted the words might be! I simply meant that you will be able to do much better than her, now that you are gaining a bit of polish. After all, she has little to wecommend her as a wife. As a social playmate, yes, but I cannot see that she would be good for much more. You could manage a peer's daughter, with a bit of effort."

The anger boiled up, forcing him to speak when usually he would remain silent. "Miss Johnson has much to recommend her, if a man is seeking a cheerful warmhearted companion. And I assure you, Mother, many more men seek that in a wife than care about whether her father was a peer."

"Nonsense." She sniffed, as if dismissing the idea as unworthy. "And even if that were twue, it still stands that a man wants a wife who will not embarrass him with outlandish modes of dress and impwoper behavior."

"Evelina Johnson is an embarrassment to no one." He was so angry, his mother's words in need of such a range of refutations, he almost did not know where or how to begin. "You speak of her flirtations, yet I warrant that her public follies have far more innocence to them than the hidden indiscretions of others whose reputations are spotless, and most certainly they have none of the cruelty to be found in the wicked whisperings of bitter women."

"Chawles! Do not use that tone with me!"

"I will use whatever tone I damn well please, if you are going to say evil things about a girl who has never done you the least bit of harm, and whose only fault lies in an excess of enthusiasm. A fault which, I daresay, many more of us could stand to have a trace of ourselves." He marched to the door and turned to look at his mother, who was gaping at him. "Good night, Mother. Do sleep well."

He decided to walk from the town house to the Johnsons', instead of riding. He needed to clean away the residue of anger with exercise, and let the breezy night air cool his temper.

After a few blocks his thoughts had cleared enough that he could almost laugh at the argument, and at his own altered condition. Three weeks ago he would not have believed that he would soon be defending a young lady to his mother, or looking forward to attending an assembly at her side.

He, looking forward to an assembly. Who would have imagined?

But of course it was not the assembly about which he cared; it was Evelina.

It wasn't just that Evelina had prettiness hidden under her paints; it wasn't completely that she seemed open to whatever advance he might soon gather the nerve to try. It was also that she talked to him . . . and seemed interested in what he had to say. She actually seemed to like him, despite his bumblings and missteps.

A carriage rumbling by startled him from his thoughts, and looking around he realized he had passed the Johnsons' door three houses back. He retraced his steps and, once in the house, was shown into a parlor where Mr. Johnson sat, sipping a whiskey and staring at the fire in the grate. They made their greetings, and then Mr. Johnson waved him to a chair.

"You may as well sit. They are going to be a while—some crisis with Evelina's hair, I take it."

"How unfortunate." He had no better response, being unable to imagine what form, exactly, a crisis of the hair might take, or how serious the condition might be.

"Whiskey?" Evelina's father offered. "I always need one to endure these evenings. Frightful bores, they are, except for the occasional card game."

"Thank you, sir." He accepted out of politeness and to have something to do with his hands.

"Hear you have some fine horses in your stables," Mr. Johnson said, and soon after that comment all formality

137

disappeared between them. Mr. Johnson was knowledge-able and interested, being a farmer at heart, and had as well an Englishman's love of racing. Two men who loved horses could not but find themselves in sympathy.

For the next hour they discussed the merits and flaws of various breeds, equine ailments, and experimental techniques for extending the natural breeding season, and by the time Evelina and her mother appeared—Evelina wearing hoops that pushed her skirts out two feet to either side—Charles had almost forgotten why he was there.

They both stood and greeted the women, Mr. Johnson doing so with a gruff, exasperated sort of affection. "All the best food will be gone by the time we get there," he complained.

"One would think you didn't get enough to eat at home, the way you carry on," Mrs. Johnson chided. "I can have Cook pack a supper for you, so you needn't eat from a picked-over buffet."

"You have entirely too smart a mouth, my dear," Mr. Johnson said with obvious fondness, holding out his arm for her to take. She did so, giggling with a hand over her mouth like a young girl.

Charles watched in fascination, his own parents having never teased each other in front of him. He wondered if, despite initial appearances, Mrs. Johnson was more like Evelina than she would like to admit—and perhaps that was why she worried at the trouble her daughter might get into.

"Charles, you look almost dashing!" Evelina said, coming up to him.

"Just 'almost'?" He had gone so far as to wear a black silk bag to hold his hair at the base of his neck; his shirt was new and had a trace of lace at the cuffs; and he was wearing proper shoes with silver buckles, not muck-encrusted boots.

"You remain distressingly short on hair powder and embroidery."

"All the better for you to shine beside me."

She made a face. "I could have wished for less attention tonight." Her hand went up to lightly touch her hair, which was sporting an extra heavy coating of powder and a quantity of silk flowers and ribbons. She also, for some reason beyond his ken, had painted faint blue veins onto her temples. "Tell me, do you see anything amiss?"

He examined her coiffure, trying to make out in the candlelight what the hair crisis had concerned. It did seem that even with the powder there was the faintest hint of green to her hair.... "No, nothing at all."

She sighed in relief and smiled. "Thank heavens. That was the last time I will ever trust the *Ladies' Guide* for a recipe for a darkening hair rinse; I promise you that."

He realized he still did not know what color her hair naturally was, but asking now would go too close to the issue of suspected greenness. She was wearing less rouge and lip color than usual tonight, and there was no sign of the mouse-skin eyebrows. Was that because of him, just as his clean shoes and black bag were because of her?

He offered her his arm, then had to extend it farther, as her side hoops hit his thighs.

"They are fashionable, but rather inconvenient, I confess," Evelina said, laying her hand on his, their distance from each other making it look as though they were engaged in a formal dance. "I had wanted hoops that were three and half feet—think of all those yards of lovely silk hanging from them, and how tiny one's waist would appear!—but Mama refused."

"I don't know that my arm could have withstood three and a half feet. It is getting tired already," he said as they followed her parents downstairs and out into the night. The assembly was being held at Mr. and Mrs. Wetherby's large house across Queen Square, and like several other guests they would be walking the short distance instead of taking a carriage.

"Nonsense. Men are marvelously strong, and not to be undone by a hoop."

"We are undone by hoops and silks and pretty faces at every turn."

She looked up at him, a smile curling her lips. "Charles! You are becoming much too charming. There will be annoying young misses swarming around you like flies."

"And that would be a tragedy?"

"Of course. They are mercenary creatures, expert at appearing to be other than they truly are in hopes of snaring a husband."

"Oh?" he asked, raising a brow.

"Do not look at me that way. I am not speaking of makeup or bum rolls. I am speaking of hearts."

"Are you wearing a bum roll?" He pretended to peer around at her backside.

She made a face of grave offense.

"I'm teasing," he said, enjoying himself. He felt more lighthearted than he could ever remember. Evelina's devil-may-care attitude drew out his own hidden playful side, and he was surprised at how good it felt.

She bumped his leg with her hoop. "I knew that."

The street lamps left much of the square in darkness, but the pockets of warm light illuminated the occasional guest heading to or from the Wetherby house. The windows were lit, the sounds of music and voices audible down on the street. They caught up with Evelina's parents, and with them went inside and paid their respects to the host and hostess.

"Now I can find something to eat," Mr. Johnson said, when they were finished with the greetings. "You'll stay with Evelina, keep her amused?" he said to Charles.

"Of course."

He was doubly glad he had been assigned to stay by Evelina's side; with her, he would not have to do any of that embarrassing milling about, trying to look as if he were talking to people to whom he could find nothing to say. When he'd been forced to attend such occasions in the past, he'd usually ended up hiding with other men in a smoky room, or hunkered around a card table, sneaking the occasional longing glance at women who seemed forever out of reach. He had thought them almost frightening in their loveliness, so different were they from men.

"What are you thinking?" Evelina asked, as they wended their way among the other guests. The assembly was being held on both the ground and the first floors, with several rooms opened up to accomodate both the large number of people and the various activities provided for their entertainment. "You look amused."

"I was thinking of men and women, and how sometimes their coming together is as surprising as would be the pairing of a massive draft horse with a spirited Arabian."

They passed a couple coming down the stairs as they were going up, the man over six feet tall, the woman well under five. "Or a draft horse with a pony," Evelina said.

He laughed. "Perhaps the offspring will take the best traits of each parent."

"One would hope so, as the alternative is not pleasant

to consider." They drifted into a room where people sat in small groups around tables, playing cards while others watched.

"Of course, it is before the wedding that such considerations should be made," she said. "Now who here would make a good pairing, likely to produce excellent offspring? There are obvious choices," she said, nodding toward a couple who were of like build and coloring, and looked to be in good health. "But we want more of a challenge than that. We are looking to improve the breed, are we not?"

He joined in the joke. "So the gluttonous," he said, slightly inclining his head toward a portly man, "should be matched with the overly thin." He directed his gaze to a young lady whose collarbones protruded and who had hollowed cheeks.

"Yes! Together, they would make children of a perfect thickness. And likewise the talkative with the silent," she said, as they passed a table where two such players sat across from one another.

They continued trading quiet suggestions as they moved through the room, then went out one door and back through another to a different room, where dancing and music filled the space. They paired the pale with the florid, the intellectual with the sentimental, the timid with the bold.

"And what manner of wife would you choose for yourself?" she asked, as they watched dancers gaily turning to music provided by a trio of musicians.

"To answer that, I would have to admit to my flaws that need balancing."

"Would you want someone who balanced you? Our pairing game has been entertaining, but no one truly chooses their mate with such things in mind."

"Horses wouldn't bother with such considerations, either," he said. "A stallion takes whomever is ready, and the mare doesn't care who sires her foal. That's why there are breeders who choose for them."

She laughed. "One might say that mamas and papas are our breeders, then, only their concerns are lands and rank, money and family ties, rather than leg length and shoulder shape."

"I'll make my own decisions when it comes time for marriage. I will not be mated by Mama to some creature of her choosing."

"Will you be allowed such a choice?" she asked, sounding concerned. "What of your horses? She will still hold them over your head."

"Marriage is for life." He thought of the affection between Evelina's parents, compared to the cold politeness of his own. He had always thought his parents well suited in their ambitious natures, but he saw now that those strivings for wealth and position had left them devoid of warmth, even with each other. They were more like partners in a business venture than companions of the heart. "I would like the chance to love my wife, and that seems likely only if I choose her on my own."

"They say that two people can grow to love one another, if there is respect and kindness. My mama and papa had an arranged marriage."

"Truly?" He would never have guessed it.

"Truly. Perhaps we are not so wise as to know who we will love, given time."

He gazed down at her, meeting her brown eyes with their cheerful, laughing warmth, and suddenly realized that he was falling in love with her. Despite the paints, despite her criticisms of his clothes, despite what he knew would be the outrage of his mother, he could imagine no one else he would want by his side, day by day. His life was brighter with Evelina in it.

He opened his mouth to speak, the power of this burgeoning emotion requiring something of him, some sign to show her what she was coming to mean to him. It was a glowing, spreading warmth he felt, apart from and yet linked to his yearning for her body.

"Charles? What is it?"

And then the moment was interrupted as a pair of young women came bouncing up, chattering at Evelina, who chattered happily in response and then introduced them to him as friends of hers.

The warm emotion drew back into his heart, hiding there in safety from these strangers. He felt his ability to converse go dead, scared into silence by the unfamiliar audience. Evelina gave him a puzzled look as his lips shut and stayed that way, and then his rescue arrived.

"Highcroft! You could have knocked me over with a feather when I first saw you come in," Edmund Beauchamp said, coming up to him. Edmund had been in his circle of friends at Oxford. They hadn't been close, but Charles had amusing—if somewhat hair-raising—memories of the escapades Beauchamp had instigated, from turning a friend's room into a one-night brothel to stealing all of a don's wigs in the dead of night.

Charles started to make the appropriate introductions, but Beauchamp said he already knew Miss Johnson, and then Charles couldn't remember the names of her friends, and Evelina had to introduce them herself.

"Splendid, splendid!" Beauchamp said. "Now if you

will be so kind as to excuse us, I need Highcroft here to settle a bet."

"Certainly," Evelina said, but she looked disappointed to see him go. "I'll stay here so that you can find me upon your return."

With an apologetic look back, Charles let himself be dragged away. Maybe by the time he returned those two friends of hers would be dancing, or chattering at someone else.

Beauchamp took him to a smallish room crowded with young men who were drinking whiskey and brandy and smoking long-stemmed pipes. A game of chess was going on at a table before the fire, observed by a few, but most were lounging around to no purpose, engaged in desultory conversations.

Charles wondered how many of them were there out of a terror of female company similar to his own, rather than from any true love of drink or tobacco. While there were some men who were naturally at ease with women, he rather suspected that most were simply better at putting a brave face on their discomfort than he was.

"I found him!" Beauchamp announced, and presented him like a fresh foxtail still bloody from the kill.

Charles recognized several of the faces, both from his time in Bath and from Oxford. "What is this bet you sorry lot need me to settle?"

"He's itching to get back!" someone said. "I'd say that points to yes!"

"It could as easily point to no," someone argued.

"Yes or no what?" he asked, smiling, wondering what this bet was that seemed to be amusing them so.

Beauchamp slapped him on the back. "Why, whether or not Miss Johnson has kissed you yet. Most think she's had enough time, and must surely have managed it with you by now. She kissed old Kingston there on the night they were first introduced. Took me two meetings to get my kiss. I was being coy." He grinned.

Charles could barely believe what he was hearing. He was stunned, taken completely off guard. He looked around at the eager, laughing faces, and felt he did not know a single one of them. He had the dizzying sense that he was separate from his body, was but a stranger looking through borrowed eyes, listening with borrowed ears as Beauchamp went on with his unreal words.

"I know you better than they do though. I remember what you were like at Oxford, and I laid my money on her not having managed it. If even a whore couldn't persuade you to touch her, I'll have to wish Miss Johnson luck."

Then all at once he was back to himself, the red fog of anger bringing him there. "How dare you speak of Miss Johnson in the same breath as a whore," he said, his words slow and deliberate. "How dare you lay bets on her. How dare you even say her name amongst yourselves." He was speaking as only a man angry enough to kill spoke, and Beauchamp knew it.

"Highcroft, hold on there! Settle down, now; we didn't mean any harm by it!"

"You hide back here, spreading lies about—"

"Wait, I say! No one here lied about anything. At least half of us here in this room have been kissed by Evelina Johnson."

A chorus of "ayes" went through the room. The volume of it shook Charles, opening a small crack of doubt in his anger. "*Half* of you?"

One by one they said how long they had known Evelina

before she had kissed them, and unanimously stated that once she'd had her kiss, she'd flitted off to find new prey.

"Surely you knew of her reputation?" Beauchamp asked.

"I knew, but . . ." He trailed off, his world spinning around him.

"But you didn't believe it? I can't blame you there. Who wants to believe that a pretty girl does not find you as charming as she pretends? Or that another will do in your place just as well?"

He realized that he *hadn't* believed much that he'd heard about her, or at least had not taken it seriously. Yes, she'd made comments about the handsome footman, and yes, she'd admitted to having kissed someone, but he had had no idea it went as far as this. Half the men in the room. *Half!*

Even Beauchamp had enjoyed a kiss from her. How could Charles look at Evelina now and not see as well the faces of all these men?

They were all laughing at him for being duped by Miss Johnson.

Most galling of everything was that Beauchamp had laid his finger exactly upon Charles's feelings: he'd believed Evelina liked him and found him attractive. *Him* specifically. Not him and half the men in the room.

His felt his face go hard and tried to hide the fact that his heart was breaking.

Her friends had invited her to go with them down to the supper room, but she had declined, wanting Charles to have no difficulty finding her upon his return.

She fidgeted alone, watching the dancers and examining details of other women's dresses. Then a young man came and asked her to be his partner in the next dance, and there seemed no reason to refuse. It might do Charles a bit of good to see that other men found her desirable, assuming he should come back before the dance ended.

He did. She caught a glimpse of him, and when the dance ended she turned her attention to the man whose arm she held, giggling at some inane comment he made. If she could make Charles jealous, perhaps he would finally gather the nerve to kiss her.

There had been many times she knew that she could have kissed him, and would not have been rebuffed. Sally's presence would not have stopped her, just as it never had in the past. With Charles, though, unlike with all the others, she needed to be the one who was kissed. She needed to be the one receiving, not the active partner.

She didn't know why there was a difference with him, but she felt it deep inside: he must come to her.

Only, he was taking a bloody long time about it. God's bodkin, but she was overwhelmed by desire for him! All her thoughts were consumed with Charles, and when the two of them were not together she was having imaginary conversations with him in her head, or daydreaming of holding him naked in her arms, as they twined their bodies together beneath the bedcovers.

She tapped her partner on the arm with her folded fan in a teasing gesture, thanked him, and departed. She returned to Charles, and saw that he was indeed distraught over her display. Perhaps more distraught than she had intended.

"Charles, whatever is the matter?" she asked as she rejoined him, pretending innocence.

He grabbed her hand and pulled her out of the room without explanation, then hurried her up the stairs to the next floor, the family quarters, where all was quiet. They stopped at the landing, and he swung her around to face him. She felt a nervous thrumming in her blood. He was passionate, but she did not think it was a kiss she was going to get.

"Tell me why you do it."

"Do what? Charles, what has happened? Why are you so upset?"

"The flirting. The kisses with half the men here tonight. Tell me why you do it."

She felt a sick sinking in her stomach as she began to suspect what he had heard while with Edmund Beauchamp. "What did Beauchamp tell you?"

"That you've kissed eight men—that he knows of!"

"Oh. Yes, well . . . I have." She tried to play it off as inconsequential, hoping that lightness would defuse the argument. "They were none of them very good at it, either. Or maybe they were, and kisses are simply not the thrill that I expected."

From the look on his face, she was not making things better.

"Why?" he asked again.

She shrugged, and felt herself squirming under his gaze. "I like men. I won't be able to kiss whomever I please after I am married."

"That is the whole of your reasoning? I like women, too, but I do not kiss them whenever the urge takes me."

"If they are willing, I do not know why not."

"Because it is not so simple as that, and you know it. Nor can I believe that you do this just because you like men. You denied once that you are trying to damage your parents' ability to choose a husband for you."

"And I deny it still."

"Then why?"

"I don't know why there needs to be more of a reason!" She felt like a student who could not give the right answer, and struggled to find one that would satisfy him. "Although if there was another reason, it might be because it makes me feel pretty."

"Pretty?" His voice was as incredulous as his expression.

"When a man wants me to kiss him, I know he thinks I'm pretty. And I certainly think he's attractive at the time, so where is the harm in it? I know not to expect more than a kiss."

"You squander your reputation for the sake of vanity?"

"That was only an additional reason." She bit her lip, considering, as a question came to her. "But you knew about all that nonsense before. It was why you were assigned as my watchdog. Why are you so upset about it now?"

He looked away and did not answer. In his silence she found the only conclusion possible, one that she had barely even dared to hope for: he had started to care about her. She felt a flush run through her, a combination of her own growing feelings for him and the anxiety that she might be on the verge of losing him, just before something wonderful truly had the chance to begin.

"Charles," she said softly, and laid her hand on his arm. He shook it off.

She felt tears come to her eyes. She reached out and again laid her hand on his arm.

He moved away and turned cold eyes back to her. "I am not going to be yet another man in your collection. If I had less respect for you I'd take what you seem so eager to offer. And if I had less respect for myself, I'd let you use me as a sop to your vanity. Wipe off your powders and take a true look at yourself, Evelina."

Hurt fired anger in her own heart. "Look at your *own* self, Charles. Dressing like a common laborer so that no one will pay attention to you, because you're too afraid of what they might see if they did! I did pay attention, and I liked what I saw, but I don't like it much right now. I cannot believe I ever thought I had feelings for you."

"Then as we apparently find so little pleasure in each other's company, perhaps it is best if we part ways."

"What a marvelous suggestion," she said. "The best you've ever had." She turned and went down the stairs before he could see the tears that were spilling down her cheeks.

Chapter Six

Evelina lay on her bed in her dressing robe, her hair loose and unpowdered, her face bare. She stared up at the canopy as she had stared up at it for the past week, alternating between bouts of self-loathing, anger, and self-pitying tears.

Mama's repeated warnings about flirting and wild behavior had meant nothing to her. The occasional hesitations she herself had felt had served only to add the spice of fear to her exploits. When a friend had told her, in an excited, semiapologetic whisper, that she was gaining a reputation for recklessness, she had been secretly flattered that people were taking note of her.

Since the time she was small she'd had an instinctive understanding that breaking rules did not matter overmuch in the long run. Most of the time the rules were there for someone else's convenience, and being a good girl meant doing what she was told instead of what she wished. Never had she realized that breaking the rules might hurt another in a way more deeply felt than the scolding disappointment of a parent.

She had hurt Charles, and lost him. And now here she lay all alone, with no one to blame but her own vain and thoughtless self.

The thought of dressing in her colorful silks revolted her. Her pots and bottles of makeup and perfume made her want to cry. The *Ladies' Guide* had been burned in the grate, and her green-tinted hair lay tangled and unwashed over her pillows.

The only thing she would look at, besides the canopy of her bed, was the drawing Charles had done of her while they were sitting on the hill. She had been painting a watercolor of him at the same time, so that they each had a picture of the one doing a portrait of the other, like two mirrors reflecting back.

He had liked her then. She knew he had. He had liked her for more than the hopes of a kiss, and she had laughed and talked with him as if he were a friend of the heart.

And then she'd gone and spoiled it all by flirting with that boy at the assembly, trying to make Charles jealous when he had just been listening to that awful Beauchamp—why had she ever kissed *him?*—relate every detail of her past. He had no reason to believe that he meant more to her than any other man ever had.

There was a soft knock on her door. She ignored it, assuming it to be Sally. A moment later the door opened, and footsteps came across the room. She glanced to the side and saw her mama staring down at her with a worried frown.

"Are you certain you do not need me to send for the doctor?"

"I am fine, Mama."

"Won't you tell me what is wrong?"

"There is nothing wrong." She felt the pull to pour out her heart, but she remembered how Mama had warned her against an involvement with Charles. She would not find sympathy here, and was afraid Mama would tell her that she had gotten what she deserved for her flirting.

Mama sat on the edge of the bed, the mattress sinking down toward her. She picked up Evelina's hand. "Then why have you not been out? Why have we not seen Charles? Why do you do nothing but lie here day after day?"

"I cannot go out with green hair. I am waiting for it to fade."

"It will not fade without washing." Mama kept looking at her, as if waiting for a deeper confession, but when none came she sighed. "I do wish you would consider going out, green hair or no. I have been speaking with Mrs. Highcroft, and apparently Charles has slipped back into his old ways in your absence, only worse. He will not leave the stables at Highcastle, and Mrs. Highcroft says she has never seen him so morose. She says that if she did not know better, she would think the boy had fallen in love. You wouldn't happen to know whom he might have lost his heart to, would you? Surely it is one of your friends, one to whom you introduced him?"

"Charles is melancholy?" She perked up a bit at the news. If he no longer cared for her, surely he would be content without her and not moping around the stables like a forlorn lover.

"Dreadfully so. Mrs. Highcroft is worried for his health."

"She thinks he is in love?"

"With a passionate desperation. You know how some men can get. They set their heart upon a girl, and then cannot eat nor sleep until they have her. They are not capable of moderation. One would think they could die of a broken heart. Perhaps if you were to see him, he would tell you what is troubling him. He will not say a word to Mrs. Highcroft."

"He may refuse to see me," Evelina said, her doubts catching up with her. "I mean, if he is so very unhappy, the promise of my company may not be enough to bring him out."

"Mrs. Highcroft is going to see if she cannot force him to attend the Atherton ball on Friday. Can I tell her that you will be there, and will try to talk to Charles?"

Evelina nodded, fragile hope beating in her chest.

Mama picked up a lock of her hair, rubbing it between her fingers. "We'll try lemon juice and sitting in a sunny window. Three days of that, and there should be not a hint of green left."

Evelina managed a smile. "Thank you, Mama."

Charles brushed Desert Rose and told himself he was *not* going to take Evelina's watercolor out of his jacket pocket again. He was *not* going to stand there mooning over it for half an hour, trying to match the happiness she had painted into his eyes with the emptiness he knew was there now. He was going to throw the damn thing away. He *was*.

He set down the brush and took the folded picture out of his pocket. He had better look at it once more before burning it.

A twinge of pain went through his heart. Who but Miss

Johnson would ever have made him look so colorful? So alive?

With the pain came the doubts that had been hounding him since the Wetherby assembly, and since he had confronted Evelina.

There was no question that she had kissed more than half a dozen men, with apparently little feeling for them personally. Was it possible, though, that with him she *had* cared? He could not forget one of her parting comments, about how she had thought she had feelings for him.

The laughter of his friends had been too fresh in his ears, though, for him to listen, as had been the sight of her dancing and flirting with another.

But what was a single dance and the tap of a fan? In truth, it was of no consequence. And what should it matter if others laughed at him for his choice of mate, so long as he was happy?

Evelina had been right when she had made those comments about his clothing. He hid by wearing them. He had been a coward, in that and with her, and he deserved every bit of misery he felt. He had spoiled his one chance at a future with a cheerful, warmhearted woman who might have been as fond of him as he was of her, and he had hurt her in the process. She probably hated him now.

A wave of utter sadness washed over him for what he had lost. He was alone now, and the company of horses could not fill the emptiness.

"Chawles? Are you in here?" his mother called from down the center aisle of the stables.

He stuffed the picture back into his pocket and picked up the horse brush. "Here."

His mother approached in her characteristic stance, her back stiff as steel stays, her nose held high as if she were above her surroundings. He imagined she would be horrified if she knew he had fallen in love with Evelina.

"What are you doing in here?" she asked. "Why have you not been spending time with Miss Johnson? I want an answer this time."

"She has not expressed any wish to go out."

"Since when does a man wait on a woman's invitation? Really, Chawles, I had thought you had come further along than that."

He said nothing.

"Regardless. Evelina is in need of your steadying pwesence. Mrs. Johnson tells me that she has been lolling about like a woebegone puppy, and she fears the girl may have had the bad sense to fall in love with someone inappropriate. You know how girls can get. They know no modewation, and one begins to fear they will make themselves ill with their emotions."

"Evelina is in love with someone?"

"That is what Mrs. Johnson fears. Would you happen to know who? You have been by her side, and surely must have seen who it was who caught her fancy."

He shrugged, trying to hide his hope that all might not be lost.

"Mrs. Johnson is going to persuade her to go to the Atherton ball, and asks that you try to speak with her. Mrs. Johnson feels Evelina may listen to your good sense, whereas she wejects it from her mother. Would you consider going?"

"Of course." A second chance! Evelina might hate him, but maybe . . . just maybe it was the opposite she felt.

His mother blinked at him in surprise. "You would?"

"I can surely bear a ball for the sake of helping a friend."

"Ah. Well. Mrs. Johnson will be glad to hear it." She

was still looking at him as if she could not quite believe he was her son.

He almost enjoyed her shock, and decided to befuddle her completely. "I'm not certain I have anything fine enough to wear. Might I borrow something of Papa's, and a wig?"

She made a little noise in the back of her throat, her mouth an O of astonishment.

"Thank you, Mother."

Chapter Seven

Evelina rose on tiptoe, searching the crowded ballroom for a head of dark hair and a mud-brown coat. She saw no sign of Charles amidst the sea of white male heads and colorful clothing, and rested back on her heels with a sigh of frustration. Perhaps he had not come after all.

She was caught between relief and disappointment, her stomach churning with a mix of anxiety and hopeful expectation. Over the past three days she had tried—and failed—to think of what she could say to clean up the mess between them. In the end she had chosen to speak without words, and to hope that when he saw her he would understand what she was saying.

She wore only the barest hint of makeup, invisible to an inexpert eye: a faint touch of color on her lips, a slight darkening on her lashes from the lead comb, the tiniest bit of powder on her nose to dull the shine. Her hair was its natural hue of golden brown, made somewhat more golden by the days in front of the window with lemon juice; a small bunch of fresh flowers was nestled in the arrangement, and their perfume was the only one she wore.

Her gown was of soft pink and cream with silver lace, her hoops the smallest pair she owned. Her brocade shoes did have paste-diamond buckles over the instep, but as they were down on her feet and almost hidden by her skirts, she didn't think they would count against her. They were the only buckles that matched the shoes and gown, and a girl had to have the right footwear if she was to maintain her confidence.

A tall man in turquoise velvet stopped a few feet from her, and scanned the crowd much as she had done, his posture denoting his frustration. He was wearing a white wig with a roll over either ear and a long tail down the back wrapped in black ribbon. She had the feeling she might have met him before, but for the life of her she could not place where.

Then, as if sensing her eyes upon him, he turned and locked gazes with her. The blue-green eyes that stared into hers could belong to only one person: Charles.

Her lips parted, but no sound emerged.

He blinked at her, and then his eyes widened in startled recognition, his gaze going from hair to face to dress, and back up again.

For a moment she thought that maybe he was dressed this way for someone else, that his supposed melancholy had nothing to do with her, that, indeed, he had dressed how she had always suggested in order to spite her, now that he was lost to her.

"Evelina?" he asked softly. The cautious hope in his voice encouraged her.

"Charles?"

A new dance was called, and Charles lifted his gloved hand in invitation.

"You can dance?" she asked. She knew there was much she needed to say, and much she needed to know about his feelings, but the dance floor was waiting and he was looking both handsome and unknown in his finery and wig.

"I was forced to learn, and I learned quickly—the more quickly to escape the lessons."

She laid her hand on his and let him lead her out onto the floor and into position with the others. The music started, and he went flawlessly through the moves as they changed partners, touched hands, circled, and turned.

Colors and changing faces, notes of music, scents of bodies and perfumes, and the light of chandeliers swirled around her. At their center was always Charles' face, with the intense blue-green eyes that held hers with a promise of touches more intimate than kisses.

She felt drunk, although she'd had nothing to drink. She was floating and dizzy, and it all seemed a dream. She was afraid to trust that she might have a second chance, and he looked too different from the Charles to whom she was accustomed to believe it was him, and that she was awake and this was real.

When the dance ended he looked around, then led her off to one end of the floor and through the pillared archways of a gallery, where a thinner press of guests milled, observing the dancing. He pulled her to one end, where a pillar and the wall afforded a modicum of privacy.

"Charles, is it truly you?" She reached up and traced her fingertips lightly over his face. He grasped her hand and kissed her palm.

"As much as it is you I see before me. Golden brown hair. I never knew!"

"Do you forgive me, then? I am so sorry for the things I said, and for flirting with that boy."

"Shhh, you are not the one who needs to beg forgiveness." He kissed the backs of her fingers. "I was the one who behaved unfairly. I was the coward that you accused me of being, and hurt you in my foolishness. Do you forgive me?"

"How could I not? It would be wounding my own heart not to do so."

His grip on her hand tightened. "Then you *do* care for me?"

She nodded, her throat too tight with emotion to speak.

"Enough that you will come away with me, now, tonight, so that we may be married?"

"Elope?" Her heart thundered in her chest.

"I will not wait on the consent of parents. Let us present them with a fait accompli, and they may do with it what they will. I want you to be my wife, and to be by my side through all my days. I cannot imagine any happiness to be had without you."

"In a thousand years I could find no man I would rather have as my husband," she said, against the tears tight in her throat.

He released her hand and lightly laid his palms against either side of her head, tilting up her face. His chest and shoulders blocked out sight of all but him, and then he bent down his head, and her eyes closed against the nearness of his image, a delicious shiver running through her as she felt the warmth of the air between them, and the soft moistness of his breath against her skin. She felt weak, and clung to his coat, her fingers digging into the velvet.

And then he kissed her.

Liquid heat poured through her and pooled in her loins at the first touch of his lips against her own. He pressed more firmly, and her legs lost their strength, forcing him to wrap one arm around her waist and pull her up against him. She felt his thigh against the mound of her sex, and a moan started deep in her throat, beyond her control.

It had never been like this with any of the others. Her desires for them had been as small and quickly dying as a spark from a fire. Never had there been this soul-consuming yearning that made her want to become part of another, blending their bodies into one.

His lips parted, and she felt his tongue trace over the joining of her own lips. She let them open, and his tongue slipped inside, rubbing lightly against her own. She felt an echoing hunger between her legs, for an entry greater than this, and wrapped her arms around his neck, pulling him closer, sucking his tongue deeper into her mouth and trying to take more of him than their clothing would permit.

Clapping and a whistle of appreciation broke them out of their web of desire. "Bravo, Highcroft! Marvelous performance! I wouldn't have thought you had it in you!"

They both turned to see Beauchamp standing in the shadows nearby, a smirk on his face. Evelina felt something turn sour in her stomach.

"Took what was owed you, you did!" Beauchamp leered. "And Miss Johnson, you are looking particularly lovely tonight. I don't suppose you'd care to put me back on your list of men to—"

Charles's fist knocked the rest of the words from his mouth. As Beauchamp's hands went up to his face, Charles punched him in his unprotected gut. Beauchamp doubled over, and a double-fisted thump on the back of his shoulders sent him face-first to the floor.

An excited murmur went through the nearby guests, who had turned to watch. Evelina stared in shock from Beauchamp to Charles.

"Whaaa?" Beauchamp groaned from the floor, a smear of blood beneath him.

"So help me God, if I ever hear Miss Johnson's name on your lips again, I will geld you like a horse and stuff your treasures down your throat."

Charles grabbed her hand and tugged her away from the scene, pushing his way through the gathering crowd and dragging her after him. "I have a carriage waiting. Let's be away before any think to stop us." And then, as if as an afterthought, he added, "Pardon my language back there."

"It is quite all right," she said, bemused, her shock being replaced now by glee. "But you know, the fashionable way to settle a disagreement over a lady's honor is a duel, not fisticuffs."

He turned and gave her a look.

She grinned, joy rising up inside her. "But I find I am growing quite fond of the unfashionable. Quite fond indeed."

Chapter Eight

Mrs. Johnson folded the letter she had just read aloud, set it beside her cup of chocolate, and smiled at Mrs. Highcroft. "They sound as if they are enjoying Scotland. I should think this is a lovely time of year to visit."

"I do not suppose they will be spending much time outside of their wooms," Mrs. Highcroft said, with such a bland expression that it took Mrs. Johnson several moments to realize that her friend had indeed just made a lewd remark.

"Dear me, no. What newlyweds do?" She giggled, covering her mouth with her hand as her false teeth shifted. "And perhaps they will enjoy those rooms for some time yet, as I believe they are half-afraid to return home."

Mrs. Highcroft's lips twitched in a contained smile. "We could have made a living on the stage, you and I. There were times I thought Chawles fairly hated me. It was hard to say some of the things I had to."

Lisa Cach

"For me, as well . . . Although sometimes my greatest challenge was simply not to confess all. I do not know if Evelina would forgive me if she knew she had been so neatly herded to her chosen husband."

"Nor Chawles." Mrs. Highcroft sighed. "I expect I shall have to play the slowly softening mama, wather than welcome them with open arms."

Mrs. Johnson sipped her chocolate, spilled a bit on her gown, and did not mind. She was feeling altogether too pleased with herself, with her cleverness, and with the fortune Charles Highcroft would inherit from his merchant father.

She looked over the rim of her cup at Mrs. Highcroft, wondering if her friend knew how very much in need of those funds the Johnsons were. Her friend would faint if she knew she had been outfoxed!

"They shall live at Highcastle, of course," Mrs. Highcroft said.

Mrs. Johnson lowered her cup. "I beg your pardon? Evelina will inherit the Johnson lands and manor. Charles will need to live there to learn how to manage the estate."

"As you wish, my dear." And then, almost idly, "One day I suppose it will be known as the Highcroft estate, when Chawles's childwen inherit in turn." Mrs. Highcroft's expression was one of quiet victory. "And no one will say *they* are the social-climbing offspring of a merchant."

Mrs. Johnson sipped her chocolate, contemplated her new in-law, and sighed within the confines of her stays.

Today

Seeking Single Superhero

by JULIE KENNER

For my mom.

Chapter One

MORTAL FEMALE SEEKING SINGLE SUPERHERO
for love, laughter, and then some. Must be charming,
witty, sexy, and willing to commit. Specific superpowers negotiable, but strength and endurance a
must! *Interested Protectors, please contact Jennifer Martin
at Employee Box #657, Mortal-Protector Liaison Office.*

Jennifer tapped her pencil faster and faster against her
desktop as she read, reread, and then *re-*reread the personal ad in the back of the current issue of the *Mortal-
Protector Liaison Weekly Bulletin.*

It couldn't be. Could it? Someone—anyone—please tell
her it wasn't so. Tell her there wasn't a personal ad in the
newsletter suggesting that she would be interested in dating a superhero. Correction: not suggesting, but flat-out
stating that she wanted to make whoopee with one of
those arrogant, self-absorbed Protector types! Continually
saving the world gave a guy one hell of an ego, and so

far Jennifer hadn't met one with whom she'd even want to have coffee—much less go all the way. *Really!* A boyfriend, sure. A Protector for a boyfriend? No way. She had standards, after all!

She exhaled in a whoosh, then looked around at the nearby cubicles, wondering if anyone else was reading the newsletter. No one was pointing at her and laughing. At least, not yet.

Tomorrow the ad would be plastered all over the Venerate Council of Protectors' Web site—that was where the newsletter items all went, eventually—and then every Protector in the world would see it. They would all think she was hunting for a superhero husband.

Absurd. Unthinkable.

And even more ridiculous since her mother was so gung-ho about hooking her up with one. Sinking farther down in her chair, she tried to get out of her colleagues' line of sight. This was a nightmare. Her own personal nightmare. And a particularly nasty one.

At that thought, she brightened. Maybe it really was just a dream. Any minute now her alarm clock would buzz, she'd wake up, and she'd laugh about the silly games her subconscious was playing. After all, since she hadn't placed an ad, there couldn't really be one.

Could there?

She'd better take another look. With her fingers crossed so tight she cut off the circulation, she closed her eyes, counted to ten, then peeked out from under her eyelashes.

Well, darn. There it was—plain as day, and larger than life.

Which meant there was only one explanation: her mother was at it again.

The metal legs of her chair scraped against the concrete

floor as she shoved it backward and stood up. Daphne Martin might have brought her daughter into the world . . . she might have helped her find her funky rent-controlled apartment . . . she might even be the main reason why Jenny had landed her great job as a press liaison here at the MLO. But this time Jenny's matchmaking mother had simply gone too far.

Tucking the newsletter snugly under her arm, she marched out of her cubicle toward the elevator. She needed to set the record straight with her mother, and she needed to do it now.

Taking a deep breath, she jabbed the down button, all the while hoping like heck that the courage she felt wouldn't abandon her during the five-story descent to her mother's lair in the computer lab.

Starbuck propped one leg on Daphne Martin's desk and watched, amused, as the older woman crawled around on the floor.

"See, the problem is the polarity," she said over the low-pitched hum of whirring tape drives and other computer paraphernalia. She followed a bright blue cable to a particularly ominous-looking machine, then slipped behind it and disappeared from Starbuck's view. "We're getting some sort of electrical interference," she called, her voice muffled. "That's what's slowing our system down."

There were a few loud grunts, followed by a metallic clanking noise, and then Daphne's head popped out from around the side, followed in short order by the entire woman. She rocked back on her heels, pushed a lock of curly gray hair out of her face, and flashed Starbuck a winning smile. "But you probably didn't come here to listen to my problems with the computer system."

171

He shrugged, hoping he looked like nothing more than the befuddled mortal employee he was pretending to be. "I'm on break. I just came down to shoot the breeze. If you want to talk shop, go for it."

In fact, he hoped she would. Daphne was a piece of work, and Starbuck genuinely liked her. For that matter, he had something of a crush on Daphne's daughter, Jenny. Unfortunately, Jenny didn't know he existed and, since she made no secret of her disdain for Protectors, wouldn't care anyway.

Also, he told himself, neither liking the Martin woman nor lusting after her daughter changed the basic fact that Daphne was his number one suspect. There was a mole working in the Mortal-Protector Liaison Office—a mole who had already dribbled pieces of Council information to the Protectors' archenemy, Hieronymous, and his band of Outcasts. And the rumor was, Hieronymous was expecting more information any day now—serious information that could only come from a spy with high-level access like Daphne. Starbuck had to find and bring down that spy.

Hieronymous's most recent scheme to enslave all mortals and take over the world had only barely been foiled— by Zoë Smith, a halfling who'd just joined the council, and the half sister of Starbuck's good friend Hale. While the girl's handling of the entire episode impressed him, neither Starbuck nor any of the other Protectors believed that Hieronymous would stop with that try. The villain wanted his power back. He wanted to crush his ex-peers, the Venerate Council of Protectors, wanted to enslave all mortals, and above all wanted to seat himself on some golden, godlike throne.

And he was nothing if not persistent.

No, the man was more than just an egocentric nuisance; he was a very real threat. He'd already turned some weaker Protectors, and he wasn't above releasing Henchmen to do his dirty work.

To mortals, Henchmen looked perfectly human—usually lawyers or used-car salesmen or telemarketers. But Protectors could see through the disguise, and it was part of their mission to fight Henchmen and prevent them from doing the bidding of whoever had set them free.

Lately Heironymous had been releasing a lot of Henchmen. Hell, lately Heironymous had been causing a whole lot of problems. Which was why, when the Venerate Council learned that the MLO had been infiltrated by a spy, they'd immediately called on Starbuck.

Lucky him. Unlike most Protectors, Starbuck looked . . . well . . . normal. Like a regular guy. His friend Hale might resemble a Greek god, but not Starbuck. Not at all. And he took no end of ribbing for it, that was for sure. However, his looks did give him one advantage: he was perfect for infiltrating all environments. Since most mortals didn't even know Protectors existed, they didn't have a clue about the things of which he was capable. And, because he looked so different and so often worked under deep cover, many Protectors didn't know he was one of them.

Still hunkered over the electrical cables, Daphne Martin muttered something under her breath, then held up a screwdriver. "This isn't working. Maybe it's in the code." She scrambled toward the monitor and keyboard set up on a makeshift desk on the far side of the windowless room. "Can you wait just a sec?"

"No problem." For good measure, he tried probing her mind, but she was still closed to him, just as she'd been for the week he'd been working at the MLO. His looks might contribute to his vocation as a spy, but his particular superpowers—reading minds and manipulating time—were really what made him good.

Unfortunately, it seemed, Daphne was one of those rare mortals whose mind naturally blocked him. And considering she was his prime suspect, that little fact was damned frustrating. Leaning back, Starbuck crossed his arms over his chest and examined Daphne the old-fashioned way.

A true flower child, the woman had been in her element back during the sixties . . . and she still dressed as if she were going to hang out in Haight-Ashbury. She was also the smartest mortal Starbuck had ever met. According to the dossier he'd memorized, she'd been recruited by the council back in the seventies after the Mortal-Protector Treaty was first signed, and she had single-handedly developed the entire computer system for the MLO.

That was not a small feat, considering everything had to be done in secret. Daphne had completed all that work without consulting any other mortals on any aspect of the project that might even hint at the existence of Protectors, the MLO, or the supersecret location in a sub-sub-subbasement of the United Nations building in New York City.

In other words, the woman was ultrasmart—and she had access to a wealth of council information. The information that was supposedly heading Heironymous's way was top, top, top secret. The kind of stuff kept deep within locked computer files. Files to which only Daphne and a select few trusted members of the council had access.

The only question was, had Daphne turned? Was she selling secrets to Hieronymous? Starbuck just didn't know, and the fact that he couldn't probe her mind only made him more suspicious. It was a shame, really, since he liked the woman, and surely arresting her for violations of the Mortal-Protector Treaty would put a damper on any shot he might have at catching her daughter's eye.

The woman was still typing away, a pencil tucked behind her ear as she chewed on the end of another.

"Hey, Daphne," he called.

No reaction.

"Daphne."

Still nothing.

He opened his mouth to yell, "Da—"

"*Mother!*"

Starbuck's breath caught as he turned to face the door. Jennifer Martin—looking very angry, and very, very adorable—stood there. Daphne's *tap-tap*ping at the keyboard stopped, and she twisted around in her swivel chair until she was facing her daughter.

"Hello, sweetie. What on earth are you doing down here in the computer room?"

"What am I doing here?" the girl echoed, the color in her cheeks rising with her voice. "What do you *think* I'm doing here?" Without even a glance in his direction, she marched across the room, her short dark curls bobbing with every purposeful stride, and slapped the current issue of the Mortal-Protector Liaison Office newsletter down on her mother's desk. "*That* is what I'm doing here!"

"This week's issue?" Daphne asked—a little too innocently, Starbuck thought. "I hear it's a good one."

Jenny crossed her arms over her chest and started tapping her foot. "Mother! What on earth were you thinking? I'm not interested in dating one of those . . . those . . . *Protectors!*"

Starbuck fought a cringe. Not that she was saying anything he hadn't already figured out in his week of undercover work here, but hearing it from the girl's own lips . . . well, so much for any chance he might have with the first woman he'd been really attracted to in a long, long time.

A wide smile passed over Daphne's face. "Now, sweetie, don't get all upset. It's high time you settled down with a good man—"

"Mother!"

"—and who could possibly be a better man than a Protector?"

Daphne's daughter ran her fingers through her hair, then shot Starbuck a look of exasperation. "You see what I have to put up with?"

He smiled, knowing the fact that she was sharing her frustration with him thrilled him more than it should.

Their eyes caught and held for one magnificent moment before she turned back to her mother. "I'm not interested in dating a Protector, Mom. We've been over this a dozen times. I want you to stop this matchmaking. You're driving me insane."

"Nonsense. You need a husband. A strong husband. Someone who can open tight pickle jars and understands loyalty and responsibility. She crossed her arms over her chest, a faraway, wistful look in her eye. "Someone not like your father."

"Mother! Aargh!" She threw her hands up and faced the heavens—well, the subbasement ceiling—as Starbuck fought a grin. He couldn't help but sympathize. He'd spent plenty of time with Daphne over the past few days, and he was well aware of how persistent the woman could be.

Daphne's expression was nonplussed. "Mother knows

best, dear." She turned to him. "Don't you agree?"

"I—"

Jenny shot him a warning look, and he snapped his mouth shut. "Mother does *not* know best," she said. "Not about this. Right, Starbuck?"

This time he had the good sense to keep his mouth closed—even before Daphne's pointed glance. Even without his superpowers, he knew enough not to get involved in a fight between a mother and her daughter.

Daphne pushed back from her keyboard, her rolling chair gliding across the floor toward Jenny. "Sweetie, what's the harm? Maybe you'll like whoever answers that ad."

"I won't." She crossed her arms over her chest, and Starbuck cringed from the note of sureness in her voice. No matter how much he might hope for a chance with this girl, it just wasn't going to happen.

Of course, what he should be doing was trying to get close to Jenny, not in order to date her, but to get a few glimpses into her mind. Surely her mother had said something to her—even something seemingly innocuous—that might prove or disprove her guilt. And if Starbuck spent enough time with Jenny—probing here and probing there—maybe he'd eventually find the clue he needed.

He'd avoided probing the girl's thoughts in the past—mortal minds were highly protected by the Treaty of 1970—but just yesterday he'd applied to the council for a warrant on Jenny, and this morning they'd given him the go-ahead. Still, he hesitated. Somehow a probe seemed unchivalrous, considering the crush he had on her. Yet a week had passed without a solid clue, and Starbuck needed to make some progress. He also needed to face up to the fact that a relationship with Jenny Martin was out of the question. She didn't want a Protector. Starbuck was a Protector. End of discussion.

Daphne put her hands on her daughter's shoulders. "At the very least, you need a date for the MLO's annual party. Go with whoever answers your ad; then that will be the end of it. That's reasonable, isn't it?"

"No . . ." Jenny frowned, and Starbuck could tell she was being worn down by her mother's persistence. "I mean, maybe. I suppose. But that's not the point. The point is, I've—"

"Already got a date." The words were out of his mouth before Starbuck even had time to think about what he was saying. Both women turned to stare at him, Jenny's ocean-blue eyes even wider than her mother's. "I mean . . ." His eyes caught Jenny's and he took a deep breath, hoping he wasn't about to get shot down in a huge way.

If she said yes, not only would he have a date with a woman he adored, but he'd also have access to the one person closest in the world to his prime suspect. Mentally crossing his fingers, he took the plunge. "The thing is, Jenny can't go with a Protector. She's already promised to go with me."

Chapter Two

What the . . . ? Jenny turned to Starbuck, her mouth hanging open. The man was either a saint or an idiot . . . and considering that he appeared to be willingly stepping into the middle of one of her and her mother's famous frays, the better money was on the latter.

"You two are going to the party together?" Her mom sounded just as surprised as Jenny felt.

"Um, yes." Jenny tried to school her features into some sort of normal expression as she cast a glance toward her savior. She and Starbuck had talked only a few times since he'd started working at the MLO, but he seemed nice enough.

His looks were definitely a plus. He was built like a normal guy, not pumped up like some Mr. Universe wanna-be. Instead, he was tall and lean with an academic's body and an attractive face. He had unruly hair that begged for a woman's fingers, and deep brown eyes hidden behind studious wire-framed glasses. Eyes she could trust. After a moment she lifted her chin. "Absolutely, we're going together."

She held her breath as she glanced over for confirmation, afraid she'd misunderstood his intentions, afraid he was now going to shake his head, back slowly away, and get himself out of this mess as quickly and efficiently as possible.

But he didn't. He just stood there—her hero for the day in wire-framed glasses, jeans, and a button-down shirt—and said, "Of course we are. I'm thrilled you agreed to go with me."

"Why?" Daphne asked.

Jenny took a step back, indignant that her mother would be asking someone why he would be thrilled to go out with her. Then she realized the question wasn't directed at Starbuck, but at her. "Why?" she repeated, trying to buy time.

"Yes, *why?* Why are you going with *him?*" Daphne turned to Starbuck, her expression of disbelief morphing into a winning smile. "No offense, Starbuck. It's just that my little girl has standards, and you're not—"

"A Protector?" he asked.

"Exactly!" Her smile broadened.

The corner of Starbuck's lip curled, as if he found the conundrum amusing.

"I do have standards, Mom. And one is that I don't want to date a Protector," Jenny said, feeling a little bit like a broken record. As she realized what she'd said, her brow furrowed. "I . . . uh . . . I mean—not that Starbuck and I are *dating.*"

"Right," he said, picking up her cue. "Since I'm new,

Jenny was kind enough to agree to go to the party with me."

"Mmmm-hmmm." Her mother managed to express a world of disapproval in that one simple noise.

"Mother . . ."

"I'm just saying that you should make more of an effort."

Jenny rubbed the back of her neck and bit her tongue to avoid telling Daphne—yet again—that she really wasn't interested in making that kind of effort.

"Piter's nice," Daphne said.

"Piter? The new Protector on staff?" Jenny's voice was rising, but she couldn't help it. "He's always looking in the mirror." She thought she heard a chuckle from Starbuck, but when she glanced over at him, his expression was perfectly bland.

"He's extremely attractive, quite polite, and very, very eligible. He even saved three Girl Scouts from getting run over by a garbage truck yesterday."

"Enough, Mom. I'm going with Starbuck." Determined to put a stop to her mother's meddling, she marched over to Starbuck and looped her arm through his. "Not Piter, not some other Protector . . . *Starbuck*."

"But—"

"No *buts*, Mom. I'm not dating a Protector. And you're just going to have to get that through your head."

Considering the daggers Daphne shot in his direction as Jenny led him from the room, Starbuck wondered if he'd just sacrificed his newly forged friendship with suspect number one. Personally, he didn't mind the trade-off. Professionally, though, he needed to keep his eye on the ball. Hieronymous was a very real threat, and Starbuck couldn't allow his libidinous feelings to get in the way of doing his job.

"Sorry about my mother," Jenny said as the elevator doors closed in front of them.

"Don't worry. I've been here awhile. I'm starting to get used to her."

"Yes, well, imagine spending the last twenty-four years with her." Jenny's smile went straight to his heart, and for just a second he reached out to gently probe her mind.

No! He pulled back, frustrated with himself for taking such liberties. He needed to know if she had any information about Daphne, but he certainly didn't need to be poking around in her brain like a schoolboy wondering if the pretty girl really liked him. Besides, that was a question to which he already knew the answer; she wasn't going out with *him*; she was going out with the apparently mortal guy who'd offered her a way out from under her mother's thumb.

Jenny squinted at him. "You okay?"

"Fine. I'm fine." He'd be more fine if she'd press the stop button, throw him up against the wall, and plaster him with kisses. But that was about as likely to happen as Hieronymous sending a message to Zephron, the council's High Elder, to say that he was really tired of all this evil stuff and he was retiring to a small island in the Caribbean.

The doors slid open, and Starbuck stepped back to let Jenny exit first. She headed straight down the hall toward her cubicle, and he rushed to keep up with her. "Uh, Jenny?"

She turned, her eyes wide and questioning, and suddenly he was overcome by a wave of nervousness.

Stop that! He was a Protector. A superhero. The envy of mortals who knew, and the stuff of myth to mortals who didn't. Unfortunately, Jenny didn't fall into the envious category, and in this case, he was the one awed by her. Thank Zeus he'd never had a crush on a mortal girl before; once was proving to be plenty difficult.

"Starbuck?"

"Right." He caught up to her. "I was wondering if you wanted to grab some lunch. We could even go outside. Maybe take some sandwiches into Central Park? Work out the details for the party?"

Even though she shot him her most winning smile, her eyes were apologetic; he knew she was going to say no.

"Oh, gosh, I'd love to, but I've got an appointment. I'm spin-doctoring that whole thing with Zoë Smith in Los Angeles, and I've got to debrief her half brother, Hale."

Starbuck nodded, remembering what Jenny's job at the MLO entailed. She worked as a press liaison, and that meant it was her job to write press releases and do whatever else it took to make sure that the general public didn't become aware of Protector activity. In other words, Jenny was responsible for putting a normal spin on anything weird the Protectors did—like flying off buildings or shape-shifting—and for covering up the whole debacle with Heironymous's last scheme. Not the easiest job in the world, that was for sure.

"I've heard of Hale," Starbuck said casually. "Is he here yet?" Right about now, Starbuck could do with some advice from his buddy.

"Any minute now," she answered, looking at her watch.

Something brushed past Starbuck's shoulder, and he waved it away, then looked around for a bug or a draft.

Nothing. He frowned, wondering what he'd felt.

"I'd better get to work," Jenny said. "But why don't I e-mail you directions to my place? You can pick me up, and we'll go to the party together."

He nodded, then stumbled as something hard bumped into him from behind.

"Starbuck?" She looked worried ... probably afraid he'd lose his balance and fall on top of her.

"Fine," he said, his arms windmilling as he tried not to topple over. "No problem. I'm fine."

Jenny didn't look convinced, but she gave him a little wave as she walked away, confusion flashing in her beautiful blue eyes.

Starbuck looked around again, hoping to find the culprit, but still ... nothing. Then the air shimmered, and he knew what it was—or rather *who* it was. "Don't you dare materialize here," he whispered to his invisible friend. "You'll blow my cover. We can't be seen together."

The glimmer in the air disappeared, and Starbuck headed toward the custodial closet. He opened the door long enough to make sure Hale had a chance to get in; then he closed them both inside. The air shimmered, and Hale materialized.

"You're making a fool of yourself," Hale said.

Starbuck rolled his eyes. "Good to see you, too."

"I'm serious. Fawning all over a mortal. It's pathetic."

"Not all of us have your particular prejudice against mortal-Protector relationships."

Hale frowned, probably thinking about his sister, who'd just married a mortal—a man Hale had grudgingly come to respect. "Maybe so," he said, "but I'd have to say the girl's on my side. She isn't exactly jumping up and down at the possibility of going out with one of us."

"Well, you're right about that. Still, I'm not here to date the natives. I'm here to find a mole. And that's *all* I'm interested in doing."

"Liar."

Starbuck grinned, knowing better than to try to pull one over on his friend. "Yeah, well, at least I'm good at it."

Hale smiled, a disgustingly charming expression. The irony of the situation struck Starbuck—he, who wanted one specific mortal woman, didn't have any of the obvious charms that seemed to attract them; Hale wasn't the least bit interested in mortal women, and with his chiseled, cover-model looks, he was a walking magnet for them.

"How's the mole hunt going?"

"Not too good," Starbuck confessed. "Daphne Martin's my prime suspect, but she's a natural blocker."

"Daphne?" Hale seemed genuinely surprised.

Starbuck nodded. "I know what you're thinking, but everything points to her."

Hale's eyebrow arched. "You *know* what I'm thinking?"

"Sorry. Bad choice of words." Mind-probing was highly illegal except when warranted, and it was particularly tacky with friends.

"Daphne's got such a thing for Protectors, I'm surprised you think she'd turn."

Of course, Hale was right. She was practically a one-woman cheering squad for Protectors. Or at least, for eligible Protectors she might fix up with her daughter. "For that matter, she's such a fan she's more than a little miffed that Jenny's going to the annual MLO party with me. She was gunning for Piter."

As expected, Hale grimaced, as if he'd just bitten into something nasty. "Piter's a jerk."

"Careful what you say. Piter's led some successful missions, he's got a ton of commendations, and he just saved those Girl Scouts. He's been one of the council's golden boys for years."

"He's still a jerk."

Starbuck chuckled. "Yeah, well, I'm inclined to agree with you." He'd done his homework on most of the Protectors, knew them though most of them didn't know him. Piter had an ego that wouldn't quit, and he was skilled at hiding it from his superiors—and, apparently, from Daphne.

Of course, even though Piter might be a jerk, he also had pecs. In other words, he was a perfect male specimen—a god of a man, like most other Protectors—whereas Starbuck more resembled the ninety-eight-pound weakling in the old Charles Atlas advertisements. "At any rate," he said, "Piter's just here doing his rotation. He's not my problem."

"Does he know about you?"

Starbuck shook his head. "No." Mortals made up the bulk of the MLO staff, but Protectors rotated in on a regular basis. Before Starbuck took this job, he and the council had decided that they wouldn't reveal his presence to the Protectors who rotated through.

"So I guess Jenny's a natural blocker, too?"

"Not on the surface."

"The surface?"

Starbuck hesitated, but then fessed up. "I haven't tried to go deeper yet. I'm planning on pumping her for information the old-fashioned way. It's less . . . unchivalrous."

Hale's usually jovial face turned stern. "I'll agree that pumping mortals is one of the benefits of associating with them—so long as you keep your head on straight. But this is your prime suspect's daughter. You won't be breaking any laws to probe her thoughts. After all, you have a warrant. Don't get all sentimental just because you've got some puppy-love crush."

Starbuck had told himself all that and more when he filed the application for the thought warrant; he sure as hell didn't need Hale to tell him what to do. He might be forced to sift through all of Jenny's thoughts to find what he needed, but if he could at all avoid it . . . "Don't tell me how to do my job."

"I'm just saying, probe in and find the information you need. This is Heironymous we're trying to stop. If you're feeling all gooey and sentimental, just avoid her thoughts about *you*." His friend grinned. "Don't lose sight of the ball, my friend, just because you've got your eye on a pretty mortal."

"I'm not an amateur, and I've never blown a mission. I'm—"

The air shimmered, and his friend disappeared.

"Hale!" *Hopping Hades!* His buddy's habit of turning invisible during conversations was so annoying!

"Starbuck?"

He froze. He knew that voice. That was Jenny's voice. *Well, damn.*

Chapter Three

Jenny stared into the dimly lit custodial closet, trying to make out what was going on. She'd heard voices, and . . .

"Jenny." Starbuck turned, his eyes avoiding hers. "What do you want?"

She peered into the closet, trying to see who else was inside. "Are you talking to someone?"

"Me? No." Starbuck stumbled out, crashing toward her as if someone had shoved him from behind.

She held up a hand to steady him. "Are you okay?"

"Fine," he said. "I'm fine. I just lost my balance." He turned around and slammed the door shut behind him, and she thought she heard a low groan.

This was all very weird. "I . . . I could have sworn I heard you talking with someone. I thought I heard you say 'Hale' as I opened the door. Is he in there? Why didn't you tell me you knew him?"

"Him? Him who?"

"Hale. My appointment. He hasn't shown up yet. Is he—"

"Nope. He's not in there. And I don't know him. I don't know any Protectors. Though I suppose I'll meet some working here."

"But I heard you. . . ." She was sure of it.

"Right. That. I, uh, I said *hell*. I'd stubbed my toe in the dark in the closet."

"Oh." That didn't make a whole lot more sense. "So what were you doing in there in the first place?"

There was a long pause; then he said, "Looking for the men's room?"

"Oh." She waved off the answer. The man was cute, but definitely odd. He gave her a sheepish smile that she found surprisingly endearing. "Well, anyway, I'm in a rush because this Hale fellow should be here any minute, but I came back because I don't have your e-mail address."

"My e-mail address . . . ?"

"To send you the directions to my apartment. To pick me up for the party."

"Right. Of course," he said. Scribbling the address on a piece of paper, he handed it to her, and their hands brushed. Her fingers tingled from the contact. Surprised, for a moment she considered staying and talking to him, but that was silly. She had a job to do, and she didn't need to be mooning over some guy she'd practically just met.

"Right. Well, I'd better go." She tucked the address into her pocket, then hurried back toward her cubicle. Something he'd said, though, tugged at her memory, and she stopped after a few steps and turned back to face him.

"What?" He looked both pleased and surprised that she'd stopped.

"I'm just surprised you haven't . . . well, met any Protectors."

He took a step back, as if her words made him uncomfortable. "Why's that?"

She shrugged. Maybe she was being silly. "I don't know. Your name? I mean, it's not an average name, now is it? I guess Starbuck is just different enough to make me think of Protectors. Well, Protectors and nonfat lattes."

He laughed. "Right. That makes sense. Well, my parents named me. Maybe they knew it was a name common for Protectors and wanted me to sound like one."

Jenny felt her mouth twitch. "Maybe your parents hung out with my mother."

He laughed again, obviously amused by her wry comment. "I sincerely doubt that."

She checked her watch, realizing that while she'd been chatting, she'd probably left her appointment waiting. And Hale was reportedly not the most tolerant of superheroes. "Look, I need to rush." The simple truth of the fact depressed her, but she really did have to go. She forced a laugh. "I'll see you tomorrow night, though, right? My mother won't be pleased if I turned down Piter for a date who doesn't show up."

"Absolutely." His smile was warm and genuine, and she found herself smiling back . . . and genuinely looking forward to tomorrow night.

Starbuck stayed on her mind the rest of the day and all through Thursday, and by the time Jenny reached her apartment that evening, she was a bundle of nerves.

Two days before, things had been simpler. Now she was dressing for a date. And though her head kept reminding her this wasn't a *real* date, her heart kept leaping to all sorts of dumb conclusions.

Seeking Single Superhero

Not that a date was such an amazing thing in itself. But considering that she had a classified job, finding a regular guy she could really talk to wasn't the easiest thing in the world for Jenny. And her weird hours meant that she never seemed to have a free weekend. She hadn't connected very often, or found herself in the position to connect, with an attractive man who shared her lifestyle. Which probably explained why she was so looking forward to going out with Starbuck.

Two days before, she probably wouldn't have been able to pick him out of a crowd; now she could sketch his face from memory. They worked in different sections of the MLO, but she'd seen him pass by three times since they'd parted on Thursday—and each was burned into her memory.

In just a short while she'd see him again, and as the minutes ticked by, the quivering in her stomach increased. A long, hot shower didn't do anything to cure her nervousness, and when she stepped out of the tub she grimaced at her reflection. "You're being silly," she said. "The only reason he asked you is because he could tell Mom was driving you insane. And the only reason you're all quivery is because he's good-looking. You hardly know the guy. This isn't what you're making it out to be."

Which sounded perfectly reasonable, but her reflection didn't look convinced. She tossed a scowl toward the mirror. Well, why shouldn't she look forward to this pseudo date? She was a grown woman. If she wanted to have a fun evening, she would. And Starbuck seemed like a nice, fun, normal guy—no matter what his reasons were for escorting her to the MLO party.

Gnawing on her lower lip, she wandered into her bedroom clad only in an oversize towel. For the first time in a long while, she stood in front of her closet, uncertain of what to wear. Yesterday she would have chosen a simple print dress—plain, comfortable, nothing that would draw too much attention. But today . . .

Before she could talk herself out of it, she dug into the farthest recesses of the closet to pull out the slinky black dress with the low neck and spaghetti straps that she'd bought on a whim two months ago. She'd never worn the outfit in public, though she'd tried it on alone in her apartment more than once. Each time, it had made her feel decadent and sexy.

The dress hadn't yet made it out of the house, but tonight . . . well, *maybe* tonight she wanted to see the way a certain pair of deep brown eyes looked when Starbuck saw her in it.

"Now you *are* being silly." This time she spoke to her reflection in the bedroom mirror, and, once again, her reflection didn't argue. She stuck her tongue out at it. "Lot of help you are."

Well, it didn't matter. She was wearing the dress, and that was that. Taking a deep breath, she dropped her towel, then slipped the garment over her head. She wasn't exactly sure what it was about Starbuck that intrigued her, but something did. And one other thing was certain: he'd notice her for sure in this dress, and tonight, that was all she wanted.

"You're *beautiful*." Starbuck whispered the words, knowing they were inadequate, but not sure how else to tell Jenny how absolutely stunning she looked.

A slow blush tinged her cheeks, making her look even prettier. She cast a subtle spell, and he was completely bewitched.

Taking a deep breath, he reminded himself of his mission. *Focus, Starbuck, focus. The point of tonight's outing isn't to get close to this girl—even though that is certainly a perk. In her eyes, I'm just a guy doing her a favor. And I need to do my job. Need to get her thinking about her mother . . . and then I need to read those thoughts.*

Hale was right. Starbuck couldn't let himself be swayed by his feelings for this woman—as beautiful as she was. Even if Daphne hadn't directly told her daughter about any illicit activities, she had likely said something that was a clue. And Starbuck had to get that clue.

Of course, it was tough to focus on work when Jennifer Martin stood right in front of him, practically oozing sex and sin. Forget about probing her mind; right now he was interested in probing much more enticing parts.

"Starbuck?" Her voice was hesitant, almost shy.

"Hmm? What?" He jumped to attention, realizing he'd been staring.

"You're staring," she said.

"Well, you're beautiful."

Again, the color rose in her cheeks. "You said that already."

He moved closer, stopping only when he was near enough to smell her shampoo. "I thought it was worth repeating." He drew in a breath, losing himself in the enticing scent of lavender.

She swallowed, then pressed her lips together. For an instant she met his eyes, then quickly dropped her gaze to the ground. "We should probably get going."

"Right. Of course." Taking a step back, he silently cursed himself. This girl wasn't interested in Protectors, which meant she wasn't interested in *him*. Or wouldn't be, once she truly knew him. He needed to keep this as they'd

193

begun it: he was simply a mortal doing her a favor. Those were the rules of the game, and he needed to keep them at the forefront of his mind.

"Is this your car?" She sounded a bit surprised, and he regretted his decision not to bring the Ferrari. Somehow the standard-issue council car—complete with an assortment of council-approved gizmos that would have made James Bond drool—had seemed a little too unlikely for his cover as a newly hired government worker. Instead he'd bought a banged-up Chevette. And right now he was wishing he'd hired a limo. Or taken a taxi. Or fought the subway. Or walked.

"Actually, my car's in the shop. This is a loaner. Sorry."

"No, no. It's fine." She smiled as he opened the door, whose hinges groaned. Getting in, she used a towel he'd draped over the back of the seat to cover a rip in the upholstery. "I don't even own a car."

"Well, I know it isn't exactly a Ferrari."

Her smile just about melted his heart, and she said, "So long as it drives, that's all we need."

He turned the key, started the car, revved the engine . . . and then listened to it die. He tried again. This time the engine started, and continued to purr. Actually it was more of a low growl, but there was definitely engine noise. That, at least, was a good sign. The Chevette's gears were less cooperative than his Ferrari's, and it took a few seconds to get the car into first. Metal ground against metal.

Jenny shifted in her seat to face him. "You *do* know how to drive, right?"

Great. She might not like superhero types, but Starbuck also doubted that Jenny Martin was looking for thin, geeky guys who couldn't drive. He could practically feel the testosterone surging through his veins and, even though he knew it was stupid, he hit the clutch, slammed the car into gear, and peeled out into traffic. A Protector's lightning-quick reflexes were handy for fighting crime, but they were also useful in the impressing-women department. Or they had been before.

Both he and Jenny leaned precariously to one side as they squealed around a corner. As soon as they were back on a straightaway, he glanced in her direction. "I can drive," he said.

"I guess so." Her hand was tight on the door handle, but her smile was relaxed. "Remind me never to doubt you again."

Their eyes met, and for just a moment he was certain he could see her thoughts without the benefit of his mind-probe. It wasn't a theory he had the chance to test, however. She gasped, and he had to look forward again. He jerked the car sideways to avoid a stopped taxi.

"Eyes on the road, Starbuck."

"But the view's so much better to my right."

"I . . . yes . . . well . . ."

He didn't have to look at her to know she was blushing again. "Don't worry, Jen. I won't let anything happen to you."

"I know." A softness laced her voice, and he knew that she trusted him.

The knowledge made him giddy, at least until he remembered that her trust was predicated on a lie. She thought this was a date with a mortal, not that Starbuck was an undercover Protector out to snare her mother in a web of deceit. It was really time to quit fantasizing that something real could develop between them. He must move on to the problem at hand—finding out if Jenny knew anything about her mother's recent activities.

195

He rested one hand lightly on the steering wheel and the other on the gearshift, trying to be casual in his interrogation. "So how long have you been working at the MLO?"

"Two years now. Ever since I got out of college."

"So far it seems like a great place." He'd learned from past experience that the best way to get information was to get a person talking about him- or herself.

"Oh, yeah. I love it."

"Even though you're not crazy about the people you work for."

Her smile was almost embarrassed. "Don't get me wrong. I'm in awe of the Protectors. When I was a little kid I used to believe in superheroes . . . and then I grew up and found out they were real." Her smile revealed a tiny dimple. "That was a very cool realization."

"But . . . ?" he asked. She'd made it so clear that she didn't want to date a Protector, there had to be a "but."

She half shrugged. "But when I started working at the MLO, I started meeting some of those real-life superheroes. Those pompous . . . Well, let's just say they're—"

"Not terribly humble?"

"That's an understatement. I mean, some of them are. I interviewed Zoë Smith after that whole big thing in LA, and she was great. But she's also a halfling, so it makes sense she wouldn't be too stuck-up around us mortals. Her brother, though . . ."

Starbuck nodded. Hale was definitely a mortal snob. He'd protect them, yes. Sleep with them, sure. Feel something for one . . . no way!

"And many others, too," Jenny continued. "I mean, I've run across a lot of Protectors in my time here. They're mostly nice enough . . . but they're not . . . *real*. Too much testosterone, too much hubris." She shrugged. "And since I've already got such a bizarre job, I think I'd like something of a normal home life—you know?"

He did know, and he also knew that he wasn't a guy to add *normal* to anyone's personal equation.

She didn't wait for him to answer. "My mom, on the other hand—"

"Thinks her little girl deserves more than normal."

Jennifer sighed. "I just want a normal guy who loves me for me . . . and I'll love him for him. I don't think that's too much to ask." She looked up, peeking at him from under her eyelashes. "Do you?"

He swallowed, wanting to tell her everything and see if she couldn't learn to see past what he was, past her preconceptions. But that was a bad idea—on so many levels. "No," he finally said. "Not too much to ask at all." He cleared his throat, determined to segue back into business. "So how'd your mom get hooked up with the MLO, anyway?"

She started to answer, then snapped her mouth shut as he whipped the Chevette around another corner. The force of the turn pressed her against his shoulder. She righted herself immediately, but just that tiny contact sent waves of awareness crashing through him. "Sorry," he said, even though he wasn't sorry at all and, frankly, wished he needed to turn again so he could feel her touch once more.

"That's okay." Her voice was breathless, but he wasn't sure if it was an after-effect of their unexpected caress or if she was now afraid of his driving. "About my mom . . ."

"Right."

"She's always been a computer genius. She and my dad designed some really cool stuff back in the sixties before I was born."

"Why doesn't your dad work at the MLO?"

A tiny shrug. "Don't know. Never met him. He ran off to join Greenpeace right after Mom got pregnant. He's doing some penguin study in Antarctica now." She turned in her seat and smiled. "I think he's another reason I'm so keen on dating normal guys. No quirks. No oddities. No penguins. No wanna-be superheroes." Again, she aimed a shy smile in his direction.

"Just your basic normal guy."

"Right. Normal." He cleared his throat, then ticked her list off in his mind. About all he had going for him was the no-penguins requirement. *Too bad.*

Back to business. "So your dad left, and your mom ended up recruited by the MLO?"

"Right. I'm not sure how they found out about her—she's never told me. I think it has something to do with some guy she was seeing before she married my dad." She turned to face him squarely. "He was a Protector, and from what I can tell, she adored him. But she dumped him for my dad, and—especially since my dad's a nutcase—she's regretted it ever since. By the time her divorce came through, that Protector guy had married someone else."

"Probably explains why she's so insistent on your dating a Protector."

"Oh yeah. Doesn't take Dr. Freud to figure that out."

"And this guy got her a job at the MLO?"

"I think so. At any rate, she's been working for the council for as long as I can remember. Top-secret clearance and all that. It's pretty neat, really."

"You're proud of her."

It wasn't a question, but she answered anyway. "Totally. She drives me nuts, but she's the greatest. If she'd just drop this whole matchmaking thing, she'd be perfect. But she's so set on fixing me up with a Protector...."

"Well, she can certainly pick from the best of the bunch."

She turned to squint at him. "I'm not sure what you mean."

This was it. Time to get down to business and get Jennifer Martin thinking about her mother—and about her mother's secrets. "I just mean that she's got access to the whole council mainframe. I mean, heck, she built the mainframe. And it's got detailed information about every Protector. Their assignments, their vital statistics, the works." Everything, that was, except for information on the Venerate Council's spies. Starbuck and the other undercover operatives weren't included in the mainframe. But other than that very elite group, the MLO's computer knew every bit of classified information about everything. And Daphne could access it.

Jenny shot him an ironic glance. "In that case, I wish that computer knew all there was to know about mortal guys. Dating a Protector—"

"I know." He didn't think he could stand to hear her say it one more time. "It's not your thing." Tapping his fingers on the steering wheel, he tried to figure out where to take the conversation next. He might as well just jump right in. "So do you think your mom ever peeks into the data?"

"You mean does she just poke around?" Jenny's voice squeaked. "In the confidential files?"

"It's got to be tempting."

"She could lose her job. Mom wouldn't do that. No matter how much she wants a Protector son-in-law, she's not about to go snooping illegally."

"Hmmm."

"What?"

He shrugged, trying to look nonchalant. "It's just that your mom doesn't strike me as the play-by-the-rules type."

Jenny scowled, clearly agreeing with his assessment, but unsure what to say. *Good.* He wanted her mind sifting through possibilities, remembering any offhand comments the woman might have made.

"It's absurd." Jenny turned to face forward, her arms crossed over her chest.

"Sorry." He'd pushed her far enough. "I didn't mean to suggest anything. Just making small talk."

Her shoulders sagged as she sighed. "It's okay. I'm probably being too sensitive. It's just that she's got such a respected position, I'd hate for any rumors to get started."

"I wouldn't dream of suggesting a thing."

This time her smile was genuine. "I believe you."

They rode in silence for a while, and he let his mind float free; then he began to let his mind connect with hers. Her surface thoughts were fuzzy and scattered, her mind taking in the city streets, scanning over the sidewalks and storefronts.

He probed a bit further, dipping into the more intimate recesses of her mind. He pushed back through a haze of fear about his driving—he stopped probing long enough to tap the brake and slow down—then he moved deeper.

Pushing aside the mists of her mind, he wandered down the mental paths that had opened because of their conversation. *Clear paths. A good sign.* Talking about her mom had blazed a trail for him.

But when he brushed through to home in on the thoughts that had jiggled loose, it wasn't Daphne he found. His heart beat faster as he focused, mentally blinking to assure himself that his mind's eye was telling the truth.

There it was, plain as day: one thought, distinct from everything else in her head. Blazing bright, like red flashing neon—*I want him to kiss me. Please, sometime tonight, let this man kiss me.*

Well, if that was what the lady wanted . . . who was he to say no?

Chapter Four

Thank goodness he can't read my mind! Jenny slunk down farther into the car seat and gazed out the window, hoping her cheeks would cool off before she had to look at him again.

She couldn't believe she was actually hoping he'd kiss her. He was practically a stranger. A cute stranger, true, but a stranger nonetheless.

Well, that was what dating was for. They were on a date. They'd get to know each other, and maybe, just maybe, it might lead somewhere—*if* her mother didn't arrange for Starbuck to be transferred to Alaska or something.

"Penny for your thoughts."

At the sound of his voice she jumped a mile, then turned to look at him as she tried to catch her breath. His grin broadened, and she had the uncomfortable feeling he really did know what she was thinking.

Absurd.

She shook off the feeling and pasted on a smile. "Just wondering about my mom. She's not too thrilled that you're accompanying me tonight."

"Yeah, I got that impression." For a moment he seemed to hesitate; then he reached over and took her hand. She tried to remain calm despite the tingling sensation the contact brought. "But I'm not out with your mother. So long as *you* want to be with me, I'm happy."

"I . . . I . . ." She hesitated, suddenly shy. Things were moving too fast. She wanted to pull back, wanted to slow down, but he'd drawn her in, wrapped her up in his spell, and she wanted him to wrap her up in his arms.

A frown touched his lips as he pulled his hand away, and she realized that he must have misinterpreted her hesitancy.

"I know I just stepped in as a favor. But I was kind of hoping this could be a real—"

"Yes," she blurted. "Real is good. I'm fine with real. Real is much better than imitation." She knew she must sound like an idiot. So much for trying to make an impression.

Fortunately, Starbuck didn't seem to mind the way she was blathering on; he just aimed a smile in her direction and kept on driving. A bit wildly.

Her fingers tightened around the door handle. He hadn't killed them yet, but the night was still young. She sneaked another glance in his direction, amazed by the way his hair seemed to beg for her fingers. Not that she intended to be so bold as to caress him like that. Better just to put her hands in her lap, turn back around, face forward and—

"Stop sign!" she yelped.

"I see it." He hit the brakes and screeched to a halt, then glanced over at her. "Don't worry. I've got it under control." His smile was bright, and she couldn't help but return it. He might be a reckless driver—no, he *was* a reckless driver—but even so, she'd never felt safer in her whole life. Odd, yes. Disconcerting. But on the whole, such illogical security was a rather pleasant feeling.

Probably for her benefit, he slowed a bit as he negotiated a few more streets, finally pulling to a stop at the valet stand in front of the Montclair Hotel. "We're here."

She sat up straighter. "So we are."

"Nervous?"

"About the party? Or your driving?"

He chuckled. "About your mom."

At that, she sobered. "I'll be fine. You're the one who should be nervous. If Mom thinks we're an item, you may find yourself working at the Alaskan transmitting facility by next week. Seriously. Mom's got clout."

"I'll take my chances," he said, his tone and expression confident. "I've got a few friends with clout, too, and I have a feeling I'm here for as long as I want to be."

Good, she thought. As the valet opened the door for her, she stifled a smile. She wasn't quite ready to admit it to him, but right at the moment, nothing would make her happier than having this wild-haired reckless driver around for a long, long time.

An annual affair, the MLO party never failed to draw a good crowd of both Protectors and mortal employees. The council sponsored the event and encouraged all Protectors to attend. After all, the MLO was the first line of defense between a Protector's cover story and the outside world.

The event was always held in a New York hotel, but

the council took precautions to keep its secrets. No uninitiated mortals staffed the party, and every Protector was warned away from any displays of power unless he or she was absolutely certain that no inappropriate witnesses were in visual range. So far no one had slipped up, and the party always proved to be great fun for mortal MLO employees and Protectors alike.

At least that was what Starbuck had been told. In his particular line of work, he couldn't admit to being a Protector, and until recently he hadn't worked for the MLO. So even though he'd been a full-fledged Protector all his life, and he'd been an active council member for years, this was his first time at this party. After taking a long look around the ballroom, he had to admit he was impressed.

Long buffet tables laden with all sorts of delicious goodies lined two walls. Thirty or so round tables, each with a freshly pressed white tablecloth and four chairs, were scattered throughout the room. Clusters of people gathered about, some sitting at the tables, some simply hanging out sampling the food.

The far side of the room had no tables. Instead someone had laid down a portable wooden dance floor. As Jenny and Starbuck entered, about two dozen Protectors and mortals were jamming to the lively tunes of Levitation, a band that several musically inclined Protectors had formed some three years previous.

"They're good," Jenny piped up. "Aren't they that Protector band?"

"I think so," Starbuck said, even though he knew for a fact they were.

"Yeah, they are. I recognize them now. Do you know

their story?" She was smiling, her face aglow as if she wanted to share a secret.

"Nope," he lied.

"I did some spin on them once. About two years ago, a mortal heard them play, and they ended up with a record deal. Pretty cool, and their manager still has no clue what they do when they're not playing gigs." Her eyes danced with amusement. "I figure that if he ever does find out, he's going to be royally pissed to have missed out on such a great marketing opportunity."

Laughing, Starbuck took her arm. "You've definitely got a point there." He nodded toward the bandstand. "Do you want to dance?"

Her cheeks flushed, and Starbuck fought the urge to kiss her right then and there.

"I'm not a very good dancer," she murmured.

As if on cue, the band wrapped up what it was playing and switched to a slow, soulful ballad. Starbuck held out his hand, smiling. "Nothing to a slow dance. Just close your eyes and sway."

The color in Jenny's cheeks increased, but she nodded, then took his hand. They moved to the dance floor. Through one song and the next, he simply held her as they swayed on the floor. Her body, soft and warm, melded perfectly with his. He was in heaven, plain and simple. There was no place on earth he'd rather be, nothing in the world he'd rather think about—then he opened his eyes and saw Daphne standing in the corner, and reality came crashing back.

Piter leaned against a wall near her, and Daphne moved closer. There was something about seeing Jenny's mother with the other Protector that made Starbuck's stomach turn. Piter knew more than just the basic council secrets, but he didn't know that Daphne's loyalty was in question. If he made just one slip of the tongue . . .

Starbuck glanced down at Jenny and sighed. As much as he wanted to spend the entire evening doing nothing more than holding her, the simple fact was that it was time to focus on his job.

That dratted mortal is dancing with my daughter! Daphne sighed, losing track of Piter's voice. Starbuck had his arms wrapped around Jenny, and—*darn it all*—Jenny seemed to be enjoying herself.

Her whole life, Jenny'd been headstrong, but she'd been smart, too. Yet about this . . . Daphne couldn't understand why her daughter didn't realize how much better her life would be with a Protector by her side. Why did she insist on making the same mistakes as her mother? Dating a mortal led nowhere, as Daphne had learned the hard way. They weren't the same breed; they weren't raised to save others, to be more than just out for themselves.

"—if you really think so."

Daphne blinked, then remembered where she was and turned to Piter. "Pardon me?"

"I said I'd be happy to go over and talk with Jenny, if you really think she wants me to. She seems quite cozy with that other fellow, though. I don't want to step on any toes."

"No! No." Daphne cleared her throat, then patted his hand. *Such a polite young man. A Protector, through and through.* "I mean, they're not cozy. They're just friends. And she's mentioned you several times to me. I'm sure she'd love the chance to get to know you better."

"She's mentioned me?"

"Absolutely." Not favorably, but that was just because

207

Jenny was headstrong. Piter was a nice guy. So cultured. So considerate. Surely her daughter would figure that out soon enough.

He took a step forward, obviously interested. "Well, if you're sure . . ."

"I'm sure. I'm sure." She made a shooing motion. "Go."

He did. Almost instantly. And something about his eagerness made Daphne frown. *Nonsense.* There wasn't anything untoward about Piter's interest in her daughter. All it meant was that the boy had good taste.

No, this was what Daphne wanted.

And she could only hope that Jenny had the good sense to see what a prime catch Piter would be.

Chapter Five

As the band played a popular love song from the eighties, Jenny kept her eyes closed, letting the music flow around them. Her cheek was pressed against Starbuck's chest, and she could feel the rhythm of his heart even through his shirt and sport coat.

There was something so peaceful—so *right*—about being in this man's arms. As if she belonged there and nowhere else. She knew she was being silly, letting foolish romantic notions get the better of her, but that didn't change the way she felt.

With soft strokes he caressed her back, and with every pass of his fingers, she fought the urge to beg him to kiss her. The touch was so casual, she doubted he even realized what he was doing. But Jenny noticed. His tentative strokes ignited every atom in her body, and if he kept it up much longer, she might just explode. Even so, she wanted him to keep doing it forever. What was a little explosion weighed against the pleasure of Starbuck's caress?

They stayed like that—two people so close they seemed almost one—until suddenly he stopped and pulled back.

With a frown, she opened her eyes, tilting her head back and looking at him, afraid she'd somehow done something wrong. He wasn't focusing on her. Instead he was watching something on the far side of the room. "What is it?" she asked.

His smile reassured her as he stroked her hair. "Sorry. It's just that your mom's watching us. I'm thinking we should go over and say hello."

"Oh." She couldn't fault his politeness, but hanging out with her mother didn't rank high on Jenny's list of things she wanted to do at the moment. In fact, it ranked far, far below continuing this dance. "I suppose we should."

He chuckled. "You sound thrilled."

"No, you're right." With a sigh she pulled free of his arms. "Let's get it over with."

He didn't bother to hide his amusement as he raised his elbow for her to take. After a second, she cracked a smile, too. "Sorry. I just know what she's going to say, and—"

"You don't want to hear it."

"I've heard it all my life. I guess one more time won't hurt." Besides, Starbuck's arm linked through hers somehow fortified her—at least enough to stand up to her mom for five minutes. Cocking her head, she looked into his deep brown eyes, drawing courage from him, then took a determined step forward. "Okay," she said. "Let's go."

They'd barely fought their way past the thick crowd at the edge of the dance floor when they were stopped again. For a split second, Jenny thanked fate for the reprieve. Then she realized who had stopped them: Piter.

"Jenny." He held out his hand, and she reluctantly took it, then cringed as he kissed her fingertips. "You look lovely."

"Thanks." She didn't meet his eyes; instead she concentrated on her painted toenails. When he released her hand, she looked up to catch him aiming a curt nod in Starbuck's direction.

"Starpluck, isn't it?"

Starbuck's smile seemed carved from ice, but he took Piter's outstretched hand. "Star*buck*."

"Right. Of course. I remember. I'm Piter. I'm the Protector on rotation at the MLO this month."

"I know who you are," Starbuck said, his voice as cold as his smile.

Jenny silently cheered. *Good for Starbuck.* Piter may have fooled her mother, but Jenny knew that he was one of the most arrogant men she'd ever run across. Even for a Protector. She was glad that Starbuck could see through him, too.

Unfortunately, Piter wasn't too put off by Starbuck's cool reception. He just chuckled softly, as if he were amused by some private joke, then turned back to Jenny. "Let's dance."

"We were just going to go talk with my mom."

She moved forward, Starbuck's strong hand at her back guiding her, but Piter stepped in front of them. "I was just with your mother. Considering how thrilled she was when I told her I was going to ask you to dance, I'm sure she won't mind if you make a little detour on your way to see her."

No way. No how. "I don't think—"

"The lady's not interested," Starbuck interrupted, taking a step forward.

211

For a second, Jenny thought the two men were about to get into it—a situation that surely wouldn't favor Starbuck, especially considering that mortals tended to fare rather poorly when pitted against superheroes in fistfights—but Piter held up his hands and backed off. The wide grin that spread across his oh-so-perfect face showed off rows of sparkling white teeth. The image reminded her of Mack the Knife, and she stifled a shiver.

"Hey, not a problem," Piter said. "I'm not trying to interfere."

Jenny didn't believe that any more than she believed her mother would stop meddling if she just asked politely. Considering the tight line of Starbuck's jaw, he didn't believe Piter either. The Protector obviously wanted to muscle in on their date, and Starbuck wasn't going to let him.

She wrapped herself in that knowledge like a warm blanket. No matter how unwelcome this encounter with Piter, it had one overwhelming benefit: now she knew that Starbuck was just as interested in her as she was in him.

Piter was on his sickly-sweet best behavior, and Starbuck's nerves were at the breaking point. More than anything he wished he could whip off his glasses, flex his biceps, and tell the bastard to get the hell out of Dodge.

Of course, there were a couple of problems with that little plan, not the least of which was that Starbuck had no biceps to speak of. Worse, revealing that he was a Protector was simply out of the question.

The only good thing about this situation was that apparently Daphne hadn't been pumping Piter for secrets. . . . Instead, she'd just been recruiting him to date her daughter. Which was good in that it didn't add any more evidence to support Daphne as the mole. It was bad in the respect that it didn't add any more evidence to support Daphne as the mole. He was still on square one casewise.

If that wasn't bad enough, he was stuck at this party watching his date be harassed by an overbearing peer, and all Starbuck could do was fend the guy off like any normal mortal on the planet. It was times like this when working undercover was damned inconvenient.

Still, he was Jenny's date, and he didn't intend to let some other bozo muscle in. With a firm grip, he steered Jenny away from Piter and toward her mother. Once again, the other Protector stepped into their path. Once again, Starbuck tamped down on his temper.

"The lady said no," he said through gritted teeth. "What does she have to do, send you a form in triplicate?"

Piter puffed up like some arrogant rooster. "I don't believe she actually said no. And the lady can speak for herself."

"Yes, she can," Jenny said. "But if I didn't actually say no, I still meant it. Thanks, but no thanks. I'm perfectly happy with the dance partner I've got."

Piter moved forward, and then the creep actually stroked the side of her arm. "Just one dance, Jenny," he cajoled. "Where's the harm in that?"

Okay. Enough is enough. Starbuck's hand fisted, and he pulled back, ready to let loose with every ounce of strength in his body.

Except he couldn't. Not only did fistfights rarely impress women, he was also undercover. He had to play the mortal role, and mortals didn't pick fights with Protectors. At least, not mortals with any intelligence.

Piter glanced pointedly at Starbuck's fisted hand. "I'd think twice if I were you."

They locked eyes for just a moment, and Starbuck hoped that somehow the anger he felt was coming through loud and clear. Maybe so, because Piter broke the stare-off first. "Listen, Starcluck, I'm not trying to steal your date. I just want to cut in. One dance. Where's the harm in that?" He flashed Jenny a winning smile, and Starbuck suddenly knew why this creep was so well liked among the council members. Not to mention how he'd won over Daphne. The man was a born politician.

"There wouldn't be any harm," Starbuck said, "*If* Jenny were interested. She's not."

"How will she know for sure until she gives it a try?" The Protector aimed his million-dollar smile in her direction. "Come on, babe. Let me cut in for just one dance." He nodded to the far side of the room, where Daphne stood next to a potted palm, obviously trying to look nonchalant. "It'll make your mom happy." Before she even had a chance to answer, he took her elbow and pulled her forward.

Jenny shot Starbuck a frustrated glance, even as she was jerking her arm away. "I said *no*. What's the matter? Too many syllables for you?"

But Piter held on. "Where's the harm in one dance? Your mom's dying to see us on that dance floor."

"She'll get over it," Jenny said, right as Starbuck decided that enough was truly enough. Maybe he couldn't fend Piter off with his strength, but there were other methods. Methods he wasn't supposed to use for personal gain, true, but desperate times . . .

With every ounce of strength in his body he focused, letting the flood of energy gather in his chest. It was special energy that only he and a few other Protectors were able to summon, a secret trait that only the council elders and his best friends knew was in his repertoire of super-powers.

Jenny squinted at him, her brow furrowed with concern. "You look horrible. Are you okay?"

He knew he looked as though he were going to be sick, but he couldn't help that any more than he could answer her. The moment was already upon him. Like lightning bugs zipping around inside him, the power bounced and fluttered, building and building until, finally, he was ready. Summoning his strength, he exhaled, breathing out all the energy he'd absorbed.

Then, as he knew it would, the world froze and time stopped.

With a low groan, he sagged to his knees. Time manipulation took a lot out of a guy, and he hadn't prepared much for this exertion. He'd be weak for as long as time was stopped. Heck, he shouldn't even be *doing* this. If the council found out, they'd have his head.

He glanced toward Jenny—frozen in the moment, still squinting toward where he used to be. Well, let the council do its worst. Some things—some people—were more important than rules. And right now, Starbuck wanted to get Piter's attention focused on something other than Jenny. Also, truth be told, Starbuck wanted to one-up Piter, even if the bastard never knew who had gotten the better of him.

The only question now was, what could he do?

Since he hadn't prepared, he had only a few minutes before the energy faded and everything continued again. With a little preparation, he might have pulled off a full half hour to poke and prod around while time stood still, but the best he'd ever managed on the spur of the moment was five minutes.

He looked about, the dancing couples frozen in mid-dip, the bubbling champagne fountain caught in midbubble, Piter reaching for Jenny and looking damn smug while he did. Well, why shouldn't he look smug? Perfect body, perfect face, perfect hair, perfect clothes. The man was a prime example of Protector genetics and breeding, and he knew it.

And since Starbuck was undercover, there wasn't a damn thing he could do—with or without time on his side—to wipe that smug expression off his face.

Or was there?

The idea was devious, true, but Piter deserved devious. And surely it would cause enough of a commotion that Starbuck and Jenny could sneak out of the room entirely before he even noticed they were gone. And it wouldn't cause any lasting damage.

He shouldn't. He really, really shouldn't.

But when he looked over at Jenny again, his heart seemed to swell, and he knew that he had to do it. Anything for her. Anything to get Piter off her back. And anything to one-up anyone who would try to steal her from him. This would be silly, but it would also be fun.

He did one last thing before he set out on his scheme to humiliate a guy who needed to be taken down a peg or two. He bent over and kissed Jenny on the lips.

Chapter Six

Piter's pants were around his ankles, his shirt was pulled over his head, and his hands were twisted up in the sleeves. Jenny had no idea where the obnoxious Protector's coat was, but under the circumstances, it didn't seem important.

She pressed her fingers to her lips, which seemed warm and tingly under her touch. This was weird. Not her lips—though, that was odd—but the whole Piter situation. Weird. Very weird. Definitely bizarre . . . especially in a dance hall full of Protectors.

Two seconds before, Starbuck had been standing right in front of her, looking quite green around the gills. Now he was tugging at her hand, whispering that they ought to get out of there before Piter pulled himself together.

"But . . . ?" She looked at Starbuck, then back to Piter, and all the Protectors and mortals gathered around him laughing. She felt entirely bemused. "What's going on?" she asked.

Starbuck shrugged. "I guess some other Protector is playing a joke on him."

"But . . . but I didn't even blink." They were moving toward the exit, but she kept glancing back toward Piter. "I mean, one minute he was standing there. The next minute he's in his underwear. I never looked away. It happened just like that." She snapped the fingers of her free hand. "It's just not possible."

Starbuck stopped, disbelief apparent on his adorable face as he leaned against the wall. "Everything you've heard about, with these Protectors' superpowers, and you say it's not possible?" He took a deep, exhausted breath. "Come on, Jenny. How would you spin this?"

"For mortals? I have no clue." The whole evening needed a spin. First she was on a wonderful date; then she was being hounded by a persistent super-nuisance; then she was caught up in the middle of something that seemed suspiciously like poltergeist activity. She shrugged. That explanation would work as well as any other. "A poltergeist, maybe? Mortals would believe that."

"Well, there you go. On our way out, we can ask the concierge if the Montclair is haunted." He took her hand and tugged her toward the exit, his grip somewhat weak.

"Are you okay?"

"Fine." His voice was thin, and she got the feeling he wasn't really fine at all. "Probably something I ate."

"But?"

He tugged at her hand. "But let's go now, while we can. Unless you'd rather stay?"

One quick look over her shoulder was all she needed to decide. Piter was almost completely disentangled, and if the flailing of limbs was any indication, he was anything but happy. As for Daphne, she'd moved to help Piter, but her eyes were scanning the room, probably searching for Jenny. "No." She zipped through the door, this time pulling him behind her. "Let's get out while we can."

Holding hands, they stumbled out of the ballroom and across the mezzanine to the marble staircase, then down the steps and out the wide glass doors to the valet stand.

"I still can't believe I valet-parked a Chevette," he said in a gasp, propping himself up against the wooden stand.

"So long as you tip, I don't think they care." She smiled over at him, having a wonderful time and willing to go just about anywhere now—even if it meant suffering through his driving again.

"You're probably right." He gave the ticket to the valet, then walked back and, very nonchalantly, took Jenny's hand. The simple gesture warmed her all the way to her toes, and she wanted to lose herself in the feeling. The trouble was, she couldn't. She wanted to focus on her and Starbuck and nothing else, but it just wasn't happening.

She sighed, shifting from foot to foot. After a moment, he noticed her agitation. "Go ahead," he prompted. "Say it."

Relieved, she exhaled. The truth was, Piter's predicament was driving her nuts. If she didn't figure it out, it would bug her all evening. She was thankful Starbuck seemed to understand—and that was yet another reason she just might fall for him. Hard.

"It's just that a poltergeist might be an okay explanation for mortals," she whispered, "but I don't see Protectors buying into it."

"No?"

She shook her head.

219

"What then?"

"I don't know." She really didn't. She'd never run across anything quite like this before. "Maybe superspeed . . . ?"

"That must be it," he said, a bit too agreeably. "I'm sure you're right."

She frowned. "Except that we still should have seen *some*thing. It all happened in the blink of an eye. I don't think any Protector can move that fast."

"Hmmm. I'm not sure." He frowned, but then perked up as his car chugged up the hill from the parking garage. "Car's here." He slipped his arm around her waist and steered her forward. His grip was no longer weak.

"Feeling better?" she asked.

He nodded. "I told you it would pass." He jerked his head toward the car. "Ready?"

She let herself be led toward it, then frowned and stopped. Something weird was going on. Starbuck seemed jumpy all of a sudden, and she had no idea why. Of course, maybe it was the confrontation with Piter. *That* she could certainly understand.

Still . . .

"Do you think there are Protectors that fast?" she asked. The truth was, as much as the MLO knew about the superhero race that had pledged to protect mortals, they surely didn't know everything.

Starbuck shrugged, tipping the valet who'd finally exited his car and left it running in the drive-through before them. He wanted to steer Jenny to the car, and he wanted her to drop this subject. He wasn't worried that she'd figure out that time had stopped—even if she did, she certainly wouldn't tie it to him—but the whole topic made him uncomfortable. For one thing, it reminded him of just how blatantly he'd broken the rules. For another, it reminded him of the fact that he was a Protector—a powerful one—and that he had lied to Jenny about everything.

He needed an explanation—one she could buy into and then forget about. Unfortunately, he was all out of convenient, rational-sounding lies.

And then he concocted the perfect answer: Hale. Maybe his friend didn't approve of mortal-Protector relationships, but he darn well would help Starbuck out of this mess. He'd better.

"Maybe not just speed," he said, hoping he sounded casual. "Maybe invisibility, too."

"Oh, right!" Her face lit up as she considered the possibility. "Of course. Hale! That's his superpower. Well, one of them. Except I didn't see him at the party."

"I think that's the point, sweetheart. You *didn't* see him."

Her eyes widened. "You think he was there?"

"I'd bet money on it."

"And you'd be right." The air shimmered and Hale suddenly appeared, scaring the hell out of both Jenny and Starbuck. As their hearts slowed down, both whipped around, looking to see if anyone had noticed the good-looking guy materializing from thin air.

Fortunately, no one seemed to be paying the least bit of attention to the trio now standing by the ugly Chevette.

She propped a hand on her hip. "*You* did that in there? In a split second? You stripped him down and got him caught up in his own shirt?"

Hale nodded, then smiled in Starbuck's direction.

"Absolutely. I'd be pretty stupid to say I did it if I didn't—especially just to cover for some other Protector.

I mean, the council would have my neck . . . and, really, who's *that* loyal a friend?"

Starbuck stifled a groan as Hale buffed his nails on the front of his own shirt.

"A heck of a piece of work, if I do say so myself," his friend enthused. "Sometimes I amaze even myself."

"I'm amazed you could move so fast," Jenny marveled.

Hale shrugged modestly. "Years of training. And when you think about it, what else could have happened? I mean, it's not as if anyone can stop time."

Starbuck tried not to roll his eyes at his friend's outrageousness.

Jenny frowned as something dawned on her. She looked from Hale to Starbuck. "I thought you two didn't know each other."

Hale stuck out his hand. "Well, we do now, I guess. I'm Hale."

"Starbuck. I've heard of you."

His friend raised an eyebrow. "Oh, really? What have you heard?"

"Just that you're a bit of a prankster . . . but that you're loyal to a fault."

Hale grinned. "I don't know who your source is, but let him know I approve of his assessment." He winked. "Although I'm not loyal enough to take credit for something as dopey as that prank up there—at least, not if I didn't really do it." He nudged Jenny and then explained. "I just know that guy needed to be taken down a peg or two."

She laughed politely, but her attention was on the car, and Starbuck was thrilled when she took a step in its direction. If she was thinking about leaving, maybe she was finished thinking about "Hale's little trick" in the ballroom. He was disappointed when she said to the other

Protector, "Uh, would you like to join us? We're going to . . . uh . . . go get a coffee." Coffee was the last thing on Starbuck's mind, and he hoped Hale realized it.

With a cocky grin, Hale perched on the hood of the Chevette. "Now, that's an invitation I wouldn't dream of passing up."

"Great," Jenny said. Strangely, her voice lacked enthusiasm. Had she simply been inviting Hale along out of politeness?

"Yeah," Starbuck echoed, looking daggers at his friend. "That'll be wonderful."

"It's a plan. I'd love to get to know you both better. Let's go." Hale slapped his palms on his legs, then jumped off the hood of the Chevette. In two long steps, he was at the door and in the backseat, waiting for them to join him.

The one thought that kept going through Starbuck's mind was that, when all this was over, he was going to kill his friend. No. Killing wasn't good enough. Torture. Maybe tar and feather him.

He pictured buff Hale running around with feathers stuck to him and decided that wasn't a half-bad idea. The idea cheered him, and he was grinning when he got into the car.

"Oh, man, I completely forgot," Hale interrupted, leaning forward. "I can't go with you after all."

"Oh, darn," Jenny said. She didn't sound particularly upset, and Starbuck decided that maybe he wouldn't tar his friend after all.

"That's a real shame," he added.

"How about I take a rain check?" Hale asked.

"Sure," Jenny agreed quickly.

"Yeah," Starbuck said just as fast, eager to get his huge friend out of his tiny car.

Julie Kenner

After climbing out, Hale walked around and poked his head back in through the passenger window. "Well, you kids have fun." He winked, and Starbuck rolled his eyes. "Don't do anything I wouldn't do."

Starbuck cranked the engine. "Thanks. Have a good one." He started to pull away, but Hale's arm was still in the car. The man held fast, keeping the Chevette from moving. *Show-off.*

"One second, you two." Hale leaned in farther, amusement dancing in his eyes. "I just want to say what a cute mortal couple you two make. And I'm touched—no, *honored*—that you asked me to join you for coffee."

Starbuck bit his tongue, resisting the urge to tell Hale to shove off.

Jenny was nicer. "Thanks. That's very—"

"I mean, there just aren't words. You'd have to *read my mind* to understand how deeply, deeply touched I am to be invited out by you guys. But since you can't . . ." He trailed off with a shrug.

Starbuck blinked, his head cocked only slightly. Surely Hale didn't mean for him to . . .

But then Hale nodded, almost imperceptibly. Starbuck wasn't about to pass up the invitation to get into Hale's head, even if only for a moment. As he probed just under the surface, he found Hale's message for him, as plain as day. *Don't say I never did anything for you, pal. And don't come crying to me when this breaks your heart.*

Chapter Seven

It just didn't make any sense, Daphne thought. Not Piter's predicament—although that too, was very odd—but her daughter's behavior. It was giving Daphne fits.

Goodness knew she had raised the child right. And the girl was smart as a whip. But despite her over-the-top IQ and her second helping of common sense, Jenny was completely oblivious to her mother's efforts to make her life perfect.

And now she'd gone and sneaked out of the party with Starbuck, leaving a perfectly wonderful specimen of masculinity behind.

Baffling.

Well, one thing was certain: it was time for Daphne to take some more serious steps.

Frowning, she glanced at Piter, who was glaring in turn at pretty much everyone in the room, as he tried to figure out which of his peers had pulled such a practical joke.

She'd need the man's help, of course, but considering how eager he'd seemed to dance with Jenny, he'd surely agree.

Her daughter might be a little miffed at first, but this was for her own good. In the end, Jenny would thank Daphne and realize just how useful a superman in the family would be.

Jenny twisted her hands in her lap, suddenly shy. She was thankful Starbuck was navigating the streets at a reasonable speed, and she didn't feel compelled to hang on for dear life. She cast a surreptitious glance toward him, then blushed when she realized he was watching her out of the corner of his eyes.

"So, uh, did you want that cup of coffee?" she asked.

He nodded. "That would be nice."

Oh. Well, heck. She'd kind of hoped they could skip the coffee and cut to the chase. But, well . . . "I, uh, know a cute coffee shop in my neighborhood." Her palms felt sweaty, and she wiped them on her dress, gathering her courage to take the next step. "Or, you know, if you'd rather, we could go to my place and I could make a pot."

She was stepping out on a limb, and she knew it. In date-speak, inviting a guy up for coffee often meant a whole lot more. But that was what she wanted, she *did* hope it would turn into a whole lot more. Still, their date had begun as a favor, and for all she knew she was reading his signals completely wrong. . . . She desperately hoped she wasn't. Something about her and Starbuck clicked, and even though she hadn't known him very long, she felt more comfortable with him than any man she'd ever known. She prayed the closeness she felt wasn't one-sided.

A slow smile spread across his face, and Starbuck took

his attention off the road long enough to fully meet her gaze. His eyes were warm and inviting, and she let out a breath she hadn't realized she held.

"Just tell me the best way to get to where you live," was all he said. Then he took her hand and gave her fingers a squeeze. Jenny trembled as a million tiny sparks shot through her body.

Somehow she managed to give coherent directions, and he even lucked out and found a parking space on the street only two blocks away. Hand in hand, they walked back to her building, talking and laughing about nothing in particular, but having one of the best times Jenny could remember having.

As she slipped her key into the lock of the main door to her converted-warehouse apartment building, she shot him an apologetic smile. "I just want you to know that I don't do this often." In fact, she'd never done this.

"Go home?" he teased.

"Invite men to my apartment on a first date."

"Well, I'd suggest *my* apartment, but since we're already here . . ."

"You're teasing me," she said.

"I certainly am."

She rolled her eyes, needing to at least put on the pretense of prudence. "Fine. But just remember you're only coming up for coffee."

He stepped closer, then placed his hand over hers as she turned the key and let them into the building. They stepped inside; then he closed the door and pressed her back against it. The heat from his body filtered through her, and she wondered if it would be rude on a first date simply to melt into the hallway's linoleum flooring. Deliriously, she wondered what Emily Post would have to say about it.

His breath burned against her ear as he leaned forward and whispered, "What if I want more than just coffee?" His lips brushed her temple, and the tip of his tongue flicked against her earlobe. Shivers raced through her body. "What if I also want . . ."

She held her breath as he trailed off.

". . . cookies?"

She giggled, but when she leaned back and saw the undiluted passion burning in his eyes, the laughter died in her throat. What kind of *cookies* was he talking about? For the record, right then, at that moment, she hoped like heck he didn't want a plate of snickerdoodles.

"Of course," she whispered. "I'd hate for it to get around that I'm not a good hostess."

Almost imperceptibly he moved closer until no air remained between their bodies. "And I certainly want to be an accommodating guest."

She hoped so. He was so warm and firm that, at the moment, she could handle being *accommodated* right there in the entranceway.

With a firm mental slap, she pulled herself together. If she wanted to melt into his arms, the least she could do was steer them out of the hall. "We should go up."

"I think that's a winning idea."

The building's ancient elevator creaked and groaned as usual, but it managed to haul them up to the twelfth floor and Jenny's apartment. With only one dim bulb, the hall was dark and creepy. "The actual apartment's a lot better than the rest of this place," she said. With her mother's help, Jenny'd landed a huge one-bedroom with a full wall of windows. She loved the apartment, though the building itself left a lot to be desired.

"I think it's got atmosphere," Starbuck answered.

"That it has." She paused in front of her door, her shyness returning. "Well, this is it."

"So it is. Shall we go in?" With the tip of his finger, he traced the side of her face, then pushed a lock of hair behind her ear. "Or should we stay outside and entertain the neighbors?"

"We should go in." She probably sounded overeager, but so what? Right then, right there, she wanted nothing more than to be alone with Starbuck in her apartment. And the sooner they got there, the better.

He was breaking rules left and right: council rules, his own rules, basic etiquette rules. You name it, Starbuck was breaking it.

But he didn't care. He should be getting close to Jenny as a means of investigating Daphne. He *knew* that; by Zeus he did! He just couldn't do it. Investigate, sure. He could—would—do that . . . eventually. But the getting-close part was purely for him, purely for *them.* The truth of the matter was, he was getting in deeper and deeper. He was falling hard for Jenny—hopping Hades, he'd *already* fallen hard—and he was setting himself up for a big disappointment.

As much as he wanted her—and Zeus help him, he wanted her desperately—in the end, she wouldn't want him. Not knowing what he was. Would she? And not after he'd lied to her about everything. Which left him in something of a moral dilemma. Did he follow the evening to its logical conclusion, with Jenny in his arms and maybe him in her bed? Or did he act the gentleman now, and step away gracefully?

He knew what he should do. It would save them both heartache and tears when the truth was revealed. But the heat of desire that burned in his veins wouldn't let him do the noble thing, the chivalrous thing. No, he *wanted* Jenny. He'd wanted her since the first time he saw her. Maybe they'd have only this one night, whatever happened, but, by Zeus, he'd live off the memory of it for the rest of his life.

"Starbuck?"

Her words drew him out of his reverie.

"Are you coming?" Her tongue wet her lips, her voice nervous, and he realized he was still standing in the hallway.

"Oh, yes." With one long stride, he stepped over the threshold, kicking her door shut behind him. She started to move toward the living room, but he caught her in his embrace and pulled her close. "About that coffee . . ."

"Actually, you can have your choice: coffee, tea, or . . . me?" Her low, sultry voice tickled his senses, and when she wrapped an arm around his neck and pulled herself up on tiptoe to brush his lips with a kiss, he just about came undone.

She pulled away, her eyes soft, but her expression one of bewilderment.

"What?" he asked.

"Nothing." She shook her head. "Just déjà vu. It's silly, but I have the oddest feeling we've kissed before."

He recalled his illicit kiss when he'd stopped time, then squashed a trickle of guilt. "Well, we haven't. So maybe it's your psyche telling you how right we are together."

Her smile started at the left side of her mouth and spread across her face. "That must be it." She caught him around the waist, then tilted her head back to look him in the eyes. "But you never did answer my question. Coffee? Tea?"

"You."

"You sound so sure."

"Sweetheart, right now I don't think there's anything in my life I've ever been more sure of."

"Well, then . . ." This time, when she lifted up on her toes to kiss him, it wasn't a soft brush of her lips. Bold and forceful, this kiss would have knocked him backward if he hadn't already been standing with his back against a wall. Passion flooded out of her and into him, as if they were sharing the same feelings, as if they were one person.

His body heated and hardened, and he slid his hands down her waist to cup her smooth behind and urge her closer. He wanted to lose himself in her arms. Hell, he wanted to lose himself in her. But not too fast. This night was for her, and whatever happened, he intended to give her as much pleasure in one night as a mortal woman could handle.

Her soft body against his was driving him crazy, and he moaned, fighting the urge simply to yank her skirt up and lose himself in her. He suddenly knew she wouldn't object—as their bodies melded, her mind opened to him— but she deserved so much more than a frantic tumble on the living room carpet.

She deserved romance. Dim lights. Champagne and strawberries. A fire crackling in the fireplace and soft music wafting through the room.

"Starbuck, please." Her whisper held a plea, but it wasn't her words that spoke to him; it was her thoughts. *Kiss me, touch me, make love to me.*

Without any effort on his part, her thoughts reached out and found his. She was begging for his touch, the emotions spilling from her reaching into his soul and stirring similar feelings that had been sleeping for years.

He wanted to love her, to protect her, to be there for her. Most of all, he didn't want to disappoint her. Her plea might remain unspoken, but the longing came through loud and clear. She wanted him, and that was all Starbuck needed. In one gentle motion, he tilted her face up to his, pressed his lips to hers, and tasted her sweetness.

Chapter Eight

As if he knew her most secret desires, Starbuck's touch took her to the very edge of sanity. She'd been silently begging for his kiss, and then his mouth closed over hers. With undisguised passion, he urged her lips apart, exploring and tasting her even while she did the same.

He tasted of red wine and something else. Something male and powerful and very erotic. As his fingers tangled in her hair, his tongue warred with hers, teasing and tempting . . . making silent promises of a night to come.

Her knees went weak, and she knew she was standing only because of his hand around her waist. Almost as if he understood her dilemma, he lifted and carried her, bridelike, to the living room sofa—as if he were Mr. Universe instead of the normal-looking guy she'd fallen so hard for. To her, though, he was the most handsome man in the world.

"Here?" he asked, setting her down.

233

She shook her head, wanting him to carry her to the bedroom. She wanted to lie with him on her satin comforter and feel the silky, cool material contrasting with the heat of their bodies.

Without her asking, he picked her up again. This time he kissed her forehead and carried her to the bedroom. When he laid her gently on the middle of the bedspread, she knew she'd died and gone to heaven.

"I want—"

He silenced her with one gentle finger over her lips. "Hush. Let me show you what you want."

And he did, tempting and teasing her with decadent desires so fresh and new she barely realized she'd imagined them. But she had. Each time his hand touched her body, only an instant before, she'd craved his touch there. Each time he kissed her, she'd been on the verge of whimpering for another taste of his lips. And when he traced his finger up her leg and under her skirt, she could only whisper, "Yes," and know that she'd been longing for him to touch her as he did.

He was her perfect man, her perfect lover, knowing her secret, sensual whims and desires without being told. There was a synergy between them, and she reveled in it, hoping her own touch brought as much pleasure to him.

With a featherlight touch, his fingertips grazed the inside of her thigh again. "Do you like that?" he whispered.

She could manage only a moan, but he seemed to understand. Gently caressing her, he slid the silk of her skirt up her leg, then pressed kisses in the soft area just beside her knee. The rough stubble of his beard tickled, somehow adding to her excitement, and she let the flood of warmth build inside her, pooling between her thighs in the one place where she ached for his touch most of all.

"Please, Starbuck, please."

His hands did wonders even while his mouth worked a magic on her she'd never experienced. His hands caressed her hips, and he lifted his head just long enough for their eyes to meet. Then he slipped her panties off and kissed her intimately. The thrill of his tongue on such a secret, sensitive place shot through her, and she moaned, her whole body stiffening against the onslaught of pleasure.

"Do you like that?" His whisper teased her, all the more because he had to know the answer.

"Yes. Oh, yes. But I want—"

"More."

She nodded shyly. "You. I want you. Now. Please, Starbuck. Please."

He wasn't about to argue. With one deft movement, he slid out of his clothes. With another, he buried himself inside her, thrilled by the absolute certainty that she wanted him as desperately as he did her. Even if he couldn't read her thoughts, he could certainly read her body. Every little quiver, every soft moan, told him that she wanted him. The knowledge made him feel more powerful than he'd ever felt simply being a Protector.

He loved this woman. So help him, he did. It was crazy to feel this intensely so quickly, but he did. Everything she did was right, everything she said was ... If she would just let herself, he was certain that she might love him, too—even despite everything. But there was no time for thoughts like that.

They moved together in a timeless rhythm, instinctual to men and women of any race. It was an expression of togetherness, an expression of love.

Julie Kenner

With an exquisite touch she stroked him, her fingers moving expertly over his skin. Every movement, every touch, ignited the sparks that burned in his blood. He wanted her, *needed* her to find her release; if she didn't soon, he was afraid he would explode.

She moaned beneath him, her ecstasy building with his, the raw passion on her face delighting him. He held on tight, not willing to lose himself without her, and listened to her thoughts. Only when he knew that she was on the brink did he let himself go. The explosion took them both to the edge of the universe and back. At last, exhausted, they lay together in each other's arms.

"That was amazing." She wrapped her arm around his chest and snuggled closer. "*You're* amazing."

A wave of guilt crashed over him. He wanted to tell her the truth—he even went so far as to open his mouth to speak—but in the end, he simply kissed her. This was their moment, and he wanted to keep it perfect. He loved this mortal woman, and his greatest fear was that this one night was all he'd have of her. Once she found out his secret . . . For at least a little while, he wanted to abandon his heritage and live an illusion.

He'd been undercover his whole life. Tomorrow he could go back to the MLO and back to the mole hunt. Tomorrow he'd be Starbuck, the super-geeky undercover agent, once again. But right now he just wanted to be himself. Not Starbuck the Protector, not Starbuck the agent. Just Starbuck the man. A man Jenny was actually attracted to. Not because he was buff like Hale, but just because he was *him*. Surely he deserved a bit of happiness. Especially when all he was asking for was one brief, cherished moment with a woman he'd found to be exquisite beyond all others.

"Hey," she called, kissing him on the nose. "You're a million miles away."

He smiled, shaking off his melancholy. "On the contrary. I'm right here."

"Yeah? You looked lost in thought. What were you thinking?"

"About tomorrow."

"Oh."

The direct mental connection between them had faded, but he didn't need to probe her mind to recognize her disappointment. Tomorrow they'd both go back to work. Tomorrow reality would move back into both their lives. Tonight had been wild, crazy, wonderful. Tomorrow would be . . .

"I was thinking maybe we should play hooky," he said.

"Really?" Delight filled her voice.

"Really."

"We'll get in trouble. No one will believe us if we call in sick."

He shrugged. "So? It's the MLO's fault for scheduling an office party on a Thursday. They've gotta know half the office'll go AWOL tomorrow."

"Hmmm. You could have a point." She rolled over until she was straddling him, naked, then rewarded him with a saucy look. "There's just one problem with your plan."

"Oh?"

"What on earth are we going to do for a whole day and another night?"

Laughing, he pulled her down and kissed her perfect lips. "I can think of one or two things."

"Yeah?"

"Yeah," he said, then proceeded to show her exactly

what he had in store for her until Saturday morning rolled around.

Daphne stood in the downstairs hallway of her daughter's apartment, drumming her fingers on the wall as she waited for the super to meet her. They were up there, she was certain. She'd seen the lights from outside, seen the shadows moving about. For the last two days, they'd been up there doing Lord only knew what. Well, after two days of them not answering the phone—despite Daphne's repeated messages—she had a pretty good idea what her daughter and Starbuck were doing.

She shook her head, frustrated by her daughter's foolishness. Clearly the girl had been bewitched—and it was up to her to convince her child that Starbuck wasn't the man for her.

Really. A mother's work was just never done.

The click of a heavy metal door sounded behind her, and she turned around to greet the building's super.

"Hey, Ms. Martin. What you doin' here?"

"Arnold." She smiled sweetly at him. "So good to see you again." The man had been the super in her own building before he'd moved to this one. He'd been the reason she'd found this apartment for her daughter.

"You're lucky you caught me. I was just on my way out."

Lucky? Actually, she'd been banking on it. For the five years she'd known him, he'd spent Saturday mornings with his sister's kids. She'd desperately hoped today wasn't an exception. And it wasn't. "Oh, I don't want to hold you up."

"No worries. I got a few minutes. So what can I do for you?"

"Well, I wanted to go up and leave some things for Jenny, but I can't seem to find the elevator key she gave me." So it was a teeny, tiny little lie.

"Ain't she home right now?"

Damn. Daphne had been hoping Arnold would just assume Jenny was out.

"Well, yes, she is." She took a step toward him and lowered her voice conspiratorially. "The thing is, she has a young man up there with her, and I don't want to interrupt. I figure they'll go out later. You know, for a romantic lunch or something. Then I can pop in and leave her stuff."

Arnold sighed and shook his head. For a minute, Daphne was afraid he'd say no. "Ms. Martin, you know how expensive these keys are. They're not standard-issue. You can't just go down to any hardware store and have a copy made. You gotta get the key from the manufacturer."

She exhaled in relief, then tried to look chastised. "I know. I'm so sorry." With a flourish, she pulled her checkbook out of her purse. "Will a fifty-dollar deposit cover it?"

With a wave, he brushed off the comment. "Don't worry about it, Ms. M. Just try to keep a hold of this one, okay?" He headed back toward his apartment, presumably to get her key.

"No problem, Arnold," she called. *No problem at all.*

He came back with the item, and after she thanked him, he headed out the front door and hailed a taxi. The building was all hers, and so was the control panel inside the elevator. She checked her watch. Piter would be here within the hour.

Time to get moving with her plan.

Chapter Nine

They were both laughing when Jenny pulled her apartment door closed behind her. "Sure you don't want to stay in a little longer?" After two solid days of lovemaking, letting up only for breaks to laugh and joke and eat, she still hadn't had her fill of Starbuck.

He faked a faint, falling against the wall. "If you had something more substantial than Cheerios and coffee, I might just take you up on that. But I'm weak. Must . . . have . . . food."

"Wimp." Delighted, she danced ahead and pressed the elevator call button. "But let's hurry, though. I want to get to the market, stock up on healthy, high-energy food, and get you back in my apartment as soon as possible. We've got almost two full days before we have to be back at work, and I've got plans for you, mister."

"Yeah?"

"Yeah." She returned his smile, realizing she was happier right now than she had been in a long time. She might have known him for only a few days, but Jenny also realized she was falling in love. She'd let Starbuck into her heart, and now she didn't want to let him go.

The elevator door opened and he followed her in. "So just how do you plan on keeping me around?" A tease laced his voice.

"Any way I have to." She quirked an eyebrow. "I was thinking maybe handcuffs. Or at least tight leather restraints." They were alone, and as the doors slid closed, she slipped into his arms. "What do you think? That enough to keep you in bed?"

"Jenny, all I need to keep me in bed is you."

She grinned. "Then you're fresh out of excuses, because that's exactly where I intend to stay."

He caught her mouth with his own in a slow, sensual kiss. Warm and languid, she could happily have stayed in his embrace, sharing his kiss, until the elevator made its creaky way down to the lobby. She wasn't expecting the lurch that brought the elevator to a sudden halt.

"What happened?"

"We're stuck." He pointed at the needle above the door. "Looks like we're between seven and eight."

The walls seemed to close in around her. "Oh, this is just great."

"It's no problem," Starbuck said. "We'll just ring the alarm. I'm sure the super will be here in no time."

But when he pushed the alarm button, nothing happened.

The walls moved in closer, or seemed to. "I don't like this."

He curled an arm around her shoulder. "We'll be fine."

"No, you don't understand. I don't like elevators. I

mean, I'm okay when they're moving, but I get really claustrophobic after a while." She aimed an apologetic smile in his direction. "Sorry."

"Nothing to be sorry about." For a long minute, he looked into her eyes as if he was searching for something. Then he nodded and smiled, but it seemed a little forced. "I'm sure some other tenant will figure out this thing's stuck soon enough," he said. At her grimace, he continued on to say, "But no sense waiting, right?"

"What are you going to do?"

He wasn't looking at her. Instead, his eyes were scanning the elevator ceiling. "I don't know. I'm making this up as I go."

Unfortunately, he *was* making it up. Under normal circumstances, he might just pry the doors open, pull the elevator car up to the next level, and get them out that way. Too bad all that prying and pulling wasn't in a mortal man's range of ability.

A mortal guy would probably wait for help, especially since this ancient elevator car didn't seem to have a working trapdoor on the roof. But Starbuck wasn't willing to wait. He'd sensed Jenny's thoughts, and she wasn't kidding about her claustrophobia. While she was doing a good job of hiding her fear, he could see it creeping up behind the mental wall she'd built. When it built up enough pressure, she wouldn't be able to fight it anymore. He didn't intend to force her to go through something like that. Not if he could help it.

And help it he could. Now he had to figure out how to do so without blowing his cover.

He let his gaze dart around the car, trying to locate something that might facilitate their escape. Nothing. Then he looked up again. The roof resembled old-fashioned ceiling tiles, and he could tell from where he stood that they were each solid and permanent. Yet, maybe Jenny wasn't paying close attention. . . .

It was worth a shot. He certainly didn't have a better idea.

"Listen, sweetheart. I want you just to sit tight. I'm going to climb up there and see if I can't get the trapdoor to open."

She nodded, and he managed to get a toehold on the handrail that ran along the edge of the interior wall. The easier thing would be just to jump, but considering his looks didn't exactly jibe with his strength, Jenny would certainly notice something amiss if he leaped ten feet into the air.

Climbing to the ceiling, he managed to grab the light fixture and hold on as he took a better look. The old-fashioned metal was molded to look like ceiling tiles.

One quick glance down confirmed that Jenny was hunched on the floor, hugging her knees to her chest. He'd move before she decided to look up.

Superstrength ranked high on his list of cool things about being a Protector, and right then he was especially happy for it. Risking Jenny's curiosity about the noise, he punched his hand through the ceiling at one of the seams, then peeled it back. With a final tug, he pulled the square completely loose, revealing a person-sized hole that led through to the top of the elevator and the gaping elevator shaft.

Since he couldn't drop the ragged piece of metal onto the elevator floor—Jenny would surely realize it wasn't a true trapdoor—he pitched it up onto the top of the elevator. With a groan for Jenny's benefit, he pulled himself up and scoped out the inside of the elevator shaft.

They weren't in too bad a predicament, all things considered. The elevator car partially blocked the door to the seventh floor, but the doors to the eighth were easily accessible by the service ladder.

He popped his head back over the opening and checked on Jenny. She was standing up now, watching the ceiling with anxiety lining her face.

"You okay?"

"I'll be better when you get back down here."

"I can do you one better than that. How about I get us both out of here?"

Her smile was answer enough, and he knew he wasn't about to disappoint her. After blowing her a quick kiss, he climbed the ladder and turned his attention to the door leading out to the eighth floor. The emergency release latch wasn't functioning, and he reached out to pry the doors apart manually. From his perch, the angle was awkward—certainly no mortal would be able to get sufficient leverage—but he managed it without even breaking a sweat.

As soon as the doors were open, he dropped silently back to the top of the elevator. Then he anchored himself with his feet, bent at the waist, and dropped his upper body into the car. Jenny reached up, her hands closing around his, as she let him pull her up onto its roof. She followed him then, climbing the ladder to freedom.

"You okay?" he asked once they were out on the eighth floor.

"I'm with you," she answered. Her smile was a little watery, and she wrapped her arms around his waist and buried her face against his chest. "How could I be anything but fine?"

* * *

Time for a rescue.

With Daphne pacing behind him, panting after their climb up the stairs, Piter stood in front of the seventh-floor elevator doors rubbing his hands. *Finally!* For almost a month he'd been sucking up to this woman, trying without success to find a chink in her rigid morality. This would be the opportunity.

So far he'd been able to provide Hieronymous only with the bits and pieces of council information he'd acquired the old-fashioned way—poking through Daphne's desk drawers after working hours and digging through the computer files his level of clearance would allow. But that wasn't enough. He'd already promised the man top-secret information that could only come from Daphne. If she were on their team, he'd have full access to the MLO's computer network. It galled Piter to have to get so close to a mortal, to pretend to actually like her and her daughter. But disappointing Hieronymous simply wasn't done.

At first, the woman seemed entirely unconvertible. His little hints and innuendoes had gone completely unheeded. The woman might be brilliant, but she was spacey as hell; it apparently never even occurred to her that one of her oh-so-wonderful Protectors might be working for Hieronymous. Instead, all the woman was interested in were her damn computers and her darling daughter. Which meant that Piter had been forced to pretend interest in Jenny. So when Daphne approached him with her latest scheme—rescue claustrophobic Jenny from a broken elevator and win her love and admiration—he'd willingly agreed. Once he had the girl safely in his pocket, the mother would be sure to follow.

The trouble before, of course, was that Jenny hadn't even been interested in giving him the time of day. *Stupid little mortal twit.* She seemed much more enamored of that scrawny Starduck fellow. Well, there wasn't a mortal male in the world who could hold a candle to a Protector. And Piter wasn't used to being ignored.

He'd get the girl. As Daphne had said, Jenny's interest just needed to be jump-started. And what better way than an effortless rescue from a broken elevator, with her mortal lover standing around like an impotent idiot?

A slow grin crossed his face. A heck of a plan, if he did say so himself!

"Ready?" Daphne finished one lap of her pacing and stopped behind him.

"Whenever you say the word." He kept his voice polite, friendly, and deferential—all the while longing for the days when he could tell Daphne exactly what he thought of her, her daughter, and mortals in general.

"Go ahead. Jenny hates elevators. She'll be so grateful she'll probably jump into your arms."

"I hope so. Your daughter's all I think about." Not exactly the truth, but not exactly a lie, either. The girl was beautiful.

"It's okay, Jenny," Daphne called toward the still-closed doors. "We're coming."

With no effort at all, Piter pried the doors apart. The elevator car wasn't lined up with the hallway, though, so he moved the car with one hand until the closed interior doors matched those of the now-open seventh floor.

"Now, Piter. Open the inner doors. Be her hero."

That was a plan he could live with. He took a deep breath—the better to accentuate his chest and arm muscles—then pasted on his I'm-a-loyal-council-member smile. If it fooled Zephron, it could fool anyone.

Set at last, he reached out and effortlessly slid the inner

doors open, ready to accept the flood of grateful kisses from Daphne's daughter.

There was just one little problem: the elevator was completely empty.

He turned to Daphne, every ounce of concentration going to conceal the anger he knew must be burning in his eyes. He needed to be calm and polite and deferential. He'd duped the woman so far; no sense screwing up all his careful planning simply because this one plan had gone awry.

Pasting on a smile, he took her hand and patted it. "I think, Daphne, dear, that it's time we moved on to plan B."

Chapter Ten

Springtime in Manhattan! All the trees and flowers were in bloom, and the air smelled fresh and alive. Starbuck breathed deeply and squeezed Jenny's hand. She smiled up at him, then squeezed back, her touch reminding him of how much he'd gained over the last few days. Everything in his personal life was going right, and for that he was thankful, even though his professional life was crashing down around his ears.

On the personal front, Starbuck was spending more and more time with Jenny. After the elevator fiasco they'd spent the rest of the weekend together, and during the next two days at the office they'd shared every break, heading back to her apartment after work.

She loved him. She hadn't admitted as much, true, but he was certain. So far he'd resisted the temptation to pry into her mind and see what she was thinking, but he didn't need a mind-probe to know how she felt. Her mouth might not have spoken the words, but her body certainly had. She loved him. And while the knowledge thrilled him no end, it also scared him. Someday soon he'd have to tell her the truth. And when he did, he could only hope that she loved him enough to forgive him his lies— and to forget her previous rule about dating Protectors. He believed she would, but he was scared.

On the professional front, things were a little shaky. He had, on some level, tried to continue his investigation. A few more select probes into Jenny's mind had revealed absolutely nothing incriminating about Daphne. Either the woman had worked hard to keep her daughter out of the loop, or she simply wasn't the mole. Starbuck hoped for the latter, but if that was the case, then he was even farther behind on his mission than before.

As for checking out Daphne directly, he'd finagled a permanent transfer to her department, but hadn't learned a thing except that she was irritated with him for dating his daughter. *That* was hardly a news flash.

She had thanked him for rescuing Jenny from the elevator, but she'd seemed a little miffed about the whole thing, too. Of course, when Jenny had told the story, she'd been delighted to be able to tell her mom that a mortal guy could be just as much a white knight as any Protector. Starbuck hadn't said a word. He'd leaned against a wall and tried not to look either woman in the eye.

His lack of progress in finding the mole was frustrating. Guilt was eating at him, but he couldn't tell Jenny the truth—couldn't break his cover—until he caught his enemy. And the longer he continued playing a mortal, the angrier Jenny would be when the truth came out.

"You're quiet tonight."

"Just thinking," he said.

"About what?"

"About you, of course."

Her delighted laughter surrounded him, and he shook off his melancholy mood. He'd known the risks when he got involved with Jenny. No sense moaning about it now.

"Want to go get a coffee or something?" She half bumped him with her shoulder. "Or do you just want to head back to my place?"

"I *want* to head to your place—but you're down to Cheerios again, and I need sustenance."

"You certainly do. I don't want you passing out." She planted a kiss on his cheek. "I've got better plans for you."

"Fast food," he said with a grin. "We should get fast food."

Laughing, she pointed across the street. "Why don't we grab something from that deli? We can take it back and have a bed picnic."

He grinned, too. "Fine with me. So long as we get to do more in bed than eat dinner."

She squeezed his hand. "I think that can be arranged."

They were waiting at the corner for the light to change when he first saw it. An old woman. Apparently confused, she'd stepped off the curb and right into the path of a crosstown bus.

Starbuck tensed. He needed to do something, but his natural superspeed and strength weren't going to help him—not unless he was willing to blow his cover. No, he had only one choice—stopping time.

Jenny noticed the old lady almost at the last second, and her scream pierced the air just as Starbuck froze time. He ran to the woman, dragged her out of the way, and set her on the curb—maybe she'd think her reflexes had saved her—then ran back to Jenny just as his power faded and time continued on its course. Jenny's scream once again rent the air.

"Oh." Her shriek faded into a single confused word. "But . . . that woman. She was in front of that bus. I . . . I was sure of it."

Starbuck couldn't speak. For that matter, he couldn't stand. The effort of such a last-moment, no-preparation time manipulation had taken its toll. He fell helpless to the sidewalk.

"Starbuck!" Jenny knelt beside him. "Are you okay? What's wrong?"

He tried a smile, but wasn't sure it succeeded. "Told you I needed sustenance," he joked.

She frowned, apparently in no mood, and pressed her hand to his forehead. "You don't have a fever."

"Need . . . to . . . sleep." But he didn't want to. Something was wrong. He couldn't put his finger on it, but every atom in his body yelled for him to fight the exhaustion. To stay awake. To help Jenny.

"Is he okay?" asked a new voice. Starbuck squinted, saw the tailored suit of what could only be a Wall Street attorney. "Can I help?"

"I don't know," Jenny answered, her tone frantic.

Starbuck tried to focus on the lawyer guy. Something was wrong. He couldn't see the man anymore. Just a tall, thin, slimy creature standing next to Jenny. And she was talking to him as if there weren't anything out of the norm going on at all.

A chill washed over him. *Henchmen.* The lawyer was a henchman!

But why would a henchman be here now?

Hieronymous.

"He seems really weak," Jenny added.

251

The henchman peered into Starbuck's face. "Stupid mortal."

Jenny gasped, her head whipping around to face the creature. "Did you say mortal?"

"And you're a stupid one, too," the creature said. His clawlike hand closed around Jenny's arm. "My master will be very pleased."

She jerked away, even as Starbuck fought to move against the blanket of exhaustion weighing him down. "Let me go!" she cried, managing a really nice left hook with her free hand. Then she got a good kick to the groin. If the creature had been mortal, her attacks surely would have freed her. But since henchmen didn't have human groins, the kick barely slowed him down.

"Starbuck!" she called.

He struggled, but his muscles wouldn't cooperate. He could only watch, helpless, as the creature dragged her away. A half dozen passersby looked on, their expressions nervous. Clearly no one was going to help Jenny.

Reaching out with his mind, he tried to probe the creature's thoughts. He got only random words: *Piter. Stopping her. Daphne. Get the girl. Leverage.*

And then the connection faded, leaving him with nothing else. From the smattering of thoughts, it sounded as if Daphne was the mole, and she was worried about Piter catching her. But why on earth would she kidnap her own daughter?

No, he couldn't believe Daphne was the mole. Logic told him his feelings for Jenny were coloring his perception, and he knew that was true, but even so . . . he just had a feeling in his gut. Daphne wasn't his bad guy. He'd been tracking her all this time, but now, in this time of trial, he saw he could never believe that of her.

But if not her, who? Piter? True, the man's arrogance made Starbuck gag, but he was a decorated Protector and an honored member of the council.

And yet, Protectors had been turned before. . . .

The basic truth was, he didn't know who was who or what was what. But he damn sure intended to find out. And he would save Jenny.

Just as soon as he managed to stand up.

Starbuck burst through the doors to Daphne's computer lab to find her hanging up the phone, tears streaming down her face.

"He's got her! That evil cretin has my baby girl!"

"Piter?" he asked almost hopefully.

Daphne shook her head. "Hieronymous."

Starbuck's mind churned a mile a minute. Could both Daphne and Piter be innocent? Could there be another suspect?

With one hand on her shoulder, he led Daphne to a chair and sat her down. "Tell me exactly what happened."

"I was just puttering around—trying to get the database uplink working—when the phone rang. This horrible creepy voice said he had my little girl and he was going to give her over to Hieronymous if I didn't do exactly what he told me."

Starbuck knelt in front of her, his hands on her knees. "What does he want?"

She sucked in a breath, then lifted her head up to meet his eyes. "He wants the password to the MLO mainframe. He warned me not to tell anyone, but, oh . . . what am I going to do?"

Starbuck closed his eyes. With that password, Hieronymous would have complete access from anywhere in the world. He'd have a wealth of information at his fingertips, including which Protectors were undercover and where—and considering his growing band of Outcasts, he could surely take the Protectors out one by one. He supposed he was glad that he knew this, that he could stop Hieronymous, but to sacrifice Jenny for the good of . . .

"Did you give him the password?" he asked.

"No!" Her eyes were imploring. "But he's supposed to call back in an hour. Starbuck, what other choice do I have? They've got Jenny."

"Yes." He stood up. "But we're going to get her back." They had one hour to do it.

"How?"

He couldn't tell her everything, but he could tell her enough. "I think I know where she is."

"You do? Where?"

"Piter's. If he's giving you only an hour, he won't risk taking her far away." And Starbuck was banking on Piter being so arrogant that he wouldn't think that anyone might yet be on to him.

"Piter? I don't understand. He's such a nice young man. And he's a Protector. Why would he be mixed up with Hieronymous?"

Starbuck didn't answer directly. Instead, he parried with a question of his own: "I need you to be honest with me, Daphne. I know you weren't too thrilled when Jenny and I started going out. I know you would have rather seen her go out with Piter."

"Well, um, yes." Her cheeks flushed crimson. "It's nothing personal, it's just—"

"I know. Don't worry about it. What I want to know is, did you seek out Piter? Or did he tell you he was interested in Jenny?"

"Now that you mention it, he approached me. About a week or so after his rotation started. He's very charming, and I tried to set him up with Jennifer, but she just wasn't interested."

Charming, shmarming. "I think his charm is rather overrated," he found himself saying.

She squinted at him through tear-filled eyes. "What do you mean?"

He took a deep breath. He was getting ready to malign a fellow Protector without any proof whatsoever. At least, no more proof than a gut feeling and several garbled thoughts of a Henchman.

Sometimes you just have to go with your gut.

"I mean, I think he works for Hieronymous. I think Piter's a spy."

At that, Daphne burst out laughing. It was not the reaction he'd expected, that was for sure.

"Piter can't be a spy. He's too . . . polite."

Starbuck ran his hands through his hair, not sure how to argue with logic like that. "Just listen to me, okay? I'm not really a new employee. I was assigned to work at the MLO to help catch a mole."

"A mole! That's impossible."

He shook his head. "All too possible, I'm afraid."

"But why you? Why would the council enlist the aid of a mortal on a mole hunt?"

That was a good question, but he wasn't yet willing to tell her the whole truth. "Equal opportunity employment. It's the law."

"Oh." She still looked baffled, but she no longer looked defeated. "So you can help me? You can help me get my little girl back?"

He took her hand. "Daphne, that's my plan."

255

Chapter Eleven

Daphne twisted her hands in her lap, not sure what to believe. Piter a mole? Starbuck an undercover agent? Everything was off-kilter, and the worst of it was that she had to rely on a mortal to help retrieve her little girl.

"Can't we get a Protector involved?" she asked.

"No time. And I can't be certain who to trust." He turned and headed out the door. "Come on. We're wasting time."

She hurried after him. "Who can't you trust?"

"Well, I can trust Hale, maybe." He paused, then said, "For one thing, I'm taking a big risk trusting you."

"Me?" Her voice was squeaking, but the idea that she'd be involved in something nefarious was just ludicrous. "Why on earth wouldn't you trust me?"

She rushed to keep up as he headed for the elevator.

"For one thing, you're the only one who works at the MLO with full access to the computer."

"Well, yes, but that doesn't make me a spy."

"No, but it makes you a suspect. And right now, things don't look so good for the guy you picked for your daughter."

They were in the elevator now, heading up through all the subbasements to the main portion of the United Nations Building.

"Would you please, please tell me why you don't trust Piter?" The thought that she might have been setting her little girl up with one of Hieronymous's bunch made her sick to her stomach.

Starbuck started counting reasons off on his fingers. "We know there's a mole. We know you have access to the information the mole has gotten . . . and likely more he wants. If we assume you're not the mole, then the mole must be someone who either has an in with you, or thinks he can get one. One who has been near you in the past. One who plans to be near you in the future."

"But—"

He held up a finger. "As for getting an in with you, you've got only one point of vulnerability that I can see, and that's Jenny. Everyone knows you want her to date a Protector, so Piter put on his most charming face and tried to get to Jenny through you."

Daphne swallowed, afraid of where this was going. Especially since everything he'd said so far made perfect sense.

"You think he's the cat's meow, and so you're obliging. Piter figures it's all going to work out. Jenny will fall head over heels for him, he'll marry her, and suddenly he'll have full access to you and everything you do."

"Except Jenny's not interested in him," she said, her mouth dry. "She's interested in you."

257

Julie Kenner

"And despite your best efforts at the party and on the elevator—"

"You knew about that?"

"I just figured it out."

"Oh. Sorry." In retrospect, that little stunt did seem pretty stupid.

"Yes, well, as I was saying, it didn't work. And Piter must have finally realized that Jenny wasn't ever going to fall for him. So he's upped the ante. He still needs Jenny to get to you. So instead of marrying her, he's arranged for a henchman to take her." He shrugged. "It all fits. I'd bet my job on Piter being our bad guy. Heck, I *am* betting my job."

The elevator doors opened and she followed Starbuck out into the United Nations lobby. "Nothing personal, but I don't give a fig about your job. I just want my daughter back."

"Then trust me. And help me."

She nodded, silently putting her trust in him. She'd rather have the help of a true Protector, but she was certain of one thing—Starbuck was in love with Jenny. She supposed that had to count for something.

"Why are you doing this?" Jenny struggled against the ropes holding her wrists together as she glared at Piter.

"Let's just say I'm a sore loser." A thin, dangerous smile touched his lips. "You should have danced with me, sweetheart. This would have gone a whole lot better for you."

"I'll never dance with you. For that matter, I'll never do anything for you. I don't know why you're holding me, but it's not going to work."

"Is that so?" He bent down, then chucked her under the

258

chin as she tried to back away from his touch. "Well, lucky for me, your cooperation isn't an issue. Your mother's is."

A cold chill crept up Jenny's spine. "My mother?"

"Either she helps me . . . or her darling daughter's going to have a very bad day."

"Helps you?" The chill increased, and she scooted back against the wall. The whole situation pretty much proved her mom was nuts about loving Protectors so much. Clearly they weren't the saints Daphne claimed. And Jenny intended to point that out to her mom at the first opportunity. Assuming, of course, that she survived this. She licked her lips. "Helps you how?"

His devious smile was nothing like the falsely charming expression he'd plied her with at the dance. "Not me, exactly. Hieronymous needs your mother's help."

Hieronymous. Her stomach churned and she closed her eyes, longing for Starbuck's strong arms around her. But he wasn't there, and she was all alone, and no matter what else happened, she was certain of one thing: she was in big trouble.

"Get away from her, Piter."

Starbuck! Jenny's eyes flew open, and there he was, standing right in front of the open window with Daphne at his side.

"I'm okay," she called out. "Run, get help. He's in with Hieronymous."

Starbuck only nodded. "I know."

"Then get out of here!" She was frantic, but Starbuck wasn't moving. Didn't he realize that a Protector like Piter would tear a mortal like him apart?

"Let her go, Piter."

Not too surprisingly, the traitorous superhero laughed. "And who's going to make me?"

"I am."

Jenny cringed. Starbuck was about to get pulverized, and he didn't seem to realize it.

Again, that devious laugh. "You and what army?" Then Piter turned to smile at Daphne. "Ah, my darling Daphne. I'm so glad you could make it. I hope you brought the password."

"I sure did," her mom said, as Jenny held her breath. "The password is *creep*. All lowercase and two Es."

"Very funny." Piter turned to Jenny. "Your mother has the most delightful sense of humor. I'm hoping it will become more refined when she realizes that she might end up childless."

"You're scum. You know that, right?"

He smiled thinly. "Sticks and stones, Jenny. Sticks and stones." And then, lightning-quick, he was beside her, lifting her around the waist. She struggled against the ties binding her wrists and ankles, but to no avail.

"Let me go!"

In a flash he was at the balcony, holding her out over the traffic rushing by fifteen floors below. The world seemed to spin in a fit of vertigo, and she closed her eyes tight, terrified, then opened them again, needing to know what was going to happen.

"Sweet Jenny, that's exactly my plan."

"Put her down, Piter." Starbuck's voice rang out calm and self-assured, and even though Jenny knew there wasn't any way in the world he could help her now, somehow the knot of terror in her stomach dissolved just a tiny bit.

"Happy to. Just give me the password."

"I'm only going to ask once more. Put the girl down."

"You're awfully arrogant for a mortal."

"You'll forgive me if I don't say what you are. There are ladies present."

At that, Piter laughed again. "I will say this, Starpuck: you do amuse me."

"I'm glad to hear it," he answered. Jenny held her breath as he moved a step closer. "I hope you'll be just as amused when I take you to council headquarters for prosecution."

"I'll give you the password!" Daphne cried. "Just give me my daughter."

"There we are," Piter said, and Jenny could hear the smile in his voice. "I knew you could be reasonable." He took a step forward, and the fifteen-story drop beneath Jenny turned into three feet as she dangled relatively harmlessly over the balcony floor. She wasn't out of the woods yet, but the situation was much improved.

"Perfect, Daphne," Starbuck said. Then he sprang forward. If Jenny hadn't been watching, she wouldn't have believed it. Somehow he pulled Piter forward, the motion loosening his grip on her, and Jenny fell with a *ker-plop* to the ground. She rolled clear, then scooted away until her back was pressed up against a clay planter. Daphne ran to her, and she wrapped her arms around her mother, then watched, helpless, as the man she loved was pulverized by Piter.

Except he wasn't getting pulverized.

She couldn't understand it. Somehow Starbuck was holding his own. Piter swung a leg out to connect with Starbuck's middle, but—*ka-thonk*—Starbuck intercepted it with his arm and sent Piter tumbling. And when Piter leaped through the air toward Starbuck—*ka-bloom*—Starbuck's foot struck Piter in the chest and sent him tumbling backward.

How could he do that? It didn't make any sense, and Piter looked just as baffled as Jenny felt.

And then she realized—the man she loved, the *mortal* she loved—was a Protector in disguise.

So much for keeping his Protector status a secret. But when it came down to catching his villain or maintaining his secret, there really was no contest. Especially not with Jenny held captive.

"You're not a mortal." Piter sneered as he picked himself up off the floor.

"You catch on fast," Starbuck snapped, avoiding another blow. He needed to hold on until backup arrived. He'd sent a message to Hale as he and Daphne had raced out of the UN. He only hoped Hale had received the message.

"Who are you?"

"Starbuck, level-five undercover agent. At your service."

"An agent," Piter said in a hiss as they circled each other. "I should have known."

"I'm rather glad you didn't. Makes things much more interesting, don't you think?" He laughed, hoping to taunt the other Protector into making a mistake.

"Things may be interesting, but I'll still win." Piter launched himself forward, and Starbuck caught him just in time to send them both tumbling backward, over and over, to the edge of the balcony. He heard Jenny gasp, but he didn't have time to reassure her. But maybe her reaction meant that even though she knew he was a Protector—that he lied to her—she still cared for him.

"I've heard of you," Piter said. "Not your identity, of course, but your reputation. You've got the ability to stop time. I suppose that little stunt at the party was *your* hand-iwork."

Starbuck glanced over at Jenny, who was listening, mes-merized, to their odd conversation. "I'll happily take credit for that."

"And mind-reading, too. Is that how you've snuggled up to little Jennifer? And why? Needed to find out if Mommy was spilling secrets? Figured it would be easier to get into her head once you were in her bed?"

"That's not true," Starbuck said, his words measured.

"Of course it's not." Piter laughed. He cast a glance over his shoulder toward Jenny. "We wouldn't want the little mortal to see the truth, now, would we?"

Energized by a burst of fury, Starbuck threw himself at his enemy. The trouble was, Piter was stronger. And fas-ter. Not only did Starbuck have a slightly less than the typical Protector physique, Piter's special gift was strength. Which put Starbuck at a significant disadvan-tage.

Apparently Piter knew it, too, because he spun around and headed for Jenny. She saw him coming, and her scream ripped through the air, as did Daphne's shriek for Piter to stay away.

Starbuck had no time to gather energy for temporal con-trol. He had only one chance, and he knew it. If Piter got hold of Jenny, it was all over. There was only one way to keep her safe, and Starbuck would have to time it per-fectly.

Knowing the risk, he raced forward, catching Piter around the waist just as his fingers were about to close around Jenny's arm. He kicked up, leaping to the top of the balcony ledge, the two of them teetering above the street.

"Don't do it." Piter gasped. "Neither one of us has a propulsion cloak."

"You should have thought of that before you kidnapped my girlfriend," Starbuck said in a snarl. At least he conveyed more bravado than he felt. The truth was, without a cloak they'd both go crashing to the ground below. Unless he used his time-stop just perfectly. And he had to pray Piter let him gather energy on the way down.

He couldn't risk Piter's getting loose any longer. With one final look at Jenny, he sent himself and Piter tumbling over the edge of the balcony and plummeting toward the ground. Faster and faster gravity pulled them down, and without their propulsion cloaks, both were almost as defenseless as mortals. Almost. Fifteen stories. They'd survive the fall, but it would hurt like Hades—if he didn't time this perfectly.

Closer and closer, the ground rose up to greet them, and Starbuck was beginning to fear he'd timed this badly when—*kerthwunk!*—they stopped in midair. Something tightened around Starbuck's waist even as he saw golden binder cuffs close around Piter's wrists. A shimmer in the air gave his friend away.

"About time," Starbuck muttered.

"Getting a little nervous?" Amusement laced Hale's voice.

"Not at all," he lied.

"Quite a risk you took there."

"I figured you'd show up." He grinned and gave a shaky laugh. "And if you didn't, I was working on Plan B: stopping time at the last second. Fortunately we'll never know if my timing was good or bad."

Hale laughed, then sighed. "I don't mean the risk on me. I mean the girl. She knows all your secrets now."

That she did. Starbuck ignored Piter's snarled curses, and hoped Jenny could love him anyway.

She had watched, terrified, as the man she loved—the man she didn't really know, it seemed—plummeted toward the ground. She had needed to touch him, needed to know that he was really safe, but by the time she and Daphne raced to the street, Starbuck and Piter were already gone, presumably to the Ops Center in Washington, D.C. There Piter would be booked and tried.

Now a day had passed, and Jenny had done little more than sit on her couch thinking while her mother wandered around burning casseroles and apologizing. Jenny loved Starbuck; so help her, she did. But was she ready for life with a Protector? Wasn't this everything she'd railed against?

"What are you going to do?" Daphne asked.

Jenny jumped a mile, then put a hand over her racing heart. "You startled me."

"Sorry." Her mother stirred something with a wire whisk. So far it smelled good. Too bad her very unculinary mom would soon destroy it. "I'm just wondering if you're still thinking."

"Of course I'm still thinking. What else have I got to do?"

"Well, you could quit thinking and start picking out wedding dresses. That boy loves you. And he's quite a catch."

Jenny rolled her eyes. "You only say that now that you know he's a Protector."

"Maybe. But it doesn't change the fact that he *is* a Protector. Or that he loves you." She paused, a gentle smile on her lips. "And you love him."

Tears welled in Jenny's eyes as she pressed her lips together. "I *do* love him." But she wasn't sure that was enough. He was a Protector, true, and she'd sworn to herself she'd never date a Protector. But Starbuck was . . . different. Or maybe he wasn't different after all, but she just loved him and so it didn't matter. And maybe she'd been a little too rigid anyway. The truth was, she hadn't fallen in love with a Protector or a mortal. She'd fallen in love with Starbuck, plain and simple.

But even if she was willing to date—even marry—a Protector, one little problem still remained. "He lied to me, Mom. He lied, and he kept secrets."

"Well, he lied to me, too, but you don't see me holding it against him."

"He read my mind."

"Maybe. Maybe he read mine, too. And he thought I was a spy. I'm not holding that against him."

"It's not the same, Mom."

"Isn't it? He was doing his job, Jenny. Don't punish the boy for doing what he had too."

Jenny sighed, giving in to the fury of emotions raging inside her. "I do understand. And I do love him. When he and Piter went over that ledge, I thought—" Her voice hitched and she drew a shaky breath. "It doesn't matter. He's alive, and so help me, despite everything I love him with all my heart and soul."

"I'm glad to hear that." *His* voice came out of nowhere. *Starbuck!*

Joy overwhelmed her. She whipped around to see him standing in the doorway. She raced into his arms, and he caught her around the waist and spun her, then planted kisses on her forehead, ears, and lips.

Behind them, she heard her mother slip out of the room and clatter around in the kitchen.

"Starbuck," she murmured, snuggling close.

"Miss me?"

"Yes." She tilted her head back. "Yes, I did. I really, really did."

A tiny smile touched the corner of his mouth. "Good. I missed you, too." He cleared his throat. "I suppose now's the time to officially tell you that I'm a Protector."

"Really?" She feigned disbelief. "Well, what do you know about that?"

"And I can stop time."

"Some people have all the luck."

"And I can read minds," he said.

"A handy trick."

"It can be."

She cocked her head and looked him in the eye. "Find anything particularly interesting in *my* mind?"

He looked a bit sheepish. "I'm sure I would if I'd poked around enough, but I promise you I didn't. I was only looking for information on your mother. Very focused. I promise."

She could hear the concern in his voice, and she lifted herself up on tiptoe to press a gentle kiss to his lips. "I believe you. You were on a job." She shrugged and sighed. "I understand. Really I do."

He stroked her hair. "And?"

"And I love you." She grinned. "You can even read my mind if you don't believe me. I was being a bit too rigid about all that Protector-mortal stuff."

His arms closed around her, obviously relieved. "I believe you."

She pulled away just slightly and cast a glance toward

the kitchen to make sure her mother wasn't listening. "I do have a little question about"—she lowered her voice—"the times we made love. You seem to know—"

"What you want?"

"Well, yeah."

"I don't suppose you'd believe that I'm incredibly intuitive?"

"Are you?"

"I wish." He stroked her cheek with the side of his thumb and smiled. "But I wasn't reading your mind, either. At least not on purpose. Your thoughts just surrounded me. There was a connection between us, a connection I never want to break." He met her eyes. "Nothing like that's ever happened to me before."

"No?" She grinned. "Nothing like that had better happen to you again. At least, not unless I'm around to share it."

"That's a promise I'm happy to make." He cocked an eyebrow. "But you're sure it's me you want? I mean, you might have a hundred offers from other Protectors."

She frowned, not sure what he meant.

"The ad. Your mom's ad. Remember?"

She laughed. "I never even checked my mailbox. And I never intend to." She held out her arms to him, happier than she could ever remember being. "Come here, Starbuck," she murmured, drawing him close. "My very own Protector."

And as they kissed, Jenny heard her mom's voice drift in from the kitchen.

"What did I tell you? Mother *always* knows best."

Don't miss these other books in the Protector saga:
Aphrodite's Kiss (April 2001)
Aphrodite's Passion (April 2002)

Tomorrow
The Day Her Heart Stood Still
by SUSAN GRANT

In memory of my courageous coworkers,
the crewmembers of United Airlines flights 93 and 175,
killed in the tragic events of September 11, 2001,
a day when all our hearts stood still.

Chapter One

The headlights on Air Force Major Andie Del Sarto's Corvette pierced the darkness smothering the road. On the last leg of a three-and-a-half-day-long car trip from Florida to her parents' dozen acres of ranch land near Roswell, New Mexico, a cell phone pressed to her ear, she listened to an answering machine play her tarot-card-reading, UFO-chasing mother's eternally perky voice: "Greetings! You've hailed Extraterrestrials-R-Us, the planet's most complete UFO museum. If you've reached this recording during normal business hours, I'm either investigating the latest sighting or helping another Earthling. . . ."

Andie squeezed the steering wheel with her left hand and quashed an accustomed flicker of impatience. Why she'd come home when she most needed her mental focus, she had no idea. She could have been in the Bahamas by now, enjoying the first week of a desperately needed month of leave before NASA announced her selection as one of six astronauts on the first manned—well, technically, one-third "womanned"—mission to Mars. Or, better yet, she could have stayed home in her cozy beachside condo, sleeping in and eating out. But rather than doing what she ought to do—acting sensibly, logically, rationally: in other words, not like her Mom—she'd followed a strange urge to come home, drawn inexorably to her birthplace like a salmon swimming upstream to spawn.

Spawn, she thought wryly. *I don't think so.* Lately she'd barely had time to brush her hair, let alone have sex.

"If you'd like to leave a message, you may do so after the beep. Thanks for calling Extraterrestrials-R-Us—where anything is possible!"

Andie forced a smile, as if it would somehow transmit along with her voice. "Hey, Mom, Dad. It's me. I made pretty good time." She was half a day early, in fact. Assessing the landmarks along the highway, she finished, "I'll see you in ten minutes."

Nine minutes and forty-five seconds later she swung her convertible into the driveway, parking in one of the slots fronting the building that was her mother's pride and joy: EXTRATERRESTRIALS-R-US: LEAVE YOUR SKEPTICISM AT THE DOOR, proclaimed a sign above the entry. When Andie was five, she'd helped her mother paint sparkly stars and flying saucers onto the museum's corrugated metal walls. The art had been retouched several times in the twenty-nine years since, but Andie's childlike hand was still evident. The sweet warmth of those memories filled her. She loved her mother.

She just didn't want to be like her.

Andie turned off the engine and the headlights, and the cool darkness of the countryside swallowed her. The glow of Roswell was visible to the east, a city that at first glance looked like any other New Mexico town. But for the past sixty years, the subject of aliens in these parts was as likely to come up in conversation as the weather. In July of 1947, a remnant of a balloon flight launched as part of a top-secret program called PROJECT: MOGUL crash-landed on a farmer's property. Many, like Andie's mother, still insisted that the balloon was in fact a spaceship, and the Air Force's story a cover-up. Andie was used to hearing the allegations; she'd grown up here. But like most of her high school graduating class who'd gone on to college, she'd never returned, aside from visiting her parents for a few weeks at Christmastime.

It was May, the week before Mother's Day. Christmas was seven months off so what on earth was Andie doing here?

She indulged in a long and weary exhalation; then she got out of the car and grabbed her belongings from its trunk. With a suitcase and a mesh bag of Florida grapefruit in her hands, she walked past the museum, toward the house. Halfway there, she felt eyes upon her.

She peered into the front yard. A veritable army of three-foot-high, green plastic creatures stared back at her.

Alien lawn ornaments. Of course. Ordinary flamingos would have been too much to hope for.

She could almost hear the bone-crunching sound of her life dismantling, the nicely compartmentalized existence that kept the weird and wacky way she'd grown up separate from her life as Major Del Sarto, highly decorated fighter pilot and astronaut. In twenty-seven days, NASA would reveal the names of those chosen for the Mars mission. The secrecy up until then was a publicity stunt, meant to revive flagging public interest in the space program, and the agency had spent months building the excitement. Not even the astronauts' families knew who would be on the mission and who would be alternates.

Andie's beaded sandals felt as though they were made of lead. As soon as NASA announced its news, press from all over the country and the world would be eager to find out more about her and her comrades. America's newest heroes, they'd be.

MARS-MISSION PILOT'S MOTHER RUNS A UFO MUSEUM!

Andie grimaced, imagining the story printed about her. It read like a headline in the *National Enquirer*. Heck, It probably *would* be a headline in the *National Enquirer*.

As much as she disliked the thought of reliving the embarrassment of her school years—that horrible shame and fear she'd felt peak when she was a self-conscious teenager—she felt a sudden and unexpected surge of protectiveness for her mother. The media would not be kind to her.

"Andromeda!"

Andie fought an instinctive cringe at the use of her given name that no one but her parents used—or even knew. The garage light flicked on, illuminating the gold 1972 Cadillac parked inside. Dressed in an oversize T-shirt above baby blue leggings, Cassiopeia Del Sarto hurried out of the house, her arms open wide. Unlike Andie, Cassie was buxom. But as she'd aged, her legs had grown thinner, making her appear even more top-heavy.

Andie set her suitcase and the sack of grapefruit on the ground, then submitted to her mother's lung-crushing embrace and all the clutching, sighs, and squeezes that followed.

Her mother grabbed hold of her hands and drew back to look at her. "I was loading the car when you called," she explained, squeezing Andie's fingers. "It's Tuesday, meeting night. Everyone would love to see you. Why don't you come?"

And spend the evening fielding questions from a bunch of eccentric, sixty-plus locals who scour the countryside searching for alien invaders? No, thanks. "I'm tired, Mom," Andie said truthfully. "Maybe next week."

"It's a date. Are you hungry? I made lasagna."

"Sure. Has Dad eaten?"

Cassie tucked a few curly, hennaed strands behind her ears and sighed. "He's working."

A pediatrician by day, Andie's father spent his evenings donating his expertise to migrant farmworkers and anyone else who couldn't afford medical care. She wouldn't hesitate to admit that he was a bit of a workaholic, but otherwise he was blessedly normal.

Her mother went on: "He needs to cut back on his hours. I'm working on him, and he's promised to try." Concern in her eyes, she smoothed her hand over Andie's sleek black bob. Her gaze was tender but probing. So easily, her mother saw past the face Andie showed the world. "You and Frank. So alike you are. You love your life's work, but too often you let it suck you dry." In a whisper she added, "But at least he has me."

Andie glanced up sharply. In all the years with her parents, she'd never heard her mother suggest that her father *needed* her—Andie had always assumed that it was the other way around. Nor had Andie ever thought about it much. Now that she did, it was clear that her father had survived all these years, able to keep up his demanding schedule, because of the emotional sustenance Cassie gave him, no matter how mismatched they appeared to outside observers.

Her mother touched fingers to Andie's chin. "My sweet,

hardworking girl," she said with a rueful sigh. "Who do *you* have, baby?"

"I'm fine, Mom," Andie assured her automatically. And then she lowered her eyes so her mother wouldn't glimpse the truth.

Cassie Del Sarto gave a skeptical yet compassionate grunt. How the woman managed to turn unintelligible noises into such complex, emotion-filled statements, Andie had no idea. Pretending she hadn't heard a thing, she hoisted her bag of grapefruit off the cement. "I'll put these in the kitchen."

"We'll have them with breakfast." Cassie grabbed her daughter in a tight embrace. "For you, there's ice cream in the freezer. Fudge brownie." She kissed Andie hard on the cheek and walked to her car.

Casting a long and solitary shadow from the light in the garage, Andie remained in place until her mother's Cadillac's taillights disappeared down the long driveway leading off of their property. *At least he has me*, her mother's words reverberated in her mind. *Who do you have, baby?* Her jaw tight, Andie grabbed her suitcase and climbed the porch stairs.

Inside the quiet house, the foyer smelled faintly like fried garlic, tomato sauce, and freshly mopped floors. She set her suitcase and the grapefruit by a twisted ribbon of charred metal. The piece of wreckage dated back to the fifties, and she was sure it had fallen off an old tractor, but her mother insisted it was part of an alien spaceship.

The screen door slammed behind her, and Spock, the family parakeet, began chirping. Andie peeked under the cloth covering the bird's cage and wriggled her finger between the bars. "Hey, handsome boy." Spock's green head bobbed up and down as he sidestepped from one end of his perch to the other.

A Post-it stuck to the refrigerator announced where her father might find his dinner for reheating but Andie's thoughts turned toward the fudge brownie ice cream. She took the pint-sized container from the overstocked freezer, found a spoon, and pushed past a pair of narrow, decades-old French doors that opened onto the patio in the backyard. The porch light was out. Quietly she ate the ice cream, alone and in the dark. Creamy chocolate slid down her throat. She licked the spoon clean and scooped up more.

The sky was gorgeous, glowing with the light of thousands of stars. To Andie, the longing to explore those stars was so powerful, so fundamental, that it was as vital to her survival as the blood in her veins. She'd wanted to be an astronaut for as long as she could remember. As a small child, she'd lain on her back for hours in the rear seat of her mother's old convertible, dreaming of discovering new worlds, while Cassie searched the night sky for "flying disks." In her head, Andie had constructed an entire future, complete with an explorer husband and a band of spacefaring kids. Their ship would be the *Mayflower* of the stars.

Andie chuckled at the memory. Everything seemed possible then.

When did you stop thinking that way?

Her smile faded. Her selection as a pilot-astronaut on the Mars mission was the crowning achievement of her life, everything she'd set her sights on for as long as she could remember. But for some reason it wasn't enough. Why wasn't she satisfied?

Who do you have, baby?

She pressed her lips together. Her loneliness was something she didn't like to acknowledge—not to herself, and certainly not to anyone else. She was strong, independent. Women like her weren't supposed to feel like . . . like . . .
This.

Andie tipped her head back and stared at the stars. She'd always studied them scientifically. Others, like her mother, wished on them. But what did one wish for when one had everything?

Someone to share it with.

Her insides clenched with a stab of yearning. If only wishes came true. . . .

Cringing, she glanced sheepishly behind her. She'd been home for all of twenty minutes, and already her mother's screwball behavior had rubbed off. On the other hand, there was something indefinably optimistic and lighthearted about the simple act of wishing. What would be the harm in it?

To keep from analyzing the deed any further, she took a steadying breath and looked for a suitable star. It took three tries to find one she didn't recognize. Then she formed the appropriate words: "Star light . . . star bright . . . first star I see tonight . . ."

She stopped herself. *Pretty pitiful,* she thought, *wishing for a man.* Sure, her demanding work schedule made dating difficult, but she wasn't about to trade her career for a social life. On the other hand, even when she *had* been able to date with the frequency necessary to develop a relationship, of all the men she'd been with—even the few who hadn't been intimidated by her accomplishments—she'd been able to take or leave every one. And so she had always left them. Eventually.

She was no social novice; she understood that a lot of

quarters had to go into the slot machine before you hit the jackpot. But the closer she got to her mid-thirties, the more she began to doubt she'd ever find that elusive, much-hyped, and probably over-rated "Mr. Right."

Who do you have, baby?

Steadying herself, she concentrated on her wish until every pore in her body chorused her secret longing: a love to fill her soul. Her spine tingled and goose bumps tiptoed up her bare arms as she imagined a lover who was her best friend, a man who didn't fear her intelligence or her strength, who'd stay by her side until they were old and gray and then some. A guy who could make her toes curl with a single look.

It was a lot to ask, yes, but as long she was wishing, she might as well go all-out.

"Star light . . . star bright, first star I see tonight. I wish I may, I wish I might, have the wish I wish tonight."

With all her heart, she focused on the anonymous fleck of light she'd chosen, focusing so hard that it made her temples throb.

Find me.

A wave of dizziness unsteadied her, and the star shimmered like a hot coal in a gust of air. Then it twitched, sailing across the sky as if it had broken free of a cosmic hook in the heavens.

Andie gave a gasp of surprise and disappointment that would have rivaled any of her mother's grunts or sighs. Over three thousand man-made satellites orbited the Earth; it looked as if she'd just wasted her wish on one.

Which meant, she supposed, that the answer to her wish was no.

Consoling herself with another heaping spoonful of chocolate ice cream, she trudged back to the house. At the back door, she stopped to take one last disgusted look at the stars. The pinprick of light gliding across the sky was accelerating.

Of the thousands of satellites in orbit, a good third were no longer in use, destined to burn up in the atmosphere. This must be one of them. Or possibly a meteorite. But instead of disintegrating like a typical falling star, the object brightened, gaining speed at an incredible rate.

Her heart sped up. *My God.* The part of her that had watched too many science-fiction movies screamed, "Killer asteroid!"

Instantly she quashed such silliness. Anything so large would have been tracked by the military. They'd have issued a warning hours ago, if not days or even weeks. The object was simply a larger-than-normal meteorite or hunk of space debris.

Eyes narrowed, she watched the growing ball of fire light up the neighboring ranches until its blaze disappeared behind the brush that sprawled for miles behind her parents' property. Darkness flooded back, and the crickets and frogs went silent.

Andie braced herself for the earsplitting roar that followed something hitting the ground with such immense force. She'd witnessed an airplane accident once; she knew what crashes sounded like. Instead, all she heard was the frogs and crickets as they resumed their singing. Whatever had entered the atmosphere in the sky over Roswell must have vaporized before it hit. There was no other explanation.

A thick, cold droplet of ice cream dribbled onto the big toe of her left foot. She'd forgotten about the utensil she held in her hand. Blinking, she licked the spoon clean and headed for the living room.

The Day Her Heart Stood Still

The purple-and-gold plaid couch in the living room was new, and it looked inviting. Sinking deep into the cushions, she kicked off her sandals and called the fire department to pass along what she'd seen. It was early in the season, but grass fires were always a danger.

The woman who answered sounded as if she'd already fielded a hundred such calls. "Thanks, we know about it."

There. She'd done her citizen's duty. Andie exchanged the phone for the television remote. She turned on the TV and tried not to think too hard about the coincidence of the star she'd wished on turning out to be a meteorite. Feet tucked underneath her, she stared at the unrecognizable series on the TV screen and smiled. Yes, this was exactly the kind of mindless activity she'd come home to find.

Long after she'd scraped the last of the ice cream off the bottom of the container, the sound of gravel popping in the driveway jarred her out of a sitcom-induced stupor. It was the Cadillac, not her father's Volvo station wagon.

"Andromeda!" Her mother appeared outside the screen door. The woman's face was glowing with excitement, and her bun was coming undone. "Andromeda! Come see what I found."

"Mom, it was a meteorite. Not a UFO."

Cassie ignored her. "Frank? Is he home yet?"

Andie shook her head.

"Well, you're a strong girl," she reasoned breathlessly. "Oh, Andie, darling, wait till you see."

With as much enthusiasm as a prisoner being led to the guillotine by a nearsighted executioner, Andie trailed her mother to the car. Cassie unlocked the trunk, and it flew open.

Susan Grant

An old quilt covered her mother's latest booty. Andie leaned forward and sniffed. The lumpy blanket gave off an acrid odor, as if what was hidden beneath had been in contact with overheated electrical equipment. There was something else, too, another scent, warm and exotic.

"Here," Cassie said. "Help me lift him."

"Him?" That was when Andie noticed her mother's scraped knuckles and dirty fingernails. "Mom, what's in there? What did you do?"

"Come on, baby. I need your help. He's out cold."

"Who is?" She swallowed against a dry throat. "What is?"

"The alien in my trunk."

Chapter Two

Andie stared at her. "Did you say . . . alien?"

Cassie grabbed a corner of the quilt and pulled. "Ta-da!"

Andie's eyes shifted from her mother's face to the trunk. The first thing she saw was a hand—with five very human fingers, she thought with relief. Strong, masculine fingers, with clean, trimmed nails . . .

Andie gave her head a shake. She was supposed to be checking his pulse, not staring at his hands, nice as they were. Pressing two fingers under his jaw, she noted the seconds on her wristwatch, studying the man as she counted out heartbeats. The old Cadillac didn't have a trunk light, and the darkness made it difficult to see. She knew he was clean-shaven, though—only the barest hint of a beard pricked the pads of her fingers—and his skin was warm and smooth.

Ten beats per fifteen seconds, she counted. Forty beats

per minute. "His heartbeat's slow . . . really slow. But strong." His respiration was equally unhurried. If anything, the man was drunk and not injured.

Cassie wrung her hands. "I helped him walk from his ship to the car, but he hasn't moved or talked since he lay down in the trunk. No matter how hard he wanted to stay awake, he couldn't. Oh, Andie. I hope he's okay. Nothing seems to be broken or bleeding. Maybe it's our atmosphere. I don't know. I'm no expert in exophysiology."

Exophysiology: the theoretical study of extraterrestrial physiology. *Right.* Andie worked hard to keep the conversation based in reality. "Was he in a car accident?"

"No, I was driving the back road, and—"

"You ran him over?"

Cassie looked outraged. "I did no such thing."

"Then how did he get hurt?"

"Why, in the crash. You saw it, didn't you?"

"I saw what I suspect was a meteorite." Though her mother had a point; the flaming object might have been an aircraft. A plane crash would explain her mother's use of the word *ship*, and how this unconscious clean-cut man had ended up in the wilderness by himself late at night. But if that was the case, where were the burns and bruises she'd expect to see on a survivor of such a fiery accident? "Did you actually see the plane crash, Mom?"

"It was a spaceship, honey."

Andie ground her teeth. "Where's the wreckage?"

"Oh, there wasn't any. The ship had a few dents and dings, that's all. Hard to believe, considering how hard it came down. It's advanced technology, Andromeda." Her mother's voice was hushed. "Very advanced. Not only is the ship almost indestructible, but you'd walk right past it if you didn't already know it was there. It has some sort of—I don't know what to call it—a disguise?"

Andie forced a shrug. Playing the game would only encourage her mother.

Cassie looked down at her scraped knuckles and torn fingernails. "I covered the furrows as best I could. The rest is up to us." She squared her shoulders. "Let's get him inside. Heave-ho!"

"Mom, we're not bringing him into the house. We don't know who he is. He could be a drifter . . . or a serial killer." Her thoughts turned to the rifle locked in the gun rack. She was an expert marksman and not too shabby with a knife, either. Of course, what good were those skills if the weapons were locked in the gun cabinet in the living room? "There's a bed in the museum, right?"

"In the spare room, yes."

"Okay, let's carry him there. Then I'll call an ambulance."

Cassie clutched her favorite cardigan to her chest. "No ambulance."

"*Yes*, ambulance. And then we're calling the police."

"No." Her mother's eyes filled with tears. "They'll do tests on him. He'll end up preserved in a row of test tubes like the aliens who crashed in 'forty-seven."

Andie groaned. Her mother believed so fervently that the rumors of a spaceship crashing in 'forty-seven were true, and that the government had covered up the evidence. But a debate over who was right and who was wrong, using almost seventy-year-old hearsay as ammunition, was the last thing Andie was in the mood for. She'd come home to disappear for a while before the impending media frenzy stole away the last shreds of her private life, not to deal with some poor man her mother had labeled an alien and brought home in the trunk of her car.

"Promise me you'll not tell a soul," Cassie beseeched her. "No one knows he's here but us."

"Okay, okay," Andie said tiredly in hopes of temporarily placating her mother awhile longer.

Cassie slipped careful hands under the man's shoulders as Andie grabbed hold of his legs. He wore a black shirt and pants, matching knee-high, socklike boots, and a pale gray skullcap that hid his hair. He didn't look to be in pain or shock. In fact, he appeared to be sleeping, as her mother thought, although his expression was more sad than serene. At that, her heart gave a little twist.

"God—he's heavy," Andie huffed as they hoisted him up and over the lip of the trunk.

Cassie staggered backward.

"Watch it, Mom, or you'll"—the man's upper body slid to the ground—"drop him," she finished flatly. His head landed on the dirt with a muffled thump, leaving Andie standing there, holding a strange guy by the ankles in a dark driveway at eleven o'clock at night. "Way to go. If he doesn't have permanent brain damage, he'll probably sue you for dropping him on his head."

Her mother bit her lip.

Andie struggled to keep from losing her temper. If NASA suspected even a speck of scandal before they announced the names of the six Mars astronauts at the end of the month, they'd quickly and quietly replace her with one of the eager runners-up waiting in the wings. She'd lose her one chance at her life's dream, participating in humanity's greatest endeavor since reaching the moon, all because her mother had decided to abduct a hapless accident victim and turn him into one of her alien fantasies.

Andie exhaled. "Let's switch places." She wrapped her arms around the man's chest and lifted. His muscles had the solid, firm feel of someone who worked out.

His clothes caught her attention in a different way. The black fabric had a pearly sheen to it and felt like her mother's quilted oven mitts. The material was warm in places, cooler in others, as if it were adjusting to the man's body temperature.

She squeezed her eyes shut. *It's not a space suit, it's not a space suit*, she chanted to herself, as if words could inoculate her against her mother's crazy ideas, which Andie hoped weren't communicable like typhoid or the flu.

"What did you say?" Cassie asked, breathless.

"Ah . . . the door. It's not open," she improvised as she stopped in front of the museum's front entrance.

Her mother lowered the man's feet and stiffly reached into her waist pouch. For a moment, the jingling of keys blotted out Cassie's labored breathing.

Once inside, Andie called upon her gym-honed strength and triathlete's endurance to drag the man's tall frame, solo, the rest of the way into a spare bedroom separated from the museum proper by another door. The man's legs swished over the linoleum floor as she pulled him past a cash register, a display case of wide-eyed plastic E.T.s with $14.95 price tags hanging from three-fingered hands, boxes of Reese's Pieces, and green sippy cups emblazoned with the phrase, *Abduct an alien in Roswell, NM*. Andie could only imagine what the man would think if he woke now.

With Cassie's help, she got him on the mattress, nearly falling atop him when his weight settled. Winded, she pushed away, gazing down at him. Now that she could study him in the light, his broad, high cheekbones and rugged features brought to mind Anatoly Butin, the Russian cosmonaut she'd trained with in Siberia, a blond god of a man who'd grown up riding bareback on the steppes of central Asia. But she'd never reacted to Butin with the pulse-pounding awareness she felt now as she watched the exotic stranger sleep.

"A hunk, isn't he?"

Andie swallowed, finding it hard to pull her attention from the man. "Not bad." She avoided meeting her mother's mischievous eyes. "I'll call the ambulance now."

"Oh, baby, no. We can't tell anyone. Promise me. We're his only hope of survival."

Headlights flashed outside the curtained window. "Good. It's Dad. He's the expert; I'll go with whatever he says." She couldn't imagine her father not sending the man to the hospital.

Frank Del Sarto appeared in the doorway, a bemused smile on his face. His silver-and-black hair flopped over his forehead as he set his medical bag on the floor.

"Hey, Dad." Andie walked into his embrace.

He gave her a tight squeeze then peered over her shoulder, seemingly pleased with what he saw on the bed. "Ah! Why didn't you tell us you were bringing someone home with you?"

"I wasn't. I mean, I didn't." She shoved her hands through her hair. "Mom brought him here."

He raised a brow at his wife.

Cassie said under her breath, "His spaceship crashed, and he might be hurt."

"Hmm," he said.

Only in the Del Sarto household would this conversation take place, Andie thought. "I wanted to call an ambulance, but Mom's afraid they'll whisk him away to Area fifty-one. He's out cold, obviously. He might be bleeding internally. Or have a head injury."

Cassie confessed, "I dropped him."

"He was already unconscious, though," Andie pointed out.

"Hmm," her father mumbled again. "For how long, do you think?"

"Oh, Frank. Close to an hour." Cassie wrung her scratched hands. "He slept in the trunk while I covered the furrows."

"Furrows . . . ?" he said blankly.

"That the spaceship made," she explained.

The discussion begged for redirection. Andie held up her hands. "Dad, I promised Mom I'd go with what you said. If you think he needs to go to the hospital"—she shot her mother a challenging stare—"then we'll bring him."

He rolled up his sleeves. "Let me have a look." Unperturbed—he'd lived with this craziness for forty years—he removed a stethoscope and a blood-pressure cuff from his medical bag. Then he sat on the edge of the bed and smoothed his hands over the man's chest. "Help me, Andie."

Andie saw the problem. The shirt had no buttons, zippers, or recognizable fasteners. She knelt on the other side of the bed and searched, running her hands over the man's chest and down to his lower abs. The man's stomach muscles contracted, and he groaned softly. Andie froze. Then she steadied herself, saying, "I'd swear he reacted to that touch." She had reacted, too.

"Keep stroking him," Cassie suggested.

Andie gave her mother a long look. Then she traced her fingertip along a seam running from waist to neck. It opened magically under the pressure of her finger. "That was weird."

Her father paused in his task. "What was?"

"His shirt. The seam opened by itself. Like a Ziploc bag, only better." She spread apart the man's shirt. Underneath, he wore a dove gray undershirt of the same soft, plush material as his sock-boots. It reminded her of long underwear. Not the kind of clothing one wore in mid-May—in this area, at least. She began to have doubts that he'd been in the area long, unless he'd come down from the mountains. "He could be running drugs," she whispered. "And sampled some of his own wares."

Her father frowned as he prepared to aim his penlight into the stranger's eyes. "Could be. He certainly isn't showing signs of trauma." He jerked up the man's left sleeve and fastened the blood-pressure cuff around his arm.

"I'll check for weapons, just in case." Andie patted him down. Nothing. Then she got to his right forearm. "Wait. There's something under his sleeve." It was rectangular with a bumpy surface. She pushed the sleeve higher. "Whoa. Look at this."

Her mother stepped closer. "What is it?"

"I think it's a computer." It looked like a very expensive piece of tech, too. It was flat and fit like a gauntlet on his arm. Riddled with optic fibers and minuscule blinking lights, it was labeled with letters in a language she didn't recognize.

Oh, brother. This was not going to help in convincing her mother that the guy wasn't from outer space.

Gingerly, she touched her fingertip to a raised ring in the center of the gauntlet. There was a beep, almost below the range of her hearing, and out popped an inch-high, three-dimensional figure.

Andie jerked backward. Her father gasped, and her

mother gave a muffled cry. Then it got very quiet as they gaped at the tiny silver man gesticulating on the gauntlet's raised circle.

This was nuts, Andie thought. She had to extract herself from the situation. Immediately. But her mounting curiosity commanded otherwise.

She rose off her haunches and leaned forward. The figure was fluid and featureless, as if it were made of liquid mercury. "Amazing," she said under her breath. At the sound of her voice, the tiny figure stopped moving, as if awaiting orders. If she took the Paper-Clip Guy—that annoying animated Office Assistant on old versions of Microsoft Word—and combined it with advanced three-dimensional holographic technology, this little silver man would be the result.

"Hello," Andie said.

"Hello," it replied in a tiny, metallic voice.

She smiled. "What are you?"

But it only repeated her words. She studied the gauntlet computer. That was when she noticed that the edges of the incredible device disappeared into the man's skin, from where information was routed God knew where. Embedded biotech. It would be decades, maybe another century, before anyone perfected such technology . . . on Earth.

The oddest sensation swept through her—part fear and part fascination. What if this really was a space voyager, a galactic traveler who glimpsed daily the distant wonders that were the stuff of her dreams?

Almost reverently, she placed her hand over the man's warm cheek. "Who are you?" she whispered. "Where are you from?" *Please tell me you're a software rep from San Jose.*

Susan Grant

A muscle in his jaw jumped; she felt it tap her palm. Then his eye lids opened, and Andie's toes curled as he focused on her with irises as bewitching and liquid-silver as the little man he wore on his arm.

Chapter Three

The confusion in the stranger's unwavering gaze slipped into curiosity. Slowly that curiosity intensified into fascination. Andie couldn't pull her eyes from him, either, though she almost blushed at his obvious bedazzlement. He was more than just good-looking. There was something indefinably compelling about him. Now that she was the target of his attention, she felt the full impact of that breathtaking magnetism.

Abruptly her father's head and shoulder blocked her view of the man's face. As he pointed his penlight into the stranger's pupils, one at a time, she exhaled sharply, thankful for a chance to gather her wits. This was insane; she couldn't involve herself. She was slipping—slipping into the quicksand that was the wild, wacky world of her mother.

Yeah, but this man made your toes curl with a single look.

That was what she'd wished for, wasn't it? Maybe he

was from space, and the sheer intensity of her plea had ripped his ship off its flight path, yanking the craft and its unwilling rider down through Earth's atmosphere and into her waiting arms.

She made a choking noise. Delusions. What came after that? Voices in her head? As if it mattered. Psychopathic episodes and harboring aliens would all weigh equally in getting her booted off the Mars mission.

Her father finished his initial examination and leaned toward her. "Take a close look at that device on his arm," he said under his breath.

"I did. It's implanted in his skin."

"Yes. Man combined with machine. Fascinating."

In his face she saw what she most dreaded. Her father's dark brown eyes sparkled, reminding her of how he looked in the photographs taken of him when he was an idealistic young resident. "You believe Mom," she said.

She waited for him to deny it, but he didn't. He'd always been Andie's ally, her partner in reason. Reflexively, she clutched her stomach. Would she be her mother's next victim?

As her father turned back to his patient, Andie fought the sensation of trying to struggle free of quicksand.

"May I remove your hat?" her father asked the stranger in a gentle voice perfected by years of reassuring five-year-olds fearful of needles and wooden tongue depressors. "I need to check for injuries." He reached for the tight cap covering the man's scalp.

One muscular arm shot up. With fighter-pilot reflexes, Andie blocked the man's hand, keeping him from harming her father if that was what he intended. Cassie cried out, and Frank lunged to protect Andie.

It was as if the four were all trapped in a freeze-frame

action scene; no one moved and no one spoke. The fear in the room was palpable.

The stranger broke the silence with a sound of dismayed apology. The little figure standing on his wrist fell to its knees, tiny hands held over its head. Its owner rolled his eyes and slapped his hand over the computer. In an instant, Mr. Mercury was gone.

Clearly worried about startling them again, the stranger slowly and carefully raised one arm and peeled off his cap, revealing an inner lining of sensors and wires—and a head of layered, dark pewter–colored hair. Andie had the sinking feeling that the striking shade was what he'd been born with, not one he'd aged into. Her hopes that he might be a computer salesman fizzled.

The stranger winced as her father examined his skull. "You've got quite a knot there," Frank Del Sarto said as he explored an area behind his head.

"He does? Oh, my." Cassie wrung her hands guiltily. "I'll get an ice pack." She perked up. "And food. Do you think he's hungry?" She hurried to the bedside and bent forward, her hands spread on her powder blue leggings. Both knees were muddy; one was torn. The huge crystal she wore on a pendant swung over her breasts. "Can I make you something to eat?" She rubbed her stomach with exaggerated motions. "Lah-zah-nyah?"

The stranger stared at her, his expression growing warmer.

Andie wanted to howl. This could very well be the end of the world as they knew it, and her mother was offering reheated leftovers. It didn't help that her father appeared to be enjoying this as a diversion from the daily grind of screaming infants and poverty-stricken migrant workers.

Only in the Del Sarto household. Any normal family

would have fled, screaming. Again, her fingers went to her temples.

Sighing, Cassie straightened. "He doesn't understand me."

The comment spurred Andie into doing something that made sense. She tried to communicate with the man. "We want to help you," she said slowly and distinctly.

Their eyes met, and her heart did a little flip. His silvery gaze intensified so swiftly that it felt as though all the air had left the room, forcing her to press her sandals onto the linoleum floor to make sure her toes didn't curl. "You've been in an accident," she told him. "This man is a doctor, and he wants to see if you're hurt."

He watched her speak, his mouth gently twisting. The fingers of his right hand twitched as if he wanted to reach for her. Failing that, he made a hoarse and drowsy attempt at speech.

The words were unintelligible. She tried Russian, then Spanish: the other languages in which she was fluent.

He shut his eyes briefly and answered with a sound of frustration. She lifted both hands and shook her head. The apology in his gaze, though, was easy to understand. Clearly exhausted by their abortive attempts to converse, he settled his head back on the pillow and closed his eyes.

She fought the almost irresistible urge to smooth his hair off his forehead. "I think he passed out again."

"He's sleeping," her father corrected.

"Oh, my!" Cassie whirled away from them. "I forgot to call the UFO group. They'll think I've forgotten them."

"You did, Cassie," her husband said drolly.

She giggled. "Wouldn't they love to know why, too? And, no, I'm not going to tell them!"

Again, Andie felt as if she were the sole voice of reason.

"Mom, when you come back, bring the rifle."

Cassie's mouth tightened. "Why?"

"For protection." Andie studied the stranger, who now looked vulnerable with his eyes shut. "Ours *and* his."

When her mother left, Andie said to her father, "I saw a meteorite earlier. Mom thinks it was this man's spacecraft." She checked her watch. "The local news ended forty minutes ago. We won't know until morning what the spin is on the incident." *Or whether the National Guard is out combing the countryside for alien invaders,* she left unsaid. Returning her attention to the man in the bed, she saw that his breathing had slowed further, but he didn't appear to be in pain. "He can't stay awake."

"My impression is that he's sedated. His heart rate and respiration are depressed." Wearily, Frank loosened his tie and undid the top two buttons of his chambray shirt. "But without lab work, I don't know what he's on."

"We're bringing him to the hospital, then?"

"No," he said firmly. At her expression of dismay, he exhaled. "Andromeda, admit it. Does he look like any man you've ever seem before?"

"Ah, no."

"And consider his arm . . . that device. Where have you seen such a thing before, aside from science-fiction novels? If we take him to the hospital, we might be placing him in danger. And us, too."

"How's that?"

"The reason no one knows what happened in 'forty-seven is because people talked about what they found. Because of that, they caught the attention of certain elements of the government—dare I say obsessed and fearful elements?—who then stepped in and put the clamp on the story. It was their own fault, Andie, those people who recovered that UFO. In their excitement, they drew the authorities to them and to what they found. We won't."

"We won't what, exactly?"

"We won't say anything to anyone. It'll only attract potentially hostile parties to this house. I will not bring that risk to you, your mother, or him." His gaze drifted to the sleeping man with his pewter hair and quilted black clothes. "This time we're doing it right."

"I don't believe this. I thought only Mom talked about this . . . this *garbage*." Andie's mother was the one who'd made her school years a mire of embarrassment. *She* was the one who'd made it impossible for Andie to invite friends home. *She* was why Andie had asked her high school dates to meet her anywhere but at the house. Not her father. "You don't believe in UFOs," Andie implored helplessly.

"I believe in what I see, Andie. And I think you do, too."

"If he's an accident victim and we keep him in a private home when he should be in the hospital, he could die. Or, if he lives, he could sue us and have every right to do so. This could be seen as abuse. Or kidnapping!"

"Ah, abduction." Her father's mouth curved mischievously. "What goes around comes around, eh? The E.T.s have been doing it to us for years. Now it's our turn."

She glared at her father. "You can't be serious."

"The bottom line is that he stays here under our protection until we find out more about him. And where he's from."

A shiver ran through her. Where *was* he from? She thought of the little mercury guy and the astronomical phenomenon she'd seen shortly before her mother had "rescued" this strange, silent man with his unusual clothing and indescribable computer. She could remain in denial as long as she liked, but dismissing the possibility that he'd crash-landed in a spaceship might be premature.

"Okay," she whispered. "Let's say he is an extraterrestrial. That makes him a threat to national security. I'm a military officer, Dad. I'm sworn to defend the country." She gestured to the bed. "That . . . *creature* could very well be his planet's equivalent of the first marines to hit the beach."

Her father lifted a brow. "Do you honestly think so? Your instincts are as good as mine, Andromeda. If he were truly evil, you would have seen it. He doesn't intend to harm us."

She lowered her arms to her sides. She'd read a lot in the stranger's eyes, more than she'd expected—or intended— but not hatred and certainly not treachery. "What if he's carrying germs for which we have no cure?"

"Why worry, then?" her physician father reasoned. "If that's the case then you, your mother, and I are already dead meat."

"True." The ice cream she'd eaten earlier sat in her stomach like a cold stone.

Cassie appeared in the doorway, offering Frank's rarely used hunting rifle to Andie as if it were a boot caked with horse manure. "Sleep with our guest tonight, baby."

Andie sputtered. "What?"

"There, on the chair. He's hurt and lost. I don't want him to wake alone and in the dark."

"Oh. Right. The chair." Andie took the rifle.

"I'll stay with her, Cass," Frank said, weaving on his feet from exhaustion.

Andie spoke up: "No, Dad, go to bed. You have to work in the morning. I, on the other hand, am on vacation." She let out a breath. *Some vacation.*

Frank glanced at the sleeping man, then back to her, and rubbed his hand over his face. He had a few reservations about leaving her, after all.

"I'll be fine," she reassured him. "Besides a gun, a black belt, and a rip-roaring case of PMS, I have a cell phone with a hot button to nine-one-one."

"Oh, dear." Cassie's expression made it clear that she now considered the stranger far more at risk than Andie.

Frank dug his hospital pager out of his pocket and handed it to Andie. "Keep this, too. If you need anything or if his condition changes, call me. The panic button rings by my bed."

Her parents walked to the door. There, her mother stopped and smiled approvingly at the man in the bed. "I started a pot of coffee brewing out in the museum." Then she winked at her daughter and left with Frank for the house.

Andie sagged onto a faded purple-checked chair at the foot of the bed. The cushion was flat, and old springs poked her rear end. With the loaded rifle sitting crosswise on her jean-clad thighs, she propped her heels on the edge of the mattress and gazed at her charge.

She was baby-sitting an alien. Worse, she might have wished the guy here.

She tipped her head back against the wall and tried to conjure the rational, sensible being she had been before she had set foot on her parents' property only four hours before. But as hard as she struggled to keep logic afloat in an ocean of absurdity, she had the sinking feeling that the stranger with the silver eyes spelled the end of her life as she knew it.

Chapter Four

In the washed-out light of dawn, Andie noticed that the
man was awake. She didn't know how long his eyes had
been open, but there he was, her mother's "alien," regarding her from the bed.

Her heart exploded with a rush of adrenaline, and her
hands tightened over the rifle. "*Aash*," he said in a loud
whisper. His hands came up, fingers spread, the gesture
clearly made to calm her.

She studied him in the light of a sun that hadn't quite
risen. The mellow illumination turned his golden skin the
color of warm honey, leaving shadows in hollows below
his cheeks and jawbone, and in the sinews of his wrists
and hands. But it wasn't his physical appearance that
captured her attention; it was something in his eyes, his
face—a hint of sadness, of loneliness, of unrequited
longing—that drew her to him on a fundamental, almost
primal level.

Susan Grant

Star light, star bright . . .

The events of the evening before came rushing back: the meteorite, her reluctant acceptance that it might have been this man's ship, her even greater unwillingness to ponder the coincidence of her wish and his appearance in the first place. Like a flood victim clinging to a piece of driftwood, she was averse to letting go of the possibility that he was an accident victim or a lost hiker. "How are you feeling? You were unconscious when we brought you here."

His reply was an apologetic murmur. He didn't understand. After attempting the same question in a variety of languages, she switched to simple sign language. Using her hands to tell a story in fighter-pilot fashion, she mimicked a craft plunging through the atmosphere to Earth.

He nodded enthusiastically and repeated her gestures, adding a few more to help describe a rough landing.

Her blood froze. Instead of denying the allegation that he was an extraterrestrial, he'd embellished it.

His next gestures were made with increasing concern, using motions that left no doubt he was asking about his ship. *Where is it?* his eyes asked. *Where am I?*

"I'm sorry. Only my mother knows where your"—she forced herself to say the word—"spacecraft is."

Interpreting her body language, if not her words, the stranger sagged back onto the pillow, his gaze turning inward. *What the hell do I do now?* was written all over his face.

He wanted to return to his ship. He wanted to leave Earth. And since she hadn't been able to give him the information he'd needed, he would believe, understandably, that he'd been taken against his will. *Now it's our turn,* her father had joked. At that, she winced. This craziness had gone too far—she wanted out. *Now.* She didn't

302

care how many housewives had been abducted by little green men in the past. She would have no part in Earth's revenge.

She spread her hands. "Tell me how to help. What do you need? I'll try to do it."

The edges of his mouth softened, and in his gaze a gentle light flickered. He must have sensed the meaning behind her words. Between the two strangers sparked an understanding, a cautious trust. With what she perceived as renewed optimism, he gestured at his gauntlet computer and then to his eyes. He repeated the motions, stopping only after it was obvious she didn't know what he wanted. Clearly stymied, he scrutinized the room's four walls, his gaze hesitating on the electrical outlets and phone jack. Again he spoke to her in his strange language. Brows drawn together, he poked his finger at what looked like a port in his computer.

"Do you need to plug in?" she asked. With technology as advanced as his, she couldn't imagine he needed to recharge his battery. But one never knew.

He raised his computer-clad wrist, this time to his mouth. Again he pointed to his eyes.

Maybe he was asking to use a computer. She tapped her finger on her chin. Was it too much to hope that he could download the English language from the World Wide Web and use that data to speak? To give him access to a PC, though, she'd have to bring him into the house, where her parents still slept. She wasn't sure if she trusted him enough to do that yet.

The man noticed her unease. Stiffly but carefully, as if she were a skittish creature that he didn't want to frighten, he swung his long legs off the mattress.

She hopped to her feet and placed her back to the door,

ready for anything he cared to try. But he appeared to be in a depleted state. Sitting on the edge of the bed, elbows on his knees, he caught his head in his hands, as if to ward off dizziness. If he'd come off a long space journey, his metabolism might have been depressed intentionally, explaining his drowsiness from the evening before and his exhaustion now.

As he lifted his head, a few locks of his thick, shiny hair spilled over his forehead. Shoving them out of the way, he spoke earnestly in an unintelligible series of syllables.

She shrugged. "I don't understand."

He followed up with a series of guttural clicking sounds. She made a face, and he switched to a language with a cadence similar to a Ukrainian dialect she'd picked up during her yearlong training stint with the cosmonauts. Unfortunately, the stranger's version was indecipherable.

Looking worn-out, he tapped a finger on the center of his broad chest. "Zefer," he stated.

"Zefer?"

His eyes sparkled, and he nodded. "Zefer."

Ah, so that was his name. She pointed to herself. "Andie."

"Ahn-dee," he repeated in a deep, rich voice.

You Tarzan, me Jane. She fought to keep from smiling, and lost. An answering grin infused Zefer's hard features with boyish charm.

She melted. He noticed.

Their mutual awareness intensified.

He was gorgeous, she acknowledged, but not in the classic sense at all. He was rugged, mature, dignified; there was nothing "pretty boy" about him. At that, she stifled a ripple of longing. She hadn't realized, until then, just how tired she'd grown of "boys."

The Day Her Heart Stood Still

"So," she said.

"So," he replied.

She laughed softly and shrugged. His eyes sparkled. She could tell he found the primitiveness of their inter- action amusing. Equally, he seemed to be frustrated that they couldn't talk to each other. How she knew that, she wasn't sure—she never imagined there could be so much communication between two people without a common language.

Zefer pressed the raised circle on his gauntlet computer. Out popped Mr. Mercury, the 3-D, holographic Paper Clip Guy. Zefer said something to it and the little figure turned to her. In its tinny voice it recited the words she'd used the evening before: *"Hello . . . what are you . . . hello."*

Zefer pondered her with an unsettling mix of interest and hopefulness. "Hello," he said. "What are you?"

"Very attracted to you."

The words simply slipped out. Only by sheer force of will did she keep herself from blushing. When it came to expressing her feelings, she was very reserved. If it turned out that Zefer understood English, she'd absolutely die.

The air outside throbbed with a distinctive sound. Zefer cocked his head as a helicopter flew over the house. Low altitude, Andie noted. Was the crew on a routine mission or were they searching for something?

Some*one*?

She came back to her senses. Freezing her expression, she worked at recovering her professionalism. She didn't want it going down in history that all it took to disarm Earth's first line of defense against malevolent alien in- vaders was a pair of great eyes and a sexy smile.

The bedroom door flew open, bumping her in the back. "Andromeda!"

Susan Grant

Andie stepped aside. Her mother breezed in, a covered tray in her hands. Her father followed, relaxed, businesslike, and dressed for a day at the hospital. *Traitor*, she couldn't help thinking, twisting her mouth.

The savory smell of breakfast filled the room. "Good morning!" Cassie sang, setting the tray on the foot of the bed. Dressed in the hooded navy blue NASA sweatshirt Andie had given her for her last birthday, she simply glowed. It was clear this was the high point of her life. She'd snagged the ultimate prize, a real, live alien, the crown jewel of a lifelong obsession with extraterrestrials. She'd be the envy of UFO hunters everywhere.

Spock the parakeet sat on her shoulder, chirping riotously. Seemingly charmed by the wriggling green ball of feathers, Zefer smiled with his eyes. He stood up. Appearing even larger in the black outfit seemingly made of oven mitts, his tall frame filled the bedroom, a chamber that made no secret of its storage-closet origins. But his manner was gracious, not overbearing. Space explorer, diplomat, scientist, or soldier—what was he?

Respectfully, he inclined his head toward her mother and father. "Zefer," he said.

Andie informed her parents, "That's his name." She made a round of introductions in Tarzan-Jane fashion.

"Hello, Zefer," Cassie enthused.

"Hello," Zefer replied. Spreading one hand over his chest, he added, "Very attracted to you."

Andie made a choking noise.

"Well," her mother said, smiling.

Frank's inquiring eyes swerved to Andie. She gave her father a look of utter innocence and said, "He has a knack for languages."

"And charm, too," her mother answered. She lifted the

306

cover off the breakfast tray. Scrambled eggs and chorizo, shredded cheese, tortillas, salsa, and plump wedges of Florida grapefruit filled plates that Andie recognized as her family's best china. There was a bowl of plain oatmeal, too, and a few slices of white bread. "In case he's not quite ready for Earth food," Cassie explained gravely.

As Andie helped her mother serve the meal, Frank somehow communicated the concept of the nearby bathroom to Zefer, but not before he checked the alien's vital signs and injuries, and asked for a blood sample. At which point even Zefer appeared dazed as he allowed her father to stick a Band-Aid on his finger. Andie imagined herself in his shoes, crashed on a strange planet, bruised, tired, separated from his ship and unable to communicate with the strange natives who had rescued him. He had a lot pressing on his mind. Despite it all, he was being one hell of a good sport. More so than she was, Andie admitted grudgingly.

"I'll show Zefer where he can refresh himself," her father said. "Then I have an early meeting at the hospital. I'll try to get back from the clinic tonight as early as I can." Andie understood too well the improbability of his fulfilling that promise.

Zefer walked with her father into the main part of the museum, gazing at the UFO sippy cups and the *Star Trek* posters with the unabashed excitement of an archeologist in an undiscovered, artifact-filled pyramid. Spying the display of $14.95 little green men, Zefer laughed. "Weezahs," he told Andie over his shoulder, as if sharing an inside joke.

The wide-eyed, price-tagged, three-fingered plastic toys stared innocently back at them. "Weezahs?" she asked.

Zefer made motions with his hands indicating flight,

307

explaining with a stream of unintelligible words that made it seem like the little green men really existed.

She didn't ask. She didn't want to know.

When Zefer closed the rest-room door, her father kissed Cassie good-bye and ruffled Andie's hair. Then he left.

Andie hid her face in her hands and counted silently to ten. The nightmare didn't go away: there was an alien using the bathroom in her mother's UFO museum.

She turned to Cassie and whispered, "We need to discuss what we're going to about this."

"This?" her mother asked innocently.

"You know." Andie jerked her chin toward the museum. "Him. He wants out of here. He wants his ship."

"Then we'll see to repairing it so he can go home."

"And it'll be that simple, hmm? I heard a helicopter fly over the house. Have you had a chance to watch the news? What are they saying about the meteorite?"

"The spaceship."

"The flying saucer. The starship *Enterprise*. Whatever."

"I haven't seen or heard anything. *Roswell This Morning* comes on at six. We'll see what they have to say." Cassie's hand fluttered over her crystal pendant. "I'm worried, too, baby. But no one saw me bring him here."

"You don't *think* anyone saw." Andie rubbed her temples. Every minute that went by dragged her deeper into this mess. It was her duty to tell someone—the military, the government, NASA—about Zefer. But last night she'd promised her parents that she would keep his presence secret. And now that she'd met Zefer, she was less certain than ever that she should divulge his identity without his consent or understanding of the possible consequences.

She hugged her arms to her chest and paced in a three-foot square. National security or her parents' trust: she had never dreamed she'd be forced to choose between two such fundamental loyalties. Moreover, she herself had guarded Zefer during the night, and was in effect guarding him still. Whether his appearance turned out to be an accident, a threat, or a hoax, she was in too deep now to escape unscathed.

Hungry for sensationalism, the press was going to eat this up—in twenty-six days . . . if they didn't find out sooner. She made a mental vow to make sure they didn't.

Her mother said softly, "This is all so fascinating. So many questions to be answered. I have to ask him about the summer of 'forty-seven, of course. And—oh!—the circles in that English farmer's field. Hmm. Do you think he knows anything about that woman's abduction in 'sixty-eight? Though it probably happened before he was born." Cassie glanced in the direction of the rest room, her voice hushed. "The rumor is that she bore her captor's twin sons, but she never allowed any DNA testing—for the sake of the children." Her voice trailed off into a sigh.

Andie whirled on her. "To you this is one big adventure!" Remembering that Zefer was in the bathroom, she lowered her voice. "Life's just a game, isn't it? You just go happily along, doing what you want, saying what you want. Have you ever stopped to think about how your actions affect me? Or my career?"

Clearly taken aback, Cassie reached for her. Andie pulled her arm away.

"Am I an embarrassment to you?" Her mother asked the question as if she'd never contemplated the possibility. It proved just how unaware the woman was of her own behavior.

The urge to answer in the affirmative bubbled up inside Andie. She thought of her school years, the ridicule, the smirks of adults and children alike. Because she truly loved her mother, she'd always held back from explaining the reason for her resentment, why she'd stopped bringing friends to the house, why she'd used college as an excuse to flee home at seventeen, why she'd spent every year since trying to show the world that she was nothing like her mother. Even now, when asked the question directly, she was compelled to soften the blow. "As a kid, I . . . I wanted you to be like the other mothers."

"I see." Spock sidled closer to her mother's head and loosened a frizzy red curl with his beak. Cassie's attention remained on her daughter. "You wanted me to view the world and its wonders in a way that was socially acceptable."

Andie cleared her throat. "Yes."

"Life is made of rocks, Andromeda. I don't think I ever told you that."

Andie's shoulders sagged. A normal conversation—they'd been almost there, she thought, burning with disappointment.

Her mother went on: "I've always been one to lift up a rock to see what was underneath, even at the risk of dirtying my hands . . . or finding a horrible spider. Am I willing to change just to satisfy others' expectations of me? No, I am not. I wouldn't want to live my life looking at only the top sides of rocks, any more than I think you—pilot, astronaut, Air Force officer—would want to spend your days as, let's say, an orthodontist."

Goose bumps trickled down Andie's arms. She never knew that was how her mother viewed her life—*their* lives.

"I'm not ashamed to dream," Cassie said. "And I'm not afraid to take risks. I don't want you to be either, baby."

Andie thought of her years spent flying fighters and then the long and dangerous upcoming mission to Mars. "I know all about risks," she said dryly.

"Not of the heart, you don't. Your father was much the same way . . . many years ago."

Andie's first impulse was to deny the charge, but her mother's remark unleashed a niggling doubt deep inside her. What if she was right?

You wished on a star and Zefer came. Crazy.

But still possible. This could . . .

No! There was more at risk here than her heart.

With timing that couldn't have been worse, the alien menace himself emerged from the bathroom. His black jumpsuit was zipped to his neck once more, the seam invisible, the exotic fabric stretched snug across his chest. He must have washed using the sink. As he combed damp hair back from his face with his fingers, he gave Andie a killer smile that made her think of long showers for two and a few other scrumptious activities she had no right pondering—not because it had been so long since she had, but because fantasizing about this god-from-the-stars, with the future of Earth possibly hanging in the balance, was downright irresponsible.

You wished for him.

She groaned. "I'm going for a run," she told her mother. She needed to think. And she thought best alone. "A long run." Maybe all the way to the airport in Amarillo, where she'd hop on the first flight to Florida. She'd be home in no time—sane, safe, and in total denial that any of this had ever happened.

Her cell phone rang. She read the caller ID and answered, her eyes lifting to her mother's. "Yeah, Dad," she

Susan Grant

said uneasily as another helicopter flew over the house.

"Turn on the radio—*Early Morning with Ed Fritch*—now. And you might as well warn your mother: she's about to get a phone call."

Chapter Five

"Ed Fritch." Andie hung up the phone. "Isn't he in your UFO club, Mom?"

"He's vice president." Cassie wrung her hands. "I don't know why he'd be calling, unless—"

The telephone extension in the museum rang. Spock chirped, imitating the sound. "Oh, dear. Andromeda, lock up the museum, and make sure the closed sign is displayed. Then come to the house. Zefer, too." She scurried off to take the call in the house.

Zefer frowned, as if he sensed the situation involved him and that it had gone sour.

"We have to go," Andie said tersely. She grabbed the rifle and the keys, and pointed to the exit. "Mother's orders."

In the entry, Zefer searched the parking lot and sky before stepping outside. Then he took her arm by the elbow, making it clear he saw himself as a cohort, not a captive.

They strode across the driveway, skirting droplets of oil staining the spot where her father liked to park his Volvo. It was still early, and the air smelled like dust and roses. Zefer noted the little-green-men lawn ornaments with amused eyes. Then, breathing deep, he soaked in the outdoors like a man shaking off a severe case of cabin fever.

A helicopter flew low over the neighboring pasture.

Its occupants were definitely on someone's trail, though she hoped not Zefer's. The helicopter was a civilian model, not Army or Air Force. However, if word spread that a spaceship had crashed, the authorities would come looking for evidence and it'd be 1947 all over again. Only this time it wasn't a weather balloon; it was real and Andie was smack-dab in the middle of it.

She gritted her teeth. "I don't want to be involved in this. I can't *afford* to be involved in this." Everything had been so simple before. Now her loyalties, her obligations, were pulled in so many different directions.

Zefer's fingers pressed gently into her skin. "*Aash.*"

"I don't want to 'aash.' " Where was he from? What was his reason for coming here? "Damn it, Zefer. This is ridiculous; we need to be able to talk!" She scowled and addressed the little silver man on his arm: "Just so you know, 'damn' is *not* a nice word."

"Ed Fritch," it droned in its robot voice.

She let out a breath. "Hmm, maybe that's not such a nice word, either." Hoping Mr. Mercury would upload her explanation for later translation, she said, "Ed and my mother have been friends for over fifty years. And I think they've spent most of it in an unofficial race to be the first to make contact with aliens." She'd never had any doubt that they'd both go to the grave defeated. That was, until last night.

The Day Her Heart Stood Still

"Ed hosts a talk-radio show on local, unexplained phenomena. It has an almost cultlike following, so you'd better believe that everyone who saw the sky show last night is going to call in. And, as always, he'll invite longtime Roswell resident—my dear mother—Mrs. Cassiopeia Del Sarto to share her expert opinion." Andie mimicked Ed's exaggerated fanfare, then continued: "Fellow seekers, join me in welcoming the president of UFO Hunters of America—senior division!"

It was clear that Zefer had no idea what she was mocking, but it seemed her animated cynicism amused him. She could feel his attentive gaze on her even after she shifted her eyes to the front porch.

They trotted up the steps. "Mom missed their weekly UFO meeting last night," she told him in a more serious tone. "Knowing Ed, he's suspicious. He'll want to find out what she knows . . . that he doesn't." She made a face. "And my mother's a horrible liar."

His fingers flexed on her arm. *We're in this together*, the gesture assured her.

Only she didn't want to be in this at all—with him or anyone else. She was an unwilling participant in her mother's greatest fantasy. *Skidding . . . sliding . . .* Reflexively, her fingers twitched; she could almost feel her nails dragging over the dirt as the quicksand pulled her in.

Inside the house the TV was on, a commercial playing. Cassie sat at the kitchen table, a phone pressed to her ear. "Actually, Ed, I think this one burned up before impact," her mother fibbed with a surprising degree of sincerity. "My daughter's visiting, the astronaut, and she thought so, too. . . ."

Spock flew across the living room and landed on Zefer's wrist. Squawking, the bird pecked at Mr. Mercury. The

315

little figure batted at the bird with tiny arms. "Damn it!" it blurted.

Andie moaned. "I'm a horrible influence."

Zefer stowed the little man. Triumphant, Spock sidled up Zefer's now-unoccupied arm to his shoulder. Like an interstellar Captain Hook, Zefer stalked around the room, peering at electrical outlets and pointing to his eyes.

"I think I have what you need. Over here." Andie steered him to the spare computer in the kitchen that her father used only to download the *New York Times* and various medical journals to which he had Internet subscriptions. No important files were saved on it, making the PC a relatively risk-free way to set Zefer loose on the World Wide Web. She brought up her favorite search engine and moved aside. "Good luck," she said, and hoped he knew what to do to get what he needed.

He ignored the keyboard. There was a soft whirring noise as the device on his forearm opened. Spock took to the air with a rustling of feathers. From a shallow compartment in the gauntlet, Zefer extracted a pair of glasses, sleek and dark, and donned them. He gave a verbal order in his language and a silvery cable snaked out from near his wrist and found the PC's USB port.

The Del Sarto computer's antivirus protection launched a fleeting, futile protest before succumbing to an assault its creators hadn't anticipated. The display on the computer screen jumped from site to site so rapidly that Andie had to work at keeping her eyes from crossing. Then the monitor blurred completely. Streams of data flickered behind Zefer's lenses. His lips parted slightly as he took in an incalculable amount of information.

The amazing sight touched upon every dream she'd ever had of the future: the unlimited promise of technology, of man married to machine, science improving human existence. Her underlying attraction to the compelling silver-eyed man melded with awe and a hunger to know the wonders he had known. And it erased the last of her doubts about his origins.

With a pop, the monitor went blank and the cable whirred back into Zefer's computer. She made a mental note to keep him away from her laptop.

"The search goes on for survivors of a possible plane crash yesterday evening. . . ."

Andie spun around. The television was playing the morning news.

"Though some local organizations insist that once again aliens have crash-landed in Roswell, search crews continue to comb the countryside looking for a downed aircraft. . . ."

"Good," said a heavily accented deep voice. "Ed Fritch does not look for ship."

Andie's breath caught. Slowly she faced Zefer. "You spoke English," she said.

"I download all languages of Earth, but I choose English. Your language, Ahn-dee," he added with a dazzling smile.

At the sound of her name on his lips, her heart did a little flip. She wanted desperately to remain unaffected by him. But the unaccountably intimate tone of his voice made her think of moonlight and kisses. "Your technology—it's incredible."

"Program will continue to improve on itself," Zefer explained, "so I speak better each time."

"Do all your people have implanted, integrated computers?"

"Not yet." He glanced at his forearm. "Still experimental. I, and many others, we volunteer. I am bachelor and in good health. Makes me perfect test subject—expendable and long-lasting." He shrugged. "Before, I do not use it much, the . . . enhancement. It brings me headaches, fatigue. But this . . . being able to speak to you"—he waved his hand at her mother—"and your people . . . it is finally worth all the trouble."

"Is that what brought you here? Exploration?"

"I do not know what brought me here." He walked to the window and peered out. "One moment I am going into deep-sleep mode used for long solitary journey. Next, computer wakes me and ship is roaring through atmosphere of a planet not on flight plan."

Andie brought her hand to her mouth. Her wish . . . ?

"I barely gain control of craft before landing it." He grimaced. "More a crash than a landing." His attention shifted to Cassie, who had, without Andie noticing, ended her phone conversation. She was gazing at Zefer, a look of blissful amazement lighting her face.

"You were there . . . Mrs. Del Sarto," Zefer said, clearly taking pains to pronounce her name correctly. "You helped me. Is my ship intact?"

"Yes," her mother assured him. "A few dents and scratches to the hull. The inside, well . . . you'll have to be the judge of that."

Relief suffused his features.

The phone rang, and Cassie answered it. Her face paled and she said, "Sure, Ed. I'll be here."

Swallowing, Cassie hung up.

"He's coming over," Andie said flatly.

Her mother nodded. "He wants to meet with me, regarding what we saw last night. I had to, Andie. If I'd acted evasive, or tried to meet him somewhere else, it would make him even more suspicious than he is already."

Andie held up her hand. "Okay." Swiftly she recovered her cool demeanor and asked, "When?"

"He'll be here after the show. In an hour or so. I'll chase him out as quickly as I can, but"—her sigh was fraught with worry and irritation—"I think you should take Zefer out."

"Out?" Andie's mouth dropped open. "Look at him! He looks like a refugee from a *Star Trek* convention."

Zefer slid a dismayed and wary glance downward at his black jumpsuit.

"I'll find him some of your father's clothes," Cassie said. "Those oversize sweats," she added, eyeing the big alien critically. "The shoes won't fit, though."

"No, and we have to get him out of here before Ed comes." Studying Zefer, Andie tapped her finger against her cheek. "I can take him with me, dressed in Dad's clothes. He'd be safe, I think, waiting in the car until I get him some shoes." If no one scrutinized him too closely, she thought. "But it's only eight o'clock," she murmured. "That doesn't leave us many choices for an emergency fashion makeover."

"Wal-Mart will be open," her mother suggested brightly.

Andie nodded curtly. "It'll have to do."

Zefer finally spoke. "It will have to," he said, humor glinting in his eyes. "I do not want to look like a . . . refugee."

Andie laughed at his self-deprecating joke, to his apparent pleasure, and then sheepishly spread her hands. "I'm sorry, Zefer. I didn't mean to insult you."

His eyes told her that he remained more amused than

insulted. "Where may I don my borrowed clothing so we may embark on our expedition?"

Andie's smile faded. Zefer's question drove home the fact that she was actually taking him into town. *Slipping . . . sliding . . .* The quicksand gripped her all over again.

He searched her face, his expression suddenly grave. "I bring you danger."

Cassie wrung her hands. "You're who we're worried about," she said.

Zefer's gaze, lingering on Andie, turned regretful. "Ah. I understand. Earth does not know the history of our race, the Progeny, or our common heritage, the Seeders. Not only does this lack of knowledge explain Earth's fear, it is against my laws to stay here without the knowledge and consent of my government. I will leave as soon as my ship is fixed."

"Wait a second," Andie said. "Who are the Seeders?"

"The Original Ones. Several hundred thousand years ago, they sowed their DNA across the galaxy. We thought we knew of all the worlds they touched; in fact, we were sure of it. But folklore recounts many tales of a lost world, one we have never seen, that became separated from us by time and distance. It was assumed to be a legend only. But"—his eyes sparked with wonder—"perhaps that lost world is Earth."

Andie and her mother gaped at him. It was as if he'd opened a volume entitled *Secrets of the Universe*, and was reading them the pages.

"I am an explorer. My parents were explorers, as were my grandparents before them. It is in my blood. Since I was a boy, I dreamed of being the one to discover the lost world, to reveal the truth of its existence to my people." He didn't take his eyes from Andie's, his face as deeply expressive as his voice. "There would be a woman there, whose soul I'd find was bound with mine. And as our worlds came together," he said quietly, "so would we."

Andie wanted to laugh out loud. She wanted to weep. She wanted to kiss Zefer hard on the mouth. She wanted to go on a run—five, ten, a hundred miles. She wanted to escape this vortex of insanity and never return.

Breaking eye contact, she twined her hands together and pressed them under her chin. If there was one thing she'd learned from her years flying fighter jets, it was this: if the rules of engagement changed, you adapted. Or else someone would turn you into—in fighter-jock terms—toast. The parallel to her current situation was clear. She was in deep—too deep to extract herself. She had no choice but to team up with her mother and, in so doing ensure Zefer's safe departure. Now all she had to do was figure out how to accomplish that without compromising her dreams, her planet, or her heart.

Chapter Six

Andie took a quick shower, while Zefer squeezed into a pair of stretchy old shorts and a T-shirt that were baggy on her father but snug on him. After he rushed hungrily through the breakfast Andie's mother prepared, Cassie shoved them out the front door to ensure they were gone long before Ed arrived.

Without Andie's needing to show Zefer how, he found the seat belt and buckled it. As she drove along the pitted dirt driveway to the road, she stared dazedly ahead. Last night she'd driven past this very spot. Twelve hours later, she was bringing a barefoot extraterrestrial to Wal-Mart.

She swallowed a groan as she drove past a man selling paintings of aliens and Elvis from the back of his pickup parked below a billboard advertising: THIS EXIT! EXTRATERRESTRIALS-R-US—ROSWELL'S OLDEST UFO MUSEUM.

"I know you want to see your ship," she said, "but I have to keep you out of sight for a while." She went into detail about Ed and her mother's UFO group.

When she finished, Zefer nodded gravely. "No problem. We will keep a low profile until nightfall."

His use and adaptation of slang was remarkable. His "program" was improving on itself, she thought as she pushed a disc into her new CD player, a device that suddenly seemed so . . . primitive. "You'll stay in the car while I buy the clothes," she said.

He nodded. "I will stay."

"And if anyone asks, you're my Russian cosmonaut boyfriend." She could have just as easily chosen *buddy*, or *business associate*. *Boyfriend?* Zefer had downloaded and, she guessed, understood the meaning of the term. Still, if he didn't seem to mind their invented relationship, neither would she. "Being Russian will help explain your accent. We'll need to pick a name for you, too." She drummed her fingers on the steering wheel. "How about . . . Anatoly Butin?"

Sunlight glinted off the dark sunglasses Zefer said he needed to wear for enhanced language translation. "He is your lover."

Her foot convulsed on the gas pedal. Zefer didn't appear to notice the sudden acceleration. "No," she said firmly. "He is not my lover." She and Butin had ended up in bed one cold Siberian night after consuming too much vodka. And they'd repeated the venture, minus the vodka, a few more times in her remaining weeks in cosmonaut training. But they'd had their careers to think about, and not enough motivation to keep their relationship going with cultural differences and thousands of miles of separation complicating the issue. "But yes, I used to see him. That was a long time ago."

"Then you have a new boyfriend?"

"Nope, no boyfriend." *Who do you have, baby?* She forced a bland look onto her face.

"Forgive me all my questions," Zefer said after a few moments of awkward silence. "But are you engaged? Married? Separated?"

She cracked a smile. "None of them. I'm single and healthy—'expendable and long-lasting'—same as you. Only no one's asked me if I want a computer implanted in my arm."

They had, though, invited her to go to Mars: an arduous, dangerous, nearly three-year round-trip. Everyone NASA had chosen for the Mars flight was unmarried. That alone summed up the nature of the mission.

Zefer nodded. "You are very attracted to me."

In the midst of passing a slow-moving truck, Andie changed lanes so abruptly that the tires shrieked. Trained to disregard distractions, she tried her hardest to do so, frowning as she followed the road into town. "Zefer, when I said that I didn't think you understood English!"

"I reviewed the transcripts."

She glared at Mr. Mercury. "Snitch," she said in a hiss.

"Hello," the little figure replied innocently.

She turned into the Wal-Mart parking lot and parked, only to leave the Corvette idling while she watched people walk in and out of the store. Normal people with normal lives, she thought wistfully.

Zefer reached across the dash. With a jangling of keys, he shut off the ignition. He stayed in that position, bent toward her, one muscular arm propped on the dashboard. "I am, too," he said with gentle frankness.

She clutched the steering wheel, as if she could hold on to something she feared she'd already lost. "You are *what?*"

"Very attracted to you."

His sincerity raised goose bumps on her arms. At the same time, sweet warmth flooded her, a sort of buoyancy; a laugh-out-loud giddiness. It was that teetering-at-the-edge-of-the-abyss sensation when you first wondered if you were going to fall in love. She hadn't felt this way in so long, and certainly never with the force and poignancy that she did now.

Her hands slid limply into her lap. "That's saying a lot," she murmured, staring out the bug-spotted windshield, "seeing that we've only known each other a few hours."

Sunshine flooded through the windshield, heating the car. But it was their heightened awareness of each other that made the temperature soar.

Her eyes dipped to his mouth. His fingers brushed over her kneecap. He wanted to kiss her. *She* wanted him to kiss her. But she had no business kissing him at all.

She'd gone above and beyond the call of a daughter's duty to her mother by agreeing to disguise him. From now until Zefer returned to his ship, he was her mother's project, her mother's worry.

Something rapped on the driver's-side door. Andie wrenched her gaze from Zefer's and rolled down the window. A woman dressed in pink-and-green floral scrubs and sensible white shoes waved frantically. "Hey, girl! Dr. Del Sarto told me you'd be coming for a visit. And wouldn't you know, I run a few errands and here you are!" The nurse winked at Zefer. "I'm sorry if I interrupted something, but I was so excited when I spotted your car. Small world, huh?"

"Very small," Andie agreed. *Sickeningly, suffocatingly, career-endingly small.* "It's great to see you, Tasha." She managed a smile. "How about we do lunch later in the week and catch up?"

"I'll call you." Tasha bent forward, peering into the car as her plastic shopping bag dangled from one arm. With a sinking feeling in the pit of her stomach, Andie realized there was no way she was going to avoid formal introductions.

Andie cleared her throat. *Meet Zefer. He's from outer space. And he's here because I wished on a star. Can you believe it? I must have one heck of a fairy godmother. I mean, look at him. Have you ever seen a sexier alien? Not only that, he's a nice guy, too.*

But of course, that wasn't the response that made it past her internal censor.

"Tasha," Andie began, "I'd like you to meet my friend Anatoly Butin. He's visiting from Russia." She turned to her composed, almost Zen-like passenger and said, "Anatoly, this is my friend Latasha Williams. She's a nurse in pediatrics at the hospital with my father."

Zefer's dark glasses made his smile seem all the brighter. "It is my pleasure to meet you, Latasha."

"*Lo-ove* his accent," her friend confided to Andie before returning her attention to Zefer. "Welcome to Roswell, hon. When did you arrive in the States?"

He didn't miss a beat. "Last night. It was a late flight."

"I bet you're jet-lagged."

"Time: it is all relative," he replied with a surprisingly Slavic shrug.

"Well, you be sure to rest up. Nice meeting you! I've got to run." Tasha called over her shoulder as she walked off, "I'll let your father know I bumped into you two, Andie!"

Andie flopped back against the seat. "Damn it."

"Damn it, is right."

"Listen to your language. I told you—I'm a bad influence."

"I saw far worse on the Internet."

"I bet you did. And look who showed you how to get there. I'm corrupting you."

He dragged his fingertip over the knuckles of her right hand. "I hope that is a promise."

Her smile faded. "Zefer . . ."

He sobered along with her. "It was a joke, Ahn-dee."

"I know," she murmured. "I . . . We . . ." She sighed a sigh that would have made her mother proud. "Zefer, it's impossible."

He sat back in his seat, his mouth tight. "You are an astronaut, one who explores space."

"You know?"

"I read the files in your computer."

She smiled at that. "My father. He's a one-man clipping service. I think he has every article ever written about me."

"You are to go to Mars," he said firmly. "The fourth planet from Sol, your star. I read this."

She gaped at him. "No decision's been made yet. That information hasn't been—"

"Ahn-dee." He acted exasperated. "You have been told. I look at you and see it in your eyes. It may be a secret to others, but not to me. Your desire to walk upon the Red Planet glows in you like fire. I know. I am an explorer, too. Like knows like."

A tremor ran through her. *Like knows like.* Was that why she was so drawn to Zefer? But she'd dated astronauts before. Even slept with a cosmonaut. And it had never been like this. There must be more to her connection with Zefer than a hunger to explore the stars.

The wish. She gulped guiltily. "Comparing you to me is like comparing a deep-sea diver to a child dipping her toes in the water. My only trip into space was a two-week stint on the International Space Station." And that was only an orbiting structure held tight to Earth's bosom. "But I've always wanted to be what you are, Zefer," she said with longing. Even his name embodied freedom. Zephyr—the wind. "I want to pioneer. I want to feel the risk, the thrill, of arriving first. Now I'm finally going to be able to see what that's like. Too bad that the space program here is still in its infancy, and Mars will be my one and only shot." She shrugged. "But life goes on."

She unbuckled her seat belt and moved to unlock the door. Zefer stopped her before she could let herself out.

"I am on my way to the Outer Fringe," he said, "the farthest known settlement known to the Progeny of the Seeders. I am to be the commander, my first leadership position—not the first such opportunity I have been offered, but the first one I have wanted to accept. Daily, surveyor vessels will depart the space city and others will arrive from areas never before explored. All will share in the wonders discovered. And I am to help determine which new worlds are to be colonized."

Again, that odd mix of hope and longing flickered across his face. Reflecting on the wish she'd made, she wondered if he saw the same yearning in her.

"Come with me when I leave here," he said. "To the Outer Fringe." The intimate way his hand moved over hers assured her she'd be more to him there than a professional associate.

"But . . . I'm going to Mars. In four months."

"I will take you there. On our way out of your planetary system. Which topographical area would you like most to see? The north pole, or south? Or perhaps the equator?"

His invitation so rattled her that she could hardly form a response. "You're offering me a lift? To Mars?" She yanked her hand from his. "I don't want anyone to bring me there. I want to go, Zefer, under my own power. Like knows like?"

She huffed, then continued, "If you really believed that, you'd never make this offer; you'd know I wouldn't give up the uncertainty, the months of boredom, the mistakes, the moments of terror, the anticipation, the thrill of participating in the greatest adventure in history—Earth's history, which was, until you came here, all that mattered." She shoved the door open. "Thanks, but no, thanks."

She planted her feet outside the car. Then she looked over her shoulder. Zefer's mouth was still hanging open. He reminded her of a little boy who'd presented a crumpled bouquet of carefully chosen dandelions only to have them cast off. Her heart wrenched. What was wrong with her? What had happened to the person she used to be? The cool, calm, *considerate* individual? Ever since Zefer had shown up in her mother's trunk, she'd been a seething knot of conflicting emotions.

She took a steadying breath. "I'm so sorry."

It was silent for a moment. Then Zefer said quietly, "You are right. I *know* you are right. Yet I said the words; I made the offer." He shoved one hand through his hair. "I am not acting in any way that is remotely like my usual behavior."

The tension seeped out of her. "I've been pretty much thinking the same thing about myself." She recalled what her mother had said about taking risks of the heart. Was that what was happening to her? To them? "Sometimes when you peek under rocks, you find some ugly spiders. Maybe this is the part where our hands get dirty." He looked totally confused. She was too drained to explain.

Slamming the door behind her, she strode across the parking lot—and didn't look back. She could pull an Amelia Earhart—right now—by disappearing mysteriously. It was tempting to keep walking, through the store, out the back, past the adjacent shopping mall, and down the block, where she'd seen a little rental-car place. As lunchtime rolled around, she'd be well on her way back to Florida and miles away from this . . . this insanity.

But once inside Wal-Mart, she veered toward the men's clothing section as if she were on autopilot. As bloody as it was turning out to be, she was in this battle for the duration. Her only hope was that when the end came, it would be painless. And quick.

Chapter Seven

Sipping a Diet Coke, Andie waited outside a gas station rest room until Zefer emerged dressed in imitation Doc Martens, jeans, and a Dallas Cowboys T-shirt. An Ace bandage covered his gauntlet. "Well. You look almost . . . local. But Mr. Mercury won't be happy, smothered under that bandage."

"Ah, but he'll still maintain all his functions."

"Including snitching?" She pretended to scowl.

He chuckled. "His simulated personality seems so genuine. I created him for entertainment only, yet even I sometimes forget he's not real."

"That's his only purpose?" she asked as they climbed back into the car. "Entertainment?"

"When you spend as many weeks as I do alone, such amusement is a worthwhile diversion."

That she could relate to—weeks alone—she thought as she drove Zefer past her elementary school and high school, and the airport where she'd learned to fly. After the minitour of her past history, and a check-in call to her mother, she picked out a buffet restaurant for lunch, so Zefer could better choose foods that appealed to him. Over a heaping plate, he answered her questions about his civilization, the ruling government, their technology and space ventures. And he eased her reservations about Earth's first contact with his people, giving her a rush of homecoming joy when he painted a mental picture of Earth's poignant reunion with the only other beings in a vast and lonely galaxy who shared their DNA.

They'd finally moved on to tales of his boyhood spent on starships and rugged, far-flung planets as the only child of explorer parents, when he stopped suddenly mid-sentence and grimaced, pressing his fingertips to his forehead. Andie's chest contracted. "What's wrong? Are you ill?"

"Not ill." He paused to catch his breath. Speaking seemed to be an effort. "It is the computer—using it to communicate verbally drains me."

"Then stop talking."

He looked as if he would protest. She held up one finger. "Enough said."

It was too early to risk going home. She thought for a moment, then perked up. "I'll take you to the movies. You can watch either with the glasses or without. And you won't have to talk."

Once there, they watched two movies in a row. Before the end of the second film, he fell asleep. He'd sunk so low in his chair that she didn't realize it at first, but his slow, steady breaths confirmed her suspicion. "I must be an exciting date, huh?" she teased. But he was beyond hearing, beyond caring.

When the lights came on at the end, she nudged him awake. "It's late and you need sleep," she whispered. "Let's go."

His face was pale as he walked slowly out of the nearly empty theater.

Once back at the house, Andie parked in front of the museum. " 'Closed,' " she read from the sign posted near the front entrance. " 'Renovating to better serve you.' " She glanced at Zefer. " 'Grand reopening July first?' Sounds like my mother plans to keep you around for a while."

Zefer did some mental calculations and shook his head. His already weary expression turned pensive. "But if I could stay until then . . . The situation for me is complicated. First I must file the existence of Earth through official channels. Moreover, I am overdue at my new assignment. Yet despite my obligations, I don't want to leave here. I am being pulled in many different directions."

Andie exhaled. "I know what you mean."

"Do you?" His hand moved behind her head and he cupped it. His sunglasses blotted out anything she could have read in his eyes, but his mouth was so close that she could see the tiny nubs above his upper lip where he needed to shave, and a small scar just to the right of the center of his chin.

His other hand lifted, dry fingertips skimming lightly down her cheek to her throat. Parted slightly, his lips grazed over hers, his breath warm, soft, and scented with buttered popcorn.

Her heart bounced in her chest. She let out the softest of sighs before she thought to suppress her reaction.

333

"Ahn-dee," he whispered. And then he dipped his head and kissed her.

The surge of rightness inside her and the passion with which she returned his kiss made absolutely no sense at all. It was reckless; it defied reason. And she had no doubt her mother would approve wholeheartedly.

Cassie always shook her head at Andie's methodical approach to relationships, insisting that logic and love were like oil and water: if you tried to mix the two, all you did was cloud the situation. Love and logic were destined to remain apart. "And that's far from being a bad thing, Andromeda," her mother would say.

Andie never in a million years thought she'd admit that her mother just might have been a little bit right. But she would have, right then, without any hesitation, had anyone thought to ask her in the midst of that blinding, heart-stopping, incredible kiss.

Breathless, they moved apart. Zefer stroked three fingers down her cheek. "I told you we do not need words."

"Shush," she whispered, her lips still tingling. She wanted another kiss, and more after that, but she forced herself to get out of the car and walk around to the passenger door.

Zefer let her help him climb to his feet. He leaned heavily on her as they struggled from the car to the spare bedroom. His eyes were half-closed by the time she helped him lie on the bed.

"Tomorrow your family must take me to my ship," he said. "I have to determine what, if any, repairs are to be made and begin making them." His face contorted and he pressed his palms to his forehead.

She pulled off his glasses. "It's worse than you're telling me," she whispered.

The Day Her Heart Stood Still

In English made halting without computer assistance, he said, "No. Tired only. Sleep will fix."

"If it doesn't, I'll call my father. Meanwhile, no more talking." She held up her hand. "And no arguing."

His mouth curved gently as his lids drifted closed. She watched him, her throat strangely tight. He'd used the computer to speak to her almost nonstop, knowing that it would do this to him.

She walked to the window to draw the curtains closed, but paused to gaze out at the stars. The sky was where all her dreams had begun, and where her heart now told her they would conclude. She'd never listened to her heart in the past. Was she ready to now?

She turned back to Zefer and brushed her fingertips over the silky strands of hair lying on his forehead. "Sleep well, star man," she whispered, and then left him in the quiet, shadowy museum.

Andie traded breakfast the next morning with her much-too-perceptive parents for a long, mind-clearing run. After returning and showering, she found her mother in the kitchen preparing tuna-fish sandwiches. Andie filled a glass with water, leaning against the counter as she drank. Roswell's relentless wind had buffeted her on her run, and she still tasted dust.

"You got in late last night," Cassie observed with a mother's concern that hadn't ebbed one iota since Andie had grown up and left home. "I was afraid you ran into something unexpected."

Unexpected was an understatement. Andie took the knife resting on the cutting block and a stalk of celery. She longed to share with her mother what she felt when she was with Zefer, the sensation of rightness that had over-

335

taken her when they'd kissed outside the museum, but she didn't quite know how. After a few moments of stripping the vegetable, she confessed, "I took your advice. I looked under a rock."

"Ah." Cassie wiped her hands on a dishtowel embroidered with E.T.s wearing little aprons. "Did you find anything interesting under there?"

Andie hacked away at the celery. "Spiders."

Her mother's mouth quirked. "Don't worry; the light will scare them off."

"I wouldn't know. I think I dropped the rock too fast."

Her mother's eyes sparkled knowingly. "Where is he?"

"In the museum. Still asleep. He's got a hell of a headache, and I don't dare give him anything for it until I talk to Dad. It's the computer. Using it to speak yesterday wiped him out."

"Oh, dear," her mother murmured.

"He wants to see his ship today."

"Best we take him tonight—under the cover of darkness."

Andie lowered her knife. "We?"

"Why, someone has to keep watch while Zefer and I are on board his starship. There's no better person than you, baby."

Andie grabbed another stalk of celery and chopped it almost to pulp with determined whacks of the knife. The sensation of being dragged toward quicksand had long since stopped. Now she felt it closing over her mouth and nostrils.

But how could she refuse to help? It sickened her to think of Zefer being apprehended by those who would fear him, stop him before he could complete his mission. And he had to get home to his people—Earth's cousins—

and tell them of the "lost world" he'd found. He had to return to his ship, repair it, and resume his journey to the Outer Fringe.

She'd accepted all of that: who he was, where he came from. Yet taking that last step, accompanying her mother to the site of an alien crash-landing, loomed in direct contrast to everything she'd believed herself to be: *not like Mom.*

The doorbell rang.

"Oh, dear," she chorused along with her mother.

"I bet that's Ed," Cassie murmured.

"Again? What is it with you two?"

Her mother pouted. "I thought I put him off the trail. But I don't think he believes me."

"And that surprises you? You can't lie to save your life."

"I'm going to have to learn . . . if I'm going to save *his*." Bravely, she gestured toward the museum with a slice of whole-wheat bread.

"Cassie, are you home?" a voice called from the front porch. Spock began squawking.

"Stay put," Andie told her mother. "I'll handle it."

Spock the parakeet dove down from the top of a potted palm tree and landed on her shoulder as Andie opened the door. Ed Fritch stood on the porch. Short and wiry with intense blue eyes, he had a leathery farmer's neck and pomaded yellow-white hair combed to the side. He smelled like cigarettes and aftershave.

She pasted a smile of welcome and surprise on her face. "Ed. What a treat. Come in."

"Andie, good to see you!" Entering the house he shook her hand, his grip roughened by years spent outdoors in a harsh climate, and they exchanged the usual pleasantries. "I'll have to have you on the show before you go home," he told her. "You and your activities are as much of a phenomenon as anything else in this town."

She winked at him. "You wouldn't believe how much."

Cassie walked up behind them. Ed told her, "The Civil Air Patrol's ready to call off their search. But I knew it all along: no plane crashed."

"No," Cassie said. "Nothing crashed at all." She slammed the front door to keep out the dust blown by the wind.

Ed's eyes narrowed. "It's not like you to give up the hunt before it's begun, Cassiopeia."

"It was a piece of space junk, Ed," Andie interjected with easy authority. "There's nothing to hunt for. I explained that to her."

Ed chewed on that. "I don't know. . . . Instinct tells me it's more. I know you're not a believer, Andie—and it's too bad, if you ask me, what with you being an astronaut and all—but if you're wrong, if something landed here in Roswell, then, by God, it's our citizens' duty to search until we find out what it is."

He puffed out his chest. The pack of Marlboros in his front left pocket made a crinkling noise, but he didn't dare smoke in the house—Cassie's law—and that told Andie the balance of power between them remained even despite Ed's overt bossiness. "As vice president of the senior division I have the right to call an emergency meeting," he said. "And so I have. Everyone but Marsha is on their way over."

Cassie's voice came out in a squeak. "Here?"

Andie elbowed her. Cassie cleared her throat, recovering nicely. "I'll make more tuna sandwiches," Cassie said, and escaped into the kitchen.

A movement caught Andie's eye. She glanced out the

window, the one that faced the museum, and saw Zefer walking across the driveway. Her stomach plunged, and she practically shoved Ed into the kitchen. "Go, Ed; Mom's tuna sandwiches are the best."

She threw a frantic glance outside but she could no longer see Zefer. *Okay. Throw Ed in the kitchen and then intercept Zefer before he reaches the front door.*

"So," she said as conversationally as she could, "where exactly do you plan to go hunting?"

"We'll start near Six Mile Hill."

That wasn't where her mother claimed Zefer's ship was hidden in a brush-covered arroyo, but it was only a matter of time—days, maybe—before the group made it to that area, too.

"Mrs. Hobbs uses a walker now; that'll slow you down, won't it?" she asked hopefully.

"Gloria Ruiz borrows her grandson's Hummer. Mrs. Hobbs rides in the front and mans the radios." Ed's body twitched with excitement. *He can smell his quarry,* Andie thought with dread. "We may be senior citizens, Andie, but if there's something out there, we'll find it. Before anyone else does."

Not if I have anything to do with it. She wasn't sure if it was possessiveness, her dogged sense of honor, or plain old stupidity that drove her decision, but like hell was she going to let Ed Fritch sink his claws into Zefer.

"Well, I wish you the best of luck, Ed." She swallowed and looked over her shoulder. Any second Zefer was going to show up on the front porch. She led the man to the kitchen and backed away, almost stumbling over a floor mat. "Don't forget sunblock. It's warm out there today. Buh-bye."

She dashed to the front door, but before she had the

chance to wrap her hand around the handle, it flew open. On the porch was Zefer, his thumbs hooked in the waistband of his new, slightly baggy jeans.

"No, no!" she whispered loudly. "Out, out!" She marched him backward. "I thought you were sleeping."

"I was. But the computer woke me. Your 'Mr. Mercury.' "

Andie saw the little guy's head trying to poke through the Ace bandage covering him. "Ed Fritch," it said in a muffled, barely audible voice. "Damn it—Ed Fritch."

"I feared you were in trouble," Zefer whispered as they stumbled across the porch. He was still unsteady on his feet. Her heart wrenched with worry for his health.

"You're the one in trouble, Zefer," she said under her breath. "Not me. Ed's here." She tried to march him backward, but his mouth spread into a brilliant grin.

"Hello!" he called suddenly.

There, in Zefer's dark sunglasses, was the distorted reflection of Ed Fritch, watching them as he stood in the doorway.

Chapter Eight

Andie had been caught with her hand in the cookie jar. But the warrior in her would not let her surrender. To prevail, she must think like a winner and act like the victor. Starting now.

Smiling, she slid her arm around Zefer's waist and turned around. "Ed, this is my boyfriend, Anatoly. He's visiting from Russia."

"Anatoly Butin," Zefer emphasized in his deep, accented voice. "My pleasure to meet you." He held out his hand to Ed and the men shook hands, Earth-style.

"Anatoly Butin?" Ed's face lit up with sudden recognition, and Andie wondered in a moment of panic if Ed would notice the differences in appearance between the two men. But he didn't. "You're the cosmonaut, right?"

Zefer nodded. "Yes. In Russia, that is who I am. But here, I am Andie's only." The breath rushed out of her lungs as Zefer tucked her firmly into his strong, warm body. Then of all things, he pressed his lips to the top of her head. Her legs turned to rubber.

Cassie appeared behind Ed, twisting her alien dish towel in her hands. "Zef—"

"Mom," Andie interrupted. "Anatoly's done sleeping off his jet lag." She gazed up at Zefer and smiled. "But you shouldn't be talking, should you? Dad said you'd lose your voice." She turned to Ed. "Anatoly's nursing a bit of a cold. If you'll excuse us, we're going for a nice, quiet walk."

Once out of sight of the house, she slowed their pace. In silence that felt more companionable than what little time they'd known each other could explain, they walked along a trail that skirted the western edge of her family's property. "This is where I like to run," she told him, pointing out interesting aspects of the harsh terrain she nonetheless found beautiful. Gourd plants and cacti stood firm in the daily onslaught of wind. Long, dry grasses hissed in chorus with a few halfhearted cicadas. And to the distant east, cumulus clouds were already boiling into thunderstorms.

Zefer was enthralled by what to him must be an exotic and alien landscape. But weariness made him eager to rest when they stopped by a rusted old pickup truck with four flat tires, abandoned years ago under a massive, ancient walnut tree. The flatbed was littered with dead leaves, broken branches, and several seasons' worth of nuts. Andie hopped onto the lowered tailgate, her legs dangling over the edge. "Try not to talk," she reminded him. "You'll need your strength for later."

He smiled as he stepped between her legs and took off his glasses. His eyes were no longer silver but smoky gray. "Words, Ahn-dee, we do not need." Seemingly entranced by her, he picked up a twig and drew its tip lightly over her cheek and jaw.

She bit back a sigh. She never used to sigh much; only her mother did. Now she made the little verbal noises constantly, it seemed. Around Zefer, anyway.

She held herself still as he replaced the twig with his hand, stroking his fingertips over her lips. She tilted her face up, giving in to the pleasure of his touch, her eyes half-closed. "I love the way you kiss, you know," she murmured.

At that he made a soft, satisfied sound, teasing her with small, nipping kisses until she wound her arms around his neck and pulled him down to her. His lips were warm, his mouth moist and hot as his tongue slipped firmly between her lips. The kiss turned passionate.

The pulse in his throat thrummed under her palm. The rhythmic beat was so reassuringly human. Yet, if what his people hypothesized was true and their races shared the same DNA, then she and Zefer were more alike than not. Did that mean they could have children together?

The thought elicited a shiver. Her space-explorer husband. She'd wished for this. For him.

But the only way she could be with him was if she gave up everything that mattered to her: her family, her goals, her career. It was more than unfair. It out-and-out sucked.

Breathless, she pulled away. She jumped down from the truck, working hard to hide her disappointment and her frustration. "Are you ready to finish the walk?"

Zefer pushed his glasses onto his face, reminding her of a galactic Superman-turned-Clark Kent. He regarded her as if she were a phenomenon he didn't understand. "I did not expect that you would want to leave already."

She didn't want to leave. But instead of admitting that,

she cast about for something that would invalidate what she'd begun to believe they shared. What it was impossible that they were sharing. "Actually, I'm thinking we should talk, instead, about this lost world of yours. You were obsessed with finding it, weren't you? But maybe even more so with your idea of finding a woman there."

The way he pressed his lips together told her that she was right.

"And now you think that woman is me."

He started to answer, but she held up one finger. "Just shake your head, yes or no."

He nodded.

"I thought so." She should have known this was all too perfect! Zefer saw her as interchangeable with any one of a million other "primitive" Earth females he might have met. " 'Worldly adventurer woos simple native woman,' " she said with disdain. "The ultimate in explorer fantasies. Awe the local girls and take them to bed. Captain Cook did it. They all did it. But I have news for you: I may be native, but I ain't simple. Find your fling somewhere else, star man!"

She lurched away to flee. He caught her by the arm before she could. "If I wanted a simple woman, Ahn-dee, I would never have chosen you." At that, he winced in pain.

"Don't talk," she ordered.

"I will do so if I like. Particularly since it appears you want my silence only so you can convince yourself of silly things, so you do not have to listen to the truth."

She tried to wrench away. He held on to her arm. "The truth?" she said in a gasp. "What is the truth, Zefer?"

He pulled her into a fierce and possessive kiss. Her knees wobbled and she saw stars the likes of which she'd never seen in three decades of studying the night sky.

Slowly, Zefer pushed her back. "Did that feel like a lie to you?" he demanded.

She lifted one trembling hand to her lips. "No," she whispered. Nothing had ever felt more real.

She steeled herself against tears. No way was she going to cry. It was as pointless as wishing for a future with a stranger she barely knew.

But your heart knows him. . . .

She made a strangled groan. "This is so . . . not . . . me." Almost pleadingly, she said, "I want my old self back."

"I do not think you want that any more than I want to return to the man I was before."

"Shush," she warned.

"No. We need the words. I want to tell you how I came to be here. How I came to be with you."

Though he stood tall against a backdrop as rugged as he was, the expression that flickered over his face betrayed an inner vulnerability.

"The past few years have been good, Ahn-dee," he said. "I had finally reached the place in my life where I wanted to be. But my success did not bring me the satisfaction, the contentment for which I had hoped—and perhaps expected."

She saw what was in his eyes, and her heart gave a little twist. "You were lonely."

He answered with a curt nod. "And it caused me more than a few moments of self-disgust. I had always viewed such feelings as weakness."

That, she could relate to.

"I had everything," he explained. "Success, professional respect, a secure future. . . ."

"But it wasn't enough," she finished for him, nodding.

"No. It wasn't." His quiet voice had joined with hers in an opera of sorts, an awkward duet of two people not used to sharing such personal disclosures. "On my journey to the Fringe," he went on, "I put myself into stasis early, because I couldn't abide my unwarranted self-pity all the way to my new assignment. But as I slipped into sleep, I tried to pinpoint what I thought—what I *hoped*—would complete my life. Then, impulsively, I took that longing and formed it into a single wish."

A wish. Bracing herself, Andie forced herself to ask the question burning inside her: "What did you wish for?"

"You."

Oh, Lord. She pressed the heel of her hand to her mouth. "This is crazy," she cried. "It makes no sense."

He lifted his hands, an almost helpless gesture for such a large man. "I *know* it does not."

She fell silent.

"What is it, Ahn-dee?" He squeezed her arms. "What is wrong?"

"Nothing's wrong," she blurted. "I'm scared because— damn it—it's all so *right*." She pressed a shaky hand to her stomach, as if the words were being wrenched from her soul. "I made a wish, too, Zefer. I wished . . . for *you*."

He gaped at her, clearly astounded.

Her innermost thoughts spilled out. "Yes. I wished for a man who wouldn't be intimidated by me, a lover and best friend, someone who'd stay by me until the very end." Shyly, she cracked a smile. "A guy who could make my toes curl with a single look."

His smoldering glance seared through every barrier she'd ever erected to guard her heart.

"Yes," she said. "Like that."

Laughing, he swept her off her feet and swung her into

the truck, climbing in after her. Embracing joyfully, they rolled over the twigs and leaves, their hands tangling in each other's hair.

Andie shut her eyes and savored every blissful second. For the first time in her life, the openness and honesty she struggled for had come easily. This must be what her mother shared with her father, she thought. And now that she'd experienced it herself, she couldn't imagine living without it.

"Oh, Zefer, what are we going to do? How are we going to make this work?"

He steadied her by placing his hands to either side of her head. "We will find a way," he said. Then, straddling her, he kissed her soundly. His jeans abraded the thin Lycra of her running shorts, and the thick, hard ridge under the denim left no doubt that this alien, at least, was built like any human male.

Their embrace heated so quickly that she knew it would end in their making love. But reality came crashing back with the sound of a vehicle driving up the trail.

They jerked apart. "Someone's coming," she whispered, her heart thumping.

Zefer's passion-glazed eyes sharpened instantly. "Ed Fritch," he surmised darkly, donning his glasses.

"He was supposed to stay at the house. If he's here, it means he's looking for something. Or someone."

Zefer's hand landed on the side of her head, soothing her. "I am Anatoly, remember? It will be all right."

Bits of leaves, broken walnut shells, and things she didn't want to think about fell from her hair as she sat up. A silver Hummer pulled up to the pickup truck and parked alongside it.

Gloria Ruiz waved cheerily from the backseat. She had

wispy white hair and deeply creased brown skin. "Enjoying the weather?" she asked mischievously, her twinkling eyes shifting from Andie to Zefer and back again.

"We were trying to," Andie said wryly. She was getting used to this. Every time she kissed Zefer, someone interrupted. "Napping in the sunshine is always nice."

Gloria didn't believe a word of her explanation, and Andie couldn't help smiling. Despite her fragile appearance, the woman emanated astonishing youthfulness. But then, any eighty-year-old who went UFO hunting, week after week, wasn't your typical grandma.

Andie's smile faltered when her attention shifted to Ed. He was sitting in the front passenger seat next to the unfamiliar young man at the wheel of the Hummer.

"My grandson Tony," Gloria explained, and a brief round of introductions ensued.

Tony had lean, muscular arms, a pencil-thin mustache, and he wore his baseball cap backward. His faded tank top was loose-fitting, exposing his armpits and half his chest as he leaned his arms over the wheel. "Nice to meet you both," he said, twirling a toothpick between his teeth, just like Ed.

Andie didn't like that the younger man had come along. A group of not-so-physically-fit senior citizens she could deal with. A guy like Tony—well, he made her nervous. He'd have the stamina to search 'round the clock—if properly motivated. How many more hardbodies like Tony had Ed recruited for a hunt that was clearly consuming him?

"What happened with your meeting?" Andie asked Ed.

"The rest of the gang hasn't shown up yet. We're killing time." He gave her a false, showbiz smile. "Do you and

Anatoly want to come along? We're taking a spin around the property."

Her parents' property, Andie longed to point out. She had no doubt that Ed was looking for signs that her mother had hidden an alien spacecraft somewhere nearby. His tenacity troubled her. Ed wouldn't give up until he found Zefer's ship. And then he'd use that coup to focus attention on himself, giving little thought for Zefer or his welfare. She didn't know that for sure, but she'd heard enough stories over the years from her mother to trust her instincts on the matter. "I think we'll stay here, Ed. But thanks for the invite."

Ed gave her a penetrating glance. *What are you and your mother hiding from me?* Her stomach chilled as she wondered just how much he was able to read in her face. But maybe her fears were due only to her burgeoning paranoia.

Tony started up the Hummer. "Well, we're off," Ed said with a jaunty salute. Gloria waved good-bye as the squat, wide vehicle kicked up dust and pebbles and bounced away across the field.

Andie glowered after them. "Pray he doesn't figure out who you really are."

"He will not," Zefer said firmly. "But tonight nonetheless I must inspect the damage to my ship."

"How long do you think it'll take to repair it?"

"The craft is capable of a good deal of self-repair. I suspect it will take another day, perhaps two, for me to fix the rest." He leaned toward her, tucking strands of hair behind her ear. "But I want more than that. A week, at least. I want to stay with you, and be with you for as long as possible."

"You can't. There's too much at risk."

349

"A week," he insisted, his voice tired and edged with pain.

"Okay," she whispered finally. They had a week.

With Ed off driving in the Hummer, it was safe to walk back to the museum. Zefer needed rest if he was to regain his strength, necessary if he was going to get anything worthwhile done on his starship later.

Soon they were back in the quiet stillness of the deserted museum. Andie no longer gave a second thought to the wacky items for sale there. Her own life had gone far beyond anything her mother could stack on the shelves.

In the doorway to Zefer's bedroom, Andie paused, feeling his gaze on her. A half hour before, she'd been ready to make love with abandon in the back of a truck. Now she felt awkward, staring at a normal bed.

When she turned back to Zefer, his expression was mournfully frank. "I want you, Ahn-dee," he said in a quiet voice. "I want to make love to you. But I don't want part if I can't have all."

She shook her head. "Do you mean you want my heart, too?" She smiled. "Well, I don't think you need to worry about that."

He stroked one knuckle over her cheek, making her shiver. "Yes, I want to win your heart. But I want your future, too. And until that is assured, I am willing to wait . . . if you are."

They regarded each other. "Think what we'll have to look forward to," he added.

She sighed. "You're a pretty amazing guy."

He smiled wryly. "I do not know about that," he said, and drew her into his arms. "But we belong together. That is a given. Now all that is left is for us to figure out how to make it happen."

The Day Her Heart Stood Still

"Yes. Even if we have to meet up on Mars."

They both froze. Then they moved apart to look at each other. Her remark had been meant as a joke, but as they both considered the feasibility of Andie's proposal, the beginnings of the wackiest, craziest plan ever attempted by the human inhabitants of the galaxy began to take form.

Chapter Nine

The day before Zefer's departure clouded over early. It was barely noon, but already thunder rumbled in the distance. The air was heavy with the tang of ozone, made stronger by the curious lack of wind.

Andie had already run ten miles, but Zefer still slept, brought low by exhaustion and headaches from his stubborn use of the computer to communicate. Compounding the problem were a week's worth of nights spent readying his starship for flight. Andie's father had treated him with nonprescription Motrin and similar meds, but he felt stronger painkillers might interfere dangerously with the biostasis Zefer would have to enter for his journey to the Outer Fringe. None of them dared risk it.

Andie brought a protein shake out to the front porch and leaned over the railing. As she watched the storms darkening the horizon, she found herself hoping the weather would be the same tomorrow and delay Zefer's launch another day. But the technology at his command didn't even blink at mere hazards like lightning and wind. *Face the facts.* He was leaving, and it would be over a year before she saw him again. If she did at all.

For their planned reunion to happen, he'd have to launch tonight without being intercepted, and then he'd have to make it to the Outer Fringe safely. She, on the other hand, still had a 259-day journey to Mars ahead of her, not to mention the landing that was up to her to make on the Red Planet, assisted by a computer that had never been there, either. . . .

Dust and the sound of an approaching car dragged her attention to the road and away from her ifs and doubts. Her mother, she thought, returning from Home Depot and Radio Shack with more goodies for Zefer's ship. Andie hadn't a clue as to where all the carloads of stuff her mother bought were going, though, because she hadn't once boarded the marvelous craft. Her duty was to stand watch, and so she had, fearing that the one time she'd fall down on the job, something would happen to Zefer or his ship. Like a Chinese border guard protecting the premier himself, she'd patrolled the perimeter of the crash site each night for a week now, never allowing her concentration to flag, until Zefer and her mother emerged in the hours before dawn.

It had been worth it, though. There were nineteen days to go until the identities of the astronauts on the Mars mission were announced, thirty-six hours remaining until Zefer's launch, and miraculously they were both still in the game.

The vehicle was closer now. She squinted at the road and made out a familiar maroon Suburban. *Crap.* The truck belonged to Ed Fritch.

The mouthful of shake she'd just swallowed dropped into her stomach like a tennis ball, and as the truck pulled into the driveway, she cast her eyes around, wondering what she should do or grab first.

Ed hopped out and waved.

"Mom's not here," Andie called. "She's shopping."

"It's you I came to visit, Andie."

She set the glass down on the railing. "What's up?"

"Oh, I was doing a little research last night, and I saw that your friend, Mr. Butin, was at the International Association of Astronautical Engineers' annual conference. As keynote speaker, no less."

She let out the breath she'd been holding. He was only curious about the cosmonaut.

"In Denmark," Ed went on.

"Anatoly's invited to speak all over the world—"

"Yesterday."

Ed eyed her coldly, daring her to prove him wrong. But God help her if she didn't try. Her blood rushed from her head, pounding in her throat, but she fixed him with the flinty glare of a seasoned warrior. "That must be old news."

"I'm afraid it's not." He pulled from his shirt pocket a piece of paper folded into quarters and handed it to her.

She unfolded the sheet. It was an ink-jet image of Anatoly, standing behind a podium. He looked good, she thought. Contented. Warmth filtered through her. Anatoly had found with someone what she had with Zefer; she could see it in his eyes.

"Your Anatoly is not who you think he is."

"No," she said. "Apparently not."

She expected Ed to take pity on her and leave. But he persisted in his inquiry. "In fact, your friend isn't what any of us originally thought." He swaggered toward the museum.

She held up one hand. "That's far enough."

His face turned purple, and he spun on her. "You have an extraterrestrial, don't you? Why else would you be so set against me going in there?"

She snorted. "I don't like the idea of you snooping. Neither does my mother." She marched over to him. "Go home, Ed."

"I have a right to see it."

"*It?*" She knew now that she'd never let him near Zefer.

"I want to know what Cassie found."

She grabbed his sleeve, stopping him as he begun again to walk toward the museum. He was stronger than she expected, and threw her backward.

Regaining her balance, she bolted after him. "Hey! You're way out of line. Get the hell off our property. I'll call the sheriff, I swear it."

He lunged at her when she tried to block him from grabbing the door handle. There was going to be no stopping him without using force. So she slugged him.

Her fist caught him under the jaw. He stumbled backward, and she shoved him the rest of the way onto his rear. "Stop it, Ed," she pleaded, gasping. He had to be past his mid-sixties; she didn't want to hurt him. "Go home. There's nothing for you to see here."

"Oh, I disagree, Major Del Sarto," he replied as his eyes glinted with the hunger of a starving man presented with a seven-course meal. "I see it now."

Cradling her throbbing fist, Andie turned around. Zefer stood in the doorway, his gauntlet computer aimed at Ed. "My apologies," he told the man. Then his computer emitted a silent, too-bright-to-look-at thread of light.

The beam pierced Ed's forehead. He stared at Zefer with an expression of startled awe. Then his eyes rolled back in his head, and he sagged onto the asphalt with the slightest of whimpers.

"Oh, God." Andie fell to Ed's side and probed for his pulse. His heart thumped away, as stubborn and indignant as its owner. "What did you do to him?" she demanded.

"I put him to sleep."

"Oh, beautiful. Now when he wakes up, he'll tell everyone how Cassie's alien shot him with a ray gun."

Zefer tugged her to her feet and gently brushed her free of grit. "He won't remember anything of the incident." He frowned. "And maybe nothing of the past few days, as well. But beyond that, his memory will be as before."

She shoved the crumpled picture Ed had shown her into his hands. "This is the real Anatoly Butin. Who knows how many people Ed showed this to? You have to leave." She swallowed. "Leave Earth."

"And not tomorrow, as we planned," he agreed. "I must go now."

The thought left her hollow. They regarded each other as the realization sank in. Zefer exhaled. "Ed Fritch will wake shortly."

He squeezed her arm, then left to retrieve his few belongings from the bedroom, while Andie requisitioned an Extraterrestrials-R-Us sweatshirt from the museum. She wadded it, wedging the garment gently behind Ed's head to cushion his skull from the asphalt. Then she folded his hands over his stomach. "Be patient, Ed. You'll find out about your aliens soon enough." *Along with the rest of Earth's population.* Maybe someday she'd even tell Ed that he'd been right about Zefer all along.

The Day Her Heart Stood Still

Zefer emerged from the museum. "Come," he said, taking her by the arm.

They scrambled into the Corvette. As she thrust her key into the ignition, she called her father from her cell phone. "Dad. There's a problem. It's Ed Fritch. He's at our house and needs a doctor . . . it's an emergency." She cleared her throat and exchanged glances with Zefer. "I'll tell you the rest later."

With an ambulance on the way, she sped onto the highway and then onto the ranch road leading to miles of rugged landscape—and Zefer's starship. Everything was happening too fast. She wanted time to slow down. She'd expected to have a night and another day before having to let Zefer go.

She glanced into the rearview mirror, and for the first time in her life she wished her mother's Cadillac were barreling down the road after her. Her mother should be here, too. Cassie would hate that she hadn't gotten to say good-bye to Zefer, and that she hadn't finished redecorating his ship.

Zefer's warm palm covered her hand. "Your mother and I will meet again," he said as if reading her thoughts.

Too desolate to reply, she squeezed his hand.

The first thing Andie noticed when she climbed aboard the starship wasn't the advanced tech of the cockpit, the gleaming white walls that formed the interior fuselage, or the runes in an exotic and alien language; it was the blue-and-white country-plaid curtains and the assortment of multicolored rubber-backed mats that her mother had bought at Wal-Mart. "Mom's added her special touch, I see."

Zefer's smile held no derision at all. Instead, his obvious

357

affection for her mother softened the sharp features of his face. "She makes my ship feel like your home."

Andie noted that he didn't say *his* home, but hers. She was so touched that she turned away, unable to speak.

Dragging her fingertips over the flight console and the pilot's chair, she drank in the incredible cockpit. The command seat was riddled with computers, sensors, and three-dimensional holographic readouts, as well as some items she hadn't the knowledge to understand. Someday, she vowed, she'd learn to fly a ship like this. Anything was possible. Hadn't her mother told her that many times?

Zefer's deep voice invaded her thoughts. "I am ready."

He had changed into his black oven-mitt flight suit. Her throat constricted. "I'm not," she said tightly.

He dipped his head and kissed her, his touch loving, tender. "I hate this," she whispered. "I miss you already."

He cupped the back of her head with one big hand. "It is time you learned my words. *Uhn t'arashah*, Ahn-dee," he murmured. "It means: 'I love you.' "

Her heart was so full she thought it might explode. "*Uhn t'arashah*, Zefer."

His expression told her that his heart was as filled as hers. Wordlessly, she dragged her finger along the seam running vertically down the front of his black flight suit. Smoothing her hands inside the parted fabric, she savored the feel of his muscled chest and firm stomach under the soft inner shirt he wore.

He took her wrists in his hands. "Ahn-dee?"

"We said we wanted to wait before we made love for the first time."

He nodded. "Only so we would have it to look forward to."

"I changed my mind. I don't want something to look

forward to." Her voice grew husky. "I want something to remember."

He drew her into another kiss, this one much more passionate. His tentative fingertips gliding up and down her throat became confident hands that explored the curves of her body, and he pressed her hard against him. Only then did he make a sound: a low, deep groan of longing.

With a shuddering breath, he pulled back. "Your father believes we will be able to have children together," he said, twisting his fingers in her hair. "And one could very well come of this. I cannot leave until we know for certain."

"The time of the month . . . and the pills I use to prevent pregnancy—I don't think anything will happen."

"You are sure?"

"As much as anyone can be. Nothing in life is guaranteed."

As he considered that, she removed his glasses and set them on the console behind her. "Oh, Zefer. We're letting words get in the way." He must have thought so, too, for he scooped her up and brought her to the bunk where he slept.

They had to hurry through the process of stripping off their clothes, when they would rather have taken their time. There was little time to savor the feel of bare skin brushing over bare skin, or the intimate caresses that preceded their lovemaking. Knowing the clock ticked relentlessly toward a future that was as uncertain as they were sure of their new love, she pulled him on top of her. As he fitted himself deep inside her body, she clutched his broad shoulders and inhaled on a long, shuddering breath.

Passion rose quickly, yet he took time to smooth his

hands over her breasts, her throat, her face, as if trying to memorize her. Heat radiated out from where they melded together. Each roll of his hips sent a shock wave of pleasure coursing through her. Taking full breaths became impossible as he brought her unselfishly to the most delicious, drawn-out peak imaginable.

Cradling her head with his palms, he watched her face contort with pleasure, a gesture that was, in its astonishing intimacy, even more erotic than the way he moved inside her. He rocked with strong, rhythmic thrusts and she pushed hard against him, until, at last, they found the completion they'd long sought . . . in each other.

Something pounded frantically on the outside hatch as they dressed. Andie struggled into her top and shorts. Donning his flight suit, Zefer checked a display showing the exterior of the ship. "It's your mother."

He opened the hatch. The sky was dark with roiling clouds, and although it smelled like rain, none had yet fallen. Waving, Cassie stood at the bottom of the entry ladder, her red hair wild in the wind. "Oh! You *are* here. I didn't see your car."

"I parked it in the brush, just in case," Andie shouted down to her. "Did you see Ed?"

"Yes. The ambulance was there. And your father told me you called."

There was a flash of lightning in the distance. Andie and Zefer climbed down from the ship. Andie tried to comb her tangled hair with her fingers, while Zefer, sporting a pair of pink splotches on the side of his throat where she might have kissed him a little too hard, worked at straightening his flight suit. It had to be obvious to Cassie that they'd just made love. But to her credit, the woman didn't scrutinize them.

Somehow Andie held her emotions in check through her mother's tearful farewell with Zefer. Then it was her turn, and Zefer squeezed her so hard that she became light-headed. Holding her by the shoulders, he moved her back. "Your journey to Mars will be safe," he said, as if willing it to happen.

Cassie's eyes widened. Now she knew what was to be announced in a matter of days, Andie thought. But with her mother and father the secret would be safe.

"I will find you on Mars," Zefer assured her. "And then we will proceed as we have discussed."

"Your ship will contact us."

"And you will pretend not to know me."

"Same with you." She nodded. "And then your people will guide us through our first encounter."

After that, she would go with Zefer to the Outer Fringe to live and work, as she'd always dreamed. And to become Zefer's wife. Odd, the image that popped into her mind was one of Zefer enjoying periodic visits from his very unconventional mother-in-law. Tears stung her eyes.

"Do not doubt, Ahn-dee. It will all come to pass."

She saw the resolve in his gaze. He'd be there, waiting. All she had to do was hold up her end of the bargain and bring her crew to Red Planet in one piece.

Zefer pointed to an embankment about half a mile away. "From there it will be safe to watch."

Andie slid into the passenger seat of her mother's Cadillac and Cassie drove to the edge of a depression carved out by a long-dry stream. In the front seat, they hunkered down. It began to rain, plump, cold drops splashing onto the windshield. Thunder rumbled. Soon the ground shook with a different kind of thunder. Zefer's starship.

Andie's hand found Cassie's. Shielding their eyes against sudden brilliance, they watched a white-hot ball rise into the coming storm. "Star light, star bright," Andie whispered in a shaky voice.

"I wish I may, I wish I might," her mother murmured along with her.

"Have the wish I wish tonight."

They sat there, hands squeezed together, long after Zefer's ship had disappeared, gazing at the sky just as they used to all those years ago.

"Mom?" Andie asked after a while.

"Yes, baby?"

"I just wanted to say . . . that you were right. About love and logic, about the rocks, all of it."

Cassie brought a trembling hand to Andie's cheek, love and pride shining in her eyes. "You surely are your daddy's girl."

"Yours, too," Andie whispered.

Tears welled in her mother's eyes. Andie compressed her lips to quell an answering upsurge of emotion. Then she realized what she was doing and threw herself into Cassie's generous embrace. Together they let their tears fall.

Chapter Ten

It was a pleasant day—by Martian standards. By mid-afternoon, sunshine had warmed the barren, rock-strewn plains to sixty-four degrees below zero. Andie rode shot-gun in the Martian rover and, peering straight ahead, she scanned their route for hazards. This was supposed to be her rest period, but, fidgety, she'd insisted on coming along with the mission's two geologists on a soil-collecting expedition.

Spread out before her was a pale, salmon-colored sky and miles of pebbly red soil, and she kept wanting to pinch herself to see if she were dreaming, or if she was really on another planet. The only dark spot on an otherwise exhilarating experience was that after two full days here, there was no sign of Zefer or his people.

He wasn't coming. Something had happened to him. Or he'd changed his mind about their reunion . . . and their future. It had been a year since they'd parted. She sagged back in her seat, her mood as desolate as the terrain.

All the astronauts had communications equipment built into their space suits, a receiver and a transmitter that were always on. Andie had gotten so used to the breathing of her companions that she didn't hear it anymore. But a sudden scratchy transmission from the other three astronauts back at the base camp came through loud and clear.

"Do you hear that!" blurted a voice that sounded like Jeff Squires, the mission commander.

Andie's heart lurched. "Hear what?"

"Oh, my God!" What sounded like chaos at the base camp exploded in her headset.

The rover's fat tires bumped over a boulder, almost knocking her out of the vehicle. "Someone transmitted, 'Oh, my God'?"

"No. Listen to this!"

Andie heard another burst of static. Then a series of beeps. Was it Zefer's signal? It had to be.

Chris Goldman stopped the rover. "Morse code I can do."

Andie and the geologist watched Chris's thickly gloved hand struggle to hold a pen as he scratched letters onto the tablet fixed to the dash. When he was through, she and Jessie, the other geologist, crowded around him to see what he'd written.

Hello. What are you. Hello.

Andie closed her eyes. *Thank you.*

"You weren't kidding." Chris transmitted back to base camp: " 'Oh, my God' is right."

"Where did the signal originate?" Andie asked Jeff.

The Day Her Heart Stood Still

"Two clicks ahead," he radioed back. "On the north-western edge of the ridge."

"I say we go take a peek," Chris proposed. "That is, if we're all in agreement."

"Yes, let's go!" Andie chorused with Jessie. Meanwhile, at the base camp, Jeff worked on contacting Houston.

They drove the rover up a gently sloping hill. The only sound from her companions was the harsh rasp of their breathing. When they crested the hill, they stopped the rover. Below was a shallow valley that scientists speculated was once a body of water. In its center was an immense starship that sparkled in the tiny pearl-like sun's light.

The rover skidded to a stop. Andie hopped out. Her limbs were weakened from too many months at zero G; nonetheless, she felt buoyant in the gravity that was one-third that of Earth. Somewhere down there Zefer waited for her.

"Andie!" The occupants of the rover stared at her in horror. "Don't go down there," Chris warned.

"What's she doing?" screamed Jeff from base camp. "Andie—we don't know who they are! We're still waiting on a response from Houston."

Morse code continued to tease them: HELLO. WHAT ARE YOU. HELLO.

Andie cast a long and solitary shadow as she faced the strange ship. The hatch opened, and she took a step forward. Then she glanced over her shoulder. "Well? Aren't you coming with me?" she called back.

After a moment's hesitation, Chris and Jessie followed her.

Jeff was having fits back at base camp. "We aren't cleared for this. It's too damned dangerous!"

"Chill, Jeff," Jessie told him. "If they meant us harm, we'd be dead already."

There was a long silence. Then a hiss of static. "Okay. Go with God, you guys."

As she and the geologists made progress toward the great alien craft, Andie perspired in her space suit, her stomach uneasy. Some might call this scheme manipulative. Yet was it so terribly wrong if it would bring benefit to Earth? When one figure separated from the rest and walked toward them, certainty flooded her.

It was Zefer. She could tell by his height and his broad shoulders, defined by a space suit so much more close-fitting and high-tech than the bulky outfit she wore. She must not give anything away. That they knew each other would be a secret they'd take to their graves. It had to be. This moment would go down in history as the first meeting between Earth's humans and the "family" from which they'd been separated for eons.

Flanked by her two companions, she stopped in front of Zefer, framed in his moment of glory by a dozen others, men and women. As she looked into Zefer's eyes, her breath caught. The love she saw there was so apparent that she couldn't imagine their companions not seeing it. But everyone's attention was luckily too diverted by the magnitude of the event to notice.

Again, she reminded herself of the significance that this day would have on both civilizations. But as she gazed into the eyes of her future husband, she realized that she no longer needed to hold on to something to remember—there was so much more to look forward to.

Suddenly Zefer took a step closer and pushed at a rock with the toe of his boot. Both groups stared politely but with some obvious confusion as Zefer flipped it over. Then he glanced up at Andie and grinned.

Andie smiled back. Her mother would surely approve, she thought. The underside of the rock gleamed as new and unspoiled as the future awaiting them.

LYNSAY SANDS
The Reluctant Reformer

Everyone knows of Lady X. The masked courtesan is reputedly a noblewoman fallen on hard times. What Lord James does not know is that she is Lady Margaret Wentworth—the feisty sister of his best friend, who has forced James into an oath of protection. But when James tracks the girl to a house of ill repute, the only explanation is that Maggie is London's most enigmatic wanton.

Snatching her away will be a ticklish business, and after that James will have to ignore her violent protests that she was never the infamous X. He will have to reform the hoyden, while keeping his hands off the luscious goods that the rest of the ton has reputedly sampled. And, with Maggie, hardest of all will be keeping himself from falling in love.

_____4974-0 $5.99 US/$7.99 CAN

Always
Lynsay Sands

Bastard daughter to the king, Rosamunde is raised in a convent and wholly prepared to take the veil . . . until good King Henry shows up with a reluctant husband in tow for her. Suddenly, she finds herself promising to love, honor, and obey Aric . . . always. But Rosamunde's education has not covered a wedding night, and the stables are a poor example for an untried girl. Will Aric bite her neck like the animals do their mates? The virile warrior seems capable of such animal passion, but his eyes promise something sweeter. And Rosamunde soon learns that while she may have trouble with obeying him, it will not be hard to love her new husband forever.

___4736-5 $5.50 US/$6.50 CAN

Dorchester Publishing Co., Inc.
P.O. Box 6640
Wayne, PA 19087-8640

Please add $1.75 for shipping and handling for the first book and $.50 for each book thereafter. NY, NYC, and PA residents, please add appropriate sales tax. No cash, stamps, or C.O.D.s. All orders shipped within 6 weeks via postal service book rate. Canadian orders require $2.00 extra postage and must be paid in U.S. dollars through a U.S. banking facility.

Name_____
Address_____
City_____State_____Zip_____
I have enclosed $ _____ in payment for the checked book(s).
Payment <u>must</u> accompany all orders. ❏ Please send a free catalog.
CHECK OUT OUR WEBSITE! www.dorchesterpub.com

✦ the
ℳermaid of Penperro
LISA CACH

Konstanze never imagined that singing could land someone in such trouble. The disrepute of the stage is nothing compared to the danger of playing a seductress of the sea— or the reckless abandon she feels while doing so. She has come to Penperro to escape her past, to find anonymity among the people of Cornwall, and her inhibitions melt away as she does. But the Cornish are less simple than she expected, and the role she is forced to play is harder. For one thing, her siren song lures to her not only the agent of the crown she's been paid to perplex, but the smuggler who hired her. And in his strong arms she finds everything she's been missing. Suddenly, Konstanze sees the true peril of her situation—not that of losing her honor, but her heart.

___52437-6 $5.50 US/$6.50 CAN

THE
STAR
King
SUSAN GRANT

Careening out of control in her fighter jet is only the start of the wildest ride of Jasmine's life; spinning wildly in an airplane is nothing like the loss of equilibrium she feels when she lands. There, in a half-dream, Jas sees a man more powerfully compelling than any she's ever encountered. Though his words are foreign, his touch is familiar, baffling her mind even as he touches her soul. But who is he? Is he, too, a downed pilot? Is that why he lies in the desert sand beneath a starry Arabian sky? The answers burn in his mysterious golden eyes, in his thoughts that become hers as he holds out his hand and requests her aid. This man has crossed many miles to find her, to offer her a heaven that she might otherwise never know, and love is only one of the many gifts of . . . the Star King.

___52413-9 $5.50 US/$6.50 CAN

Aphrodite's Kiss

Julie Kenner

Crazy as it sounds, on her twenty-fifth birthday Zoe has the chance to become a superhero. But x-ray vision and the ability to fly are only two things to consider. There is also her newfound heightened sensitivity. If she can hardly eat a chocolate bar without convulsing in ecstasy, how is she to give herself the birthday gift she's really set her heart on— George Taylor? The handsome P.I.'s dark exterior hides a truly sweet center, and Zoe feels certain that his mere touch will send her spiraling into oblivion. But the man is looking for an average Jane no matter what he claims. He can never love a superhero-to-be—can he? Zoe has to know. With her super powers, she can only see through his clothing; to strip bare the workings of his heart, she'll have to rely on something a little more potent.

___52438-4 $5.99 US/$6.99 CAN